·MOUNTAIN·
Ranch

·MOUNTAIN·
Ranch

Johny Weber

Hildebrand Books
an imprint of W. Brand Publishing

NASHVILLE, TENNESSEE

Hildebrand Books an imprint of W. Brand Publishing
j.brand@wbrandpub.com
www.wbrandpub.com

Cover design by designchik.net

Mountain Ranch/ Johny Weber — 1st Edition

Available in Paperback, Kindle, and eBook formats.
Paperback ISBN: 978-1-956906-90-5
eBook ISBN: 978-1-956906-91-2

Library of Congress Control Number: 2024900208

CONTENTS

To my brother, Tom, and my sister-in-law Dayna.

One is my "rock" and the other my trusted first editor. I'm so glad I have you both to lean on.

MOUNTAIN RANCH FAMILY TREE
AUGUST 1880

JACOB BATES — BROTHERS — HENRY BATES

Jacob Bates line:

- SABRA HOLDEN WELLES — BLUE KNIFE
  - KADE WELLES
  - JAKE BATES WELLES — SP. ANNA (CURTIS)
    - THOMAS — SP. BETH (BATES)
    - MOLLY — SP. JACKSON COWDEN

Henry Bates line:

- JIM BATES — SARAH
  - MARTHA — SP. SAM TENBROOK
  - WILL
  - BETH — SP. THOMAS WELLES
  - BONNIE — SP. SWIFT HAWK
  - JAMES
- MATTIE BATES JORGENSEN — MATTHEW JORGENSEN
  - JEREMIAH
  - LATHE — SP. KASA
  - CATHERINE — SP. BUSTER
  - RACHEL — SP. ARMY TALBOT

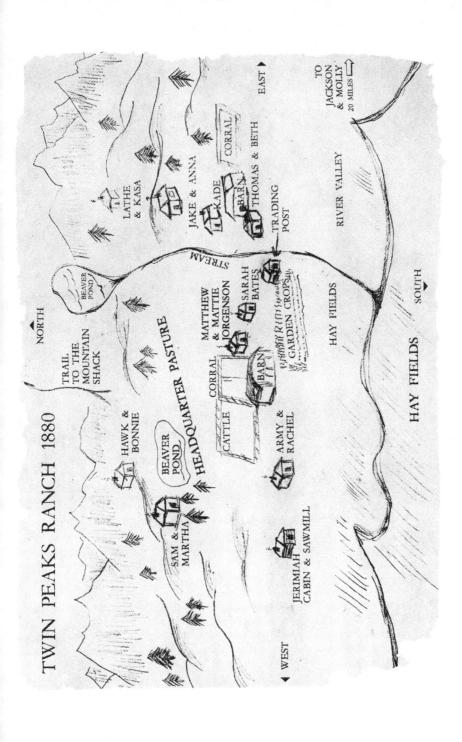

CHAPTER 1

Waiting for the Dawn – August 1880

He sat in the gloom of the cabin, waiting for the dawn to begin to break outside the window. It was still too early to see the mountains. With no moon this night, the mountains were still shrouded in darkness, but there was a faint brightening of the sky. It wouldn't be long before the sun in the east would begin to outline the peaks. Sabra lay in his arms, cradled against him as if she were a sleeping child. They sat in the rocker old Tom had made for Sabra when the children were little.

"Take me out in front of the window," Sabra had whispered during the night, "so I can watch the sunrise over the peaks." *Breath.* "I want to watch the dawn come in with you."

And so, Kade had gently picked up Sabra, wrapped the quilt around her, and carried her to the main room of the cabin. Here they sat together by the window, waiting for the dawn. But Kade would be the only one to see daybreak on this day. Sabra had breathed her last less than an hour before. He knew immediately when she took her last breath. He didn't panic or shake her or try to wake her. He knew that it was fruitless. Sabra simply drifted off, her body relaxed against him, and her labored breathing was stilled. He lay his chin on her head, holding her as close as possible as if the more parts of him that touched her would help. But, in his heart, he was hit with an almost physical hurt. She was gone, and he was alone.

Kade knew Sabra would need to be laid out; that the women would come and wash her and dress her. But he also knew he could not take Sabra to the bedroom and lay her down. Someone would have to come and take her from him. Kade could not put her away from him. He would wait for Thomas to return. He would let Thomas take Sabra from him, but not until after dawn.

"Go home, Thomas," Sabra had whispered through labored breaths late in the night. "Your family needs you now." *Breath.* "Your father and I need to be together." *Breath.*

"I'll be back in the morning, Ma," Thomas told her gently. "You hang on. Jake will be back with Molly."

Sabra had smiled weakly at that. "You tell Molly not to feel bad she wasn't here." *Breath.* "Tell them I want to leave this world," *breath,* "remembering her as I saw her last," *breath,* "when she and Jackson rode away." *Breath.* "They were riding side by side and they were teasing each other," *breath,* "and they were laughing." *Breath.* "I don't want to see her crying." Sabra had closed her eyes then, weary from trying to breathe and speak. Thomas had grasped her hand in his and kissed her forehead.

"Love you, Mother," he whispered, and Sabra smiled and squeezed his hand, but her eyes remained closed. She didn't want to see Thomas' face, see his pain at saying goodbye.

Kade thought about these things as he sat. He could start to see the outline of the mountain ridge to the east. It was still dark, but dawn was not far away. He rocked Sabra gently. It was too warm for a fire, so the cabin was dark. He had no candles or kerosene lamps burning. Mattie slept in Molly's old room, banished last night by Sabra even before Thomas was sent away. As Sabra's oldest and best friend, Mattie had been staying most of the time to help take care of Sabra. But it was clear, well before midnight, that there was no more to do. It was too late. None of the poultices or medicines or love would keep Sabra alive.

For the past several days a slew of people came to give their regards to Sabra. At first, they came to encourage, but yesterday, even those who didn't know how sick Sabra had become could see that this was Sabra's last fight. Yet she greeted them with a smile, weak though it was. She would often fall asleep between visitors. But if she heard Kade or Mattie turn someone away, Sabra would wake and call out. Sabra turned no one away.

Just before Jake left to bring Molly home, he had turned to Kade and told him he would make a quick stop at the teepees before heading out. Sabra had perked up at that.

"Teepees," she had asked. "Who is here?"

"Hawk's mother, Snowbird, is here," Jake told her. "There are about a dozen other Utes who are here with her. Yellow Dog's son and a cousin to Brown Otter and some others."

"Do they know I am sick?" Sabra had asked.

"That is why they came," Jake answered. "One of our hands met some Utes out hunting and told them."

"Have them come in," Sabra had whispered. "They are your people and my friends. Have them come."

Kade, at first, objected to more visitors, but Sabra

would have none of it. "Yellow Dog let me live in his mountains. Brown Otter was like a son to me. Snowbird is his wife," she struggled to speak. "I want to see them."

And so Kade relented, and the Utes came. They had heard that Woman with Many Horses was sick. They would keep a vigil on her cabin and family until she got well, or until she went to the spirit world. She had been the wife of Blue Knife and was mother to Jake, who they called Rides the Wind, because of the good horses he always rode. Jake was the son of Blue Knife and half-brother of Blue Knife's other son, Brown Otter. Even the younger Ute people, who never knew Sabra when she lived in the mountain meadow, knew the stories of her and her horses. Brown Otter, a respected warrior, was buried less than a year earlier. Jake was the son of a Ute warrior, and, despite growing up with his white family, he was accepted by the Utes. And so, they came and paid homage to the woman who had been Blue Knife's woman, was Jake's mother, and who had earned their respect.

Kade sat, remembering these last few days and this last night with the woman he loved. When she was alone with him, Sabra struggled to talk. He tried to hush her, to help her save her strength, but she would have none of that.

"I need to talk now," *breath*, "while I can. You need to let me." *Breath.*

And so, he had.

"When I am gone," *breath*, "you need to be strong for Molly and the boys." *Breath.* "They will worry about you," *breath*, "and you can't go off like you did with," *breath*, "Jim and Tom. You can't take this," *breath*, "on by yourself. There is no one to blame here."

He had smiled at her then, though his heart was breaking, and promised her.

"And you need to let Sarah," *breath*, "help you. That will help her too." *Breath.* "She is still hurting."

"I can take care of myself, Sabra," he had replied, but she cut him off.

"Let Sarah help you." *Breath.* "She will want to." *Breath.* "It will comfort her." *Breath.* "She will understand what you feel." *Breath.* "She is still hurting from losing Jim." *Breath.* "Let her comfort you." Sabra closed her eyes again, then opened them and fixed her gaze on Kade. "Promise me."

Kade could see it was important to her, so he nodded. "If it helps Sarah, I can do that."

Sabra relaxed in his arms then. Mattie had brushed Sabra's hair out that night and it hung long and loose over her shoulders. Kade brought his free hand up and stroked her hair, gently moving his fingers through the fine dark strands. With his other hand, he held one of hers, fingers entwined together. They sat in silence, and he thought she might have drifted off to sleep until he heard her whisper, fainter now.

"I have had such a good life with you." *Breath.* "I have been so happy here with you." *Breath.*

Kade squeezed her hand, unable to answer her, and felt her fingers tighten on his. And then, shortly after, he felt Sabra go limp. He knew that she had left him. Kade knew she would not see the dawn. They would never see the dawn together again, but Kade would not release her until the sun was up. Sabra might not watch it with him, but he would watch it one more time with her.

Dawn was Sabra's favorite time of the day. So many times, when he didn't need to leave early, they would stand by the window in winter or go outside in the summer to watch the peaks around them light up.

"It's a new beginning today," Sabra would smile. "Think what we can do with a new day!" And if they were alone, she would pull his shirttail out of his trousers and run her fingers inside and up his back. She was always doing that if they were alone. He would feel her fingers dance along his muscles, or up his spine. He would grin down at her then and see the mischief in her eyes. If there were time, when they were younger and the children slept, they would find themselves back in the bedroom with sunlight streaming in the tiny bedroom window.

And so, Kade sat with Sabra in his arms, waiting for the dawn. It was like this when Thomas returned. Thomas didn't need his father's words to know his mother was gone. One look at Kade's tortured expression, and Thomas knew that life would never be quite the same for any of them.

"When, Pa?" he asked.

"Reckon 'bout an hour or so ago."

"You want me to take her and lay her out?" Thomas asked softly. "I can wake Mattie and get Sarah and Martha."

"No, leave her for a few more minutes," Kade replied. "We are going to watch the dawn first; watch the peaks light up."

Thomas gave Kade a sideways glance, and Kade caught it.

"No, I'm not daft, son," Kade said sadly. "But I promised her last night we would watch the dawn together.

So, we will do that one last time. Maybe wherever she is right now, she can look upon us and know."

Thomas pulled up a chair beside Kade and his mother, facing the window. "I'll sit with you both then," he said softly. "We'll wait for the dawn together.

Thomas sat alone outside the cabin in the sunlight. He expected Jake and Molly to come rolling in anytime now. He had his father asleep, and if Kade needed anything right now, it was sleep. Thomas knew that his father had had precious little sleep for any of the last week. Kade had seldom left Sabra's side and mostly sat vigil over her, as if he could keep her alive by watching her. So, Thomas hoped to intercept Jake and Molly away from the house and keep the cabin quiet.

Kade resisted going to bed. But Thomas had insisted, "Molly will need you to lean on when she gets home. You can't be staggering tired, or she will notice." Put that way, and remembering Sabra's words to him the night before, Kade relented.

"I'll lay a bit in Molly's old room until noon or until Jake an' Molly come," Kade had grumbled. "But I reckon I won't be able to sleep. Maybe jest restin' will be good." So, he had gone to Molly's room and laid down on her old bed while Mattie, Sarah, and Martha began to wash Sabra. He needed to let the women do for Sabra now.

When Thomas peeked in an hour later, his father was fast asleep, lying with the tintype portrait of him and Sabra in his hand. They had taken family pictures at Thomas' wedding several years before, and Kade had wanted a photograph of Sabra alone, and she had refused unless he stood with her. Kade had taken the portrait from the mantle and carried it to the bed with him. That surprised Thomas, not because he wasn't aware of how much his father loved his mother, but for the first time, Thomas saw Kade as vulnerable.

It was not yet noon when Thomas saw Jackson's buggy coming up the valley. He figured they would come in the buggy. Molly was as good a rider as Sabra, but having two-year-old little Jack with her would make coming easier with the buggy. Jake was driving the team, and Molly, cradling the baby, was beside him. The team was coming up the valley at a high trot and Thomas could see they were wet with sweat. He knew if they had left at first light, they made good time getting here before noon with the carriage. There were detours that had to be taken when driving, making the trip a bit longer than that of a man on horseback.

Thomas went down the slope to the barn to meet them. Jake saw Thomas coming to meet them, so he pulled up at the corrals instead of driving to the cabin. Jake would know, Thomas thought, that they were too late.

"How's Ma?" Molly asked, trying to clamber down from the seat with her toddler in her arms.

"Honey," Thomas said gently, going to his little sister. "You're too late. She left us this morning, before dawn."

Molly froze. She looked wildly between her two brothers. Jake leaped down beside her and took the sleeping child from her while Thomas folded Molly into his arms. The two brothers looked at each other over Molly's shoulders. Jake was not surprised. He didn't think they could make it home in time, but he had hoped, for Molly's sake, that he was wrong. They stood, waiting for Molly's sobs to quiet.

"Why didn't you come for me sooner?" Molly asked when she had control of herself again. "Why didn't you send for me?"

"Ma knew you and Jackson were in Cheyenne. She didn't want to call you away from there," Thomas told her. "We promised her we would wait until yesterday when you were supposed to be home. It was what Ma wanted."

"Why didn't she want me here?" Molly wailed. "I should have been here."

Thomas looked fondly at his beautiful little sister. "Honey, she didn't want to see you crying. She told me that last night. She sent me away too, before midnight even. And she sent Jake to get you. She wanted all of us away. She wanted to be with Pa. You know how they were. Ma just needed Pa at the end."

"Where's Jackson?" Thomas looked at Jake.

"They were just pulling in at dark last night," Jake replied. "He was going to get some things taken care of and will be here before dark today. Catherine and Buster will be along with him. Maybe some other hands will come." Jake looked away and back before asking, "Did Pa say when he wanted to bury her?"

"Pa wants to take her to the burial ground at first light tomorrow. Dawn was Ma's favorite time of day. He wants to see her for the last time then."

Jake, Thomas, and Molly sat, saying little, in their parents' cabin. Martha took Molly and Jackson's little boy home with her for the afternoon. It was quiet in the cabin. For the moment, they were alone, apart from their sleeping father in the next room. Jake had asked Martha to spread the word that Kade was finally sleeping and to stay away until at least late afternoon.

"Where's the picture of Ma and Pa?" Molly suddenly asked, seeing it missing from the mantle.

Thomas pointed to Molly's old room. "Peek inside. Pa took it in with him."

Molly got up and moved quietly to the door. She peeked inside before returning to sit with her brothers. "This is going to shatter Pa," she murmured. "I don't know if he will survive this."

"It will be hard, yes, for a time at least," Jake spoke, quiet contemplation in his gaze, "but he will survive."

"How can you be so sure?" Molly asked.

"Because Ma made him promise," Thomas answered for Jake. "She made Pa promise he wouldn't go off half-crazy like when Jim and Tom were killed. Pa would never break a promise, especially to Ma. Jake's right, Pa will survive this, but it's going to be tough."

"We're going to have to cut Pa some slack here," Jake started slowly. "He's going to be hurting, and the way he deals with it might not be the way we want him to. We're going to have to understand that."

"What do you mean?" Molly inquired.

Jake looked out the window before answering. "He'll go to the mountains. And I know you won't want him to go off alone, but that's what he will do."

"Did he tell you that?" Thomas asked.

"No, but he will. That's his way. He will go back to his life before Ma. He'll go back to the mountains to be alone. When he's able, he'll come back and learn to be alone here as well. We have to be ready to let him do that."

"I don't want him to go off," Molly stated. "What if he got hurt? I can't lose him too. He's not a young man, after all. He's almost sixty now."

"Well, he's actually fifty-eight, but that's what I mean," Jake answered patiently. "You won't want him to go, and he will anyway. We'll worry about him, but we can't hold him here. Trust me on this."

"You have always understood Pa better than Molly and me," Thomas said thoughtfully. "You'd think it would be the other way around because we are blood, and you aren't. But you are more like him than either of us."

Jake smiled at this. "I know. Maybe it's just that I grew up with him more when this country was still growing up. Or maybe we just had a bond that had nothing to do with blood. But I know him, and I know his ways. We have to respect that."

Kade woke up shortly after the sun reached its zenith. The three siblings heard the bed creak, and his boots hit the floor. Thomas got up and went to the door.

"Pa?" he spoke softly. "Molly and Jake are here. We are out here sitting."

Kade looked at his son in the doorway and nodded. "Give me a minute. I'll come join you."

Thomas could see the sleep had done his father some good. When Kade came out, the aura of sadness was with him, but he was not quite as haggard as he was that morning. When Molly saw her father, she rose and went to him, and Kade pulled her into an embrace.

"Oh, Pa," Molly whispered, "I don't want her to be gone."

"Don't reckon you are the only one thinkin' that way, daughter," Kade looked at his sons over her head. "I'm thinkin' this might take some time to get used to."

"I'm never going to get used to it," Molly said fiercely.

"Don't reckon you are alone on that either, honey," Kade replied softly.

Kade went into the bedroom to see how the women had dressed Sabra. The boys and Molly went outside. They knew Kade would join them after he had viewed Sabra. Martha and Sam's cabin and Thomas and Beth's cabin were in sight, and once Kade was seen up and outside, the visitors would start to arrive. The teepees of the Utes were below Jake and Anna's cabin and they were also in view. The Welles cabin would not be quiet again until after the burial in the morning. Food would be brought, and people would come and go. But there would always be someone here. They had all done as much as they could for Sabra. Now they could only do for the loved ones Sabra left behind.

They buried Sabra as the sun came over the mountains, bright light streaming out, lighting the day. Jackson, who had arrived late in the afternoon, stood with Molly, letting her lean into him, giving her strength, and holding little Jack. Beth and Thomas stood beside them with their two-year-old Jennie, and Anna and Jake, with their two little girls and one little boy, made up the line. Kade stood between his daughter and Thomas, silent and resolute. Behind them fanned out the other community members, the Jorgensens, the Bates, their children, and their children's spouses, all distant relatives of Jake and friends of Kade and Sabra. Intermixed with the white community were the Utes. These also were primarily relatives of Jake. Jake stood between two cultures, and the people he cared for the most came to pay respects to his mother.

Matthew Jorgensen led the service. He had been the spiritual leader of their community for the past thirty years, ever since Sabra and Kade settled here and brought Mattie and Matthew to join them. Matthew had led them in weddings, baptisms, Sunday prayer services, and funerals, but this funeral was a tough one for him. Sabra had been loved by all.

"I have known Sabra for over thirty years," Matthew began solemnly. "She first came to the doorstep of my in-laws in Illinois with her newborn baby in her arms. She stood before us, telling the family about their Uncle Jacob and his western family. Sabra became the wife of Jacob's Ute son, and she held her mixed-blood baby in her arms. She was not ashamed. But she was afraid of being rejected because of it. This family I married into loved her, accepted her, and I did too. I respected Sabra that day for her courage. I never lost that respect for her in all the years I have lived in these mountains with Sabra and Kade and their family. Sabra was a spirit. The Utes call her Woman with Many Horses. That is a fitting name for her. Her family and her horses were her whole life. We will miss seeing her riding, hair flying under her slouch hat, graceful and proud. We will miss her joy of life, her wisdom, her gentleness, and her laughter. We will miss her unfailing love for her family, of which we all feel we are part. We will miss the music Sabra played on her piano and the songs she sang. We have lost the best friend any of us have ever had. I have no words strong enough to express the sadness we all feel with this goodbye. We can only be glad that we had the joy of knowing her, that she was one of us."

Kade sat quietly, listening to the stories being told around him. He was wearing down. While it was only early afternoon, the past week and this morning's burial had taken its toll. He was weary and heartsore. He wanted to go home to his cabin, yet he dreaded it. Sabra was not there anymore.

He watched his friends and family around him. Thirty years ago, he, Sabra, and old Tom had settled this valley. Tom had gone that spring to St. Louis and brought Sabra's best friend, Mattie, and her husband Matthew, here to settle this land with them. Then the following summer, Jim Bates, Mattie's brother, and Jim's wife Sarah had joined them, backtracking from the Oregon territory. Jim and Matthew took the lead in farming, mainly garden truck and hay. Old Tom and Kade took the lead with the cattle, oxen, mules, and horses they raised to trade with the immigrants on the Oregon Trail or with the army at Ft. Laramie. They had all prospered here. Now the married offspring of all the families made this more than a farm, more than a ranch. It had become a community. Cabins spanned up and down the river valley and the low meadows that extended from it.

And with every community, there was a burial ground. Jim and Old Tom, with his wife Clara, already laid there. The stillborn children of several of the families lay waiting for others to join them. Now Sabra was there, beside her two stillborn children.

Jeremiah made a fitting box for Sabra's final journey. Jake told Kade the night before how Jeremiah feared for Sabra days earlier. Jeremiah, the oldest son of Matthew and Mattie, had a small lumber mill. When he saw how sick Sabra had become, he started working on boards, sanding them, staining them with beeswax, and polishing them with a clean rag. When it was apparent that Sabra would not survive, he stayed out all night, putting the boards together and making a coffin befitting her. His younger brother, Lathe, went looking for him and seeing what Jeremiah was working on, the two brothers stayed up all night to finish the coffin. Sabra had been laid out in the main room of Kade's cabin until they carried her to the burial ground this morning. It was a lovely coffin. Kade was touched that the boys, both distant cousins of Jake's, would make something so fine for Sabra. And now, the box was in the ground, the cabin was empty, and Sabra was gone.

Molly's voice startled Kade from his thoughts. "Pa, I'm going to walk up to the cabin. Would you walk with me?"

Kade looked around. He was finished here. He nodded at Molly and rose to his feet. "Reckon I could use some rest, daughter," he said softly. "No one will leave until I do, so I best get a move on an' let people get on with their lives."

They said their thanks and farewells and started the walk towards home.

"Who's got the baby?" Kade asked as they walked.

"Jackson has him. Jackson will come soon. Little Jack just went to sleep," Molly answered.

"How long you plannin' on staying?" Kade broke the silence after a few minutes.

"We'll stay tomorrow and then head home," Molly responded. "Jackson wants to get some of the cowboys out bunching up some of the cattle. But I will help you go through Mother's things tomorrow," Molly gave her father a sideways glance. "I'd like to help you with that."

Kade nodded. He didn't think he'd be much help with that. It was fitting that Molly stay and take care of that task.

"Pa," Molly took hold of his hand, "would you come home with us for a bit? It's been a time since you came and," Molly hesitated, unsure how to say what she felt, "well, with Ma gone, maybe you should come stay with us."

The request didn't surprise Kade. He knew his daughter. She would want to try to ease his hurt. What she didn't understand was that she couldn't. He had to find his own way.

"Daughter," Kade began slowly, "I will visit soon, but I need to work this out myself."

"But, Pa," Molly spoke quickly, "You could play with little Jack. He needs to grow up knowing his grandpa."

Kade gave a short laugh. "I don't reckon I know much what to do with such a young'un, but I'll be a visitin' a lot as he grows. He'll need to learn 'bout these mountains. I'll come visit, daughter. When the time is right."

The evening passed better than Jake expected. Thomas and Jake brought their families to Kade's home, and along with Molly, Jackson, and little Jack, the main room of the cabin was overflowing. The toddlers tumbled over each other, playing with balls of yarn, cups, and saucers from the cupboard. When they got tired, they crawled into a parent's lap and dozed off. The grown-ups sat quietly for a while, not sure where to let the conversation go, until Jake asked Kade a question.

"Pa, tell us again about you and Mother coming here." Kade contemplated the question, looking into the fire for a moment. Then a small smile touched his face, and his eyes took on a faraway look.

"Tom was with us when we said our vows at Jacob's cabin," he started slowly. "Tom figured he wasn't going to be much use to a newly married couple in a one-room cabin, so he decided to set off for Ft. Laramie. From Ft. Laramie, Tom headed to St. Louis. I had a letter sent back with him to my brother, Joe, to outfit a wagon with supplies an' buy up some starter cattle an' a few horses. Then Tom was going to wait there for Mattie an' Matthew to reach St. Louis in the spring. We wanted to let them know we were not going to Oregon, but if they wanted to farm with us, Tom would bring them out. It would be half the trip for them to come to Wyoming territory rather than goin' all the way to Oregon. Tom an' I had the idea of trading with the wagon trains as they went west on the Oregon Trail. We thought that might make a good business, an'," Kade paused in his story, eyes distant, "we were right about that."

"Yer ma wasn't real happy to leave Jacob's mountains, but she knew it was for the best if our plan was to work. I was glad to go. I struggled in my mind 'bout Sabra living there with Blue Knife, yer pa," Kade looked over at Jake then. "It was good for me to start our married life there, though. If I could get through my thoughts there, then by leaving them ghosts behind when we left, I knew we'd be good. But it was still hard on Sabra. I'm glad we got to go back this past summer. Sabra was happy to be there again an' I long ago quit worrying about Blue Knife being her first husband.

"We left Jacob's cabin in the springtime after the worst of the snows had melted. We came this way by the hot springs an' stopped a couple days by one. Those were some good days for us," Kade smiled in the remembering.

Jake, watching his father, saw Kade relaxing. Talking about the past brought back good memories, healing memories. Jake glanced at Thomas, and they grinned at each other. They could both imagine the good times their parents had camped by the hot springs near Steamboat. They knew their parents. It was no secret how their folks loved each other. They could imagine what their father was remembering about those days.

"Tom an' I had wandered much of this land an' years before we had followed the Little Snake River looking for beaver. I remembered there were lush river valleys an' many upland meadows that rose up from the valley. This is where I headed with yer ma that spring. We found this place. We camped just about where Jim an' Sarah's cabin is now an' searched up an' down the river for the best spot to settle. Finally, we decided on buildin' a cabin up here along this meadow a piece. When Mattie an' Matthew arrived, they decided to be closer to the lowland bottoms along the river.

"Mattie sent a letter with the wagon train they were with to Jim, who was already in Oregon. Mattie wanted Jim an' Sarah to join us the next summer. Suddenly it was three families an' Tom. I think yer ma was happy to have friends here, but we never wanted more people to crowd in on us. At least not until all you children grew up, an' then we were glad you didn't leave," Kade stopped then, finding himself talked out.

After a time, Kade started again. "Your ma had no other living relatives that she knew of. I only had my brother, Joe, and a sister, both in St. Louis. They both were settled in St. Louis, so having the Bates and Jorgensens here was good for us. With Jim an' Mattie being niece and nephew to old Jacob, an' Jacob being your grandfather," Kade glanced at Jake, "it was like we were part of their family. That was good for all of us. Your ma loved having friends. Between that an' having you children an' her horses, I don't think she ever wanted more."

They sat until the shadows faded to black outside before Thomas and Beth returned to their cabin with their sleeping daughter. Little Jennie Rose was already the apple of Thomas' eye. If the Welles boys were good at anything, Jake thought, it was birthing girls. Jake had two girls first before, finally, getting a boy. Only Molly and Jackson had a firstborn son. Sabra was overjoyed with the babies, boys and girls. For that matter, Kade was too. Jake's two girls, Kestrel and Sabra Lark, were Kade's shadows when he visited. Five-year-old Kestrel would hound Grandpa to take her out to ride Smoky. She was going to be another Sabra, for sure. Right now, Jake knew that this would be a comfort to Kade. Maybe that was the best they could do for Kade. Help him remember the good times and give him something to live for in the future.

Molly and Jackson stayed one more day. Kade and his boys took Jackson through the horse herd and then rode upriver to check on the steers grazing there, waiting to be driven to Laramie soon. It gave Kade a purpose and the boys wanted to keep him busy. Jackson bought a couple of horses, and they sorted them out, ready to tether to the buggy the next day to get them home. Buster, Jackson's foreman, headed out early that morning with the few cowboys who had come for the funeral. Buster's wife, Catherine, was Mattie and Matthew's daughter. Catherine would ride back with Jackson and Molly the next day. Catherine wanted to visit her parents the extra day. She had come by horseback but welcomed riding in the buggy going home. Catherine was expecting a child in the late winter and thought the buggy would be easier traveling for her.

When the men returned to Kade's cabin late in the afternoon, Molly, Anna, and Beth had a big supper waiting. Kade's sitting room was almost overflowing with his sons and daughter, their spouses, and children, so they built a fire outside and sat around it, mountain man style, eating. They didn't need the fire for warmth until the sun went down, but the coffee pot sat on its grate, ready for refills when needed. The little children, all too young to understand the sadness that filled their parents, played and rolled in the grass around the grown-ups. Kestrel and Sabra Lark had both cried for their grandma, but as it is with little children, the pain was soon forgotten, at least, until they missed Sabra again. The permanence of death was hard for little children to understand.

"Jackson, when are you driving your herd to Laramie?" Thomas asked when the conversations around him lagged.

"I was thinking in about two weeks," Jackson replied.

"I have most of my men out gathering now and sorting off the cattle I want to sell. You could bring yours up closer in about ten days if that works for you."

"How's that sound, Pa?" Thomas looked to his father. "Should we gather and start moving the steers next week?"

Kade looked at Thomas vaguely, "Whatever you think best, son."

"Well, how many hands do you think we should take with us?" Thomas kept on, hoping to draw his father in.

"Thomas, you handle the cattle," Kade responded somewhat impatiently. "You been doing that for a couple years now. You an' Jake can make the decisions."

Thomas and Jake exchanged glances. They would have preferred to get their father interested again in business. Give him something to think about rather than thinking about being without Sabra. But Kade was pulling back; they could both see that.

Molly and Jackson pulled out shortly after daybreak the next day. Kade was up and outside with his sons to see them off. Thomas hitched up the buggy while Jake got the horse herd in to cut off the two horses that Jackson bought. Then together, the three men watched the buggy fade away toward Mattie's to collect Catherine and be on their way.

The buggy was not far when Kade turned, and without a word, he went back to the cabin. Thomas and Jake watched him go without comment and then went to the corral to pick out the horses they wanted to work with that day. They would keep the herd in until their father returned in hopes he would also pick out some horses to ride with them.

But when Kade returned, it was apparent that riding colts was not his intention. Over his shoulder were thrown saddlebags, stuffed full, and a rolled-up blanket was over his arm. Kade dropped these items by the corral and went into the barn. When he returned, he was carrying a rolled-up canvas sheet, some trading supplies, and a pack saddle. He went into the corral and surveyed the horses. When he came out, he had his most trusted saddle horse with him and a younger, but steady gelding.

"So, where you planning on heading, Pa?" Jake asked. This was what he had expected; his father would head out alone. Jake was not surprised, only saddened that he was right. Like Molly, Jake didn't want his father going off alone.

Kade didn't pause from saddling, "Reckon I'll head up to check the cattle in the high country. See where I want to mosey from there."

"You coming back from up there?" Thomas couldn't resist asking.

Kade didn't answer at once. When he had the cinch tight and picked up the pack saddle for his second horse, he looked over at Thomas, "Tom, I don't reckon I know where I am going right now, but I'll be back for fall gather. You two can handle things. I am not needed here," he stopped talking, working with the latigos. "Hell, I just need to work this out myself. I'll be fine. But I need to go to the mountains. I need to be alone."

CHAPTER 2

Miss Tillie's – August 1880

J ames rode drag on the cattle, feeling grimy and dusty. It was dry in August and hot on the plains. Being the youngest of the crew, he often got stuck in the drag, eating the dust of a thousand steers. But he never complained. Whining wasn't going to help any and would only make the rest of the men think of him as a kid. He had been a trusted member of the Twin Peak's ranch ever since the Cheyenne attacked the ranch when he was fourteen. By his own people, he was considered a man. He held up his end in all his chores. But here, riding with the cowboys of Jackson's ranch, helping to push Jackson's and Twin Peak's cattle to market, he was often ribbed by the seasoned cowboys who worked for Jackson. But James didn't mind. His time would come.

James was a stringy, lean, eighteen-year-old with still a good deal of filling out to do. His arms were well-muscled beneath his homespun shirt, but he still looked like a kid. His ma said he'd flesh out soon and be a good-looking man, but it couldn't come fast enough for James. He was lithe and quick, and he was trusted to ride the Welles' young colts now, but outside of his own community, he still looked nearer fourteen than his eighteen years and often found strangers treating him that way.

Only he and Thomas rode with Jackson's Anchor

J crew on this drive. Jake, Sam, Lathe, and Army had helped gather the cattle and drive them to the Anchor J, but they were needed at home. Haying wasn't over yet, and with Jackson's cowboys, only Thomas needed to be along to deal with the cattle buyers. But it was the custom of the three Twin Peaks families to always have someone from one of the other families along on any business trip. Echoing words of Kade's long ago that it was safer to have several names on a bank account, there were always at least two, if not more, members of the ranch who took livestock to sell. James was proud that he was chosen to go along this year.

"Time you learn some of the responsibility of an owner, James," Uncle Matthew had told him. "You help Thomas and learn the ropes. You might be needed for more than just riding colts someday."

James was grateful to his uncle for the words. He was interested in knowing more about the business part of the ranch than just the work part. He knew all he needed about haying, and he hated farming. Riding horses was his first love, but cattle were the biggest part of their ranch. With his father buried on the hill, James and his brother Will would hold the reins for their mother, Sarah. Will was a farmer at heart. Will hated to spend even a day rambling the river looking for cattle. Instead, Will would walk the fields, checking the growing things and where the best hay could be cut. Will was like Uncle Matthew in that way. But James was like his great uncle Jacob, the mountain man he never knew. James would mount a horse and head out if he had a chance. Hell, he had been home three weeks since he, Kade, and Sabra came home from Jacob's cabin in the high mountain land Jake loved. James was already restless and wanted to make tracks.

He'd rather go with Jake to the Ute villages, but he'd settle for a town this time. He hadn't been to Laramie since he was fourteen. But he remembered the town. He remembered seeing the girls there and how his heart pounded when they sashayed by him. He was eighteen now and he was more experienced. He had heard the cowboys talk. He knew there were women there to be had. He intended to find some.

He had gone to Jacob's cabin for three summers now, always stopping to visit Jake's relatives in a Ute village. Those Indian women were pretty nice to him, not caring that he was barely more than a kid. Hell, he didn't feel like a kid when he was there, and they didn't treat him like one, either. It took a good portion of his pay to buy the ribbons, knives, and baubles that were prized by the Indian women or their husbands if it came to that, but what else did he have to spend his money on?

James wished Jake was with them on this drive instead of Thomas. Thomas was always teasing the younger kids, and like his namesake, Old Tom, he was a great story-teller. But when it came to the women, Thomas was always the steady one. Jake married Anna when he was twenty-five, and that hadn't been planned. Thomas had courted Beth for almost two years before they married when Thomas was twenty-three. James wasn't even sure if Thomas ever visited the Utes with Jake. Thomas took cattle to Laramie once with Lathe and Jackson before Thomas married, but those three never talked much about that trip, at least not what they did there. James hoped Thomas didn't expect him to hit the hotel by dark. If James only had one night to spend in town, he meant to make it a good one.

They got the herd into the stockyards at Laramie in good time. The men needed to sort the Twin Peaks cattle from the Anchor J cattle before finishing for the day. Jackson's cattle were the longhorn cattle that originally came from Texas. Longhorns were lean and sometimes wild-eyed, living most of their lives on the range. Twin Peaks cattle represented years of breeding that initially came from the settlements in the east with the pioneers on the Oregon Trail. The Welles traded rested stock for worn out animals with the emigrants for years. As the Twin Peaks herd increased, the best cattle were kept and bred, climbing the mountain slopes in the summer and fed on hay in the winter. They were beefier than the longhorns and would bring a better price. Even though Twin Peaks brought fewer cattle to town each year than the big ranches, they earned almost as much money as the larger herds.

It was early evening but still daylight when the cowboys finished the sorting. Thomas waved James over after talking with Chadwick, the livestock buyer.

"I'm going to supper with Jackson and Chadwick tonight. You want to join us, or do you have other plans?" Thomas asked.

James felt instant relief. "I can fend for myself, Thomas," he answered, glad that he had the evening to himself.

"I'll get a room for us at the hotel then," Thomas told him. "You can ask the desk clerk for the room number." Then reaching into his pocket, he pulled out a wad of bills. Counting some out, he handed them to James. "This should be your pay for the month. If you need more, then you come see me, and I can write it down. We can settle up when we get home."

"Thanks, Thomas," James said. "I reckon this will be enough."

"James," Thomas said seriously. "You watch yourself. This ain't no Indian village."

James grinned, "I know that. Ma lit into me before I left."

James walked into town from the livery with a couple of Jackson's cowboys. These were the youngest of the crew and new men to James. They had hired on with Jackson sometime in the spring, and James hadn't run into them before. He wasn't sure he even liked them. They were a foul-mouthed pair and constantly teased him for being so young, but the rest of the men were quite a bit older, and James didn't fit in there either.

"You goin' looking for a poke tonight?" the man called Cleat asked, grinning wickedly.

"Reckon I'll find a bathhouse first and maybe a steak," James responded, not looking at the two men.

"Hell, you're too much a kid to find a woman yit," the second cowboy, Harvey, laughed. "You best jest go to bed early and leave the carousing to men."

"What men would that be?" James asked quietly. "Think most the men are still getting their pay at the corrals."

The two cowboys laughed, not one bit insulted by James' insinuation. They walked on a bit more before Cleat started in again.

"Harv," he asked, "you goin' to Miss Tillie's tonight?"

"Tell you what," Harvey responded, "why don't we three jest meet at the café after we get cleaned up? We can get us a good meal and then walk over together.

What about you, James? Are you in with us?"

James knew what Miss Tillie's establishment was, and intended to go there anyway, so why not go over with these two? He didn't hanker on walking into the fanciest bordello in town and not having a clue what to say. Yes, he knew what to do, just not what to say to get to the doing part. James nodded to the two with him, and they hit the edge of town.

James rolled off the woman and stretched out beside her on the bed. He felt loose and easy, relaxed. Damn, he just plain felt good.

"Thank you, ma'am," he said quietly.

The woman was already getting up and dressing. She looked curiously at the young cowboy. "Didn't think you'd know what to do, cowboy, you being so young, but you ain't bad," she smiled at him. "And you don't have to thank me; I work for it."

"Yes, ma'am," James answered, watching her dress. The woman was not young, but not old either. She still had a figure that a man would hunger for. She probably was still in her twenties, but times had hardened her. Still, she had not teased him when he asked for her. He had seen her lounging on a settee, surveying the room when he entered the parlor. Her name was Rosie and she cost more than some of the other girls. Rosie was clean and shapely, catching James' eye. He had the money and the time, but he didn't pay for a whole night with her. He wasn't used to spending money, so having some left in his pockets felt good. He was going to make it count.

"You best get yourself dressed and come down," the woman told him. "I'll be needing the room again soon 'nough. You can get a drink downstairs if you want."

"Thank you, ma'am," James repeated. "I'll be down." He rolled his legs off the bed and stood, reaching for his pants. Damn, he thought, it was over so soon. Maybe he should have paid for the whole night. In the village, sometimes, he spent the whole night with an Indian woman. He liked that.

The prostitute was out the door, and James was not far behind her. Entering the elaborate parlor, he saw Cleat and Harvey sitting near the bar at a small table flanked by a settee and cushioned chairs. They waved him over. James stopped at the bar to get a beer from the bartender who worked it. He was the first Black man James had ever seen, but he remembered his manners and didn't stare.

"You look quite satisfied," Cleat began. "What was she like?"

James looked across the room where the woman was already sitting on another man's lap. "She was nice," James' upbringing wouldn't allow him to talk badly about a woman, including what they did in a closed room. His Pa had been death on that, and Ma too. And to be fair, he didn't want to talk to these two about his evening.

The men needled James for a few minutes but got nothing out of him. He refused to rise to the bait. Finally, they gave up and watched the activity around them. The parlor of Miss Tillie's was only for those men who were regulars or had already paid money for a roll. It was quiet and had good alcohol and comfortable seating. It also had a goodly number of women in the room, and they weren't shy about either attire or activity. The show, alone, was worth sitting there sipping a good beer.

Suddenly, the door opened behind the bar, and an immense woman came out. James didn't think he'd ever seen a woman so large. As if that wasn't enough, she wore a tight low-cut dress and her bosom stuck out, straining at the silky material. James couldn't help but stare this time. Cleat noticed James staring and laughed.

"You know who that is, don't you?" Cleat asked.

James just shook his head. She was dressed just like the other prostitutes, but he couldn't believe that a man would ask for her.

"That's Miss Tillie," Cleat told him. "She owns the place. Watch this."

Cleat beckoned to the barman for another whiskey. "Watch now," he repeated. Taking out a bill, he waved it at the woman and set it down by him on the table. James waited, seeing the barman set the small shot glass on the bar and fill it. Then Miss Tillie picked it up and placed it in the crevice of her bosom, pushing it in. Without hesitation, she sauntered over to Cleat, and getting close, she leaned over him.

"There you go, cowboy," she said, plucking up the bill, "if you're man enough."

She made no effort to take the little glass out and serve Cleat. He grinned at her, and slipping his hand carefully into her dress front, he slowly eased the glass out. There wasn't a drop spilled. Without another word, the woman turned and returned to the bar. As they sat, this ritual was repeated over and over. Apparently, it was an everyday activity. The whiskey cost double that way, but it didn't seem to bother anyone.

A pair of dice rested on the table, and Cleat picked

them up and played with them. He looked over at Harvey, and they smiled at each other.

"You know, Miss Tillie still takes customers at times," Cleat started. "Course, some boys are some scared of going anywhere with her. If she fell on you, she'd kill you." Cleat didn't lower his voice, and it made James uncomfortable. They were sitting close and could be overheard.

"That's a mean thing to say," James commented quietly.

"But I hear tell that jest to see them bazoos hanging is worth the risk," Cleat cackled at this. "I gotta admit them is the biggest pair I've ever seen."

"Drop it, Cleat," James said again. James would have been enjoying himself just sitting and watching the soiled doves work the men, but he was uncomfortable with these two. He was ready to leave, and scooted his chair back, downing the rest of his beer.

"Hey, how about we just roll the dice for it?" Cleat said, sensing James' intention to leave.

"What are we rolling on?" Harvey asked, but his grin seemed a good clue that he already knew what was up.

"Let's roll the dice. Low man has to go upstairs with the elephant woman," Cleat replied.

"You roll. I'm gonna call it quits," James said. He wanted no part in this.

"I told you, Harv, that this kid would be scared," Cleat egged. "He comes back from upstairs walking like a goddamn peacock but scared to go upstairs with a sure enough big-busted woman."

"I'm not scared, jest don't need to do any betting on it," James replied. He didn't like being called a coward.

"Then roll the dice, cowboy kid," Cleat pushed them

31

toward James. "Show us you ain't scared to see them big watermelons."

James felt cornered. He was going to ride for two days toward home with these two. This story would be told over and over by the campfire that James was chicken. Maybe he'd be lucky and not be low man. He picked up the dice and rolled. It was a fair roll. He had a six, a deuce, and a three for eleven points. Harvey picked up the dice next. He shook the dice in the cup, and just when he was started throwing them, Cleat punched James on the shoulder.

"Look over there!" he said excitedly, pointing to the far corner where a girl was sitting on a man's lap, facing him, and slowly rocking back and forth.

"Damn," Cleat breathed, "that about gets me in the mood to go upstairs again." Then he looked down at the table. Harvey had thrown two sixes and a one for thirteen.

"Normally, I'd take that as an unlucky number," Harvey said, "but in this case, I pretty much like it."

Cleat picked up the dice and slowly put them in the cup, shaking it slowly as he gazed around the room again. Without looking at the table, he dumped the dice out, but in the process, he bumped Harvey's beer roughly, and it sloshed over, running down the table towards James. James pushed back quickly to keep the liquid from running onto him.

"Well, hot damn, look at that!" Cleat grinned. "Two fives and a four. You lose, cowboy. Get your money out and take a walk to heaven upstairs!"

James stared at the dice and the beer running down the table, the realization that he had lost the bet setting in. Resolutely, he stood and went to the bar.

"Ma'am," he said. "Reckon if you was willing, I'd like

to go upstairs with you."

Miss Tillie looked at the barman quickly and then back at James, "I'm no cheap working girl like Rosie," she said. "It takes ten dollars to go up with me."

James swallowed deeply. He had paid five dollars for Rosie. A whole night would have cost him twenty. Still, a bet was a bet, and he had lost. He nodded. As James followed Miss Tillie out the door, he heard Cleat and Harvey cackling. James had the overwhelming desire to put a fist in a face, but instead, he just followed this immense woman up the stairs.

As he climbed the stairs behind Miss Tillie, James' thoughts whirled. *What the hell was he to do now,* he thought. He had absolutely no desire for this woman. If anything, her immense bulk turned off all amorous thoughts. He figured he could pretend to like her, but he knew one part of his anatomy that was going to make a liar out of him. She was going to think him just a boy unable to get it up. Shit, how did he get himself into this?

They entered a very nice room on the second floor. The bed was immense, befitting the size of the woman. It was made up with a colorful quilt, matching the bright frilly curtains on the window. It was bigger than the room he went to with Rosie and far better furnished. A dresser against the wall and a couple of chairs were at the foot of the bed. A porcelain washbasin and a pitcher were on the dresser, which he soon found out were full.

"Stand over there, cowboy," Tillie commanded, pointing to the basin. "Drop them britches and lean back and enjoy this."

"Ma'am," James began, "I been to the bathhouse already . . . and to Rosie. I been washed more today than in the whole past month."

"Well, we don't want no damn diseases in my place. So, you best get used to it," Tillie took no nonsense off her customers. She pointed to the wall.

James skinned out of his britches and boots, feeling embarrassed. At least with Rosie, he was already showing his desire. He leaned back against the wall. James remembered something his Pa told him once when he complained about a chore. "Being a man is doing things you don't want to do," his Pa had told him. "Sometimes you just got to buck up and take whatever is thrown at you," James remembered. In two short months after this conversation, his father lay dead with a bullet in him. *Well, he was going to buck up here,* James thought, *even if it killed him.* At least what went on here would be just between this woman and himself. He leaned his head back against the wall and closed his eyes.

James felt the warm water, silky with soap, touch him. With his eyes closed, maybe he could imagine Rosie with him. James had to admit, it did feel pretty good, but it wasn't making him come alive. The towel she used was soft, and she knelt, sliding it slowly up and down his legs. Tillie's fingers moved along him. She was an expert James could tell. *If he didn't think about having to crawl into a bed on top of her, maybe he could keep from shaming himself,* he thought. It was then, when he thought that this part of the process would be finished, that he felt her mouth on him. James went rigid; all of him went rigid. His last clear thought before he let himself simply enjoy the sensations was that he was not going to shame himself this evening after all.

James was glad for the wall to keep him upright. He stood, gasping, feeling the sweat on his body. Tillie laughed at him.

"Didn't expect that, did you, cowboy?" she grinned. "Now climb in that bed."

"Ma'am, I think I got my ten dollars' worth," James said. "You've been fine."

"I got a bottle of champagne here. You ever had champagne?"

"No, ma'am," James replied. He'd heard Jackson and Molly talk about champagne, but had never had any himself.

"Climb up in that bed, and we'll have us a glass," Tillie commanded again, pointing. James climbed.

The champagne had a different taste, but he liked it. He leaned back against the piles of pillows, sitting upright, and Tillie climbed in next to him. They sat in companionable silence while they sipped the drink. When James' glass was empty, Tillie filled it again.

"You didn't want to come up here with me, did you, son?" Tillie said softly.

James thought of lying, but he knew that wouldn't suit. "No, ma'am, but I lost a bet. But ma'am, it was the best bet I ever lost. I got no regrets."

Tillie laughed outright at that. "You didn't lose that bet, boy," she said. "They cheated."

"No shit?" James was surprised. How could he have been so dumb? "I'm sorry, ma'am. I shouldn't have said that."

Tillie laughed harder. "Cowboy, I'm just a whore. I have heard that language before."

James thought about that before he answered. "Maybe so, ma'am, but still, you deserve the same respect I'd give any lady. There is right and wrong, and using that word in front of you was wrong. But it just slipped out."

They sat in silence again. Tillie reached to the side table and took out a cigarette. "Smoke?" she asked.

"No, ma'am. Thank you, but I never got around to smoking yet."

Tillie nodded and lit a smoke for herself before she began to speak. "Not many men come in here treating us women like a lady. Sometimes we forget what it was like before we fell from grace. Rosie told me you were just a proper gentleman, and I believe she was right on that score. A lot of us women in the red-light district might have been ladies once. Most of us didn't choose this profession, but once you are in it, it is hard to get out."

"Did you choose it?" James wondered. He found it pleasant sitting in this soft bed talking to this woman.

"No, it was just circumstances that got me here," Tillie went quiet. James was content to sip the drink. He wasn't in any hurry to leave anymore. He looked around the room. On the dresser was a tintype picture of a beautiful young girl, posing in her finery, smiling for the camera.

"Who is that pretty girl?" he asked.

Tillie looked over at the dresser and smiled. "That, my boy, is me, about twelve years ago."

"Holy," James whispered. "You were beautiful."

"I had just made a big bundle of money working a mining town and had that picture taken. That money and the money I made after was what built this house."

"Is that why you kept working at this?" James asked.

"The money was just too good? Didn't you ever want to quit and get married or anything?"

"It does happen that women like us get married sometimes and live a normal life, but it doesn't happen a lot," Tillie mused. "It just didn't happen for me. I was smarter than a lot of women, though. I saved my money and when I was getting too old and too fat to turn tricks, I had enough money to build this house and run it."

"Didn't you ever love anyone? Want to quit?"

"I was born in the South," Tilly began, "and while my family was not wealthy or plantation owners, we did good. The first battle of the war ran right over our little farm. My mother was dead already, and my pa went to fight with the rebels. I had to run for it. There was a man who I took up with then. His name was Randall. He had a horse, and he took me with him to get away from the fighting. It wasn't more than a couple of days before he was telling me he loved me, making advances. He was well-dressed and spoke like a gentleman, so I thought he was dashing. We traveled for several days and finally stopped outside a town where it turned out he had a little house. It had two rooms, a front room, and a bedroom. That night he told me we should get married, but we had to find a preacher first. But he didn't want to wait, and by morning, well, I was ruined, so to speak. He promised he loved me, and I believed him then. We were away from the fighting, and I felt safe. He went off to town every afternoon and came home late at night. He said he worked as a bouncer at the saloon, but I found out later that he was a gambler. We were maybe at that little house a week and Randall came home earlier than usual. It was after dark, though, and he had a man with him. They sat for a while at the table having a beer, and he told me to go in the bedroom and leave them alone. When he came in, not too much after I went in, he came to me and helped me out of my dress. I thought we were going to go to bed, but then he tells me the other man was going to come in. Well, I was appalled and told him so, but he kissed me and held me and told me if we wanted to get away and get married, we needed more money than he was making, so this would be our shortcut to a future together. We argued, and he coaxed until finally, I said yes. He promised that he'd be right out in the other room so no harm would come to me. That was the first night," Tillie stopped talking and poured herself more champagne.

"The next night, Randall brought home another man, then it happened again and again. One night, he came home with two men, then three. Finally, I got mad. I fought with him in the morning and told him I was finished. He slapped me around then, threatening me. I asked for the money the men were paying him, and he refused that too. I thought about running away, but I had nothing but the clothes I wore. He always brought just enough food for a day or so." Tillie lit another cigarette.

"There was a little shed out back, and one afternoon, I was out walking and heard moaning coming from it. There was a man inside with a bad leg and head wound. I cleaned him up, bound the wounds with rags, and told him to stay there, and he'd be safe. His name was Marcus, and he was running away from someone. I brought him food. As he got better, I would go out and sit with him during the day when Randall was gone, and we would talk. Then one morning, Randall got really angry at me. I had resisted with one of the men he brought home the night before, wanting me to do something I didn't want to do. Randall was beating me when suddenly Marcus hit him over the head with the blunt side of an ax. He didn't mean to kill him, just stun him. But the blow must have broken Randall's neck. Anyway, we took off Randall's clothes and dumped him in the well. I got the money out of his pocket that he got from the men the night before. Marcus put on Randall's clothes, and we had the horse, and we took off. We hit off west. Marcus didn't want me to sell myself to other men, but we also had to live, and times were hard. Marcus helped and protected me, and I made money. So here I am now," Tillie finished her story.

"So why didn't you get married to Marcus? What happened to him?" James was curious now.

"Some things just aren't meant to be, cowboy, and that was how it was with us," Tillie looked away. By her body language, James knew that the subject was closed.

"So, you want anything else from me?" Tillie asked. "You want a peek? Was that part of the bet you lost?"

James smiled at her. She was still a big woman, but she didn't seem repulsive anymore. Maybe just knowing her story made her seem more human. "I don't need anything else," he said. "But I'm curious. Is Tillie your real name?"

"We red-light girls don't usually use our given names," she responded. "I am no exception with that. But my real name is of no consequence here."

James nodded, then said, "I should get going."

"No, you stay," Tillie retorted. "I don't sleep in this room, and there is no one else coming up here tonight. You can have this whole bed to yourself. Enjoy the champagne. This bed has to be better than those in the hotel," she smiled at James, got slowly out of bed, and went to a side door. "This is my closet, and my private room is on the other side." She opened the door and went through it.

"Ma'am, Miss Tillie," James called, stopping her. "Where do I leave the ten dollars?"

Tillie grinned at him, "I ain't been treated so respectful for years," she said. "You got yourself a free one tonight." She turned to go, and then as if thinking of something, she turned back, "If either of them other cowboys had lost, even fair and square, I would have charged them double this and not shown them half the time you got. They are vulgar men, and I would make them pay dearly. So tomorrow, when they try to laugh at you, you tell them just what they were missing."

James interrupted her, "No, ma'am, I can't do that. What happened here isn't their business."

Tillie smiled fondly at James, "You, my boy, may look like a kid, but you are a man, in more ways than one. But this one time, you can speak about it. Make those two ringers feel bad. You got my permission," she turned to go. Over her shoulder, Tillie said, "You can come back anytime and visit me."

Tillie walked through her closet to the room next door, starting to unbutton her bodice. The Black barman sat in a rocking chair, reading a book.

"You're done with the young man?" he asked.

"I am," Tillie replied. "He was a nice boy. Going to be a good man when he fills out some."

The Black man stood up and came to Tillie, helping her with her buttons. "You look tired tonight, Susan.

Time you get in bed. Let me rub your back for you."

The woman looked fondly at him, "You ever wish it could have been different for us?" she asked.

The barman looked seriously at Tillie, "Someday, a Black man and white woman may be accepted together, but we live in a world that won't allow that. I am just glad for what we have."

Tillie climbed into bed, sighing. "Curl up here, Marcus," she said softly. "We can pretend we live in different times."

James woke in the morning to a soft tapping on the door and the sun streaming through frilly curtains. He looked around, trying to get his bearings, then remembered where he was. Damn, he had been sound asleep.

"Yes?" James said to the closed door.

A black head poked in. "Mister James, there's a boy below, from the hotel, asking about you. He says the rest of your ranch crew is eating and wondering if you are here."

James shook his head again to clear his thoughts. He had been sleeping hard. "Tell him to go back and tell the boss I'm on my way, please."

"Yessir," the Black barman answered. "And Miss Tillie say for you to go out through the kitchen and take a sweet roll with you."

James grinned and nodded. He was learning it paid to make friends with a variety of people. Up quickly and dressed, he headed for the door to leave. James looked back at Tillie's room with its oversized bed and chairs and frilly curtains. He smiled and digging in his pocket, he came up with ten one-dollar bills and laid them neatly on the dresser, tucked underneath the picture of Tillie in her youth.

When James walked into the hotel eatery a half-hour later, the conversation around the Twin Peaks and Anchor J table stopped abruptly.

"'Bout gave up on you," Thomas growled. "We are done eating now."

"Oh, that's alright, Tom," James answered easily. "I just finished eating on the way over here. They had sweet rolls that were really good. I'll just run up to your room and get my things, wash up, and meet you at the livery." James turned on his heel and left. He saw Cleat and Harvey grinning, then losing some of their smiles as it was apparent that James was no worse for wear from staying out all night. James thought he would just let them keep guessing for a while.

The crew rode out as soon as Thomas and Jackson collected supplies at the mercantile. They had a day and a half ride to Jackson's and another half day farther to make it home. James had his horse saddled and was waiting when the rest of the crew arrived at the livery. Thomas noticed that James stayed away from Cleat and Harvey, instead keeping close to Thomas, asking how the sale of the livestock went. Thomas got over his impatience with his young cousin now that James had turned up in good shape. It gave Thomas quite the turn to wake up and find that James had never returned to the room the night before. Over breakfast, he had questioned the hands, and Harvey and Cleat mentioned that James was still at Miss Tillie's when they left after midnight. So,

Thomas had paid a boy to run to Miss Tillie's and in-quire after James. He had a sobering thought that he might have to return home and tell Sarah that he lost her youngest son, and the last he heard of him was at a whore house. It wasn't a comforting thought.

They rode a long day trying to get as far as possible before they stopped to camp. It was almost dusk, so a campfire was quickly started. One of Jackson's hands was a cook of sorts and got coffee, beans, and bacon fry-ing while the rest of the men took care of the horses.

The sky had turned black by the time they sat around the fire, sipping hot coffee, and scraping their plates clean. Most of the men were tired, both from little sleep the night before with their carousing and from the long ride this day. Still, they sat telling stories over supper, winding down from the day.

"So, James, how was your night?" Cleat had to ask. "Did you ride the big bucking pony?"

James fixed Cleat with a solemn stare thinking care-fully before he spoke. He knew Cleat was burning up with curiosity about the bet James had lost.

"Actually, I think I had one of the best nights of my life," James said carefully. "Miss Tillie is quite an accom-plished lady."

This brought peals of laughter from most of the men who frequented the place, but it was Harvey that spoke, "Well, at least she didn't fall on you."

James looked mildly at Harvey. "No, she didn't do that. I never had to fear for my life. She was very . . . well, accommodating . . . experienced. That was the best bet I ever lost. I have to thank you, boys, for helping me see that joy."

Cleat's eyes narrowed. "You're lying. You must have

ducked out."

James sat up a bit straighter at those words, and all conversation at the fire fell silent. A muscle in James' neck twitched in anger, but he took a breath, calming himself. He was tempted to tell the men what happened with Miss Tillie, but his conscience, despite Miss Tillie's permission to speak of it, wouldn't let him. His Pa had been death on saying anything bad about a woman.

"You don't know me well," James started, speaking low, "but if you did, you'd know the only time I ever told a lie was when I was nine and put ants in my sisters' beds. Didn't sit down for a week after that." James leaned back again. "I don't lie, I don't smoke, and," he hesitated and then looked directly at Cleat, "I don't cheat at dice. When you can say the same about yourselves, then you can call me out again. But until then, you don't ever say that to me." James' voice was almost a low growl when he finished. He saw the flicker of surprise in both Cleat's and Harvey's eyes at the statement about cheating at dice, and they flicked glances at each other. The subject was closed, and the rest of the men looked at James with new respect. They understood the implications, and they respected James' response. James had become more than a green kid to them on this trip.

CHAPTER 3

White Trash - August 1880

Thomas led an extra saddled horse on the first day out from Laramie, but offered no explanation to the men where it came from or why he had it. The horse was not an Anchor J or a Twin Peaks horse. But Thomas had it with him, and no one asked. On the second morning, as they were breaking camp, Thomas pulled James aside.

"This is Greybull Creek we are camped beside," Thomas told James. "I got a job for you, so you will not be going farther with us. There was a man killed night before last in a brawl in the saloon. Seems he broke his neck when he fell. He was plenty drunk. It's his horse that I been leading," Thomas gestured at the horse. "Knowing we go out this way, the sheriff asked if I'd take this horse out to his place and tell his wife. I want to get home, and settle up with Matthew and your Ma, and get to haying, so I am going to send you."

"You want me to go tell a woman her husband is dead?" James was dismayed. This did not appeal to him.

"Reckon you can just give her the letter the sheriff sent with me. See if she needs any help, and if you have to stay a day or two to help her, you do that. Sheriff said he didn't know the man well, but knew he had a wife and several kids. The man had been in town once and had a couple boys with him, maybe ten or twelve years old. He didn't know much more," Thomas looked off toward the west. "Sheriff thought the woman lived maybe a half day or so up this creek. Couple punchers used to work out here told they have a soddy out there. They didn't think it would be hard to find if you stay along this creek. Take this horse back to the woman and give her the letter. Then see if she needs help before you head home."

James nodded. He would do it and not complain, but he didn't like it. He didn't want to face some woman with a passel of kids when she learned her husband was dead. He wished he was back with Miss Tillie.

James saw the soddy in the prairie horizon. It was hot this day, and he wished he was closer to the mountains. The closer he came to the homestead, the more he wished he were going the other way. The man who died was nearly fifty Thomas told him, so maybe there were older children at the homestead, and James could get on his way after dropping off the sheriff's letter. He hoped that older kids could take over.

As he came closer, his horse jogging smoothly, he saw a figure of a woman hoeing in a field. He saw her look up and see him, and he saw a little child scurry toward the house and then back to the woman. He guessed the child was sent for a gun. As he came closer, James saw the woman motion to the child to go back to the house. The woman held a revolver in her hand, but didn't raise it toward him. James slowed his horse to a walk and approached slowly.

James studied the woman as he approached. He was

instantly relieved. This was an older girl, a daughter, he thought. With luck, maybe they would not need him to stay and help with anything. The woman was rail thin and plain with no welcoming smile. She was deeply tanned, no sunbonnet on her head, and her hair was black, curling wisps escaping the knot of hair on her neck. She wore the most surprising outfit. At first, he thought it was just a dress with no sleeves, but as he came closer, he saw the woman was clothed in flour sacks, stitched together to make a shift of sorts. Over the cream-colored material, with the word "flour" interspersed on several panels, she wore an extremely tattered apron belted at her slim waist. The woman was barefoot, and her hands and feet were filthy from working in the garden. Her apron was dirty too, and the hem of the sack dress, hanging almost to the ground was black with dirt.

"Is this the homestead of," James pulled the letter out of his pocket and read the name on the front, "Mr. Albert Snyder?"

"It be," the woman answered, her face a mask.

"I am looking for Mrs. Snyder," James spoke politely.

"You found her," the woman was grim.

James looked at her in confusion. This woman appeared no older than he, and he was eighteen. They said the man was near fifty.

"Excuse me, ma'am, but you are the wife of Mr. Albert Snyder? These are your children?"

"I'm the wife, an' this is my stepdaughter, 'cepting the baby," the woman gestured behind her at the little girl, and James realized the child was standing by a wooden box. Little arms and legs stuck up kicking and waving from the box.

"Ma'am," James started again, stepping down from his horse. "I brought you a letter from the sheriff." He held out the letter to the girl, taking a step forward.

The girl did not step forward to take the letter. She did not smile or have any expression on her face. Instead, she asked, "Be he dead or in jail?"

James was loathe to tell her. Instead, he stepped closer, holding out the letter. "I think the sheriff explains things in here," he said.

The girl just stared. Finally, she said, "I can't read big words. If there is big words there, I cain't read 'em."

James thought about that. "Would you like me to read it?"

The girl nodded.

James unfolded the paper and studied the sheriff's message. Then he began to read, "Dear Mrs. Snyder, I am sorry for telling you this, but your husband was killed in a brawl on Saturday night prior. He sold livestock that afternoon, but he has debts to settle. So, I am holding the money until you can come to town at your earliest convenience. I am sending your husband's horse home for your transportation, but his dog is being kept at the livery until you arrive. Sincerely, Sheriff Tank Taylor."

James looked up at the Mrs. Snyder, anticipating her reaction. It didn't come. She made no move, not to cry, or faint, or even acknowledge that she understood his words. She just stood there. Finally, she started to turn away, then hesitated.

"Albert's two boys are out with the sheep. They need to know."

James first heard the word "sheep" and started involuntarily. Sheep could be a dirty word out here on the plains. But he was told to help. He had to remember that.

"Would you like me to go find them and bring them in?"

"Yes, they are west of here somewhere. They won't take kindly to me telling 'em this, at least not the older one. I'd be obliged iffen you'd tell 'em," she turned from James then and walked back to the little girl and baby.

James watched her walk off. She was what his mother would call "hard," old before her time. He watched her stoop to the little girl's height and draw the young one to her, sitting in the dirt. James knew she was telling the little girl the news.

It was time to go and look for the sons. James looked off to the west. He wondered if the boys were herding sheep on horseback or by foot. He would lead the horse along with him and find out. It wouldn't hurt to lead the man's saddle horse a bit farther.

James rode west about two miles before he heard the distant bleating of the sheep. Slowly, he saw the cream-colored shapes appear in the distance. As he came closer, he saw the two boys. They stopped throwing dirt at each other when they caught sight of the horses and watched as James rode up to them.

James skirted the small flock of ewes and lambs and rode directly to the boys. James studied them as he got close. One was taller, looking about twelve, while the other was younger. James guessed the younger boy might be eight or nine. They were dressed in worn and tattered clothes, not more than rags. They wore no shoes. They stood solemnly waiting for his approach warily.

"That's my pa's horse," the oldest boy said when James pulled up before them. "What ya doin' with Pa's horse?"

James dismounted, taking a moment before he answered. "The sheriff in Laramie sent him back. Your pa got in a fight, got hurt bad." James hesitated, trying to find the words to tell these boys the truth before simply saying, "Your pa died."

The younger boy's lips started to tremble, eyes filling with tears, but he stood silently, just staring. The older boy turned away, kicking the ground with his bare toe. After a few minutes, the older boy turned back to his brother.

"We gotta git these sheep to water," the older boy's voice broke, but he just ducked his head and moved around James toward the sheep.

"What are your names?" James asked, stopping them.

The older boy looked up at James, studying him before answering. "Noah . . . an' my brother is Emmett."

"I'm James," James held out his hand to the older boy solemnly, "James Bates. I'm from the Twin Peaks Ranch about a day southwest of here."

Noah looked at the outstretched hand, thinking. Then hesitantly, he held out his grimy hand to James, and they shook solemnly. James stepped closer and shook hands with Emmett as well.

"Might as well get you on this horse of your pa's, and I'll help you get the sheep brought in. But you boys are going to have to teach me what to do," James smiled apologetically at the boys. "I've no experience with sheep."

The boys rode the Snyder horse double and got the sheep moving toward the water in the creek. James didn't figure moving sheep was going to be much different than cattle, but thought giving the boys a chance to be the "bosses" would help them concentrate on the job at hand rather than their pa being killed.

James studied the area as they rode. The boys were not taking the sheep directly back to the soddy. He let them take the lead and watched to see what the routine was. About a quarter mile from the soddy, they came to an old oxbow of the creek that had filled with water in the spring runoff and still had water for the stock. The creek wound closer to the soddy, but it was a wet weather creek, drying up in the summer heat. The soddy was a long way from water in the summer when the creek dried up, and probably most of the winter also.

James already had a distaste for the plains, its heat, bugs, and lack of water, but when he came to this watering hole, his dislike increased. After a hot summer, it had dried up to a mud-encircled, stagnant hole where the sheep waded out to drink. James walked his horse deeper into the water, where the animal could find some water that wasn't mud swirled by the hooves of the sheep.

As his horse drank, he watched the boys. They found a bucket, apparently left in the grass in the morning, and picking it up, they waded into the pond looking for clean water. James spurred the horse nearer before asking, "You need a bucket of water?"

"We gots to bring a bucket home with us. We are out of water at home," Emmett responded.

James leaned over to the boy, "Here, give it to me. It's too dirty here." Riding his horse belly deep into the middle of the pond, he leaned over and filled the bucket before the silt from the bottom was stirred up by his horse and reached the top.

"I can carry it for you," James told the boys, knowing they probably couldn't get a whole bucket of water home without sloshing half out. "You know your sheep. You do the herding."

The boys nodded. Noah got on the horse, and with Emmett whooping along on foot, they got the sheep headed toward the distant soddy. After the sheep were underway, Noah rode over and pulled his brother up behind him. They dropped behind and rode beside James, letting the sheep lead the way, snatching mouthfuls of grass as they went.

"You a real cowboy?" Noah asked.

"Reckon you could call me that," James smiled. "At least you could before you put sheep in front of me."

"There's been other cowboys by sometimes, and they aren't nice like you," Emmett offered. "How come cowboys hate sheep?"

James thought about that. "Don't really know why, boy. People are afraid of what they don't know, I guess." Noah stared ahead, watching the sheep's slow movement toward home and not trying to speed them up.

It was Emmett that broke the silence. "You told Mary 'bout our pa?"

James nodded. "She told me where you were and asked me to get you."

Noah snorted at that, "Reckon she jest wanted you gone so she can laugh. Reckon she's jest plain happy now."

James looked curiously at the boy's twisted, angry face. There was bad blood here between the woman and her eldest stepson. "She didn't look much like laughing when I told her," he replied mildly. "Don't think being out here with young'uns alone is anything to laugh about."

"Well, she kin jest go away now," Noah growled. "We

don't need her."

Emmett looked concerned. "Noah," he began, "iffen she goes, who's gonna cook fer us 'er git us clothes 'er anything?" The boy's voice rose as he spoke.

But Noah refused to answer that. Instead, kicking the horse forward, he pushed the sheep to a faster pace. James watched them go. It was apparent the sheep knew exactly where to go, and by the time he got to the soddy with the bucket of water, Emmett was sliding off the horse and shutting the gate to keep the sheep in the corral.

The woman came out of the soddy then. Seeing James with the bucket of water, she reached up for it.

"Thank you," she said softly, noticing it was a full bucket. "We couldn't go for water with the buckboard until the horse got back. We've been makin' out with what we kin carry on foot fer a while now."

James just nodded and began to dismount. "Ma'am," he started, "you mind if I camp nearby tonight? We can hitch up both the horses tomorrow and I can help you fill your barrels." James noticed that the buckboard was loaded with two big barrels for hauling water. But the wagon was set up for a team, not a single horse. He imagined it made for a tough haul hitching just one horse to it. He knew his blue roan wasn't a driving horse, but he figured the horse would learn in a hurry.

"I'd thank ya fer that," the woman mumbled, turning away. "You can make a bed in the lean-to. There's some hay there. I'll have supper ready in a bit."

James watched her go. She had found water some-where before he came back and had washed. Her hands and face were clean, and her feet were not black, at least. Her dress was the same flour sack shift she had on before, but she had a clean apron over it. The apron was plenty tattered, but it was clean. That was at least an improvement. James turned away to unsaddle his horse.

The little girl found James in the lean-to later and told him to come to eat. She was a skinny little thing with stringy brown hair and big eyes. She had a dress on that was at least not made from flour sacks. It appeared to be made from faded cotton cloth of several different patterns and colors, probably patches of worn clothing.

The children were all seated at a table when James entered the soddy. It was a rough-hewn table with benches at each side. The two boys sat across from each other, and the little girl sat beside Emmett. James sat down next to Noah. The children each had a cup filled with milk. As they waited, Mrs. Snyder spooned beans onto plates and set them in front of each child. James noticed that the servings were not large.

"Please, ma'am," James spoke up, "I was chewing on jerky while I rode over here today so I am not that hungry. Don't give me a lot." He thought he wouldn't starve to death in a day here, and it looked like the family was eating on the frugal side.

The plate James was handed was filled slightly more than the children's but not man-sized. He eyed the mixture, noting it was mostly beans, but a few chunks of salt pork were floating in it. When he tasted it though, he could taste that it had been seasoned with onions and some kind of herbs. It was surprisingly good for such meager fare.

"We have plenty of milk if you want," Mrs. Snyder offered. "I am out of coffee, but there is still water in the bucket."

James shook his head. He'd get something to drink after he ate. He had a canteen on his saddle. Then looking across at the little girl, he spoke to her.

"What is your name?"

"Alice," she said shyly, looking down.

"And what is your baby's name," he asked. Other than seeing the little legs kicking out from the box the baby lay in, he didn't even know if the baby was a boy or a girl. Even now, inside the soddy, the baby was laid out in a box cradle in the back corner of the room.

"Gideon," Alice murmured. Then as if she just thought of something more to say, she looked up at James and said, "He were born in the winter."

James smiled at the little girl. Then looking at Mrs. Snyder, he asked, "Would that make the baby four months old?"

"Five months old or there 'bout," she said, but she did not look up at James while she spoke.

James didn't try for more conversation. This did not look like a family who talked much, and with the news he brought, he was not surprised there wasn't chatter around the table. Instead, he finished his meal and stood up.

"I'll be outside if you need anything tonight," he spoke to the woman. "If I bring you in some coffee, would you heat me some in the morning? Maybe you want some too?" James had a packet of coffee in his saddle bags. It would be a poor camp not to have coffee when traveling so it was a staple that he usually had with him. He watched the woman think about that, and then glancing quickly up at him, she nodded solemnly.

The lean-to's back wall was one of the walls of the

soddy. There was a small window high in the wall for ventilation and air movement, but it also allowed James to hear the activity inside the house. When morning came, he heard the stove top rattle as the woman started a fire. James had sent the coffee in the night before with Emmett, who went outside to the little privy before going to bed. It wasn't long before James could smell the coffee. He rolled off the hay and pulled on his pants and shirt. As he was pulling on his boots, he heard the woman call the boys, asking them to milk the cow. It was the strident voice of Noah that made James stiffen with anger.

"You ain't our ma, nigger woman," he snarled at her. "Go milk the cow yerself."

James heard the woman inhale sharply, but she made no reply. Instead, he heard the wooden door scrape open, and she came out, bucket in hand, heading to the corral where the milk cow stood.

"Ma'am," James spoke up, "give me the bucket. I'll milk the cow. I don't want my breakfast to burn."

Again, the woman didn't look at James; just nodded and turned back after handing James the bucket. But even then, James saw the hurt in Mrs. Snyder, eyes filled with tears she was fighting to keep back.

The cow was gentle and waiting to be milked. Its calf bawled in the next pen, so James knew they still let the cow and calf together. He started milking, gauging how much should go in the bucket and how much should be left for the calf. He was finishing up when Noah came out, and seeing him in the corral came over.

"Didn't know cowboys milk cows," he said in a neutral tone.

"Be surprised what cowboys do," James spoke calmly.

"What they don't know, they usually can learn." He looked over at the boy. "For instance, I figure I already know how to drive sheep after one lesson. I can find game and bring it home to the pot. I can even cook it if I need. But there are some things a good cowboy never does."

Noah was interested. "Like what?"

James looked thoughtful. "Well, I never eat before I take care of my horse. He's my partner, and if I want the horse's help, I need to take care of him. I never leave my saddle out in the rain unless I get caught in a storm and can't help it," James looked back at the soddy, then fixed a severe eye on Noah. "And I never, ever, speak disrespectful to a woman."

Noah flushed slightly, but his back got straight, and he pushed his lip out before he said, "She ain't nothin' but trash. Pa said so. She ain't nothing like our mother."

"Well, boy," James's voice was curt, "I don't know what demons your pa had, but he was wrong. You don't talk bad to a woman, any woman. What you called your stepmother this morning was bad." James stopped talking for a minute, then continued. "And then you get to one thing a good cowboy always does. They never allow anyone to speak poorly of a woman in their presence. I hear you talk to your stepmother again like you did this morning, I'll backhand you," James watched the boy to see if he understood. "Noah, there is right, and there is wrong," he said more calmly. "You talkin' like you did this morning is wrong. I don't want to be the one to make it right, but I will. You will not speak like that again."

The boy looked up at James, but he nodded sullenly. It struck James that this boy was probably a miniature of his father. It didn't appear Mr. Snyder had been a model husband or father.

Breakfast was a quiet affair again. There were small biscuits that Mrs. Snyder took out of a pan, placing one small one on each plate. Then there was milk gravy to pour over. The milk gravy was more plentiful, but it had no meat in it. Again, each child had milk to drink. At least they had plenty of milk.

After breakfast, the boys let the sheep out to wander down to the water, nibbling prairie grass along the way. The cow was turned out to graze, too; it would not go far with its calf penned up in the corral.

James gathered the two horses, and finding the harnesses, he began to hitch them up. One harness fit the Snyder horse, and James had that on quickly, but the other harness had evidently been on a larger horse than his roan, so it took some time to get it adjusted. Emmett wandered off, following the sheep, but Noah came to see if he could help James.

"I may need help to hold Blue before I get him hitched," James told Noah. "He's a pretty broke cow horse, but when that wagon starts chasing him, all hell could break loose," James looked over at the young boy.

"What's your pa's horse called?"

"Brownie," Noah answered.

"Well, we got a team of two colors then," James laughed. "Mine's called Blue."

Noah stood holding Blue while James adjusted the harness, taking up the slack. In a few places, James had to take out his pocket knife and make some holes to make the harness fit the smaller cow horse. It took some time, and after a bit, Noah began to talk.

"Did you ever get in trouble for speaking bad?" the

boy wondered.

James laughed. "I don't suppose there is a boy who ever grew up who didn't get into trouble. But I didn't do it often," he smiled, remembering his youth. "I remember not being able to sit down for days once."

Noah thought about that. "Pa usually took a belt to us'n. Not a lot 'cause we usually watched an' knew when to jest stay out o' sight. Iffen we saw him getting' in a black mood, Emmett an' I would head fer the loft. Pa wouldn't climb up there to git us."

"Lofts are good for that," James commented, more intent on adjusting the harness than in the boy's talk.

"Mary got spanked once this winter," Noah went on calmly.

"Hmmm . . ." James replied, Noah's words not really sinking in. Noah, however, took the response as interest and continued his story.

"Pa were in a black mood, so Emmett an' I beat it up to bed. Alice were asleep already in her bed. I heared the cups an' plates crash to the floor, so I put my eye to the crack in the loft floor an' I could see part of the table an' Pa had thrown Mary across it. I could see her head laying off the side. Mary must have made Pa mad 'cause he said, 'Least this way you won't give me no nigger baby,' an' Mary was crying an' saying no, no, but Pa jest kept slapping her, but it must not have been hard 'cause it didn't sound hard, just bam, bam, bam. I couldn't see, but I heared her crying an' . . ."

"Boy," James cut Noah short, "pay attention to this horse now. I am going to hook him up!" James suddenly realized the significance of the tale the boy was telling. Revulsion rose in him. God, what had this family had for a father and husband who would do such things to his wife and call her such ugly names? He wondered if Noah even knew what the word "nigger" meant that his pa had used and Noah picked up. James did not want to hear more.

Blue stood quietly while James hooked him to the traces. James knew this was just the lull before the storm that would break when this wagon started to move.

"Hold them both steady now," he told Noah, "until I get up in the seat. Then when I say let go, you get as far away as you can. I don't know what this blue horse will do for sure."

James climbed over the wheel and told Noah to let go. The team stood quietly. James slapped the reins softly against the rumps of the two horses. Brownie knew that cue and stepped forward. Blue, however, was waiting for a heal to touch his sides, sending him forward. He stood stock still until the evener hit him in the rump. Then he jumped forward only to get to the end of the reins and into the collar and be brought to a jerky stop. Brownie continued his forward motion, unmindful of the wild-eyed cow horse beside him. This brought the evener bumping against Blue once more, and the process began again. Blue plunged, stopped, and plunged again. James caught his balance, and timing the next plunge, he whipped Brownie to a gallop, and together the team bolted forward. Brownie ran on steadily, and Blue, wild-eyed and high headed, plunged alongside until the two began to pull together evenly. James let them run out a good quarter mile. He wouldn't have minded letting Blue run longer, but he could see the old brown horse did not have the stamina of the younger cow horse. James drew up on the reins and brought the team to a trot, moving steadily for a few more minutes before making a wide turn and heading back to the soddy. By the time they arrived, even Blue was puffing, although he still swung his head back and forth trying to see what was following him. Thankfully, the blinders kept the horse from seeing behind him and panicking more. By the time James pulled up before the soddy, he figured the starts would still be a bit rough, but he was confident he could keep from overturning the wagon and killing his passengers.

Mrs. Snyder was waiting with buckets when James pulled the horses to a stop. She had enough horse sense to know James wouldn't want the horses to stand long, so she threw the buckets in the back of the wagon.

"Get in, Alice," she said. "Help her in, Noah. Hurry."

James saw Noah's face flush in anger at the order, but then Noah glanced at James, and without a word, he helped his sister into the wagon. James saw Mrs. Snyder grab the baby in the cradle box and put it in the back of the wagon, the little tyke bundled up to protect him from the sun. Then, the woman climbed into the back herself, sitting at the far end of the wagon with the baby.

"Hold tight now," James called and slapped the reins on the horses. Brownie began steadily with Blue plunging beside, but this time without the intensity the horse had during the first start. The horse still thought a monster was behind him, but so far it hadn't eaten him. James talked constantly to the horse, and he could see Blue's ears twitch back and forth. Blue knew James was near but couldn't quite figure out where. They weren't far from the soddy when the two horses found their rhythm together and trotted toward the water hole.

James let out a deep breath. He wasn't much worried about himself, but he sure didn't want the little ones to get hurt. As they passed the sheep and Emmett, James called to the boy to get in. Quickly, Emmett ran behind and clambered up into the wagon from the back. When they reached the water hole, James pulled the team down to a walk and then a full stop.

"Get out quick," he cautioned his passengers, and they did just that. "Now, stay out of the way, and I'll get this wagon close to the water. Noah, find a rock or a log to stop up the wheels."

James urged the team forward, and they moved unevenly in a large circle before Blue got the rhythm of Brownie beside him. When James came to the water hole, he had already picked the best place for the wagon so that they could get closest to the deeper water. He drove the team down a steep incline, the remnants of the creek walls when this oxbow had been running water. At the bottom, just before the wheels touched the water, he turned the team at a right angle and headed them up a gentle rise. He had just gotten the wagon turned with its back near the water, when he pulled the horses to a halt.

"Here, Noah, stop up the wheels so it won't roll into the water, and come help me hold the horses," James called to the boy.

Noah threw a log behind one wheel, and by the time he reached the team, James was already out of the wagon. With Noah at the horses' heads, James quickly unhooked first Blue and then Brownie and led the team away from the front of the wagon, tying them to a side. He breathed a sigh of relief. He got the whole family here safely.

James surveyed the woman and kids, assessing the best way to get the water.

"Can you swim?" he asked Mrs. Snyder.

"No. None o' us kin," she answered quietly.

James thought about that and then came to a decision. "The best water is out there in the deep. This along the edge has been fouled by the animals," he said, gesturing at the shore. "I'll go out the farthest. If you wade in to about your waist, I can pass you the bucket. These wooden buckets float pretty good, so you could just float it to Alice, and she could float it to Emmett, and he could lift it almost to Noah." James fixed an eye on the older boy. "You might have to lean over and help Emmett. He's not so tall yet."

Noah nodded, understanding. James sat down and pulled off his boots and socks. He was going to get wet, but his pants would dry. He didn't intend to ruin his boots, though, or have to scrub out muck from his socks. He waded in until he was quite far out. He waited, watching the silt swirl around his feet. He had to wait for the dirt to settle down. They had three buckets. James carried them all out and filled the first. Holding it upright, he floated it an arm's length toward the woman who reached out, took it from him, and floated it to Alice. Alice reached for the bucket and passed it on to Emmett and Emmett had to wade a step or two out of the pond to Noah, who reached down from the wagon box to grasp the bucket and lift it, emptying it into a barrel.

James watched the process unfold with the first bucket and then nodded. "Looks like this will work. I will send buckets along faster now, and you will have to pass them back down the line, but we can slow down if we have to."

It went well. Slowly the first barrel got filled. Noah started emptying water into the second barrel. The kids were more experienced now and started working faster at moving the buckets along. Suddenly, Emmett, who passed the empty buckets back to Alice, pushed one back too quickly and Alice, who saw it coming when she wasn't ready, jumped to try to catch it. Instead of catching the bucket though, her movement in the water only made a wave that sent the bucket careening off her hands and into the deeper water of the pond, away from Mrs. Snyder and James.

"I'm sorry!" Alice screamed, her face a mask of terror. "I'm sorry, I'm sorry," she kept repeating, watching the bucket float off into deep water.

James saw the bucket on the loose and heard Alice scream. Looking up, he dove into the water and swam the three strokes to catch it, before it capsized and sank. He couldn't touch the bottom there, so he just turned easily and swam back to his place. As he was standing, waiting again for the water to clear beneath his feet, he glanced over at Alice and smiled. That was when he noticed her look. She was terrified. Over and over, she repeated, almost to herself, "I'm sorry, I'm sorry."

"Honey," James said, "it's fine."

"I got you wet," Alice's lips trembled as she spoke.

"It feels good to be wet," James laughed. "Here, try it yourself." He cupped his hand and threw a handful of water on the surprised little girl. She drew in a quick breath, still unsure if he was mad or not.

Emmett laughed, "You got yers, Alice!"

James looked over at Emmett. Taking his bucket and filling it partway, James threw the water at the boy, dousing him.

"Oh! You got me," Emmett sputtered.

James dipped the bucket in again, and with a hard toss, he was able to reach Noah. Now they were all wet, but the boys were laughing, and Alice was too. Crisis averted.

When both barrels were filled, James sent them all to gather some of the weathered downed timber along the creek bed, dragging what they could back to the wagon. He had seen the gunny sacks the boys carried when they walked the plains, gathering cow chips for fuel. But there were some pieces of wood here that he could chop up and leave for them, as well. There was room in the wagon to haul some wood back with them.

James noticed that Mrs. Snyder went to the baby's box, took the infant a distance away, and sat with her back to the pond. He knew she was nursing the baby, and he occupied himself helping the kids haul in the heaviest of the old timber. When Mary Snyder put the baby back in the box, she called Alice and had her sit with the child, dangling sticks to entertain the infant. Then Mary fell to helping gather wood.

The wagon filled. They put branches and logs and twigs in every crook and crevice. Finally, James said they could get no more in. He looked at the family, panting in the summer heat around him.

"Maybe it's time you learned to swim. Come on young 'uns. Back in the water with you," James walked down to the bank. Looking back, he saw four pair of astonished eyes looking at him.

"We can't swim," Emmett spoke for them all.

"Exactly," James countered calmly, "and I'll teach you. Come here Emmett. You first."

The little boy walked hesitantly toward James. James

took him out into waist deep water. "It isn't so deep here that you can't stand," he told the little boy. "But I'll hold you too."

Patiently, James held the little boy, instructing him to put his face in the water, to relax and learn to float. It wasn't long before he had Emmett dog paddling around in the shallows. Noah followed and then Alice. Alice was more timid than the boys, but she was at least floating by the time they were all tired. James did not coax Mrs. Snyder into the water. She had moved back up the bank to sit by the baby and watch. He was uncomfortable with the woman. She was so close to his own age that he was uncertain how to act. She had just lost a husband, and while the man might not have been a good husband, James was sure the woman had much to worry about living out here with these children.

James would not let any of the family into the wagon until he got the team and wagon up on the flat and had made a swing. Blue was not liking his new job, but he was acting better. As James swung the team around in a big circle, he saw the family waiting for him. As he came to a jerky stop, the boys and Alice clambered up beside him, crowding onto the front seat. Mrs. Snyder set the baby and box onto the logs at the back of the wagon and climbed in beside it, facing backward. When they were all settled, James clucked to the horses, and they made a clean start.

It was well after noon when they returned to the soddy. When the horses were unharnessed, the boys saddled Brownie and took off after the distant sheep. Noah needed to move them farther out to better grass for the remainder of the day. James also saddled his horse. He saw rabbits this morning along the creek, and he thought that it might be nice to add some extra food to the menu. He saw Mary hand each of the boys a small biscuit with butter as they left, riding double on Brownie. As James swung into the saddle, Mrs. Snyder brought him a biscuit, too.

"Ma'am, save that for the children," he told her. "I can get by. I'll bring home some rabbits for supper if I am lucky."

"You've helped us," she answered gravely. "Take it. We are used to having little."

James nodded and took the biscuit. He could see it was important to her to be able to give something back. They have virtually nothing, he thought, but she still needed to make some effort to pay back.

James returned with four rabbits and had them gutted and skinned before taking them to the house. He watched Mary Snyder's eyes light up seeing the meat. How long had it been since they had fresh meat? For that matter, how long since they had had anything more than salt pork and milk gravy?

James set to work on the wood, then, unloading and stacking the smaller pieces in the lean-to and the larger ones by the chopping block. Alice came outside and helped with the smaller pieces, never saying a word.

When all the timber was unloaded, James started chopping the big logs into smaller sections. Alice picked them up and took them to the lean-to to stack. It was late afternoon when Mary Snyder came out and called Alice to her.

"Go in and watch the baby. He's sleeping. I am going to walk out and find the cow," she looked over to James.

"I won't be gone long. The cow is usually in a draw not far from here where the grass is greener."

James nodded and kept on chopping. James wasn't sure how long he worked. He was hot and sweaty again. *How did people stay clean out here in this heat?* he thought. He took off his neckerchief and mopped his brow.

While he stood there, James heard the cry of the baby. He waited to hear Alice, but instead, he only heard the baby crying harder. He looked around, and Mary was nowhere in sight. James set the ax down and walked to the door of the soddy. Inside, he heard the baby from the back corner, and Alice lay on a pile of blankets on the floor. Like so many small children, she was sound asleep, not hearing her baby brother cry. James smiled. Let the child sleep. She'd already had a long day hauling water and wood, and learning to swim. He walked over to the baby.

In his own community, he was the youngest of all the children, but the older ones were married now with children of their own. He knew how to hold a baby. He knew if he picked the child up, there was a good chance that he could soothe him for a little while until Mrs. Snyder returned. As he drew near the box, he leaned down to scoop the child up, and that is when he actually saw the baby for the first time.

"Hey little man," James crooned softly, "no sense in . . ." The baby was completely naked and had wet himself. But that is not what gave James a start. Suddenly, he knew why Noah and his pa had used such an ugly name when speaking to Mary. Because this baby he looked down on, with his tight black curly hair and his dark complexion clearly showed his heritage. A fleeting image of Black Charlie at Miss Tillie's came to James.

Like Black Charlie, this baby was of African heritage. The child's color was not a deep dark black, but more a dusky olive. But with his features and skin color, Gideon would always be recognized as a Black man.

The crying baby brought James back to the present. Glancing around and seeing no rags close by James took his neckerchief off and wiped the baby before picking it up. Almost instantly, the baby's cries lessened. Gideon nuzzled James' shoulder.

"Bud, you ain't getting anything like that from me," he whispered. "Don't you pee on me either." James bounced the baby gently, looking around the room. He knew that walking with the baby was only a temporary fix. Spying some jars on a shelf, James investigated. There were three, and all were almost empty. He found flour in one, salt in another and a tiny bit of sugar in the last. Finding a wooden bowl, he put a pinch of sugar in and got a small dipper of water. Swirling the mixture around, he took it and the baby outside into the shade of the soddy and found a place to sit, leaning against the house.

Eying his fingers, he scrubbed the cleanest one on his trousers and dipped it in the sugar water. Laying the baby in his lap, he let the child suck his finger. Each time the baby gave the finger up, he swirled it around again, and the sweetness made the child forget how hungry he was. He was sitting this way, finger in the child's mouth, when Mrs. Snyder came around the house. Seeing James with the baby, she stopped abruptly, staring.

"Alice is sleeping," James commented softly. He knew now that this woman had been hiding the baby from him, keeping him covered up in the box. "I found some sugar. Seems to comfort him, but I think he needs you now."

The woman nodded, and reaching down, she took Gideon and went into the house. James sighed. He wished he had his cousin Jake here right now. Jake would understand this, being White and Ute himself. Jake always understood people. Jake would know what to say, or what not to say. James had no idea.

James went back to the woodpile. He saw Mrs. Snyder come out with a bucket to milk the cow. But instead of going directly to the corral, she came over to stand off to the side, waiting. James put the ax down.

"Ma'am? You want me to milk?" he asked.

"No, I kin do it," she said softly. "I jest wanted," she stopped, thinking, "I jest thought you . . . well, you seen Gideon, so you know, but . . ." she couldn't go on.

"Mrs. Snyder, you don't have to tell me anything," James spoke gently. "Nothing to tell."

"I just wanted to say that Gideon is my husband's child. I didn't get with anyone else. Negro comes from my side," she said in a rush like she was afraid she'd run out of courage to talk. "My great-granny were a slave. She were took by the master. Then my granny and my ma was took too before the war was over. My granny was took by the master, but ma was took by the overseer. I don't show that side much, but it's there," Mary Snyder looked out across the prairie. "My ma said all them women before me was pretty Black women, an' the masters would want 'em. But the overseer that took ma was a ugly man, so I didn't turn out pretty like my grannies and ma. Ma said maybe I'd be lucky, an' I wouldn't get noticed," Mrs. Snyder stopped and took a breath. "Reckon I didn't get lucky, neither."

James had no idea how to respond to this. He stood awkwardly, looking off to the distance as she did. Finally, he came up with words.

"Mrs. Snyder, I have a cousin, a man older than me," he started slowly, thinking through his words. "Jake's father was part White and part Ute. When Jake's blood father died, his mother, who was a white woman, married a mountain man. They are the ones who lived out here and brought the rest of our families out to live in the mountains with them. Now our ranch has many families. But what I want you to know is that Jake, my mixed-blood cousin, is one of the finest men I have ever known. He is one of the bosses of our ranch. He is respected," James looked at the woman. "You don't have to be ashamed of your son or your background. Not with me, you don't."

When Mary Snyder came back from the cow with the milk, James called to her.

"Mrs. Snyder, would you want me to take you to town tomorrow to see the sheriff?"

The woman looked back at James, and her face registered her alarm. "I can't go to town!" she said vehemently, looking down at her feet.

"Ma'am, the sheriff said to come as soon as possible," James reasoned. "I could take you and the two little ones in, and the boys could probably watch the sheep and cow until we get back. We could make it there and back in three days if we push it."

"I can't go to town," Mrs. Snyder repeated, alarmed. "I can't go in this." She pulled on her flour sack shift.

"Don't you have a dress?" James was dumbfounded.

He had assumed she wore the flour sack dress to save wear on a better dress.

"Alice is wearing what were left of my last dress," Mary Snyder said. "I told Mr. Snyder we needed cloth, but he never brought any."

"Ma'am, you are going to have to go to town sometime. You are almost out of supplies. You can't stay out here alone with no supplies."

Mary Snyder looked around wildly. Suddenly she was struck with an idea. "You go for me," she said hurriedly. "I don't 'spect there are much money left from what my man sold, but you could take the rest of the sheep in an' sell 'em an' bring back supplies. You could talk to the sheriff an' see if there are any money to send home."

James' first thought was that he wouldn't be caught dead going into a cow town like Laramie with a flock of sheep. His second thought was more considered. "Ma'am, the sheriff is not going to release anything to me. If he wanted to do that, he would have done that with our range boss." James noticed the woman's stricken look. "Ma'am let me think on this for a bit. Maybe I can come up with something."

Supper was the most animated James had seen since he had arrived. The children were excited to see fresh meat and plenty of it. Mrs. Snyder had made it into a stew, flavored with onions and herbs, and poured over little biscuits. James thought all the children would go to bed with full stomachs for once.

After supper was over, James sat outside the soddy,

enjoying the prairie as it cooled off. He knew that Mrs. Snyder would come out once before she went to bed. James had an idea and wanted to talk to her about it.

The sun was setting when Mary Snyder emerged from the cabin. James called to her, and she joined him. She stood, uncomfortable in the growing darkness. He realized that she did not know if she should sit with him or stand. Instead, she fidgeted.

"Mrs. Snyder, please sit for a minute. I have an idea, but you are the one to decide," James indicated the ground.

Mary chose a spot along the wall to sit, but not close. She waited silently.

"If it is true that you want to sell the sheep, I know where I could sell them. It would be closer than Laramie too," James watched for a reaction.

"I would like to sell 'em," she responded. "We don't have feed fer them through the winter. We might be able to feed the horse an' cow but not the sheep."

"My Uncle Matthew was a farm boy before he married and came west," James explained. "I remember he once mentioned that he liked sheep and wouldn't mind having some. I am pretty sure he would buy your little flock. It is closer to get to Twin Peaks than to drive the sheep all the way to town."

James watched the woman. She nodded slowly as he spoke.

"I could ask my ma if she had a dress you could use and bring it back with me," James said. "You could go to town then and see the sheriff. You would have money to buy supplies while you were there."

Mary Snyder nodded again. "I'd pay fer the dress," she said. "I ain't never took charity."

"We can talk about that later, but first, we have to figure out about getting the sheep to the ranch," James told her. "Can you spare Noah for a few days?"

Mary Snyder snorted at that. "I could spare him fer a few months or years. We don't get 'long. When he is 'round, Emmett don't know if he should hate me or not. Noah was too much his father's son. It's hard to have him 'round now."

James thought about that. "I see how he is around you. Why does he dislike you so much?"

"His pa didn't want to marry me. He made that clear from the start. But Albert's older brother said he had to have a woman to help with the children. Albert's sister-in-law been stayin' helpin' out with the children. They both wanted to go home. Albert's brother made Albert get help an' it jest weren't fittin' to have a woman living with 'em an' not be married. Albert's brother came an' talked to my brother the day before, made arrangements. They drove over the next day an' got me. We stood up before the magistrate an' there it was done. Albert got me to help with the children, an' his brother an' wife went home."

"How long had your husband been a widower before you got married?" James asked.

"Two days."

James stared at her. "Two days!"

"Albert an' his brother came for me as soon as the funeral guests done gone home. That's the first reason Noah hates me. He sees me movin' into his ma's home afore his ma was even cold in her grave."

"Are there other reasons?"

Mary looked thoughtful before answering. "My brother showed the Negro blood. People around there knew 'bout us. We both worked odd jobs in the area. Mr. Snyder was shamed by me, even though I kin pass fer white. We moved shortly after that, coming out here. I think Mr. Snyder's brother done something 'bout that. Albert weren't that good a provider before his first wife died. I think his brother helped 'em a lot. This place . . ." here the woman waved her hand at the soddy, "were bought by Mr. Snyder. I think his brother give him the money. He hoped that Albert could do better out here. Albert was barely making out back there. An' out here, no one would know 'bout me.

"When we moved a few days later, Noah didn't want to go. I heard him ask his pa why we had to go away, and his pa only said, 'We gotta move 'cause of her.' I don't think Noah had any idea what that meant, only that his pa blamed me, so he did too. Things never really got better after that."

"How were things after you came out here?" James wondered.

"Albert never really noticed me much at first. He jest told me to do this an' that, watch Alice an' git supper. We got the ground tilled up last fall fer the garden this spring. Albert had a few cows an' the sheep. We had a team of horses an' Brownie. We had food enough. Once in a while, Albert would talk to me. Not really conversation, but he'd say he was goin' out to hunt, or he was goin' to check cows. Things like that. But then the baby came," Mrs. Snyder stopped talking and took a big breath before continuing. "He got black moods before but after Gideon, he . . ." Mary couldn't go on. She stopped and then began again, "By spring, we didn't have the cows anymore, the team was gone, and this last trip, he took half the sheep. I know he were gamblin' an' drinkin'. Even a day an' a half ride to town couldn't get the whiskey stink off him.

"Noah doesn't understand why his pa hated the baby so," Mrs. Snyder covered her face with her hands. "But he blamed me for that too. That's when his pa started calling me names. Noah is just doing what he learned."

James sat quietly, thinking about what she had told him. What a life she must have had. Being free of the man would not make life easier either, not with the children to care for, no money, and no way to make a living.

"We have a lot of work that needs to be done at home," James said. "I think I could get Noah a job there, at least through haying. He's not very big yet, but he's pretty stout, and he can learn. Would you want me to leave him at the ranch for a while? How old is he? I've guessed him about twelve."

"Noah is twelve an' Emmett is eight. Little Alice jest turned five. She wasn't much over three when her ma died. She don't remember her ma much, but the boys do. Noah resents me, but Emmett jest wants to be loved. He is a good boy, especially when Noah is not around. It would be easier if Noah were not here."

"I'll take Noah then and the sheep and head for the ranch tomorrow. I'm going out hunting at daybreak first so the boys can take the sheep to water and then hold them nearby. I'll bring you back something to eat while we are gone. My cousin and her husband work for the Anchor J ranch, and that's about halfway to Twin Peaks. With the sheep, we can make that by later afternoon, even if we get a late start. We will go there and spend the night. We can get the sheep home by noon the next day. I'll get Noah settled, and the next morning I'll head back here. I can make it back in a day. So, unless there's a problem, I'll be back in three days. Then I'll take you and the children to town."

Mary Snyder nodded but wouldn't look at James. "Mr. Bates, why you doin' all this fer us?"

James didn't expect the question. He had to think about it. "I don't reckon I know what else to do," he said simply. "It isn't right you are left out here to fend for yourself with the children. It wouldn't be right to go off and leave you either." He looked over at her and grinned as he rose, "Guess it's just the way I've been raised."

CHAPTER 4

Back to Town – August - September 1880

J ames was saddled and off to hunt by daylight. He
didn't know how much food the family had but
knew it couldn't be much. It didn't appear as if they
were eating substantially. James hoped to see a herd of
antelope and bring one back. That would keep the family in food while he was gone, even if something held
him up. James kept remembering how the children rel-
ished the rabbit stew. It had to be a nice change from
milk gravy.

By midmorning, James was back. He had been lucky
and had a big buck antelope tied on behind the saddle.
He would help the woman hang the carcass and then let
her do the butchering. James would catch up to Noah
and the flock and start southwest. He had no idea how
much stamina sheep had. He wanted to make it to Jackson's ranch before nightfall. James dreaded going there
with this little flock of sheep, but there were corrals
there, and he and Noah could get a good night's sleep
as well. It would be good to see his cousin Catherine
and her husband. He knew his mother and Aunt Mattie
would be pleased to hear he had stopped.

⚜

Moving the sheep was not hard. They stayed relatively together, trotting forward and then stopping to nibble grass and trotting forward again as the riders caught up with them. By early afternoon the little procession came to the foothills and found water where the sheep could rest and graze for a bit before heading on again. James had jerky in his saddle pack and took some out to share with Noah. The boy sat on the edge of the small creek they were at and cooled his bare feet in the water.

"This water is cool," Noah said, splashing water with his toes.

"It will get downright cold as we get deeper into the mountains," James laughed. "A body gets used to cold water in the mountains."

Noah thought about that, then changed the subject. "Maybe I'll jest move to the mountains someday," he said. "I aim to run away soon. Maybe when Emmett grows a mite more, we'll go together."

"Maybe I just leave you at our ranch, and you can work there for a while," James commented, watching for Noah's reaction.

"Yes 'em, I'd do that fer sure," Noah was enthusiastic about the idea.

"Well, if you are going to work at our ranch," James told him seriously, "you need to speak right. It isn't 'yes 'em' and 'no 'em', it's 'yes, sir' and 'no, sir.' Or if you are talking to a woman, it is 'yes, ma'am' and 'no, ma'am.'"

Noah shrugged his shoulders.

"Don't shrug at me," James was curt. "Say it right."

Noah looked at James. "Yes, sir."

"That's better. Remember your manners when we see people."

Noah hesitated and then said, "Yes, sir."

James had a fleeting thought that the boy just needed guidance. Maybe with time, Noah would turn out better than what the father had been.

James and Noah made it to Jackson's Anchor J ranch a couple of hours before the sun went down. To James' immense relief, Jackson had his whole crew on the range that week. The only ones left at the ranch headquarters were his cousin, Catherine, Jackson's wife, Molly, and one old hand who was left in charge of the homeplace in the absence of the rest of the men. Catherine and Molly were overjoyed to see James. They were lonely for news of the outside world and were glad to have company. The old hand grumbled about the sheep, but left it at that. James was relieved he wouldn't have to hear the razzing some of the other hands would give him after seeing him with a flock of sheep.

Catherine and Molly made a big supper, and they all spent a nice evening in Catherine and Buster's house. Noah was all eyes seeing the nice home, and also Molly's even more spacious home. It was evident to Noah that this ranch was well off. Besides the two houses, there was a big bunkhouse where the cowhands slept and ate, a big barn, and an elaborate set of corrals. Jackson had spared no expense in setting up his headquarters.

James rousted Noah from his bed before dawn. They ate a cold breakfast that Catherine put together for them of biscuits and jam. Catherine wrapped up some biscuits for them to take. James noticed Noah licking his fingers to get every little bit of the sweet jam. James promised Catherine he would stop by quickly on his return trip to give her news from home. He carried with him a letter Catherine had written to Aunt Mattie, and one Molly had written to Jake and Thomas. Molly hoped that on James' return he would have news that Kade had returned home. Molly worried about her dad.

James opened the corral gate to let the sheep out just as the sun was touching the peaks around them, and the river valley was coming awake in the early morning gloom. It was a half-day ride from Jackson's to home, and James wanted to make it home by noon. He knew all the men would be in from the hayfields for the noon meal. He could talk to Matthew about the sheep. There was also the matter of Noah staying on that had to be discussed with the heads of the families.

The sheep moved steadily all morning, grazing, trotting on, and grazing again. It was just noon when James saw the cabins come into sight. He saw the hay wagons parked in front of the twin cabins of his Uncle Matthew's and his Ma's. The workhorses stood with feed bags on, getting their noon meal while tied up in front of his mother's cabin. As warm as it was, the cabin door was open, so he knew the men would hear the approach of the sheep. Sheep didn't seem to move very far without their incessant blatting. And just as James suspected, he and Noah weren't far out when he saw Jake emerge from the cabin and survey the area.

By the time James got the flock close, all the men had filed out to watch. James saw his Uncle Matthew and called to him.

"Uncle Matthew, I hope you meant it when you said you wanted some sheep," James grinned, "because I brought you some."

"I'll take them, boy. Just put them in the corral, and we can talk about them inside. Food's hot now," Matthew called back.

James showed Noah where to wash up outside after they shut the gate on the sheep, and once clean, they made their way inside. Sarah had a big table that took up a large part of the central room's living space, and around this table the hay crew was assembled. James' sister, Bonnie, was helping Sarah today with the meal. The hay crew was fed in either the Bates or Jorgensen's cabins because of their proximity to the hay fields. If they were working cattle or horses, the men would take their noon meals at one of the Welles' cabins up the valley.

When James and Noah came in, the men scooted closer together on the benches to make more room available. James saw that Noah was almost instantly cowed by the number of men who sat there, if not by the size and comfort of the room. Then Noah's eyes fell on Jake and Hawk, and James saw the boy's startled look as he took in the Indian features of these two.

"Sit here," James said, pointing beside him. "I'll introduce you to everyone."

James went up and down the table, pointing out the men. Beside James sat his brother, Will, and then there were the three extra hands they had hired for the summer. At the far end was Sam, who was married to James' oldest sister, Martha. Across the table sat Uncle Matthew, then Luke, a hand that had been with the ranch for several years, and next to Luke sat the half-brothers, Thomas and Jake Welles, and next to Jake was Jake's nephew Swift Hawk. Last on that side was his cousin

Lathe Jorgensen.

"Hawk's married to my sister, Bonnie," James said nonchalantly, noticing Noah's eyes widen at that news. "And that's my sister, Bonnie, over by the stove and my Ma, Sarah. You probably won't remember everyone, and there are others that live out here that aren't haying right now, but at least you get an idea about who everyone is."

Sarah came with plates heaped with food for James and Noah, and they fell to eating. James glanced at the boy next to him and grinned. Noah attacked the food as if he hadn't eaten in weeks. James looked up, caught the eyes of Jake and Thomas and grinned and shrugged. He wondered how long it would take before Noah started to take food for granted.

Most of the men were finished before James, having started earlier. The men thanked Sarah for the meal as they finished and headed out to the porch for a smoke or to rest in the shade. Finally, the only men left behind were Uncle Matthew, Thomas, Jake, and Will. James looked down at his young companion, getting ready to dive into a big slice of apple pie.

"Noah, why don't you take that pie out to the porch and eat it and let us men talk business for a bit?" Noah nodded, and without a word, he left, intent on balancing his pie so as not to lose a crumb.

James waited for Noah to be out of earshot before he began to talk. "That's the oldest kid of that man who got killed," he started. "These are the sheep they had left. His widow has no way to keep them over the winter and figured they'd need to sell. She's got three other kids, one just a baby, so she really has no way to get them to town," James looked over at Matthew. "I thought of you.

Hope you meant it that you would like some sheep."

Sarah and Bonnie came over and sat with them around the table. "What are they planning on doing then?" Sarah asked. "Do they have family they can go to?"

James shook his head. "I don't think so. I'm just trying to sort it all out. Getting the widow to talk about anything is hard," he looked out the door to the boy sitting on the steps eating his pie. "Ma, they don't have anything. I haven't ever seen anything like this. That's the only clothes the boy has. His brother is no better. There's a little girl and she's wearing a rag of a dress, made from scraps from other clothes," James stopped and took a breath. "And the widow, she's wearing what she's made from flour and sugar sacks. I never seen such an outfit. They don't any of them have shoes. There isn't much food. And the sheriff wanted the woman to come to town and she won't because she doesn't have proper clothes," James looked over at his mother. "I was hoping maybe you or one of the other women had a dress I could take back to her so I could take her to town to see the sheriff."

"So, you're planning on going back?" Thomas asked.

"I don't see any other way," James replied seriously. "I know you need me here to help with the haying, but if I don't go back, I know they will starve to death. I have to take their horse back if nothing else."

"I kind of saddled you with this job, sending you with the sheriff's letter," Thomas said thoughtfully. "Reckon I can spare you."

"The poor things," Sarah murmured. "I will find her a dress. How big a woman is she?"

James looked over at his sister. "She's not as tall as Bonnie, but about built that way," he said, then colored slightly. "I mean, I think she is anyway."

The men chuckled at that, noticing James's discomfort.

"There's another thing," James went on. "This boy here is the husband's, with his first wife. Noah don't get on with his stepmother at all. I was hoping maybe I could leave him here. You could put him to work. He's a resourceful young'un, and stout. He's talking about running away anyway. It would be easier not to have him go back with me and probably safer for him in case he means it about running."

James looked over at his mother. "I wouldn't mind if he slept in my room with me for now," James went on. "I know it would make more work for you, Ma, but I don't think Noah should be up in the bunkhouse with the hands. He needs some good guidance before he runs with older men. His pa doesn't sound like he was a good influence, but that is all the kid had."

Sarah nodded in agreement. "He can stay. There's enough menfolk around to put him in his place if he steps out of line," she smiled at this.

It was decided then. Noah would stay, and James would head back at first light. Sarah and Bonnie rustled up a dress to send back, along with some extra supplies. And, just at dawn, when James was saddling up, Jake rode up with a pair of moccasins that Anna was sending.

"See if these work for the woman," Jake told James. "At least she won't have to go barefoot in town until she can buy something of her own. She won't be the first to turn up to town in moccasins."

James grinned at that. Several years ago, their families had traveled to Laramie for Thomas and Beth's wedding. At that time, none of the Welles wore shoes in the summer. They always wore moccasins. So, the first night in town, they all trooped into the hotel restaurant in moccasins and caused many an eyebrow to raise. At the time, Molly told Sabra they had the best-looking menfolk anyway, but James saw it differently. Even though he was barely in his teens then, he knew they had the best-looking womenfolk. He noticed such things.

◆

James made it to the soddy before dark the next day, even after stopping again at the Anchor J. He bagged a deer early that morning and had the best cuts tied on Brownie. At least there would be fresh meat. In his saddlebags, there was a jar of jam, a small sack of flour, some sugar, salt, and a couple tins of peaches and sardines.

Mrs. Snyder was working in the garden when he came in sight. He saw the cow grazing in the distance and Alice and Emmett in the garden. When they saw him, they jumped up and ran to meet him.

"You came back," Alice called to him.

"I told you I would, didn't I?" James teased. "Did you think I'd forget where you lived?"

"Where's Noah?" Emmett asked.

"He got a job at the ranch," James told him. "He is going to stay there for a while."

The woman came to meet James. He took the saddlebags off Brownie and handed them to her. "Ma sent some things for you. And I got a deer this morning, so I have some meat chunks in there for supper. Maybe cook up extra to take with to town."

Mary Snyder looked uncertain. "I don't know . . ." she started to say, but James cut her off.

"There is a dress in there for you to wear," he told her, nodding at the saddlebags. "It will be alright. And I brought you back money for your sheep so you can get supplies. My boss knows I'll be gone, so we can take your wagon and start tomorrow."

She met his eyes hesitantly. Finally, she nodded.

It was no easy task getting the water barrels off the wagon. One was about half full by that time, so they dipped out all the water they could with the three buckets and an assortment of bowls. Then James and Emmett carefully edged the barrel to the back of the wagon and let it fall as gently as possible to the ground. It was clumsy, but James and Emmett were able to move it to the side of the soddy. They put the water from the buckets and bowls into the barrel. Then they filled it, taking water from the second barrel until it was brimming full. Using the same process, they got the second barrel on the ground and next to its twin. Now the wagon was ready to be loaded for the trip to town.

James' blue roan still had to snort and roll his eyes the next morning when James hitched him to the wagon, but he stood still. Mary Snyder got Alice and Gideon loaded onto the straw tick mattress she had put in the back and climbed in with them, sitting next to a box of foodstuffs she had packed. Leaving Emmett to hold the horses, James climbed up in the wagon seat.

"When I say let go," James told Emmett, "you jump back. If we start slow enough, climb on the back. If it's a runaway, I will circle around and pick you up after I calm Blue down."

Blue plunged once but settled then beside old Brownie and Emmett scrambled up into the back of the wagon box. Climbing over his stepmother and the two children, Emmett joined James on the front seat. All morning they rode that way, with the horses alternately jogging along steadily or walking when they were either winded or the terrain was rough. The sun was high in the sky, past the noon hour, when they came across a bit of water in a wide spot of a dry creek.

"This should be a good stopping spot," James commented. "These horses need some water, and you can stretch your legs a bit before we head out again."

Mrs. Snyder found some biscuits and jam she had packed, and they ate quickly before James hooked the horses back to the wagon and they were off again. Blue started steadily this time, apparently resigned to being part of a team.

Again, Emmett climbed up beside James with the woman and two youngest huddled on the straw tick. It wasn't long before James felt Emmett nodding beside him. Glancing back, James saw Gideon and Alice were sound asleep on the mattress.

"Ma'am," James spoke quietly, "I think you better take Emmett back there before he falls off this seat," James smiled down at the little boy. Emmett nodded wearily and let himself be helped over the seat to the back. When James looked back soon after, he saw all three children sleeping on the mattress, and Mrs. Snyder huddled in the back corner of the wagon on the hard wooden slats.

"Mrs. Snyder, you'd be more comfortable if you ride up

here," he said. "They don't leave you with much room."

Mary Snyder looked warily at James, and James caught her look. "You should know I won't hurt you by now," he said. "I'd be pleased to have you join me."

Slowly, Mrs. Snyder stood up, and catching her balance, she stepped over sleeping children and made her way to the front of the wagon. James reached out to steady her as she stepped over the seat, but she pulled away, sitting as far away from him on the seat as she could.

They rode silently that way for a time until James noticed that the woman was worrying her dress, wadding up part of the skirt and dropping it, then wadding it up again. He could see it was a nervous habit, and he wondered about it. Was the woman afraid of him? He never really got that feeling when he was in the soddy for meals.

"Mrs. Snyder," James finally asked, "are you afraid of me?"

She looked startled at the question. "No 'm," she said slowly, "I just ain't never rode up front w' a white man before?"

"Ma'am," James was incredulous, "you were married to a white man! For all accounts, you are a white woman. Certainly, you rode in the front of the wagon when you and your man came out here?"

Mary Snyder nodded back at the baby before answering. "You know I gots the Negro blood in me. Everyone knew that where's I come from. My brother showed it. Mr. Snyder hated me fer it. I rode in back w' the chilluns."

This was new territory for James, and he just couldn't understand it. "He couldn't have hated you. He married you."

"He were shamed o' me," Mary went on simply. "He married me 'cause his brother made him. We moved away so's no one'd know. Then I have me a Black baby, an' the hate come out. He'd a turned me an' Gideon out but fer Alice. He did love little Alice, an' Alice needed me. The boys did too, I reckon."

"He loved them enough to drink and gamble their lives away," James spoke angrily. "That is not the way a man should act."

They rode in silence for a long time. Finally, as if the conversation had never laid dormant so long, James said, "You ride up here with me whenever you want. I'm not ashamed of you or your baby. No sense in you worrying about it either."

They drove all afternoon, until the sun was just beginning to settle in the horizon. James knew there were creeks where they could get water, and when he came on one late in the day, they stopped. They had tinned food that James had brought from home and while James and Emmett took care of the horses, Mary fixed supper for them. They ate quickly before heading for their blankets. James and Emmett laid blankets on the ground leaving the wagon to Mrs. Snyder and the youngest two.

Dawn found James harnessing while Mary fixed a cold breakfast. James knew they could make town before noon if they got off early enough. He wanted to take care of all their business in the afternoon and be ready to turn around toward the soddy the following morning.

When they got underway, Emmett rode in front again, but about an hour from town, James told the little boy to go back and send his stepmother to the front of the wagon. James reached under the wagon seat to pull out his saddle bags when Mary was settled. From within one pocket, he drew out the moccasins that Jake had given him.

"My cousin sent these for you," James told Mary. "He thought maybe having these on your feet might be better than going barefoot when you got there. You can buy some shoes after we settle up with the sheriff."

Mary fingered the soft leather tops and looked at him questioningly. "Won't I look . . ." She didn't know how to finish.

James laughed. "Several years ago, most of my people went to Laramie for the first time. One family never had shoes in the summer. They always wore moccasins. So, the first night they just traipsed into the hotel in moccasins, and no one said a word. They bought shoes the next day."

"They hadn't money fer shoes neither?"

"They had the money, but they were used to moccasins. Some of them had lived with the Utes and that is what they liked to wear."

Mary thought about that and then slipped the moccasins on, tightening the leather thongs securely. "They feels good."

The dress was too big for Mrs. Snyder because she was shorter than James' mother, so it dragged a bit on the ground. The nice part of that was that her feet were barely noticeable. Because she was obviously nervous about coming to the town and being dressed in hand-me-downs and moccasins, James drove the team right up to the hotel hitch rack. He didn't want the family to walk from the livery at the edge of town.

"Let's get you checked in here first, and then Emmett

and I can get these horses to the livery for a good meal and rest."

"Mr. Bates," Mary said softly, "I don't have money fer no hotel."

James looked at her calmly. "It's taken care of. Don't worry about it."

James reached over the wagon box and scooped up little Alice. "Come on, Princess. Let's get you a place to rest." He led the way into the hotel, leaving Mary little choice other than gathering up her baby and following him.

At the register, the clerk was the same one who had waited on Thomas when they were here with the hands ten days earlier.

"Back with more cattle?" the clerk asked.

"Not this time. Have some neighbors I'm helping," James answered easily. "I need a room for the woman and children and another for me." James looked over at Mary for a minute and then added. "The lady would like a bath up in her room for herself and the little ones. I'll take the boy with me down the street."

Mary looked startled and started to protest, but James cut her off. "It's been taken care of," he said. Turning back to the clerk, he said, "I expect you to see her to her room." And to Mary Snyder, James said, "Emmett and I have some things to do, and we will get cleaned up. I'll send for you when we get back, and we can go to see the sheriff."

James could see the woman was disconcerted, but she was at a loss for what to do other than follow directions. Waving at Emmett to come with him, the two of them walked out to the horses and wagon, leaving Mary no choice but to follow the clerk up to her room.

After James had the horses squared away at the livery, he and Emmett made their way up the street. Coming to a corner a block off the main street, he motioned to Emmett to stop and sit on the boardwalk.

"Sit right here and wait for me," James said. "I don't want you to move, you hear?" he said sternly. "I have to stop and talk to someone for a minute. I won't be long."

Emmett, eyes wide at the strange surroundings of the bustling town, nodded. It was too scary for him to go anywhere by himself. He sat where James pointed.

James crossed the street and went in the door of the big house and into Miss Tillie's parlor room. It was too early to be busy and the only one in the parlor was Black Charlie who was stocking bottles on the bar's back wall.

"Mister James, you are back again so soon?" the old man smiled.

"Not for what you think," James grinned back. "But I really need to talk to Miss Tillie, if she's here."

Charlie studied the young man and nodded. "Wait here," he said.

It didn't take long for Miss Tillie to emerge from the back. She also smiled widely to see James back so soon.

"James, I thought you were out of here until next summer," the big woman laughed at him. "You going to be a regular now?"

"No, ma'am," James was quick to say. "Well, not yet anyway," he grinned. "I need your advice, though."

Miss Tillie gave James a long look and then indicated a corner table. "Set down then and tell me your problem."

"Ma'am, I brought this woman and her kids to town with me," James started.

"Damnation," Tillie exclaimed. "You are getting married already!"

"No, ma'am!" James was startled at her take on his statement. "This woman is the widow of that man who got killed in a brawl when we were here. My boss sent me with a message from the sheriff to have her come to see him, and that's what I am doing. I am just helping her come to town."

"Ah, you would fit that job," Tillie smiled. "So, what is your problem?

"Well, this family is real poor. They don't have much," James began. "I was wanting to get them each a set of clothes so they wouldn't look so poor while they are here," James hesitated, coming to the problem. "I can take the little boy in the store with me, but I don't know how to tell any store clerk about getting clothes for a woman. I don't even know if I can buy women's clothing. And I don't think this lady would accept them if I took her into the store myself. I was hoping someone could take her what she'd need, and if the clothes are paid for, then she'd have to take them."

James watched Tillie. When she didn't react, he struggled on, "I don't know how to say what this widow lady would need. I mean," he began almost to stutter now, "she'd need a dress, and then she'd need, well, you know, she'd need more," he finished helplessly, turning a flaming red.

Now Tillie started to laugh. "Boy, for someone who loves the women as much as you apparently do, you are a dear. Do you know that?" Tillie looked over at Charlie. "Would you bring me some writing paper and a pen?" she asked him.

Tillie took the paper and went right to work, her pen moving over the paper furiously. She would stop to read and then write more until finally, she looked up at

James. "Here, read this and tell me if this is what you need. You can read, right?"

"Yes, ma'am," James replied, relieved. He bent to read the note that Tillie handed him. It said, "Cora, this young gentleman wishes to do a favor for a neighbor. He needs you to pick out a dress and all the underthings a woman will need and send it to her. He will pay for the clothing in advance, and you are to insist that the woman accept it. Thank you, T."

"Yes, ma'am, this looks fine," James breathed deeply, "but could you add a dress for a little girl and something for a baby boy."

Tillie laughed harder at that, "What have you gotten yourself into, young James?" she appraised him. "You will have to give Cora some idea of how big these clothes have to be." Tillie wrote more on the paper and then handed it to James. "Go down the street to The Fine Lady Shoppe and ask for Cora. She is a seamstress and always has some dresses and skirts ready to go with a little altering. Just give her the note. She is a good woman and will take care of you. Don't shame her by saying my name out loud."

James nodded, understanding. "Thank you, ma'am. For some reason, I knew you could help me."

"Go on with you now," Tillie waved James off brusquely, "since you aren't going to spend your money here." But her words were softened by her smile. Just as James was almost at the door, she called after him, "You make me believe in the goodness of men again, young James. Come back and see me again when you are in town. Even if just to say hello."

❧

Mary put on her borrowed dress after bathing, had Alice dressed in her rag dress, and was just washing the baby when she heard a knock at the door. Putting the baby on the bed, she went cautiously to the door and peeked out. There stood a kindly-looking woman with a stack of clothes in her arms.

"Mrs. Snyder?" the woman asked.

"Yes'm," Mary replied warily.

"I have some things here for you and the children. Can I come in?" the woman smiled.

"I don't understand?" Mary was confused, but she opened the door and let the woman in. "I didn't ask fer nothin'."

The woman smiled at her. "These things are from my shop. You are to pick one dress and accessories for you and the little girl. They are paid for already," the woman laid out the clothes alongside Gideon. "I was told you are in mourning, so the colors are dark, but we didn't have anything completely black. These will be pretty on you with your olive complexion. What do you think will suit you best?"

Mary Snyder was astonished. "I . . . who?"

"Honey, just pick what you fancy. You have to take a set. I can't take it all back because it is paid for already," the woman said gently. "Sometimes, you just have to be glad someone is nice."

It was two o'clock when James tapped on Mrs. Snyder's door. Emmett stood proudly beside James in new denim jeans, shirt, and cowboy boots, barely able to conceal his excitement at having all new clothes. Mary peeked

out, and seeing James and Emmett, she shyly opened
the door. Turning, she gathered up a sleeping Gideon,
and taking Alice by the hand, they walked hesitantly
out of the room.

"You look very nice, Mrs. Snyder," James commented,
trying not to make much of it. Seeing the woman in
shoes and clothes that were clean and fit properly was
quite a transformation. Her expression was still solemn
and fearful, but she stood straighter with her head held
high. Little Alice shyly emerged in a pale yellow frock
and reached for James' hand. He smiled down at the
little girl. Alice too was overwhelmed with her new
clothes.

The sheriff was in when they got to his office. He
came right to the point. "We need to go to the bank
first. Your husband had some outstanding bills, and the
bank is holding the money he had with him when he
was killed."

At the bank, James stood and leaned against the
back wall, holding Alice's hand with Emmett beside
him. Mary Snyder sat in a chair across from the banker
with the sheriff next to him. The news was not good.
Mr. Snyder had outstanding bills at the general store
and the livery. The livery even charged her for keeping
their sheepherding dog that helped Mr. Snyder bring
the sheep to town. The banker showed Mary the ledger
and explained that more money was owed than they
had recovered from Mr. Snyder's body when he died.
Mary fumbled in her pocket and drew out the money
that James had given her for the sale of the sheep.

James stepped forward and touched Mary's shoulder,
stopping her from handing over the money. He looked
at the figures over Mary's shoulder. What the banker

was showing Mrs. Snyder would take all her money, leaving none for supplies. It would be a long, cold, bleak winter without money for supplies.

"I think you gentlemen are forgetting that Mrs. Snyder did not create these bills," James began. "You are showing quite a lot of interest too. And if we'd been told about the dog, we could have taken it back with us when our crew was here. I think you should consider that she came here on her own accord and is willing to make things right, but you have to work with her too. She has children to support."

The banker cleared his throat and looked at the ledger. "Well, young man, I am not sure what your position is here. Are you related to Mrs. Snyder?"

"The Snyders are neighbors to our ranch, Twin Peaks. You have the Twin Peaks accounts here. I don't think my boss would take it kindly that you weren't fair to our neighbor when she is not the one who created the problem," James spoke confidently, even though he didn't feel so confident. "We are doing our part at Twin Peaks to help the family. I would think a bank that wants to keep our business would also want to help out."

The banker looked hard at James, assessing him, then took the ledger back and did some figuring. After a considerable length of time, he turned it back to James and Mrs. Snyder and showed it to them. "I can do this much," he said reluctantly.

James looked at Mary Snyder and nodded slightly. It was enough that she would have money for supplies and maybe a little for fabric to make clothes. One set of store-made garments for each of them wouldn't last long.

Mary nodded at the banker. She was relieved that James had spoken. She had no idea what was on the ledger that the banker showed her.

From the bank they went to the general store. When they arrived, James could see that Mary was also unsure of herself in this environment. "Do you know what things you might need?" he asked.

"Maybe some flour?" she asked rather than stated. "Maybe a big sack?"

James looked over at the storekeeper. "Let's have one hundred pounds of flour then," he told him.

"What cost would that be?" Mary asked, taking her money out of her pocket.

"A pound of flour is a nickel, so one hundred pounds is five dollars," the man answered over his shoulder.

Mary looked at her money, hesitating. Suddenly, James understood. Mary had no idea how much money she had. He knew she couldn't read, but she also didn't know numbers.

"Mrs. Snyder, let's just get all your items on the counter first and then see what we have," he told her. "If we have to put some back, we can do that."

Mary Snyder nodded. "I reckon some cornmeal," she said hesitantly, "an' some sugar."

They looked together at the shelves, and the pile got bigger. They added coffee, beans, molasses, and rice. James looked at the tinned food and picked out some fruit. He knew the garden by the soddy would give the family fresh vegetables, but it would not contain fruit. Finally, when Mrs. Snyder was looking at the yard goods, James leaned over and spoke quietly.

"Mrs. Snyder, would you like me to count out the money you will be owing the man? You seem a little unsure dealing with a stranger," he had a feeling she wasn't worried about the stranger, but instead, did not understand the money and was embarrassed about that.

Mary nodded, giving James the money that she carried in her hand. James thought how quickly she trusted him not to cheat her. He could see almost immediately that she did not have enough to pay for all that was piled on the counter, even if she did not buy any material. He quickly reached into his pocket and pulled out a twenty-dollar bill. He looked at it wistfully. It signified several nights of carousing at Miss Tillie's. James sighed and put it with the Snyder money. He doubted he would be in town again any time soon. He could afford to help.

When Mary came to the counter with several yards of shirting material, denim, and cotton flannel, James added a small bag of hard candy to the pile. He wondered how long it had been since the children had candy. He added a set of pants, boots, socks, and a shirt for Noah. It would be a cold winter with only the rags Noah was wearing when he went to the ranch. Finally, they picked out some heavy blankets that could be fashioned into coats for winter.

"There be enough fer all?" Mary whispered. "Looks like a lot."

"Well, it is a lot," James tried to look like he was contemplating the pile, "but I think you might even have a little left over. For emergencies," he finished.

The trip home was good. They picked up the dog at the livery along with the horses. Alice and Emmett were ecstatic to see the dog, and the dog felt the same way. The horses were rested, and James pushed them long into early evening. Emmett was full of comments about what he saw in town, what he thought about his new clothes, how he liked the public bathhouse, and how irritating the four chickens were that James had bought in town. Telling Mary Snyder that he was buying them for his mother, James planned to leave the chickens with her. He would tell her he forgot he was going the rest of the way home on horseback, and Blue might be broke to drive now, but he would never haul four chickens in the crates behind the saddle. James would ask her to take care of them for him until he returned to get them. He figured he could have another excuse later.

Alice was also full of stories about what she had seen and done in town. She was especially excited about eating supper and breakfast in the hotel dining room. She was again wearing her rag dress but was thrilled about her new dress. Her stepmother told her they would keep it for good.

Mary Snyder was still wearing her new dress while they traveled. She had folded up the borrowed dress and returned it to James when they got in the wagon at Laramie. But as soon as she got home, Mary went into the soddy and changed into her flour sack dress. She, too, wanted to save the new dress for good. Mary had remarked solemnly that she intended to sew each of them another set of clothes as soon as possible with the material she had purchased. James noticed the pinched worry lines on her face were not as evident on their trip home. Having a wagonload of supplies was a comfort. For the foreseeable future, the family had food and clothing and a roof over their heads. Maybe that was the best James could do for them at this time.

James stayed one more day with the family. They

loaded the water buckets and a wash tub and brought home as much water as they could. Mary said the water would last them for quite a while. She would go to the water hole to wash clothes now, and every trip they made they could carry a bucket or two of water back to keep their water supply somewhat replenished. After that, old Brownie would have to pull the wagon alone. James tried to rig up a single hitch for the wagon that would help the old horse, but without proper shafts, it was a poor attempt.

While they were coming home from the water hole, James decided it was time to talk to Mrs. Snyder about his leaving. While she never asked his council after leaving town, he suspected she was beginning to depend on him. And he knew he had to return home. Fall was coming, and fall was a busy time at home.

"Mrs. Snyder," James began gently as the horses plodded toward the soddy, "I will leave in the morning. Is there anything else you can think of that I can help you with before I go?"

Mary did not answer at once, instead looking off towards the house. "I reckon I knew you'd be a goin'. You've helped us. Reckon I can't think o' nothin' else."

James watched her face. The worry lines were back. The endless prairie had to be worrying to a woman alone with children. It dawned on James that in all the time he had been with the family, he hadn't seen Mrs. Snyder smile.

"I'm glad you have your dog. He will alert you to strangers coming or animals too," James paused before going on. "I'll ride over and check on you before winter hits hard," James told her. "I'll want to make sure you can make it through until spring. Maybe get you some more firewood hauled in. But I have work to do at home. They are expecting me back." Mary Snyder nodded. "I'd not want to be the cause a' you losin' yer job," she commented.

James refrained from telling her that his family was one of the ranch's owners, and that being fired wasn't a possibility. Instead, he simply said, "I'm not afraid of that. They know where I am." James looked up at the sky. "Still, plenty of daylight left. When I unhook these horses, I will go out and get you some meat. You ever make jerky?"

As it turned out, Mary had never made jerky, so when James returned with a big antelope, two rabbits and three prairie chickens, he helped her rig up a rack to dry out strips of antelope meat, essentially preserving it. The rabbit meat was chunked to be used in stew, and the birds were cut up and fried for supper that night. It was still too warm on the prairie to keep the meat fresh for long. The jerky may get tiresome, but it would be food.

And at daylight, James had Blue saddled and ready when the woman and children came out to say good-bye. Little Alice cried, not wanting James to leave, and Emmett fought hard not to do the same.

"I'll be back," James told the children. "Now, I want you both to help your mother. Emmett, you are the man of the family now. I am depending on you," James noticed that Emmett did not tell James that Mary was not his mother. Instead, the little boy nodded solemnly.

James looked at Mrs. Snyder. He smiled and stuck his

hand out to her. "You take care of yourself now. Keep a gun handy too. You shouldn't have trouble, but it's safer with a gun nearby." When the woman nodded, James added, "I'll come back before winter."

As James rode off, he glanced back once and saw all three of them still standing, watching him go. James studied the little family. One woman with three small children trying to survive this land. She was probably not much older than he, yet she seemed like an old woman to him with her pinched, plain face, hands hardened by work, gaunt frame, and grimy clothes. He hoped they would survive until he came back. He couldn't do much more.

CHAPTER 5

Fall Gather - End of September 1880

The air had a chill these fall days, and climbing into the high country only made it chillier. The sun was lowering in the sky when the men reached the high-country shack where they stayed during fall gather. The shack was just that, a shack. It was small and drafty, but their foodstuffs could be put inside and barricaded from any wandering bears.

In the past, Sabra and Molly, until Molly was married, accompanied the men. Anna, Jake's wife, had also joined them some years, but Anna with three little ones, now stayed home. All the Welles went to fall gather from the first year they used the mountain ranges in the summer. Sabra hauled the children when they were little. It was a family affair then. Now, the number of cattle they were gathering and the vast expanse of the mountain slopes they had to ride to bring home their large herd meant hiring extra men and bringing many saddle horses.

"Luke, are you doing the cooking?" Lathe called to one of the hands. Luke had been with the Twin Peaks Ranch for two years and was a mainstay.

"Yea, I told Jake I could do it," Luke replied, starting to unload a pack mule.

"Well, I'll take care of the animals and the unloading then," Lathe told him. "I'm hungry. Get to cookin'."

There were chuckles from the other men, but they agreed. When Sabra was there, she would start a meal and have it ready soon after the men had the horses unpacked, tents set up, and supplies in the shack.

There were no new hands this year, only young Noah and the older men all knew their jobs. The unpacking went well, and tents went up quickly. The shack was usually used as a storeroom and a bunkroom for any women who came to help. The men didn't quite know how to treat it with Sabra dead and buried and no other women along this year.

Thomas got the last pack mule unloaded and looked around for Jake. Thomas had hoped they would ride up to the shack and find their father waiting for them. It was disconcerting not to find him here.

"Where do you think Pa is?" Thomas asked Jake.

Jake looked toward the high ridges surrounding this mountain meadow where they made their camp. "No telling. Big country out there. He's wandering somewhere."

"Aren't you worried?" Thomas asked.

Jake looked at his younger brother, "Tom, there is nothing I'd like more than for him to be here, but he'll come back when he is ready. I'm thinking we will see him soon." Jake looked back at the sky, watching the darkness fall. "And, if he doesn't come, we just have to hope he's finding something to make him happy. This is something we have no control over. Worrying won't make it happen. Come on, let's eat."

The fire crackled, and the beans and bacon that Luke had cooked up had been filling. All the hired hands and Noah had gone to their tents to get an early start in their beds. Around the fire, James, Lathe, Sam, Swift Hawk, Jake, and Thomas sat quietly, sipping coffee, or puffing on a pipe. All, but Sam and Hawk, had grown up together. This was their ranch, their business. As for Sam and Hawk, they had married into the family. They were family now too.

"Seems strange as hell not to have Sabra and Kade here," Lathe broke the silence.

"Don't hardly know how to act," Sam agreed. "I keep thinking yer ma is going to jest up an' come out of that shack with something good she packed for us to eat."

"Seems strange not to see her and Kade sitting together around the fire too," James commented. "When they were in camp, they always ended up sitting about as close to each other as they could."

"Sitting together is an understatement," Thomas chuckled quietly. "They lived for each other. There was never any doubt in our cabin that those two loved each other."

"That makes it hard for Pa," Jake said softly. "I don't reckon he ever thought he was going to outlive her. He's probably wandering these mountains looking for her," he hesitated, "or looking for memories of her . . . memories of them together."

Swift Hawk watched the others, his black eyes solemn. Finally, he spoke, his voice low and rich, "She's here with us now. Kade will come back. He will know she is here with the ones she loves. She lives in you," Hawk looked at the brothers.

They sat silent then, each with his own thoughts. Suddenly the quiet of the mountain was broken by distant whooping and hollering. The men looked at each other, and then a smile broke out on Jake's face.

"Pa's bringing in the first package of cows. He's lost them in the dark, but you can bet he has some in front of him," Jake stood up.

Soon enough, they heard the cattle crashing through the deep-wooded hills. Out of the blackness of the forest came dark shapes. Cows, calves, yearlings, and two-year-olds erupted from the wooded slopes onto the meadow. The whooping quieted, and it wasn't long before they saw the buckskin horse Kade rode emerge from the darkness like a ghost. The horse turned, and Kade trotted over to the fire.

"I take it you haven't started yet?" he inquired, smiling down at his sons.

"It rained," Thomas grinned back. "We got a late start."

Kade stepped off his horse. He was gaunt, but not emaciated. His eyes, although sunken a bit, were not desperate. His smile at reuniting with his sons and friends said volumes to Jake and Thomas. Kade was back. The loss of Sabra would never leave him, but he would stay for the living.

"Good to see you, Pa," Jake said. "There's some beans left. Come get something hot. It is getting chilly tonight."

"I'll take your horse, Uncle Kade," James said, reaching for the reins. "You must be hungry."

When Kade got a plate of beans and bacon, the men settled again by the fire. They let Kade eat for a while, answering his questions about how things were at the ranch.

"So where did you head out to, Pa?" Thomas inquired when Kade put his plate down.

Kade took out his pipe and lit it, using a branch from the fire. "I hung around here for a few days, checking on the cattle. Did you see the mountain lion pelt pegged to the back of the shack? I got him before I left," Kade puffed on his pipe. "Then I just headed out. Thought about going back to Jacob's cabin, but decided against that since we'd just come back from there."

Kade and Sabra spent part of the summer at the high mountain cabin. It was coming back from there that they rode through a midsummer cold rain, and Sabra got chilled. Shortly after they returned home, her slight cough had gotten worse. And then worse again, until it was too late.

"I just wandered mostly. I went over by Dixon," Kade remarked. "They got a post office there now. Spent a day there. I got some paper at the little store an' wrote a letter to your Uncle Joe an' Aunt Katie. Figured they'd want to know 'bout Sabra." Kade's eyes had that faraway look as he thought about what his words meant. "I run into a Ute village an' stuck around there a couple days." Kade looked over at Swift Hawk. "I saw your mother and sister. They asked about you."

"They are good?" Hawk asked.

"Mostly," Kade replied. "But they are getting moved. Government is moving them to Utah sometime after the winter. Not too many Utes are happy 'bout that."

"I was afraid of that," Jake commented softly. "I knew the Meeker affair was going to be bad news for our people," he looked over at Hawk. Then addressing Kade again, Jake asked, "Apparently, the Utes didn't get much negotiating done in Washington?" Jake was referring to the handful of Ute leaders who traveled to Washington, D.C. to talk to the white leaders there.

"No, an' I'm not surprised," Kade replied. "There was an outcry over the Meeker incident. Right or wrong don't matter. It's a damn shame."

Hawk looked over at Jake. "Maybe you should have gone with them, talked for our people."

"We discussed that already. You know that wouldn't work," Jake remarked.

"Why?" James wanted to know. "You are well-spoken. You might have been able to change minds."

Jake shook his head, "The whites would just use me against my own people. There goes an Indian that is doing just what we want him to do, they would say. The government wants the Utes to farm, or at least, settle on a piece of land and make a living. Pretty much that is what we are doing here, only sort of on a larger scale," Jake paused. "But I was raised white. I was raised in this life. It doesn't come hard for me. But my life isn't the life the Utes want. The whites would just point at me and say if you can live this way, why not the rest of the tribe?"

James looked over at Hawk. "Well, you do it, don't you?" he asked the young Ute.

"I do," Hawk agreed. "But it is a hard change for me. Having a white wife, and an uncle, and sister here have helped me fit in. There are times though, when I want to go back to my old life. Only, I know it isn't there anymore."

"Did you hear how Ouray was taking it?" Jake asked, changing the subject. Ouray was a respected Ute leader who had a home in the Uncompahgre Valley, far south of the White River Agency, where the Meeker incident had occurred. Ouray was well-known, educated, and respected by both whites and Indians. He had been part of the contingency that traveled to Washington.

"I don't think the plans were finalized in time for him to know," Kade told them. "Ouray died in August."

Hawk sat up. "He died?"

"I heard he got sick, maybe kidney. But he didn't want treatment by white doctors. Maybe it was his way of staying in his homeland," Kade mused. "It is a loss to your people and to the whites too. He was a good man."

The men were quiet after that, thinking of the changes coming, and soon they headed for their blankets. The news that the Utes were being relocated to Utah was hard for Hawk and Jake to hear. Lathe's wife, Kasa, would also be sad when she heard the news. Kasa was Hawk's sister, and the two were sure to want to go and see their mother before the tribe was moved the next year.

The next morning, Kade noticed Noah among the men and inquired about him. Thomas filled Kade in on their newest hired hand. The boy was fitting in, trying to learn to be like the older men. They might tease him some, but they also taught him more than just riding and working with cattle. James gave the men enough information about Noah's father for them to know that the boy had had little for a decent upbringing. James had sternly warned the hired hands that he didn't want them leading the boy astray. They were to watch what they said as much as they could around Noah.

The men spent the next week gathering cattle, spread out through miles of upland meadows and forests. They bunched the cattle they found into the meadow by the shack. Finally, the meadow was getting pretty crowded with cattle, and the animals were starting to wander, looking for better grass.

"I think we should send these cattle down tomorrow," Thomas commented that night around the fire after most of the men and Noah had gone to bed. "We are going to have to gather them again pretty soon if we don't move them."

"I think a handful of us can stay and go through these mountain ridges again looking for strays, but you are right, these need to go down," Jake agreed. "Thomas and Lathe, you have families. Maybe you should head down and see how everything is faring down there." Jake looked over at Sam, "How about you, Sam? You think Martha and the kids are watching for you?"

Sam grinned, "I can stay a few more days. Martha was going to go stay at Sarah's, so she's not alone."

"Jake, would you mind if I headed down with Thomas and Lathe?" James asked. "I been worrying some 'bout that widow and her kids," he added. "I thought to maybe head over and check on them before winter hits. I'm feared they won't survive the winter. I think they may have enough food to eek it out if their garden came in well, but if there is snow, they won't even find cow chips to burn. It's hard to find wood to burn out there, and I know they don't have enough."

Jake contemplated this, looking over to Thomas for his opinion. James was taking this family a bit seriously, he thought, but then James was the only one who knew the family. It would be hard to have known the children and find them starved or frozen out after a hard winter. James seemed to like the kids.

"So, what is the situation there?" Kade asked. "Can't she take the kids an' go to town?"

"There's no money for town living," James said. "And I don't think she has family to go back to. She's scared of town people anyway. I don't think she's had many good experiences." James thought about that and added,

"Noah once was telling me his pa called his wife "white trash." I asked Ma what that meant. I'd never heard that before. Anyway, I'm not going to comment on that, but to say that the woman can't read or write and has no real skills. I don't have any idea what she could do to make a living."

"Can she keep a good house?" Kade inquired.

"Well, she tries," James said. "But a soddy with a dirt floor is always dusty. When she has water handy, she got herself and the kids scrubbed up. But that is another thing. The water will be froze solid in the cold this winter. If the plains have an open winter, they will be hard-pressed to get enough water without snow to melt."

"She's got three kids?" Kade asked.

"Well, three kids are with her, and then there is Noah."

"Tell you what, James," Kade spoke slowly. "See if she'd be willing to hire on as a housekeeper. I'm not hankering to ramble around in that quiet cabin this winter, an' the sound of kids' feet would be a distraction. She an' the little girl an' the baby can have Molly's old room, an' the boys could have the loft. I'll take her on for room an' board for her an' the children an' give her twenty dollars a month if she's willing to give that a try. I know that isn't a big wage, but I can't hardly give her more than what we give the hands working for us, an' they only get their pay plus room an' board for themselves."

"Pa, are you sure about this?" Thomas interjected. "What if you can't stand them?"

Kade grinned at his son, "I reckon if it comes to that, I could move to the bunkhouse for the winter an' send the woman on her way in the spring. But if she keeps the house up an' puts food on the table, I think it would work. I don't need company, just the noise."

James looked between Thomas and Kade. "So, I'm to offer that to her then?" he asked.

"Well, it's up to Pa," Thomas said grumpily. "He don't need my permission."

James looked between Thomas and Kade, and then taking a deep breath, he looked at Kade and spoke, "There's just one more thing. She's a white woman by her looks, but way back her family come from slaves. She carries the Negro blood. Her baby shows that."

Kade looked mildly at James before answering, "You don't think that matters with me, do you?"

CHAPTER 6

A New Home – October 1880

J ames left the Anchor J at dawn four days later, heading to the Snyder's. He had gone as far as Jackson's ranch the day before, staying overnight with Catherine. Heading out early, it was a brisk but sunny day, and he had shed his winter coat soon after the sun was up. But it wasn't to stay that way. By midmorning, angry dark clouds completely covered the sky, and the wind blew cold. Shrugging back into his heavy coat, James felt the sting of sleet against his face. He had a feeling the last three hours of this trip would be very uncomfortable for both him and his horse. As the hours went by, the winds increased, and the sleet turned to heavy snow. By the time the Snyder soddy came into view, the horse was starting to struggle through drifts, and James was an ice-encrusted figure hunched over trying to stay warm. As he came close, he saw the soddy take shape with smoke coming from the chimney. Visibility was poor, so he was relieved to make it. He couldn't reach it fast enough.

Mary Snyder answered his pounding on the door and stood, astonished to see him. He looked like a snow monster with this hat pulled down low and held on with his neck scarf to keep his ears warm. He was covered with ice and snow.

"Hello, ma'am," James said. "I seem to have picked the wrong day for a ride."

Mary Snyder looked back into the soddy and said, "Emmett, bundle yerself up an' go take this horse 'round to the lean-to an' get him unsaddled an' fed." Then looking up at James, she said, "I reckon you better come in an' warm yerself."

James sat sipping hot coffee and warming himself by the fire. He was chilled to the bone. He'd heard of early October blizzards coming to the plains, but never experienced one. The mountains were probably getting the same snow, but the winds would not be as fierce. There was always somewhere in the mountains where a body could find shelter. Out here on the plains, the wind seemed to own the land, whipping and slashing anything that got in the way. Sitting by the fire, he could hear the wind wailing outside as if frustrated it couldn't get in to reach them.

"You said you'd come back," Mrs. Snyder said softly. "But maybe you should've come earlier."

James grinned, "I just came off the mountain four days ago. The rest of the crew was coming down today. I hope they aren't fighting this weather too. This shouldn't last though. At least, I hope it don't."

"When I seen them clouds comin', I sent Emmett to bring the cow an' horse in," Mary said.

"Mrs. Snyder," James started. He thought it would be best to get right to the point. "You can't stay here this winter. This snow may not last, but winter will be hard anyway. I'm worried you can't get enough fuel for your fire, or water either. If this snow stays, you could melt snow, but if we get a chinook wind and it melts the snow, it will still get cold, and your water sources will freeze."

"I don't reckon I got a choice," Mrs. Snyder looked down. "This is all I got."

"I got an offer for you," James went on. "There's this man at our ranch. His wife died a couple months ago. He'd hire you for a housekeeper and put you and the children up, room and board. He'd give you twenty dollars a month too."

Mary Snyder looked doubtful. "I don't know," she started slowly. "What do a housekeeper have to do?"

"Well, he'd like you to keep the house clean, and when he's around, have you do the cooking. You could do that. You do that here. There's a bedroom there for you, Alice, and the baby, and the boys can sleep in the loft," James answered. Then he added, "Kade has his own room."

"A single man, you say?" Mrs. Snyder asked doubtfully.

"Ma'am, you won't find a more honorable man. You don't have to worry about that. You'd be safer with Kade than you are with me," he smiled at her, "and you know I'm safe."

"What's this man gonna do when he sees Gideon?"

James smiled. "I told him about Gideon. Kade don't see color. He's been a mountain man long before he was a rancher. He traveled with Indians and even a Black trapper once. His adopted son is part Ute Indian. You don't have to worry about that."

"I don't know . . ."

"Ma'am, you can save your earnings all winter and go on in the spring if it doesn't work out. But you have to take a chance. You and the children most likely won't survive this winter here," James was serious. "You trusted me in Laramie with your money. Trust me in this . . . it's your lives."

Mary Snyder looked into the fire, thinking. Finally, she looked up at James, and he saw her eyes brimming with unshed tears. Slowly, she nodded her head.

There was much to be done before James could take the family to the ranch. First, the weather had to change. The blizzard raged that day and into the afternoon of the next. It was too cold for James to make a bed in the lean-to with the animals, so he crawled into the tiny loft with Emmett. It was cramped, but it worked.

While the storm continued the next day, James and Mary fought their way to the cellar door, and using old food sacks, they bagged as much of her garden truck as they could, moving it into the house. James tried to tell her they had plenty of food at the ranch, but she insisted on taking what she had. She didn't want to go empty-handed.

Inside the soddy, there was little that Mary Snyder needed or wanted. The table and its bench seats were poorly built and wouldn't be needed in Kade's cabin. The family didn't have much for clothes, either. Mary was able to pack all the family's extra clothes in one packing box they had used when they came from town with supplies. Mary had made another set of clothes for each of the children, herself, and something she had intended to send back with James for Noah. It didn't take long to pack these few items. By the time the blizzard had blown itself out, they were organized and ready to go.

In the afternoon, when the blizzard finally was spent, James threw extra hay in the wagon box after wrestling the water barrels out. The barrels were almost empty, so that helped. There was no need to haul the barrels with them. The hay would be warm for the children to burrow into on the trip if the cold continued. Plus, they could feed it to the cow and horses if they didn't make it to the Anchor J in one day. James was unsure how fast he could travel dragging the milk cow along.

The day after the blizzard dawned sunny and mild. By midday, the snow was melting, and the prairie was becoming a sea of mud. James knew the wagon was not heavy but pulling it through the snow and mud would still be hard on the horses. They waited another day for the least of the drifts to melt and the windswept areas of the prairie to dry out. The trip home would be a constant challenge between dry ground, snow drifts, and mud holes. But James wanted to head out before Mary Snyder lost her nerve and backed out.

"Do you have any of the jerky left?" James asked the night before they were going to leave.

"There's a little bag on the shelf," Mrs. Snyder nodded.

"We can take that and have it handy, but let's mix up some flour to make some biscuits too," James said, thinking about the trip and what could go wrong. "I'm hoping we can make my cousin's by nightfall and eat there but if we can't, I don't want to be without something handy to eat. We might not find dry wood to burn for a fire."

Mary nodded, and together they went through the foodstuffs they had. There were fresh vegetables from the garden that could be eaten raw. But if the night temperatures got bitter cold, the vegetables would freeze. Still, if all went as planned, they would only eat quick meals on the prairie during the day and make it to Jackson's the first night and home to Twin Peaks the next.

The first day was the hardest, coming across the plains. The blizzard had dumped a lot of snow, but the wind had driven it hard, piling it up in drifts in some places and leaving bare ground in others. Many times, James had to drive the horses around drifts rather than through them. Sometimes he came on mud holes where a drift had melted, and he drove the horses hard to get through them. Blue was a seasoned member of the team now and pulled strong and true alongside the old brown gelding. The half-day ride to Jackson's Anchor J ranch became a full day, but even with the shorter daylight hours of late fall, they made Jackson's ranch just before dark. Horses and humans were tired by then. James was glad to pull in.

Catherine was watching for them, knowing that James would come back this way as soon as it was possible. As they drove up, Buster came out and helped James put the horses up for the night. While they were in the barn, Kade walked in.

"I came to see Molly," Kade told James. "I knew she would be worried about me, wondering if I turned up. So, I rode over after coming down with the herd. Got here the day after the snow quit. I'll ride back with you tomorrow."

James insisted that Mrs. Snyder ride up front with him the next day. With her baby in her arms, he pointed out landmarks along the way, trying to lessen the uneasiness he felt in her. The initial meeting between Mary and Kade went well. Kade was so laid back, neither ignoring the woman nor showing more than quiet regard for her either. But James could see the surprise in Kade that the woman was so young.

Alice and Emmett took an instant liking to Kade. His easy manner and gentle teasing had them smiling and laughing in no time. Between the two, Kade seldom rode alone that day. James and Mary could hear the children chatter as one or the other would ride double with Kade. James had a feeling this was going to be a good move for Kade to have the children in the cabin. James knew Kade was a good grandpa to Jake's and Thomas's children. Kade had all the patience in the world for children. Every kid who grew up in the community knew that. This arrangement was going to be good for Kade.

When they drove past Sarah's cabin on the way to Kade's, Sarah came out on the porch and called out to them, "I'll come and visit soon and meet you proper, Mrs. Snyder. Glad you made it." Mary, eyes wide, could only nod back.

At Kade's cabin, James helped Mary carry her few belongings inside. Kade helped James unload the garden produce into Kade's root cellar. James saw Mary looking at the cozy cabin with its fireplace and cook stove, wood plank floors, and two bedrooms. James had the feeling that this was a nicer home than Mary had ever experienced. When Mary saw Molly's room with the off-the-floor bed, she drew in her breath in surprise.

"Mr. Welles," she softly murmured to Kade, "this are awful nice. You sure you want us'n in this nice room?"

Kade just smiled. "I hope you are comfortable here."

James left them then. Promising he would stop in the next day to see if Mrs. Snyder needed anything, he headed home. He knew his mother would be waiting to hear how the trip went and he wanted to talk to Noah. Whether Noah liked it or not, he was moving in with his stepmother and siblings tomorrow. But James wanted to talk to him first.

The sun was peaking over the mountains when James met Kade and Jake at the horse corral between Kade and Thomas' cabins. These last few days of fall were good days to get the first outside rides on the three-year-old colts. The cold nights had mostly killed off the flies and the snowstorm that came through got rid of any that survived. Thomas and a crew were out with the cattle, sorting and separating calves from cows and branding summer born calves, but Jake, Kade, Lathe, Hawk, and James were back to riding the young horses.

Jake, Lathe, Hawk, and James picked out the young horses they would ride, and Kade sorted out an older trusted gelding to ride. If there was trouble, Kade had a solid horse under him. At fifty-eight, Kade had stopped riding the youngest of the colts, leaving the bronc-busting to the younger generation.

"How'd it go last night?" James asked Kade casually as they saddled their horses.

"Good," Kade replied, glancing at James. "It'll work."

James dropped the subject, relieved for that much. He wasn't sure why he cared so much. Maybe it had to do with little Alice and how she held his hand in Laramie when they went into the bank. She was afraid of the people and the unfamiliar surroundings, and she came to his side, fishing for his hand for comfort and support. Her stepmother was with the stern sheriff and bank manager, and Alice needed someone for security. She had already picked James out to be that security. *Kids had a way of worming their way into your life*, James thought.

The four colts getting their first ride outside were settling down well by the time the men turned and made a wide loop, heading back toward home. The first hour out was a little dicey at times, but only once did Kade have to rescue a rider when the colt got a branch flicked on its rump on a mountainside and began to buck his way to a wreck. Jake was riding the colt and when the storm subsided, they all had a good laugh, but they weren't laughing when it happened. Mountains can be easy to fall off from on a bucking horse.

When they hit the meadow and were heading toward home, Kade rode up and alongside James.

"She's quiet, I'll give her that," he commented nonchalantly to James. "I don't think she said two words all night."

James smiled at that. "She's not the chattiest woman I have ever met," he said. "But I don't think she means anything by it. I think she feels, I don't know, maybe like she isn't worthy, so she just keeps quiet."

"You ever seen her smile?" Kade inquired.

"Never," James answered. "I always felt pretty good if it didn't look like she was going to run from me, but never a smile," he reflected on that for a bit. "What I pieced together from what she did say to me and what the kids said, I don't think they have had much to smile about lately. I would think that would be a burden that is hard to carry for long."

"Well, I've lived too much out in the mountains alone to worry about someone being quiet," Kade said. "That little girl an' boy are good to have around. I think Alice an' Emmett just want someone to be nice to them."

"I am going to send Noah up to stay in the loft with Emmett. I think the brothers need to be together," James told Kade. "But watch Noah. I am going to put the fear of James in him if he is disrespectful to his stepmother, but he might need some reminding. If he doesn't work out there, he can come back or go to the bunkhouse. I don't want him poisoning Emmett to his stepmother. Emmett likes her, but is afraid to when Noah is around."

"Send him," Kade agreed. "I'll watch him."

James was just getting home when he saw Noah trudging up from Matthew's. Noah was sent to help Matthew often since he was familiar with farm chores and sheep. Besides that, Matthew was a good role model for the young rascal.

"Noah, I need to talk to you," James called to him as he entered the cabin. When Noah had shrugged out of his coat, James led him into the bedroom that James was sharing with Noah.

"You need to gather your things and head up to Mister Kade's," James told the boy. "They are expecting you. There is plenty of room in the loft with Emmett for you, and tomorrow we will sort out a horse for you to use to get back and forth to Matthew's or to help with the cattle. Jake and Thomas said you did a good job on the fall gather, so it is time you get your own horse assigned to you. All the cowboys have their own string picked out when they work here."

"You mean it?" Noah asked, excitement in his voice. "My own horse?"

"It will be the first horse in your string," James explained. "It is a Twin Peaks horse, but it will be yours as long as you work for us. But that includes going to Mister Kade's and living with your stepmother and your brothers and sister."

"Couldn't I stay here?" Noah implored. "I don't like that bitch."

"Noah, you listen to me hard now because I am not going to say this again," James' look was hard, and his words came out angry. "You will never ever call your stepmother that or any other degrading or insulting name. Right now, you have to decide if you belong here or not, and that is one of the conditions. You are going to go live in that cabin, and you are going to be polite and respectful. If I hear differently, there will be a come-to-Jesus moment that you will not like. And I can't say it will be any better if Kade hears you talking trash. Don't press your luck."

James' tone and words were enough to frighten the young boy, but Noah still looked at James with smoldering eyes. James could see Noah was fighting between his desire to stay on the ranch, with its good horses and a job, and his dislike for his stepmother. James thought maybe he was too harsh with the boy, but he felt it would take harshness to drive the boy's father's ways out of him.

"So, this is what you will do," James said, thinking that by outlining what expectations he had for Noah, it might help Noah to know how to act. "I can't make you like your stepmother. But you will eat at her table. You will thank her for the clothes she has made for you. You will be polite when she asks for your help. You don't have to start a conversation with her. You can talk to Alice or Emmett or Mister Kade. But you will be civil, and you will answer when she talks to you. And finally, you will do all of that respectfully. It's that, or when the next cowboy heads to town, you can take your pay, ride double with him, and make out on your own once you get there. It's your choice."

Kade was coming up from Thomas' cabin when he saw Noah trudging along with his small bundle of extra clothes, mostly the rags he arrived in. Kade was expecting the boy. James had filled him in on the boy's relationship with Mary, and Kade knew what James was expecting from the boy. From this point on, Kade and James would watch the youngster for any backsliding.

"I understand you get to pick out a horse tomorrow," Kade said as they walked up the hill to the cabin.

"Yes, sir," Noah said, but a smile came to his face with the thought of it.

"Well, guess if you are going to be a hand on this outfit, we best go get some good food in you," Kade smiled down on the boy.

The smell of frying meat hit them as they came in the door. Standing at the stove, Mary didn't look up, though Kade was sure she knew they had entered. Alice glanced at the door and smiled at Kade, then seeing Noah, she squealed with delight and came running to him.

"Where's Emmett?" Kade inquired.

"He went to the brook fer some milk. I put a jug in this morning to keep cool." Mary still didn't look at Kade.

"Your cow still giving milk?"

"Yes'm, but she's dryin' up. It won't be long an' we won't have any," Mary responded.

"Let me know when that happens," Kade told her. "Matthew and Will both have milk cows. That can be Emmett's job to trot down there every day to get milk."

"I don't have money to pay for that," Mary said softly.

"It's just part of our ranch. We get milk an' eggs from the farmers an' they get beef from us. We pay them for the hay an' garden truck when we sell cattle. It is all part of what we do here," Kade told her. "Sarah has chickens, as you know, since you brought some more for her, an' we get the eggs from her. So, Emmett an' Alice can go to Sarah's and collect eggs. I reckon we will end up getting mutton from Matthew someday too."

Kade and the children sat, and Mary put a skillet of meat and a kettle of mixed vegetables on the table. She had plates set out, but Kade could see she was one setting short. He was sure he had told her that Noah would be coming. But when Kade and the kids sat down, he saw Mary move to the back of the kitchen area and wait. Suddenly, Kade knew she didn't forget but didn't intend to sit with them.

"Mrs. Snyder," Kade said firmly, "we will not eat until you get a plate and join us. We all eat together here."

Mary looked at him and the children, and then without comment, she brought a plate to the table and sat next to Alice.

The food was good, and the children fell right to eating. It was a quiet supper and Kade didn't try to start any conversation. He was content to eat and watch the kids. They still ate like this was their last meal. When Kade finished, he took out his pipe and moved to a chair.

He left Sabra's rocking chair to Mary or the children. He wasn't ready to sit there yet.

The sun had long since set when the boys went to bed, and Alice and Gideon were put down in Molly's room. Kade thought he would have to think of it as Mrs. Snyder's room now rather than Molly's room. Mary returned from putting Alice to bed and shrugged on a coat to go out to the privy. The fire crackled in the fireplace, and Kade thought of all the years he had sat watching the fire and hearing the family go off to bed. Now he was listening to another family perform the nightly ritual. It wasn't the same, he knew, but it helped. When Mary came in, he spoke to her before she could disappear into her bedroom.

"Mrs. Snyder, I appreciate that you brought all your garden produce here with you," he said, watching the fire, "but when it runs out, we get garden things from Matthew and Will. You don't have to worry about how much food you cook up. There is no shortage here. We always have access to beef and wild meat. I'll talk to Sarah tomorrow about Emmett and Alice coming for milk and eggs, so you get fresh each day."

Mary stood in the middle of the room listening, but her eyes were on the floor. She nodded at his words but made no sound.

"Mrs. Snyder," Kade said gently, "I am not used to having anyone do for me other than my wife. You will have to be patient with me as I get used to this arrangement." Again, Mary nodded. Kade went on, "Another thing I am not used to is having someone I am talking to not look me in the face. I am not sure if you are afraid of me or don't like me, but I'd appreciate it if you would look at me."

Kade saw his words startled the woman. Her eyes raised from staring at the floor and looked at him. "No'm, I'm not afraid a' you," Mary told him softly. "But I jest don't want to overstep . . ." she wasn't sure what to say.

"Well, ma'am, you aren't overstepping," Kade explained. "Out here, you are just one of us. This has to be your home too, if this is going to work. I'm not much for having servants. But I appreciate your help in the house." Kade got up and went for his coat to go outside, but he turned back to the woman. "I'm pleased to have you and the children here. I can't tell you how much I enjoy having the children underfoot." He left then. The words were like opening his heart and letting the loneliness out. It was true, he was glad to have the children there. He knew that without them, he would be staring at the fire every night and probably hitting the jug. Sabra would be disappointed with him if that happened.

When Kade got up in the morning, Mary was already cooking a hot breakfast. The baby was awake in his cradle box near the warmth of the fireplace, but the other children still slept. Kade went to the loft ladder, took the broom that hung near, and pounded on the ceiling.

"Noah, if you want a job, you'd best get yourself up and get some breakfast while you can," he called to the boy. "Think we will get the horses in first thing."

Kade heard movement above almost immediately. He knew the young boy wouldn't want to miss the chance to pick out the first horse for his "string.'" Kade had raised two boys. He knew how to motivate them, either by getting them excited about what they were going to do, or occasionally, by a kick in the pants.

It wasn't but a few minutes, and Noah was sliding down the ladder. Mary put eggs and fried beefsteaks on the table, and Kade slid into a chair. Noah had not reached the table when suddenly Alice came to the bedroom door, rubbing the sleep out of her eyes.

"Can I have some milk?" she asked plaintively.

Almost simultaneously, the baby began to squall from the cradle, wanting his own breakfast. Mary looked at Alice and nodded, but went to the baby. Without thinking, Mary saw Noah approaching the table.

"Noah, you run out to the brook an' bring in the milk jug," she said distractedly.

The transformation on the boy's face was almost instant. It was like an ugly grimace spread over his countenance, and he began to snarl, "I ain't your . . ." Noah stopped suddenly, glancing at Kade.

Mary seemed to shrink into herself. "Never mind," she said quickly, "I'll get it."

There was a brief silence and then Noah spoke again, "No, I'll get it. I jest gotta git my boots on." He sat on the floor, pulled his boots on, and headed out the door.

Kade looked at Mary, seeing the tears brimming. "Give him time, Mrs. Snyder; he will come around."

Kade watched Thomas and Jake pick through the horses, cutting out the horses they thought would work for Noah. When they had five horses sorted off, they called Noah in to look at the horses.

"Pick your first horse from these," Jake told the young boy. "If you get to riding enough that you need a second horse, we will worry about it then. But for now, the horse you pick will be kept in the small pasture here so you can wrangle him every morning and ride down to Matthew's."

The young boy's eyes lit up at the horses. Jake had picked out seasoned horses that were well suited for a younger rider, but he had also looked for some colorful horses. Jake knew the boy would want a flashy mount, if possible. So, the five horses included a paint, a buckskin, a red roan, a blood bay, and a sorrel with a flaxen mane and tail.

Noah studied the horses, but Kade was pretty sure the boy's expertise with horses didn't go much farther than the old brown gelding of his father's.

"Look at the big heart girth on that bay," Kade told him. "He will have great lung capacity. Sometimes you need that if you have a long distance to travel in a short period of time. They all have good legs, or we wouldn't keep them. The sorrel is sort of flighty. You can see that the way he carries his head, looking for things to spook at. He'll be a good working horse, but you'd have to watch him, or you might find yourself on the ground sometimes." Kade smooched at the horses, making them move around the corral. "The paint is pretty tall. If you can't reach the stirrup, you might find yourself walking a far piece if you have to get off him where there aren't logs or rocks around to help you mount. The buckskin an' red roan are steady geldings. You can see how calm they move, but they have speed an' agility too." Kade paused. "It all depends on what kind of horse you want. Time to choose, cowboy."

Noah looked seriously up at Kade. "Iffen you were to choose, which one you reckon would work the best for me?"

Kade was pleased the boy asked. It showed that the boy knew he lacked the knowledge and was willing to ask for advice. "I reckon, if I was as tall as you, an' jest learning 'bout good cow horses, I'd look at either the buckskin or the roan. They are damn fine horses that will teach you as much as they can. But they are also pretty, an' I always hanker to ride a handsome horse."

"I'll take the red roan then," Noah said. "James rides a blue roan. Be nice to ride a roan too."

Kade wanted to smile at that, but he didn't. James had made his impression on this young boy. Kade remained serious. "Yes, I think that is the best choice for you. That's a good horse. I use him a lot when I'm riding with these bronc busters. He's one of my first choices. Guess I'll have to look for a replacement now," Kade smiled down at the young boy.

"Boys, pick me out what you want me to ride today, an' I'll be back in a bit," Kade raised his voice to carry to his sons. "I'm needin' to tell Mrs. Snyder something." Kade started toward the cabin but turned back, "Catch up that old Brownie horse of the Snyder's too. Emmett an' Alice can use him each day to go an' fetch milk an' eggs."

Mary was finishing cleaning the breakfast dishes when Kade entered the cabin. "Mrs. Snyder," he began, "I was never good at the fancy cookin' you womenfolk do. I couldn't make a cookie to save my life. But my wife used to make this sweet thing an' a couple times in the winter, when I was jest lazin' around, I helped her peel apples for a crisp she made. She'd get apples out of the cellar, peel an' slice them an' put them in a cook pan. Then she'd mix flour an' sugar an' butter. She'd put this on top an' put it all in the oven an' cook it until the top was golden looking an' the apples were soft. It was pretty good too. The young'uns always loved it." Kade paused, looking out the window. "You are goin' to get company an' it is sort of expected to have some coffee or tea an' something to eat. There's plenty of apples in the cellar. Maybe there are things around here that make some other sweet treat that you know about."

Mary stood still, listening to Kade. When he finished, she looked up from the dish she was wiping out. "Why would I get visitors?"

"Ma'am, they will come to meet you. The womenfolk here will want to welcome you."

"But I don't know what to say to them," Mary whispered.

Kade saw the panic rising in her. "Mrs. Snyder," he began, then stopped, thinking before continuing. "Would you mind if I called you Mary? You have to be thirty-some years younger than me, an' it jest don't shine to be so formal in my own home. But I don't want for you to think I'd do it to be disrespectful, either."

The change of subject calmed the young woman. "Reckon that would be jest fine," she said softly.

"Well, good then, and you can call me Kade, or if you choke on that, you can say Mister Kade, but that's as formal as you are allowed," Kade smiled at that. Mary did not smile back, but there was a faint twitch on the corners of her mouth. Kade considered that a beginning.

"Now as for what to say to the womenfolk that come, well, I reckon first you say 'please come in' an' 'pleased to meet you' an' 'please sit down.'" Kade thought about what Sabra would do. "Then you put out plates an' cups an' put out whatever you have. The women might ask you questions 'bout where you grew up an' such like. You don't have to talk 'bout anything you don't want to talk 'bout. Jest say 'that was a long time ago,' ifffen you don't want to go there. If you get asked about losing your husband an' you don't want to talk about it, you jest say something like, 'it was a shock.' People here won't pry, an' they won't judge. They jest want to be friendly. You might have to meet them halfway."

Mary watched Kade intently as he talked, trying to put to memory the phrases he used. She hoped she would remember them when she got visitors. She'd had few visitors in her life and none that she had to entertain. This was new ground for her.

Kade turned to go. Just as he was at the door, he turned and spoke once more. "Mary, this is your home now. You look through the foodstuffs an' find whatever you need. If we are getting low on something, you tell me, an' we will go 'bout getting more if we have it on the ranch." He smiled and said, "You will be fine today. Just try to relax. The women will want to be your friend. Let them."

CHAPTER 7

Fitting In – Late Fall 1880

Mary walked outside to meet the children coming home with the eggs and milk. She learned from experience not to let them try to get off the horse before she met them. The first time, they dropped the eggs and almost lost the milk jug. Now, Emmett rides to the cabin and calls out. Then Mary goes out to meet them and gets the basket of eggs first and then the jug of milk. Emmett and Alice have a circuit they ride each day on old Brownie. They have a "job," and they were mighty proud of that.

Each day, Emmett goes to the corrals between Thomas' and Kade's cabins and saddles Brownie returning to Kade's home to get Alice. Then the two of them would set off with empty milk jugs and an empty basket for eggs. They rode to Sarah's cabin, where she would meet them and load them up with fresh milk and eggs. Next, they would ride carefully back up the valley and stop at all the cabins, delivering the produce. Beth, Martha, Anna, Bonnie, and Kasa would come out at their call and take what they needed. On some days, the children picked up Martha's oldest boy, Thomas James, or TJ as he was called, and the three children would ride triple on old Brownie to Anna's. There they would linger, tying up Brownie and playing with Kestrel and three-year-old Lark. Both TJ and Kestrel were almost five and with Emmett and Alice, they always found things to do. Finally, the children would deliver TJ back to Martha and ride home to Mary with the eggs and milk left for them. For this delivery route, Kade promised them a penny a day for each of them.

On this day, the children were bundled up against the early winter chill. There was snow on the ground now, but winter had not sent its worst yet. When it did, the children's job would end for a while, and one of the men would ride for the eggs and milk. Mary helped Alice down and sent Emmett off to take care of the horse. It was just noon, and Alice was bubbling over with what they did when they stopped at Anna's. Anna always welcomed the children, probably because for a few minutes, her two oldest were occupied by playing with the newcomers.

Mary set the eggs and milk on the table. She didn't need to put the milk in the brook now. The weather was cold enough to put the milk outside the door during the day, but it would freeze out there overnight. Mary didn't expect Kade home for dinner. He seldom came home for the midday meal. They were butchering at Matthew's today, so he would take his meal there. Mary set the table for Emmett, Alice, and herself.

She thought about these last two months. The children had lost the pinched look of those who lived on the brink of always being hungry. They had also lost the fear they often had when their father was alive. They wore clothes that were not rags, but new clothes made for them. They laughed and played and loved "Mister Kade" when he teased them at night. Mary still could not take this life for granted. Every morning, she woke wondering if her world would come tumbling down again. And every night, she went to bed with a prayer of thanks that it had not happened on that day.

The first few weeks were hard. As Kade had warned, she got visitors. The first to arrive were James' mother, Sarah, and her daughter, Bonnie. Bonnie had been married a little over a year and to Mary's surprise, she was married to a Ute man. Swift Hawk was Jake's nephew and the first time Mary saw him, it was quite a shock. But now, two months later, he was just part of the people that made up this ranch.

The next day, Mattie and her youngest daughter, Rachel, came by. Rachel was younger than Mary but not by much. Married at sixteen to Army, one of the ranch's hired hands, Rachel had a baby girl about the same age as Gideon. Mary found it easier on the second day of visiting as the three women watched the two little ones tumble around on the cabin floor. The talk went to baby clothes and favorite foods, and Mary felt more comfortable discussing those topics.

Only Martha and her two little boys visited on the third day. Martha was James' sister. Older than all the other young people, Martha had married Sam five years earlier when she was twenty-seven. Mary had seen Martha moving slowly across the meadow, and as she came closer, Mary saw that one of Martha's arms was misshapen. Martha came by midmorning and stayed well into the afternoon. When Martha finally realized the time, both women were astonished at how fast the day went.

With Martha, Mary found a kindred spirit. Crippled from an accident when she was a child, Martha always felt different. Unhappy and ashamed of her deformity, Martha was well on her way to becoming an old maid when Sam, fifteen years her senior, came to their valley in search of his mother, Clara, who was married to Old Tom. It was Sam who gently bullied Martha into taking a chance, learning to dance, and learning to love. With Clara and Tom dead now, Sam and Martha lived in their cabin across the meadow.

When Martha left that first day, she turned to Mary and remarked, "I am so glad you are here. It is so nice not to be the only one different here." Then with a look of horror, she continued, "Oh, I'm so sorry. I hope that doesn't offend you. I didn't mean it that way." Martha paused, trying to gather her thoughts. "I know it is just me that sees my short leg and crippled arm as different, but I do. Jake always understood me because he is different too, in his own way. But he's a man. You can't talk to a man like you can with a woman. And I think you are the only one who sees your baby as making you different, but there you have it. We see our own insecurities. So, I don't mean to be disrespectful, but it's just I knew right away you would understand. Please say you are not offended!"

Mary was not offended. She immediately knew that this sweet, kind woman was a friend. It was a new experience for Mary to have a friend. She hadn't had a real friend since she was a child living in the Black quarters with her mother and brother. With Martha, Mary felt at ease.

On the fourth day, Anna and Kasa came with their children. Anna, with three children, and Kasa, with little two-year-old Slade and another well on the way to being born during the winter, came in the afternoon and their children played around them for several hours. Kasa was Jake's niece and Swift Hawk's sister. A pretty Ute woman, Kasa felt the most comfortable with Anna. A white woman, Anna had been abducted and raised by Indians until she was seventeen when Jake traded with the Cheyenne for her, and she became Jake's wife. Anna and Kasa understood each other because they were both learning to live in a new culture.

By the time Mary got through the first days of visiting, she was becoming more relaxed around the people here. Her attempt at making an apple crisp had been successful, and the women had praised the sweet treat. Mary also found the ingredients for a molasses cookie and baked that too. And as a bonus, there was enough left over each night of one or the other of the desserts for the children and Kade.

The late fall was mild, and the snows held off. The first week that the Snyder family had come to stay, Jake detoured up to Kade's cabin one day on his way home. Mary was dipping water from the brook when she saw Jake coming. He rode a nice bay gelding that had a ground eating walk, head swinging from side to side as it came. Jake rode the horse into the front yard and smiled down at Mary.

"On Sundays, some of us go to Matthew and Mattie's. Can't say it is really a church, but we get together and do some talking about God and our beliefs. Some get to singing. Things like that. Matthew leads us. Anna and I would stop by on Sunday and get you, if you and the children wish to come with us. If it is nice, we walk, but if it is cold, I'll have a wagon hitched," Jake smiled at Mary. "We'd be pleased to have you join us."

Mary looked doubtful. "Not sure we should," she murmured.

"Yes, you should if you want," Jake told her. "You'd be welcome."

"Does Mistah Kade go?" Mary looked at the cabin.

Jake reflected on that a minute. "He has some in the past. He is sort of sporadic. I'm not sure I'd count on his attendance right now."

"But you go?"

Jake looked off to the mountain slopes briefly before answering, "Let's just say I was raised there. My ma took us as kids," Jake looked back at Mary. "A few years back, I got in a bad scrape, and wasn't sure I was going to get out of it. I had some long talks with my Maker that night. When help showed up at dawn, I figured I had more than just one reason to be thankful. I try to get there on Sundays now as much as I can." Jake turned his horse and moved off. Before he got too far, he said over his shoulder, "We will be by about eight on Sunday morning. We will stop for you."

Kade rode to the cabin and stopped by the root cellar door. The men had butchered some steers, and he had a couple quarters to hang up in the cellar. It was mid-morning, and he knew Mary had gone to Martha's with the children. Martha had taken an instant liking to Mary, and Kade could see they got along well. They were sharing recipes, sewing clothes, and learning from each other.

Jake had told him that Mary had fared well at Matthew's on Sunday. She was scared in the beginning, but everyone welcomed her. Noah knew so many people now, and even Emmett and Alice knew several in the community through their job of delivering milk and eggs. Emmett and Alice received plenty of attention, and with Jake's little girls and Martha's boy, there was plenty of interaction between the children. Kade thought of going that Sunday to Matthew's, but he knew he wasn't ready. He'd be looking for Sabra's ghost the whole time, sitting in her favorite spot. No, he wasn't ready for that.

Kade took a quarter of beef and shouldered it down the stairs to the cellar. Kade and Sabra had expanded and refurnished the cellar in the decades they lived there. Kade built shelves along the walls and along these sat bags and barrels of supplies and produce, stored from the winter cold and the summer heat. He went to the back of the cellar, hung the first quarter, and climbed back up the stairs to get the second.

When Kade had the second beef hung, he glanced around at the shelves. He didn't come down here often except to bring in more supplies. The cellar had been Sabra's domain, and she would tell him if any of their food stores were getting low. With Mary now, Kade wasn't sure she would tell him if they needed something. He studied the shelves, gauging how much they had of the needed staples.

There, on one of the top shelves, something caught his eye. He reached up, pulling down heavy papers and looked at them curiously. He was looking at a wanted poster. It was lying flat, but it had been folded, the creases showing. He looked at the name. It was a man named

Walters, wanted for horse theft in Cheyenne. He didn't recognize the man or the name. He placed the poster on a low shelf and looked at the next page. This was an old poster. It told of a meeting in an unfamiliar town in Missouri. While it now lay flat, the poster had been folded and refolded so many times that it was cracking along some of the folds. He set this aside too. The third poster was about a town festival near St. Louis. Kade set it on the top of the others and looked at the fourth and final poster. This was a poster advertising a farm auction.

Kade looked at the posters and wondered what in the world these could have in common. James had told Kade that Mary couldn't read. Why had she saved these posters? He knew it had to be Mary who placed these on the root cellar shelf. Sabra would not have had access to all these places to acquire the posters. Kade set this last poster on top of the rest when the one on top fluttered to the ground. When Kade reached down to pick it up, he saw it had landed on its front. There on the back of the poster, he saw pencil marks. He picked up this poster and moved closer to the light coming down the steps to see better.

Kade studied the back of the poster. It was covered in pencil drawings. He recognized the children in the drawings. There were little sketches scattered across the page haphazardly. At the top was a picture of Alice asleep in a narrow cot, a blanket pulled up around her chin. In another, he saw Emmett and Noah curled up together in what appeared to be a wagon bed. Again, they were asleep. They looked peaceful. Kade turned the poster a bit to see the next scene. He saw a man in a chair, gently holding Alice. The man's face was blank, his eyes closed as if he were sleeping, and Alice lay asleep in his lap. Could this be Alice's father? The last picture was almost upside down from the others. Kade turned the poster to see it clearly. Emmett and Noah were both in it, climbing up the ladder to the loft. Just at the edge of this picture was a hand pointing upward. A man's hand. Kade could almost see the little boys scurrying up the ladder. The final picture on this page was of a soddy, with a milk cow standing by the fence and some sheep grazing nearby.

Kade went back for another poster. He took the town meeting poster, which had to be the oldest, with its cracks along the folds and its frayed edges. He turned the poster over. Here too, were pencil sketches. The first picture was a line of shanties at the top of the page. He could see people sitting on porches; an old man and woman were smiling. Two men and a woman were walking between the little houses, bent with age and work but still smiling. The artist had shaded the people, all of them were Black. Kade rotated the poster to see the next scene. He recognized Mary, but she was much younger, still a child. She stood with a pretty woman with slight African features and shading and an older boy. The boy too, showed his Black heritage, although he was not shaded as dark as the people by the shanties. Finally, there was a white boy, younger than ten, for sure. He was in a sketch by himself, and he was smiling. He looked out of place with the other drawings containing Black people.

The third poster that Kade turned over was the poster about an auction. The sketches on this page gave Kade pause. There were only two sketches on this page. The first was of a girl, although Kade couldn't tell how old a girl. Her face was not drawn. The drawing started at her neck and went down from there. The bodice of her dress was torn, but she was still mostly covered. Two young boys sat, one on each side of her, holding her arms and shoulders down. Kade couldn't be sure, but he thought the one boy resembled the white boy on the poster he'd just set down. But the angles were wrong, so that he couldn't be sure. Another man, or at least a much older boy, knelt on the girl's legs. He had her skirt hoisted up, and he was reaching under it. His face was grinning, like he was laughing. Kade felt sick.

Kade turned the page and looked at the second picture, drawn upside down from the first. This time it was a woman's body, or part of a woman. He studied the image and then suddenly realized what he was seeing. The woman was lying on a bed with knees bent and a blanket haphazardly covering her except for her bare knees. Between her legs lay a baby, and instantly Kade recognized little Gideon. Gideon was just a tiny mite, naked and crying. And leaning down over them both was a man. Kade recognized the man as the one holding Alice in a chair. At first, Kade thought the man was reaching for the baby, but as he studied the picture, Kade knew he was wrong. The man wasn't reaching for the baby, but rather he was scrabbling to get away. The look on the man's face told Kade that. The man's face was a mask of horror and revulsion. This was Mary's husband, and this is what she saw when she gave birth to her baby.

Kade took a deep breath. He was almost afraid to look at the last and final poster. Slowly, he turned it over, hoping he didn't see more horrors on it. He let out his breath, studying these sketches. In the first image, his cabin was sketched in the early morning with the sun coming over the peaks. There was a picture of Martha walking up the hill. There was a drawing of James, next to the soddy from a previous sketch. James was chopping wood, and Alice was picking scraps up from the ground. James had his shirt off, and even with only the pencil marks, Kade could see James was sweat covered. Kade rotated the poster to see the last picture. It was of himself. He was sitting at the table with Emmett beside him, and the two of them were laughing at something.

He knew that these sketches had to have been done by Mary. While the sketches were somewhat primitive, he could see that she drew well. All the feeling and detail she had put into these were amazing, and in some respects, frightening. Not having any paper, Mary had evidently taken posters off walls and used the back for her artwork. Kade wondered if these were all she had done or if there were others, possibly lost somewhere in her travels. Apparently, she hid these sketches, folded up to keep them safe. Now she had them laid flat to save them. The oldest one was falling apart already. Kade gently piled them up and returned them on the shelf.

Kade wondered where she got pencils. Some of these were drawn quite a while ago. Kade knew he had a pencil on the small table he and Sabra used for a desk. He thought there was another pencil in a drawer. That was Sabra's domain. Kade seldom wrote the letters to Joe unless he wanted Joe to get him something. He wrote the letter to Joe and Katie about Sabra's death, but he sat at the Dixon post office to do that. He hadn't written since. Kade knew he should. Joe and Katie would worry if they didn't hear from him. He could get something ready, and someone would wander over to Dixon and post it before winter hit. It was a new sensation to have a post office less than a day's ride from them.

But now the question was, should he mention to Mary that he'd seen the pictures? He decided it was too soon. She was still too new and unaccustomed to living with them. He would leave this discovery for another time.

Later that night, though, when the children were in bed and Mary had come in from an evening trip to the privy, Kade looked up and spoke to her.

"Reckon as the nights get longer, an' the children don't have much to do," he started casually, "you might like to have some paper an' a pencil for them or you to use, to draw pictures or maybe later to work on letters or such. There's paper an' at least one pencil over there," Kade pointed toward the desk. "You help yourself. I won't need but a sheet or two to write to my brother. I can always get some from Sarah too. Help yourself."

Mary listened solemnly, then nodded. "I thankee. I think the children might like that. Miss Sarah were saying Emmett an' Alice should start takin' lessons. She are teaching Kestrel an' TJ on some days. Emmett an' Alice haven't had any teachin' yit. I can't help 'em."

"Well, you just use what you want," Kade repeated, getting up. He went to the mantle and took down the picture of him and Sabra. He often carried it into his bedroom at night. He liked looking at Sabra one more time before blowing out the candle.

"You miss her?" Mary said softly.

Kade looked up, surprised. Mary seldom started a conversation. "I do," he said simply.

"She were pretty," Mary commented. "Where were that taken?"

"We were at Thomas and Beth's wedding in Laramie. I wanted a picture of just Sabra alone, but she wouldn't do that," he smiled, remembering. "She insisted we both would be in the picture, so I had to stand with her. She was pretty strong-willed when it came to some things."

◆

The winter set in long before Christmas. The river valley was deep with snow, but many days were mild. Unlike the prairie, the winds were not as big a problem for the mountain people. Molly and Jackson, along with Buster and Catherine, were coming for Christmas. They would bundle up, putting hot bricks by their feet in their light wagon. Filled with hay, the men would drive, and the women and little Jack would snuggle in the hay under buffalo robes. The light wagon, fitted with runners in the winter, would be easy for the team to drag across the snow-covered river bottom. They would arrive on Christmas Eve and leave the day after Christmas. This year, Molly and Jackson would stay with Beth and Thomas in their newly built second bedroom.

Kade was surprised to find that he was looking forward to Christmas. It would be different without Sabra, but he wanted to see Molly, Jackson, and his little grandson. He always enjoyed watching the children. Little children made Christmas rich, despite the changes that hit them this year.

Without Sabra to do Christmas gifts, Kade had to think through what presents he needed. The adults did not usually exchange gifts. It had always been too hard to get supplies at Christmas time, so the ranch families had only celebrated with presents for the children. When his children were young, most gifts were home-made, unless they thought a long time ahead and hid items they bought during the summer when visiting Ft. Laramie. Now, with a post office and general store not more than a half day's ride at Dixon, they could get mail and supplies more often. It was late October when Kade rode over and ordered gifts for Christmas. While Kade was there, he studied the wall where the storekeeper put up posters that came through the mail. Kade picked out two outdated posters. They would be thrown away anyway when the shop owner went through them. Kade thought he would add them to Mary's pile of posters and let her form her own opinion on how they got there.

Kade's order was ready to be picked up when Luke went for the mail the next month. Kade warned Luke to take a pack mule along. Kade expected it would take more than a man on a saddle horse to get supplies home with everyone ordering Christmas items. Kade wouldn't be the only one sending out for gifts for the holidays.

It was easy to get things for the Snyder kids. They had nothing. He was particularly tired of seeing them fight the winter cold in homemade coats made from blankets. It was time they had real coats. Kade ordered a winter coat for each child, even Gideon, although it would be too large for the baby this year. But the coat would have growing room and fit next year when Gide-on would be more mobile when he went outside. This winter, he could be wrapped up in it. Sarah had helped Kade decide on sizes.

In each coat pocket, there would be a small bag of hard candy. Just before he sent off the order, Kade added one more coat. He would break the rule about no gifts for adults and get Mary one too. She was his employee, after all. He could give her a coat. And in the pocket of the coat, she would find new pencils, some of different colors. He ordered plenty of paper to share.

Kade asked Sarah to sew Kestrel a new riding skirt like Sabra used to wear. He approved of them for one thing, and for another, little Kestrel was already getting to be a good rider. Sabra would have been so proud of her. He also ordered little dolls for Kestrel, Lark, and Thomas and Beth's little Jenny. As for the boy babies, he had no idea what to get. But the store owner had told him drums were popular, so Kade ordered in a drum for Jake's little boy, Kade Brown, and another for Molly's son, little Jack.

On Christmas Eve, Kade walked to Thomas and Beth's. Jake, Anna, and the children were there as well as Molly and family. Between the adults, toddlers, and babies, the cabin was overflowing. Molly remarked earlier that she was dreading Christmas without her mother, but they all admitted that while it was different, and they were all saddened by the loss of Sabra, they couldn't say that the evening had been unpleasant. There were a lot of memories shared. There were some tears, some laughs, and lots of stories. Sabra was gone, but she was still very much a part of the family.

"What did you and Ma do for Christmas when you were first married?" Thomas asked Kade as the family sat before the fire after supper.

Kade smiled at the memory. "Well, the first year, it was just the two of us after old Tom went back to Ft.

Laramie," Kade glanced over at Jake, "except for you an' you were mostly sleeping an' eating at the time. Neither your ma nor I had thought about Christmas when we left the settlements, so we mostly just had a nice meal and," Kade grinned at his sons, "we just enjoyed being with each other." Kade paused, a faraway look in his eyes. "But by the second year, we were here with the Jorgensens, an' the Bates joined us the year after that. It was just the three families, so we did a lot together. When Jim an' Sarah joined us, Jake an' Martha were the only kids, an' we could all gather at one cabin or another. I think your ma really enjoyed those times. She had lived pretty lonesome before that, so she enjoyed having friends. As our families grew, we spent our Christmases more in our own homes, but I don't think we ever forgot those early days when our three families were all we had. Maybe that is why our ranch families are so close now. This ranch is not just one operation, but several, with all three of our families an' our offspring, but we all seem to work it out, whether we are talking business or pleasure."

It was late when Kade left, trudging up the rise to his own cabin. The cabin was dark, and he built up the fire to warm it. Mary and her children were invited to Sam and Martha's for the evening, and were not back yet. Kade left the fire crackling, warming the cabin for when they returned. Satisfied the fire would last for several hours, he went to his bed. He had his own plans for Christmas morning.

Kade was up early on Christmas morning, beating Mary. He found hot coals in the fireplace, got a fire going along with the stove, and started coffee. In front of the fireplace, he laid out the five winter coats with the pockets filled. When the coffee was ready, he sat at the table and waited, sipping the hot brew.

He didn't have long to wait. Mary came from her room in a hurry when she smelled the coffee.

"Sorry, Mister Kade," she blurted out, "I'm late gittin' up."

"It's Christmas morning," Kade answered mildly, "so you don't have to rush for me."

Mary started to reply and then saw the five coats spread out on the hearth. She stopped and stared. Kade could see she was confused. She might not know much about numbers, but five coats matched the number of her family members. It didn't match the rest of Kade's family.

"Merry Christmas, Mary. You reckon you an' the children can fit those coats?" Kade asked.

"Mister Kade, you ought not to spend yer money on us'n," Mary almost whispered.

Kade sipped his coffee before replying, "I reckon I can spend my money in any way I want, an' I wanted to do this. Go on now, try on that one on the end."

Mary didn't have to be told twice. The coat fit well, and she hugged it to her. She slid her hands in the pockets, testing their warmth, and then her fingers felt the pencils. Slowly she fished them out and stared at them.

"These have colors to them," she murmured. She looked up at Kade. "You put the extree posters in the cellar. You seen my pictures."

"You have quite a talent, Mary. I hope you don't mind I saw your drawings. You're good. I hope you will show me more pictures if you draw some," Kade cradled his coffee cup, studying it. "But best you wake the children now. I'll be heading out soon to help feed."

The children came grumbling and yawning from their beds until they saw the coats. They, too, stopped and stared. It didn't take much prodding from Kade for each child to find the coat that fit and try it on. Kade went to his room and found the little mirror of Sabra's. He held it for the children to see themselves. When they found the candy in the pockets, their joy increased.

The children were taking off the new coats when there was a pounding on the door. James stumbled in brushing off newly fallen snow as he shook off his coat. He was carrying a pack.

"Crazy thing happened," James said as he accepted coffee from Mary. "We got up this morning, and there were presents by our fireplace, but we knew they weren't for us," James grinned over toward Kade. "I figure poor old Santa must have gotten the wrong house. So, I brought these up here to see if they maybe were supposed to go here."

James pulled two sets of spurs out of his pack and looked around at the children. "You reckon you two boys might need a pair of spurs?" He smiled at the surprised nods from the boys as they saw the shiny rowels on the spurs. James handed each boy a pair. "You might want to see if they fit your boots," he prodded, "or I might have to look for a different set of boys." The boys were off instantly, sitting on the floor by the door trying the spurs on their boots.

"Let's see, there are these blocks," James comment-ed. "Suppose Gideon would like blocks to play with?" James asked Mary, pouring ten little homemade wood-en blocks on the floor. Mary smiled, something she was doing more often now, and set the toddler on the floor by the blocks. They all watched the little boy as he ex-plored the shapes.

James looked around then, seeing Alice watch the boys get their presents. He could see the hope in the little girl's eyes that she too might receive a gift, but also the doubt. James didn't want to draw it out.

"Then I seen this one thing laying out, and I just knew where there was a little girl who would take care of it, so I brought it here," James pulled out a little wooden doll. It had a painted face and wore a long dress. He held it out towards Alice. "You think you could take care of this little thing?" he asked.

Alice's eyes widened as she looked from the doll to James and then to Mary.

"A real dolly," she whispered, then looked at Mary. "Mama, it's a real dolly," her voice held all the won-der of a little girl who never believed she would have such a wonderful gift. She looked to James, "For me? Really?"

James knelt to Alice's level, "Yes, honey, this dolly is yours." He handed it to the little girl, and she clutched it to her. Then, without a thought, the child threw herself at James and hugged him hard.

"I have something for you, ma'am," James said to Mary as he patted Alice's head and rose. He reached into his pack, pulled out a small package, and handed it to Mary. She took it gingerly, unwrapping the paper. Inside, there was a hairbrush with a decorated handle.

"This is beautiful," Mary murmured. "I've ain't never had sich a nice thing," she said looking up at James. "I thankee fer this."

The men were silent, letting the Snyder family enjoy the gifts. Then suddenly, Mary spoke again.

"I have something fer you both," she didn't look at the men but went to her room.

When she returned, she had sheets of Kade's writing paper in her hand. She solemnly handed one to James first. Kade could see the picture she had drawn as he looked across the table. It was a picture of James, half-risen in the seat of a buckboard, legs braced and reins in hand as the team he was driving was plunging wildly. She had caught the action of the horses and the effort of the young cowboy as he struggled to control the horses. James looked in wonder at the drawing.

"Holy," he murmured. "You did this?" he looked up at Mary. "This is really good."

A shy smile lit Mary's face. She nodded back at James. Then she grew serious again and looked at Kade. "I ain't sure this are good enough, but I kin try agin iffen you don't like it," she said doubtfully. She handed Kade the sheet of paper.

On the paper, Mary had sketched the face of Sabra. It wasn't copied from the picture of Sabra and Kade together though, but instead, it was drawn from Sabra's likeness in the wedding picture of the whole family. In that photo, right when the photographer took the picture, Sabra had run her fingers up Kade's back, then looked up at Kade and smiled mischievously. When the photograph was developed, Sabra was afraid that she had ruined the picture by smiling. The custom at the time was for solemn demeanors. But Kade liked seeing her smile and wished she had smiled in the photograph of them together.

In her drawing, Mary must have studied both pictures to capture Sabra's image, the tiny smiling face from the photo of the whole family and also the larger picture of Kade and Sabra together. And between the two, Mary had captured Sabra. It was a head shot of Sabra and it took Kade by surprise. It captured her smile, the twinkle in her eye, and her beauty. Kade studied the drawing, almost holding his breath. He couldn't speak.

Mary watched him nervously. "I kin try again," she whispered.

Kade rose from the table, shaking his head. He cleared his throat, trying to get control of his voice. "This is," he stopped, searching for words, "it's 'bout the best present I ever had." He turned and stepped toward his room. "I'll make a frame for it so I can hang it in my room. I can see her that way every night and morning." He turned back and both Mary and James could see the emotion in the man. "Thank you, Mary. This is fine."

January came in cold. Winter dragged on with short days and more snow. When the weather allowed, the children walked to Sarah's for lessons. Mary took to walking them, or if she finished her chores, she went to meet them on the walk home. Sarah welcomed Mary in to sit and watch the lessons. Sometimes, Sarah gave Mary mini lessons in reading and arithmetic. On other days, Mary would take Gideon and walk to Martha's, or Martha would visit. Both Sarah and Martha recognized the longing that Mary had to improve herself by learning to read and speak better.

She felt comfortable with Martha and asked Martha for help, so while they worked together sewing or knitting or going over recipes, Martha would talk to Mary and help her practice better speech. Mary's speech improved slowly, finding the correct verbs and putting sentences together more correctly.

It was on a day in late in January when the sun was strong, the temperature was mild, and the children were restless over their studies. When the men came in from feeding hay, Sarah sent the children home and told James and Jake it was time they got out their sleds and took the kids out to some hills.

So it was that shortly after the noon hour, the younger men and women and the little children began congregating at Kade's hill. Kade had the best sledding hill in the community. They could climb up behind his cabin and glide right by the front yard or start in the front yard and slide down the slope to the meadow below. Every family had sleds of some sort, most made by old Tom. James, Sam, Jake, and Thomas saddled horses and took turns pulling the sleds and children back up to the yard to slide down again. Mothers with little toddlers could go into Kade's cabin to warm up if needed, but a big bonfire was built in the yard too.

When Gideon awoke from his nap, Mary brought him out, bundled up in his oversized Christmas coat, and asked James to take him down the hill on the sled. As she stood watching James and Gideon slide away, Noah approached her. Over the months, Noah had kept his distance from Mary, but the animosity he had shown her in the summer had dissipated. Pulling a sled, he handed the pull rope to Mary.

"Best you take this down," he said seriously to his stepmother. "Gideon might be watching for you down there."

"I cain't do that," Mary protested. "I never done sledding before."

"I'll help you," Noah said, pushing the woman towards the sled. "Sit there in the back and cross yer legs. I'll sit in front of you so I kin steer."

Mary warily approached the sled, but prodded by Noah, she sat as instructed. Noah climbed on in front of her, and grasping the rope, he pushed off with his feet. The sled gained speed, and Mary gasped, clutching Noah from behind.

"Ohhhhhh!" Mary screamed, ducking her head behind Noah to keep from seeing where they were going. It didn't take long for them to descend the hill, and steering for a snowdrift, Noah tipped the sled over in the fluffy stuff, throwing them both off the sled. It was then that people first heard Mary laugh. She lay in the white powder and laughed, looking over at Noah. He looked back at her, and face relaxing, he also laughed.

James was getting Gideon off the sled when he looked up and saw Noah and Mary, skirts flying, careening down the slope towards them. Picking up the toddler, he moved quickly out of the way and watched as they tumbled off the sled into the snowbank. But it was Mary's laugh that caught him by surprise. He had seen her smile occasionally but never had she laughed.

James studied her as she lay in the snow. He had never noticed before, but she looked so different from when he first met her. Gone were the worry lines and the grim look. Her eyes had been sunken then from tension, hard work, and little food. Now her face had filled out and with surprise, James realized it was a comfortable face, even pretty, when she laughed. He had never noticed that before.

CHAPTER 8

Courting – Spring/ Summer 1881

Kade noticed the subtle difference in James as January turned into February. James had often visited Kade's cabin since the Snyders moved in but had mainly interacted with the children. Alice and Emmett were both fond of James. Kade suspected James felt somewhat responsible for the children since he had brought them to the ranch, but Kade also knew that James truly liked the children.

After the sledding party, James began to come and visit more in the evenings, playing chess with Kade or just sitting and visiting with Kade and the children in front of the fire. But James also tried to draw Mary into conversations more, not letting her keep to herself. He brought books for the children and read to them, and lessons Sarah sent for him to go over with Mary, making her sit with him to study.

By April, when there was snow only in the protected areas of the mountain valley, and the evenings were mild, James would stay and visit until Mary had Gideon and Alice tucked into their beds and then he began to ask her to walk with him outside. There had been a good thaw in March, and then in early April, a snowstorm dumped several inches of snow. The day that followed was cold, but a warm chinook wind blew across the valley late in the afternoon.

"It is going to be a beautiful night tonight," James commented after the children were in bed. "The temperature is warming, and most of this new snow will be gone by morning. Have you ever seen the full moon sparkle on the snow in the winter, Mary?" he asked, turning toward her. "I mean, really walked out onto the meadow and looked at it, not just in here looking out the window?"

Mary looked solemnly at him and shook her head. "I've seen it from the cabin and the front yard. Is it different out there?"

"Well, come and see," James went for his jacket, plucking Mary's off a peg as well. "It's pretty to walk out there and see it sparkle, and the moon is full tonight."

"I don't know," Mary began doubtfully, "the children might not go to sleep."

"You go," Kade told her firmly. "The kids are no problem, and if they look for you, I'll be here. Emmett and Noah are in the loft."

So, Mary and James walked out together. Kade wasn't sure how much they talked, but Mary didn't come back inside for over an hour. She smiled shyly then and thanked Kade for being with the children, and went to bed. After that, James made a point of coming to visit several times a week, and at least one of those times each week, James persuaded Mary to walk with him. Kade had a feeling he might lose his housekeeper one of these days.

❦

James was anxious to be back home. He had been moving the steers up the river valley to summer pasture. It had taken four days to sort and push the packages of cattle two miles from home where he and Luke camped near each night to keep the cattle from wandering home. When the last steers were sorted off the cow herd, Luke, James, Thomas, and Jake pushed the herd ten miles west on the river. Here the cattle could graze the lush grass along the river without threatening the hay fields near home. Once the herd was settled, Thomas and Jake went back to their families, leaving Luke and James to stay to keep the steers located. Luke had gone home for an overnight once to resupply them, and now it was James' turn to head home. In a couple of days, Luke would follow. For the rest of the summer, one or two of the men would make weekly treks to check on the cattle and throw them back west if they drifted too close to the home. But for the most part, the steers would stay put. The grass was plentiful and there was water everywhere. It was cattle heaven. Late in the summer, when Jake and his crew returned from Jacob's cabin, the herd would be gathered and taken to Laramie to sell. But for now, the cattle had the summer to eat and gain weight.

James knew he could make it home well before dark. He needed a bath and his ma's good supper, but then he was going to see Mary. He didn't fool himself any longer that he was going to see the children, although he loved being with them. He was going to see Mary. He wasn't sure if she knew it, but he knew now what he wanted. He wanted to marry her and settle down.

Over the past several months, he had learned a lot about Mary on their walks. At first, Mary had been quiet, not prone to conversation, but James had persisted, quite often doing a lot of the talking himself. Over the weeks, he began to draw her out. He learned that Mary was born into slavery. Her mother never left the plantation when the war broke out, not knowing where to go. The plantation was never close to fighting or threatened. Before the war started, the father of Mary's brother had been sold. He was a field hand from the next plantation, but was married to Mary's mother. Mary's mother worked in the plantation kitchens. After her husband was sold, the white overseer visited Mary's mother. The family got more benefits, better food and clothing because of his attentions. The overseer was Mary's father. Mary vaguely remembered him. He left during the war to fight and was never heard from after that. After the war, Mary's mother died of lung disease and left Mary and her older brother alone. Mary was almost ten at the time.

Mary's brother was six years her senior. The two lived in the same shanty they had lived in while their mother was alive, and Ezekiel, Mary's brother, worked as a field hand. As a child, Mary sometimes worked in the fields during harvest. But the plantation owner had a son a year younger than Mary. When Mary's mother was alive, Mary often went to the plantation kitchen with her mother to play in the corner while her mother worked. The little boy would come and play with her. Even after her mother died and when Mary worked in the fields, little Robert sometimes came to get Mary to play with him. It was accepted by the foreman that Mary be allowed to leave if Robert came for her. It happened less and less as the children got older, but Mary always considered Robert her friend.

It was because of that friendship that Mary and Ezekiel ran away. Mary had just turned eleven. She wouldn't tell James exactly why they had to run away. All she told James was that Robert had come for her and that she was attacked by Robert's visiting cousin. That very night, Ezekiel had gone to the foreman and drawn what little pay he had coming, and they had headed west. They didn't stop until they reached Missouri. There they found an old couple who had a toolshed they could live in for helping around the place, and Ezekiel could get day work at farms nearby. This is where they were living when she married Albert Snyder.

Mary had shown James the poster with the pictures of her mother and brother and the shanties that she grew up in. She didn't remember living in slavery, but her mother told her it wasn't much different from what they had after the war, except that they could leave. The problem was they didn't know where else to go.

James thought of all of this as he rode toward home. He could barely get a kiss out of Mary, but he intended to change that and soon. James didn't understand why Mary was so put off by his advances. He decided it was time to push it. He was sure Mary looked forward to his visits. She willingly went walking with him. She even started conversations now. Mary was speaking better, reading a little, and knew some numbers. James was proud of how far she had come since living in their community. He just wanted to make life easier for her, more secure. And to be honest, James was attracted to her in more ways than one. As the worry lines faded from Mary's face and she smiled more, he saw the pretty girl she was. That she carried a slight bit of Negro blood meant nothing to him. With her olive skin and dark hair, Mary was quite striking. That was all James cared about.

It was a mild May night with a bit of mountain chill when the sun went down but nothing to keep a person inside.

"Walk with me, Mary," James said after the younger children were in bed.

Mary looked at Kade, and he nodded. "You go off. I'm jest goin' to sit and smoke a while. I'll be up."

So, Mary put on a shawl and she and James went outside. James took her hand and led her down the slope to the meadow and into the moonlight toward the brook. The grass was green and growing, but not too tall yet to struggle through on foot.

"I have been gone too long," James began, "and I missed you."

Mary nodded solemnly before saying, "The children have been looking for you too."

"I hope it wasn't only the children that missed me," James retorted, stopping, and pulling Mary around to look at him. "I hope you missed me too."

"I reckon I did," Mary admitted.

James leaned in and kissed her then. At first, Mary responded, kissing him back. But when James wrapped his arms around her, pulling her towards him, she resisted, pulling back.

"Why, Mary?" he asked, exasperated. "There ain't nothing wrong with a kiss. What's making you pull away?"

Mary turned away from James before she answered. "I jest don't want you to think that there be any more to this. I mean, I'm glad to see you, but that is all."

"What do you mean?" James was perplexed. "Mary, don't you know I want more? I want to marry you."

"I can't marry you," Mary was firm. "I ain't never goin' to marry agin. I made myself that promise a long time ago."

James was astonished. "A long time ago! You ain't that old to make a promise like that a long time ago. You can't be much older than me and I'm nineteen. How old are you?"

"I'll be twenty this fall, and I made that promise to myself a month after Albert got me to the soddy. I promised myself, someday when he was gone, I weren't never goin' to be married agin. Him being so much older than me, I figured I'd live longer than him. I aim to keep my promise."

"Mary, I don't know what he did to you, but you should know I am not like him. It don't make sense you refusing me because of him."

Mary stuck her chin out stubbornly. "I ain't never gonna be a slave to no man agin," she said angrily. "That's all I was, jest like my ma and granny and great granny. We's all jest slaves to men, doing what they say. I ain't gonna do that no more."

"Mary! I'm asking you to be my wife! I don't want a slave. I just want you," James was confused. This was not the way he thought this evening would go.

"Same thing for someone like me," Mary replied stubbornly.

"Like you? Mary you are a handsome woman. You aren't in the South anymore. To me, you are the woman I love," James hesitated. "Marry me, Mary. I'll be good to you."

Mary stood rigid and shook her head.

"I've been courting you! Surely you knew that?" James's voice rose in frustration.

"I never asked you to," she replied resolutely. "I figured we could just be friends."

"Friends!" James's voice rose as his frustration turned to anger. "Friends! I got friends! I don't need more friends. I need a wife! I want a wife!"

James saw Mary's eyes fill with unshed tears in the moonlight, but her reply was firm. "I ain't never goin' to lay with no man agin," her voice broke. Then she turned and began to run back to Kade's cabin and away from James.

James met Kade, Jake, and Thomas at the horse corral the following morning at the usual time. However, the men all noticed that there were saddle bags and a bedroll tied on behind James' saddle. He didn't dismount when he got to the corral, just spoke to all of them.

"Reckon if you can get by without me for a week, I'd like to ride into Laramie," James didn't look at any of the men, staring over them toward the corral.

"We're done moving cattle for a bit now," Jake said mildly, "so might be a good time to take a break if you're so inclined."

"You got business in mind to do there?" Thomas inquired.

This time James looked down at Thomas as he answered. "No," he said, his voice tight, "I just feel like getting drunk. Been a long winter."

"Watch your back then," Jake told him.

James nodded, and wheeling his horse, he cued it to lope. The men watched him go.

"What you suppose bit him?" Thomas asked.

Kade looked solemnly up the slope toward his cabin. "I think there is a woman up there in my cabin that has something to do about it," he said. "I don't think all is fine between those two. Thought there might be some sparks between them, but it looks like the fire is out."

"Hmmm," Jake murmured, "looks more like that young man got burned before it went out."

James hadn't gotten over his anger by the time he reached Laramie early the next afternoon. He had spent much of the last thirty-six hours telling himself he didn't need any wife, and if he did, Mary just didn't fit the bill. He had other options and intended to take advantage of them first thing. He dropped his horse off at the livery and carrying his packs, made his way to Miss Tillie's.

It was early, and the parlor was vacant but for a couple of girls waiting for their first customers of the day. Rosie was one of them. James nodded to her, and she rose and took him by the arm and through the door to the upstairs. James wasted no time when he got to the small room upstairs. He wanted to rid his mind of the olive-skinned woman who spurned him, and he thought Rosie would do the trick. But when he rolled off Rosie, while the tension in his body was gone, his heart was still heavy. He left quickly and headed to the parlor. Maybe he just needed to get drunk.

Charlie was the only one in the parlor when James walked in. James went to the bar and ordered whiskey, taking the bottle. Charlie gave James a curious look, but passed him a glass. He watched James find a table in the corner, sit alone, and brood. After a while, Charlie left the parlor for a few minutes. When he came back, Tillie came with him.

Tillie studied the young man for a few minutes, noticing his attention was not on the room around him. She saw the methodical way he lifted the glass to his mouth, and the way he sat and stared at the bottle. She made her way to James' table.

"Looks like you have a burden, cowboy," she said softly. "Rosie said you were a different man. You lose your best friend?"

James looked up, just noticing that Tillie had joined him. He shrugged and poured himself another drink.

"When did you move to the strong stuff?" Tillie inquired, touching the bottle.

"Today," James replied shortly.

"Speak to me, boy," Miss Tillie commanded bluntly. "You got something nagging at you. Sitting and drinking whiskey won't change anything."

James looked up at her then and relented. "I reckon it won't change anything but I'm hoping it makes me feel better."

Tillie chuckled at that. "I can guarantee it won't. It might make you forget for a time whatever is eating at you, but you won't feel better now or in the morning when you wake up. Now what bee has flown up your ass?"

"It's a woman," James said moodily. "I asked a woman to marry me. She not only said no, but her reason just doesn't make sense."

Miss Tillie nodded at this and waited. James took another sip of the whiskey and then looked up at Miss

Tillie. She could see the hurt in his eyes. Quietly, she listened while James began to talk.

"She's that widow woman I helped last summer," James began. "Only she is my age. She was the second wife." James told Tillie the little he knew about Mary when she was married to Albert Snyder. "I know it wasn't a good marriage. She didn't mourn him when he died. But I don't understand why she's so damned set against marrying me. She should know I will be good to her. I like the kids too."

Tillie sat quietly for a bit before answering. "Sometimes, when a woman has bad happen to her, she sees bad in those things. Sometimes a body just can't get over it."

"But I know she cares for me," James burst out. "When we are with other people, I catch her watching me or coming to stand by me sometimes. Even my older sister, Martha, has remarked on it. But then I ask her to marry me, and she not only says no, but she says never." James looked up at Tillie, pain in his eyes. "Mary says she just wants to be friends. I just don't understand that."

"Exactly what did she say when she told you no?" Tillie asked gently. "Did she give any reason?"

James grunted. "She said she wasn't ever going to lay with a man again," he looked away from Tillie, embarrassed. "I know her man mistreated her," James went on. "Noah once told me something he heard his pa doing, but he didn't know what it meant. I did, but I'd never treat her like that. She should know that." James took another sip of the drink.

Tillie studied him. "You've filled out over the winter, cowboy. You are starting to look like a man instead of a boy just growing out of short pants."

"Lot of good it did me," James shrugged.

Tillie laughed at that. "Feeling sorry for yourself won't help," she said. "Nor will getting drunk. You got to have a plan." Tillie took the bottle, and calling for Charlie, she had him bring James a beer and take back the bottle.

"I'm fresh out of plans," James groused, holding onto his half-filled glass.

"Well, I have a plan," Tillie responded firmly. "So here is what you have to do. You go back, and for the next month, you be that girl's friend. You act like it is all fine and dandy between you, like being a friend is just good. Then you get her here for the Fourth of July doings. Bring the kids. Use them as the excuse to get them all to come."

"You think taking part in Fourth of July activities is going to change anything?" James interrupted her.

"No, but talking some sense into that girl might," Tillie persisted. "I need to talk to her, find out what demon she's got in her mind that keeps her from marrying you." Tillie looked shrewdly at James. "You going to take it well if she's got eyes for another man and not you? You sure she has feelings for you?"

James shrugged again. "I don't know what I know anymore," he said moodily. "And how would I get her to talk to you? I can't very well escort her in here."

"No, you can't do that," Tillie agreed. "But I often have Charlie take me on long drives in the country to get away from town. Think I might just be doing that on the third of July or maybe the fifth. Might be we'd happen upon you if you were to take the lady for a drive."

Tillie watched the hope come into James eyes as she talked. She grew serious. "James, I don't know if it will change the girl's mind, but if she's afraid of being with a man, there is no one better to talk to than an old whore. I've seen it all and heard it all. She can lay her burdens on me where she can't talk about them with a good woman." Tillie hesitated, taking a breath. "Bring her to town and I'll try. Might work. If not, I still have Rosie and that bottle of whiskey here."

"I reckon I've waited this long; I can wait another month," James grumbled.

Tillie laughed outright at that. "You are all of nineteen!" she exclaimed. "You haven't lived long enough to 'wait this long!'" she shook her head. "You're just wanting that body in your bed every night and not have to come to town! You cowboys are all the same."

James did smile a bit at that. "Well, it ain't just the body in bed that I want," he hesitated, thinking. "I want those kids to have a good home, and I want a kid of my own, and . . . ma'am, I just want what I grew up with like I had with my ma and pa and all. And I want all that with Mary."

Tillie looked sympathetically at the young man. "Be patient, young James. I think it will come. We'll give it a try anyway. But for now, stick to beer, go home, and be her friend. Don't pressure her. Then in July, we will try to get to the bottom of this." Tillie looked around the room. The girls were filing in, getting ready for the late afternoon business. "I got a new girl," she commented. "You might like her. Do you need one more roll to take the pressure off before you head out? You can be home tomorrow anyway if you leave right after."

❧

James had to enlist his sister, Martha, to help him get Mary to agree to go to Laramie for the Fourth of July. And first he had to get Martha to agree to go too. Martha had never been to town. With one leg shorter than the other and a crippled arm, Martha had never felt comfortable around strangers. But now, married to Sam for six years and with two rambunctious little boys, Martha was more confident. Sam was her rock. Over a decade older than Martha, Sam had been a mountain man before he came to Twin Peaks Ranch. Calm and steady, Sam had brought Martha out of her shell and shown her that she could be happy, despite her deformities. James had Sam's backing, and between them, they got Martha talked into taking in the festivities in town. Then it was only a matter of time before Martha helped James talk Mary into going.

They took the democrat wagon with the spring seats and the small area in back where the children could lay out and sleep or play. They also took a couple of saddle horses. Neither James nor Sam could see themselves riding the whole way to town in a wagon. But James also took a good horse of Kade's to enter a race on the morning of the Fourth. It was a good excuse to be going. Noah and Emmett rode horses too, and they fairly shook with the excitement of going to town for the holiday. Little Alice rode in the back of the wagon with Martha and Sam's two little boys and Gideon. Alice was getting to be quite a little mother to the young ones, which allowed Martha and Mary to enjoy much of the trip. Even camping the one night was fun, sitting around a campfire telling stories to the kids. Sam was an excellent storyteller and kept them all intrigued with the stories of his early days in the mountains.

They arrived in Laramie early in the afternoon of July second and reserved rooms in the hotel. James got a room for Mary, Alice, and Gideon, and another he shared with Noah and Emmett. They had a pleasant meal in the hotel dining room together before going to bed. No one seemed to notice Gideon's dark complexion, and as they ate, James could see both Mary and Martha begin to enjoy being there.

After the little boys were asleep, James slipped away and went to talk to Tillie and set up a time and place to meet the next day. In the morning, James took Sam aside to enlist his help. Sam and Martha knew that James had been courting Mary, but now James filled Sam in on his problem. James had a buggy rented from the livery, but he needed Sam and Martha to take Mary's children so the two of them could drive out of town together without the kids.

After breakfast, Sam suggested to Martha that they take the children to see the town. At the same time, James brought up a buggy ride to Mary.

"I jest spent much of two days riding in a wagon to get here," Mary protested, "I don't need a buggy ride."

"Oh, but a buggy is much more comfortable than a wagon," James coaxed, "and we can go off for a bit, just the two of us, and see the sights around Laramie."

"You go," Sam told Mary. "Martha and I will watch the kids. You jest need a bit of quiet time, an' there's no better than a buggy ride to see the sights."

Martha approved, and reluctantly, Mary agreed. It wasn't often she got to get away from the demands of the children. She was surprised that the idea of a quiet ride appealed to her.

James talked little as they drove. Charlie had told him directions to a stock dam three miles out of town where there were some trees. The grass was still green, and the day was pleasant. When James came to the dam, he stopped the horse and tied it to a tree. Helping Mary down, they stood looking out at the great expanse of flat prairie. In the distance, James could see a carriage coming. He was hoping it was Tillie.

Tillie's conveyance was an enclosed carriage with windows. If she drove in town, she could close the drapes over the windows to give herself privacy. Today, she had the drapes pulled back. James and Mary watched the carriage approach until Charlie finally pulled the team to a stop a short distance from James' buggy. James took Mary by the arm and began to walk her toward the carriage.

"This is a friend of mine," he said softly to Mary. "I'd like you to visit with her a bit while I talk to Charlie."

Mary looked at James quizzically. "That's a right fancy carriage. Who'd have something that nice an' want to talk to me?"

James took a breath. This was the tricky part. "Mary, I'm not going to lie to you. This lady owns Miss Tillie's in town." James saw Mary's eyes widen in alarm. "She's a good person. Please, trust me. Just talk to her. I need you to do this for me. Maybe she can help us." He was so earnest and insistent, that Mary relented and nodded. James went to the carriage door and opened it, helping Mary in.

"James, you go off with Charlie now and let me visit with this nice lady," Tillie's voice came from inside. James nodded and closed the door behind Mary.

Tillie studied the girl in front of her. Mary was nervous, wringing her hands around a handkerchief as she sat. Her dark hair was curly, escaping the pins that pulled it back into a bun. Tillie could see she had a deep olive complexion and dark brown eyes. While she wasn't quite on the pretty side, Tilly suspected that changed when, or if, she smiled. But the girl was uncomfortable and wouldn't raise her eyes to look at Tillie.

"Honey," Tillie began gently, "you might be wondering just how come I know that young man out there, and I'll tell you straight out that I met him last summer when he came in with some other young cowhands after a drive. And I'll tell you this too," Tillie hesitated, then went on firmly, "if that is something you hold against him, then you aren't worth the salt that James thinks you are. There aren't many young men who don't find their way to my establishment when they are not attached. It's more important how they act after they are attached that counts. That is one fine man out there."

Mary didn't look up, but she nodded. "Yes'm, I know that," she said softly.

"So, do you also know that he loves you?" Tillie asked.

"Yes'm, he done tole me that a while ago," Mary answered.

"He told me you won't have him," Tillie said. "You mind telling me why?"

"I jest ain't goin' to be no man's wife agin," Mary was almost whispering now, her face reddening.

Tillie studied the girl. "Why?"

Mary shook her head, not answering, tears filling her eyes.

"Tell me this," Tillie spoke firmly, "do you love James?"

Mary peeked up at Tillie then. "Maybe. I think of him a lot. He's good."

"Then why won't you accept him?"

Mary just shrugged, looking down at her lap again.

Tillie decided to take the conversation in a different direction. "You didn't have a good marriage?"

Mary shook her head.

"Tell me about it," Tillie commanded.

Mary looked up, wide eyed. "I cain't." She dropped her gaze again almost immediately.

"Honey, look at me," Tillie commanded, and again Mary looked up. "You can tell me. I have heard it all. Might be it has already happened to me. Tell me about what happened to you. Start at the beginning. Why did you marry that man?"

Mary took a deep breath, holding Tillie's gaze. Then coming to a decision, she began to talk. "Albert's brother made him marry me, so's to have someone to care for the children. I was the only one available that would take him. I carry colored blood. My brother shows his colored blood, having a different daddy than me. My brother an' me was not doing well. Living was hard for us. Marrying a white man seemed like a step up. My brother said I should marry, so I did. Then a few days later, Albert packed me an' the kids up an' moved to Wyoming to a soddy Albert bought. Albert was ashamed of me, but in Wyoming, no one knew I had Negro blood in me.

"I don't think Albert ever thought of me as his wife. First night he says to me, 'Go sleep with Alice an' keep her quiet. She cries a lot in the night.' So's that's where I slept, with the little girl. I was fine with that. I liked the children, leastwise the two youngest. The oldest, Noah, resented me.

"We'd been at the soddy maybe a month or more, an' one night Albert was sitting in the rocker an' rockin' Alice. He had a soft spot fer Alice an' when he was in a good mood, he'd hold her an' rock her. I always waited fer Albert to go to bed an' blow out the candle 'fore I got myself ready but that night, he sat there rockin' an' rockin' an' watchin' me. Then he suddenly told me to go get ready for bed," Mary looked down then, wringing the handkerchief again.

"What happened that night," Tillie pressed.

Mary took a deep breath. "He watched me shuck my dress right down to my shift. He jest kept rockin' an' rockin' Alice. He gets up an' brings Alice over to the bed an' puts her in an' says, 'Make sure she stays asleep' so I's get in an' lay with her. But Albert, he don't get into his bed. He sits back down in the rocker an' he keeps rockin' an' rockin', but I see his hands movin' up an' down his front side," her voice broke, and she couldn't go on at once. After a moment she started to talk again. "He jest keeps staring at me. Then he gets himself up an' comes over to the bed. He reaches down an' takes me by the arm an' says, 'Take yerself to my bed' an' he blows out the candle. He shucks his pants off an' climbs on top of me an' jest starts a pumpin'. It hurt. I cried out, an' he grunted an' told me to shut up, or I'd wake the children. When he was finished, he pushed me off the bed an' told me to go back to Alice."

When Mary stopped, Tillie stayed quiet for a while, letting Mary gain her composure. "How often did that happen?"

"Every month or so, maybe," Mary replied softly. "I'd see it coming after that. But it was always the same, at least before Gideon. He'd jest drag me to his bed, get on top an' do it, then push me away. When I began to show the baby, he left off then. But he would sometimes talk to me, tell me he was going somewhere or what he was going to do. Weren't like no conversation, but he'd talk some."

"Was he pleased about the baby?"

"He never said one way or other before Gideon was born. I once said I was afraid to have the baby out there alone, an' he said he had three chilluns with his first wife, an' he had been there fer all of them. He reckoned I could do the birthin' same as her. So's when Gideon came, he sent the children to bed, Alice up to the loft with the boys, and he helped me . . . until he saw Gideon, started cleaning him off. Then his face got dark with rage. I feared he'd throw my baby against the wall or kill me or both. I ain't never seen anyone so mad before."

"James told me the baby shows his ancestry," Tillie said softly. "That bothered your husband?"

"He couldn't pretend I was white anymore," Mary replied. "He blamed me for having a darkie for a child."

"What happened then?"

"He saw my dress hanging on a hook an' he went into a rage. He took his knife, an' he ripped an' slashed that dress into such little pieces I could hardly piece them together for a dress for Alice. That were the only dress I had. I had to get flour sacks I kept for rags to piece together for a dress. That same night, he put his coat on an' went to town. Didn't come home for over two weeks. Took the team an' came home without them.

The next trip to town he took the cows, then part of the sheep. Each time, even though we lived over a day away from town, he came home smelling of whiskey an' sometimes still drunk. He was short with the children, more than usual, an' we all took to keeping our distance. I told him once I needed material for clothes an' he struck me an' said I didn't need anything but to keep his kids fed. Then one night he sent the children all up to the loft. He threw me over the table, and he . . . he said I couldn't give him no nigger child this way." This time Mary simply couldn't go on. She sat, shoulders slumped, softly crying into the handkerchief.

"James told me," Tillie said gently. "You don't have to speak it."

"Oh, sweet Jesus," Mary moaned, "James knows?"

"The oldest boy told him, not knowing what he was telling about. James put the pieces together." Tillie watched Mary. "Honey, you know James would never treat you like that."

Mary took a deep breath. "No but laying with a man is nothing but ugly an' hurtful. I don't never want to be hurt like that agin. An' I ain't never goin' to birth a baby to have its daddy look at it like it was a monster. I ain't never." Mary covered her face with her hands and sobbed.

Tillie waited until Mary quieted and then spoke softly. "Mary, look at me. I been with lots of men; it's my profession. I been hurt by a good many men. But it's the man who hurts you, not the act. You ain't had a man like that. When you have a man who loves you, he makes sure you don't hurt. A man who loves you will make you want to be with him in the marriage bed. You'll find a joy you never thought you could have.

With the right man, there is no hurt. If anyone should know that, I should. You got a man out there who loves you and would never hurt you. You let him go, and you lose the chance at happiness that you deserve. Not only does he love you, but he will take care of you. You have to trust him on that."

"Til I birth him a Black baby," Mary murmured.

"You ever see James treat your Gideon any different than the others?"

Mary shook her head.

"You won't either. I've talked with James quite a bit, and he don't see color, not white, not red, not Black. He just sees the person. He sees you and you are who he loves. Honey, you gotta take a chance, or you will lose this good man. You will lose your chance at a good life."

"I'm afraid," Mary whispered.

"Well, you have a right to be afraid," Tillie replied kindly. "But being afraid is just not enough to keep you from taking a chance. You got a whole life to live. You got to be brave and take this chance. He'll take care of you. He loves you."

James stood beside Charlie at the horses' heads, waiting. They talked of the weather and the festivities to come and how the town was growing. When these safe subjects had been exhausted, they stood for a while in companionable silence.

"You been with her a long time?" James suddenly asked.

Charlie smiled. "I have. Been with her since before we came west even."

"Why you suppose she let herself get so fat?" James asked. "I saw that picture of her when she was young, and she was really pretty."

"When Tillie got her house established, she had the other girls there." Charlie looked back toward the carriage. "She didn't need to take any men upstairs herself. She got fat so they wouldn't ask. Maybe she did it so no man would desire her."

"Did it work?"

"Reckon it did for most but not for all," Charlie said reflectively. "There's been some, like you, over the years that she took upstairs, but it doesn't happen often."

"I'm grateful, you know," James said, "for that night. I got to know her. She's quite a lady, despite what she is."

"Yessir, she is that," Charlie grinned back.

"Why do you reckon she never quit the business and settled down?" James asked.

"I think she thought of it, but the money was good. It just doesn't always work out for a woman like that. She had her big house and her private places in it. Reckon that is what she wanted."

"She told me she loved someone once," James commented. "Why didn't she get married?"

"Son, life don't always work out the way we want. As you are learning, I hear," Charlie answered, looking away.

Suddenly, James put the pieces together, the pieces of conversation that Charlie was saying and what Tillie told him the night he met her. "You're Marcus, aren't you?" he said softly.

A little smile quirked the sides of Charlie's mouth, but he didn't answer.

"You couldn't marry. It wouldn't have been accepted," the sudden realization came to James. "I wonder, but does Tillie think the same for Mary and me?"

"James," Charlie said seriously, "a person can lose himself on the frontier. You can become a new person and leave the past behind. Your gal there can be white. Can be accepted as white. Your friends accept her. It ain't the same for me. I'm Black. I can't hide it. I can't marry a white woman," he hesitated. "No white woman. Especially I can't marry her if I love her and want the best for her. But I can be a barman and bodyguard in her establishment. Sometimes we just have to play the cards we are dealt."

The carriage door opened, and Mary climbed out. James and Charlie went to help her.

"Charlie, escort this young lady to her buggy," Tillie said. "I want to say a few words to James."

When Charlie and Mary were out of earshot, Tillie looked out at James. "I think you may have a chance. She's afraid. She's afraid of all that marriage holds. She needs to know you won't hurt her, not in the marriage bed or as a father to her children, no matter what color they come. You need to make sure of that. She's like a wounded deer. If she is hurt again, she will run and maybe never stop. Remember this, James." Tillie looked sternly at James. "Be gentle. Be patient."

It had been a good two days in town during the festivities. The children bubbled over on the way home with all the things they saw and did while in Laramie. James had placed second by a nose in the horse race on the morning of the fourth. He didn't even feel bad about that since the horse that beat him was an imported horse owned by an English investor in the ranching business. James and the Twin Peaks' bred horse certainly gave the expensive thoroughbred a run for the money, and everyone was impressed with James' horse. James' horse was also a good cow horse, earning its keep through ranch work. The ranchers and cowboys were more impressed with the Welles' horse than the high-dollar racehorse. It was good advertising for the Welles horses.

The fireworks had been spectacular. James had seen fireworks the year they came for Thomas and Beth's wedding, but none of the others had seen fireworks before. Emmett, Alice, and Noah were thrilled, and the adults were content that no Indian war came about during this trip. All in all, it had been a good trip.

James hadn't pressed Mary on the way back from talking with Tillie. He just drove along slowly, letting her relax. He felt she had enough to deal with that day. Tillie had told him to have patience. So, patience was what he was trying to have.

The night they camped on the way home, James got up the nerve to speak to Mary. They camped along a little creek that still had some flowing water. It was a place they had camped before, and it had a few trees and an old beaver dam in the creek where water was backed up. James waited until the little ones were put down before he talked to Mary.

"Walk with me, Mary," he said, taking her arm. "Martha and Sam will keep an eye on the kids."

They walked off, quiet between them until they came to the bank overlooking the beaver pond. James suddenly found himself tongue tied. If she refused him this time, was that it for him? He was afraid not to ask, and also afraid to ask.

"Mary, you know what I want to ask you, don't you?" he said finally.

She nodded but didn't help him by indicating what her answer would be. James knew he had to ask her the question and live with the answer.

"Mary, I want to marry you. You know that. I want to make a good home for you and the children. Marry me, Mary. I'll be good to you," he finished lamely.

Mary stood, looking out across the water, watching it glimmer in the dim moonlight. Finally, she turned to James. "Why? Why you want me? I ain't good enough fer you."

That was not what James was expecting. "I love you," was all he could think to get out.

"An' what's gonna happen to that love iffen yer child comes out a lookin' like Gideon?"

"Mary, you are the only one who thinks Gideon is someone to be ashamed of. To me, he's just a cute little boy. He will grow to be a handsome man, and I'll be proud to call him son. Won't change when we have our own," James said sincerely.

"An' what about when people come here an' settle an' they come a visitin' an' yer wife speaks like a slave?"

"Mary, I don't care how you talk. I know it bothers you, and I know you have been having Martha help you speak better. You already sound better than you did. But I don't care about that. You are just fine the way you are." James hadn't realized the extent of Mary's insecurities. He decided to ask his own question. "Mary, do you love me?" he spoke softly, going close and taking her hand.

She couldn't answer, but instead looked at him then slowly she nodded her head.

"Then marry me. I want to be your husband."

Mary backed away, her eyes widening. "I'm scared," she whispered.

James smiled teasingly at her. "Hell, if that is all," he said, "I'm scared too."

That surprised Mary. "What are you scared of?"

James came close and folded his arms gently around Mary, pulling her to him. She didn't resist. "I'm nineteen years old, and I love a woman that has four kids. That is enough to scare any man. But mostly, I am scared I can't make you happy. I'm scared the kids won't want me in your life," he stopped, thinking. "What I am not scared about is being able to take care of you all. I'm part owner of this ranch and these cattle and horses have done well for us. We might not be rich, but we are doing just fine. We have a good ranch built up, enough for all the families, and we are spreading out too, claiming more land. I know I can take care of you. Let me try."

James felt her begin to relax in his arms. He did not press her. He just gently held her. When she finally laid her head against his chest, he spoke again.

"I know what you are afraid of. I won't hurt you like he did. But if it helps you decide, I'll make you this deal. We will get Matthew to marry us. We won't tell anyone except maybe my ma and one person that you choose. Two people can stand with us when we say our vows. Then the morning after we marry, if I hurt you in any way, we just go back to Matthew if you want to call it off. I reckon if he can marry us, he can unmarry us," James stroked her hair, waiting for her answer. She hadn't pulled away. That had to be a good sign.

It seemed like ages that he waited, but James knew it was only minutes. Finally, he felt Mary nod her head against his chest. Then softly he heard the words he had been hoping for.

"Yes, I'll marry you. We kin try."

They reached the ranch in the late afternoon the next day. There was plenty of daylight left, so after James threw his packs in his room, he went off to watch for Kade to come in from riding. Kade was the person Mary had chosen to stand up with them before Matthew. Most of the horses were out of the corral, which meant that Sam, Thomas, and Kade were out on their last horse for the day. It wasn't long before Kade came riding in.

James caught him before he unsaddled and asked him if he'd ride down with him to talk to Sarah. James wanted to tell Kade and his ma the news together and ask them to be witnesses. He and Mary had also talked about where they could live, and James wanted to discuss that with Kade. Mary was willing to get married right away, and James didn't want to give her time to change her mind.

Sarah warmed a pot of coffee and when it was hot, they all took a cup and sat at the table. Kade and Sarah could see that James had something important to talk to them about. Sarah knew her son well enough to see he was nervous. They sat for a few minutes discussing the time in town and the race James had lost by a nose. When there was a lull in the conversation, James cleared his throat and began to talk.

"You both know I've been courting Mary. You know she's been reluctant. We got some things ironed out on our trip and she said yes." James couldn't keep from grinning then.

"Son, I'm happy for you," Sarah said, smiling back. "She's a nice girl. But you got your work cut out for you with all those children already."

"I know, ma, but I don't mind the kids. And Mary has been doing it pretty much alone for over a year. It won't be so hard. Those are good young'uns," James said sincerely.

"Stealing away my housekeeper, are you?" Kade grinned. "I had a feeling that was coming. I'm happy for you both, boy."

"Well, that is one thing we wanted to talk to you about," James said. "Mary feels bad about leaving you, and we really don't have a place big enough for all of us, so we were thinking maybe if it suited you, I could just move in that room with Mary, Alice, and Gideon. We could start on a house this summer and move into it when it is finished."

"Oh, hell, James," Kade chuckled at that. "I'm not sure bunking with a newly married couple is what I want to do. You take the cabin. We can work something out on it eventually. I'll take what I need and go bunk with the hands. I know there are empty beds in the bunkhouse."

"You will not," Sarah exclaimed. "If James is moving out of here, you'll take his bedroom. Will has the girls' old room, so you can have James' room all to yourself. Will is moving into his own cabin before fall, and I am not anxious to have this house all to myself. I have extra room, and it makes cooking a meal much easier when there is someone here to eat it."

Kade gave Sarah a long look. "You sure about that? Sabra said I was never really broke to a house."

"I'd like to know what man is?" Sarah laughed, then quickly turned serious. "You and Sabra have been friends to me since we came here thirty years ago. I think having you in James' room would be right."

They talked out a few details and then James brought up his next concern. "There is still a problem," he said. "Mary's husband didn't treat her so well, as a wife, I mean." This was trickier for James, speaking about such things with his mother. "What we have planned is a secret wedding, sort of. We just want to stand with Matthew and have you two as witnesses."

"I'm not sure what you are getting at, son," Sarah was puzzled.

"Well, I sort of made a deal with Mary. I told her we'd get married on the sly. We'd spend the night together, and if she was still scared of it all, we'd go back to Matthew, and he could unmarry us."

"I don't think that is how it works," Kade remarked, "with Matthew, that is."

"Well, to be truthful, I don't intend that to happen, but it eased Mary's mind to think that if she was unhappy, I'd back out. I am going to be damned sure that doesn't happen, but to be honest, we won't really know we will stay married until tomorrow morning," James finished. He couldn't look at his ma.

Kade glanced at Sarah then and gave her a slight smile. "So, you plan on telling anyone else?" he asked James.

"Well, I figured we'd tell tomorrow, and maybe we could have a wedding dinner in a couple days. Nothing big since Jake, Lathe, Hawk and their families aren't back from the mountains yet, but just something to say we went and did it," James was more comfortable talking about this.

"You planning on tonight?" Kade asked.

"If you two and Matthew are willing," James answered.

"You telling the kids?" Sarah asked.

"Well, no, not 'til morning," James said. "We figured it this way. Maybe Matthew, Ma, and I could ride up to your cabin, Kade, after the kids go to bed. We thought it would be right nice to get married outside, under the stars. Then, in the morning, if I'm still there, we'd tell them then."

"Sounds like a good plan," Kade said, thinking through the events to come. "I'll go home now. You can come after dark. I'll come out with Mary when the kids are in bed. I'll take what I need for the night, and you two can have my bed. Reckon that might be more comfortable than having to share with two little kids."

James looked at Kade. "I will take you up on that," he grinned. James was starting to think this might actually happen.

James thought getting quietly married in the dark in front of the cabin was a pretty nice affair. Mary wore what she had worn all day, the dress she had traveled in. But James had bought her a pretty shawl on the sly in Laramie, and he gave it to her before Matthew began the ceremony. She wrapped it around her shoulders fingering the softness of it. James knew it was a fine shawl and was glad he had thought of buying it for a wedding present.

After they said their vows, Kade shook James' hand, and Sarah hugged them both. Then Kade and Sarah left with Matthew, leaving James and Mary alone. James took her hand and led her to the bench outside the cabin. Mary's hair was loose and it curled around her face. In the moonlight, he could see her eyes, wide and uneasy.

"Don't reckon with children, we will get many peaceful times like this," he said softly to Mary. "This might be our alone time from here on out," he stroked her hair.

"I thankee fer the shawl," Mary whispered. "It is awful pretty."

"No prettier than you."

They sat in silence for a while, and then James took her hand and helped her up. "It's getting cold out here. Let's go inside."

Taking a candle, James led Mary into Kade's room. He turned her to him and took her in his arms. "Mary, I love you," he said softly. "Let me love you."

His fingers played in her hair, pulling it back from her face. He bent down and kissed her, and he felt her, ever so slightly, kiss him back. Feeling his blood pump, James wanted to rush it then, but Tillie's words, "Be patient," echoed in his mind. So, patient he was.

He unbuttoned her dress, slowly folding it back. He was puzzled then. There was another layer of clothes underneath, maybe two layers. With an Indian girl or a prostitute, it wasn't so hard to get the clothes off. He wasn't quite sure how to go about this, especially when he didn't want to scare her. He kissed her again before saying softly, "You have to help me here. I'm not sure how to get all these clothes off you."

To James' relief, Mary smiled at that. Between the two of them, her dress slid to the floor. His shirt came off next and then her shift. Shyly she stood before him. He shucked off his britches and drew her to him, feeling her warmth, skin against skin. She didn't resist. He wasn't sure how they found their way to the bed. He just knew he was mesmerized by her body. He lay beside her, feeling her gently, caressing her softness, her curves. He was gentle and patient. His lips found her nipples and gently he played with her. Then he slid his hands deliberately down her sides to her legs. When he drew his hands up her thighs, he felt her move towards him, ever so slightly.

"Mrs. Bates," he whispered, "I love you."

"Mr. Bates," she replied, "I love you too." And this time, she came to him to be kissed.

Morning broke, the sun finding the mountaintops. James felt Mary stir and get up. He gave her a few minutes then he too got up and dressed. By the time James went outside and came in again, Mary had the fire started and had breakfast cooking. He could smell the bacon and hear it sizzle in the pan.

"Go wake the little ones; I'll pound for the boys and watch the bacon," James told her. "I want to talk to them before I head out."

Mary gave him a worried look. "I'm thinkin' Alice an' Emmett will be fine with us," she said. "But I'm not sure of Noah. He's pretty attached to you an' not sure 'bout his feelin's 'bout me anymore. He thought I took his mother's place when I married Albert. Not sure how he is goin' to take this."

James nodded and prodded her towards the children's room. "We'll face it together."

James took the broom and pounded the handle against the ceiling. "Boys, breakfast is ready soon. I hear the horses coming in," he called loudly.

It didn't take long before Mary came out, carrying Gideon with Alice following. The boys gave James a funny look before heading out to the privy. "Hurry up outside," Mary told Alice and then came over to the stove to check on the cooking.

James took out the bacon and began to crack eggs into the pan. Mary took over with the eggs. James had a loaf of bread his mother had sent the night before, so James sliced it and set it on the table. The boys came back in but were silent, watching him. When Alice returned from the privy, Emmett was the first to question.

"How come you are here so early, James? Where's Mister Kade?"

James looked at the three older ones, standing together, watching Mary and James getting breakfast. Gideon had no idea this was an unusual morning, but the other three did.

"Last night, after you were in bed, Matthew came and married Mary and me," James told them. "Mister Kade went to sleep in my old bedroom in my old house."

The three children just stared. Emmett looked to James and then to Mary before saying fearfully, "Where do we go now?"

That question took James by surprise. He had no notion that the children would be afraid they'd be sent somewhere else. "Well, I hope you want to stay right here with Mary and me," he said gently.

"You gonna be our pa?" Alice asked, wide-eyed.

James knelt to her level. "I'd be proud to be your pa if you want me to. Nothing would make me happier. But," here James glanced toward Noah, "I don't have to be your pa if you don't want. I can just be your friend like before."

"I'd' like it if you were my pa," Emmett said seriously. "You'd be a good pa."

"Well, it's settled then," James smiled at the little boy. "I can be your pa if you want."

"Be my pa too," Alice said, starting to smile.

James rumpled her hair and picked her up. "I will, honey. I'll be glad to."

Noah stood watching, but said nothing. James didn't press him. He felt the fact that Noah wasn't outwardly angry was better than he had hoped. Noah had just turned thirteen. James knew if Noah was hostile about the marriage, he could move to the bunkhouse with Luke and the other hands, but James hoped to keep the boys together for a few more years. James looked over the heads of the children to Mary. She was still by the stove, filling plates, but he could see the relief in her.

"James is late this morning," Thomas groused as he sorted off the horses they would work that day. "First, he goes off on a holiday, and now he's sleeping in."

"Give the boy a break," Kade said. "He's had a lot on his mind lately."

"I don't think it's his mind that's been bothering him," Sam grinned at Kade. Kade caught his look and grinned back. Sam knew something was up. He knew he and Martha had been prodded into going to Laramie with James and Mary as more than just chaperones. He and Martha both knew James was wooing Mary, and they both knew she was resisting.

"Here comes James now," Kade said. He had been watching for James and knew he would come from Kade's cabin. James was walking down the slope with

Noah, Emmett, and Alice. This took both Thomas and Sam by surprise, but neither made a comment. On the other hand, Kade was watching the young man, and when he saw James smile at him, he knew the outcome of the night.

James just nodded to Kade, and they shook hands. "Congratulations, James," Kade said sincerely. "I'll go and pack up." Turning to his son, Kade told Thomas, "Sort me off what you want me to ride today, Thomas. I'll be back in a bit to saddle up. I got to see Mary a minute."

"Boys," James couldn't quit smiling, "I got myself hitched last night. Think we need to have a party soon."

Kade climbed the rise to his cabin. He looked at it with a fresh perspective. He had built it over thirty years ago, the core of it at least. Over the years, Kade had added on a bedroom on each side, and a lean-to off the back. He saw his children grow strong and tall in this cabin. He had loved his wife here. Now it would become James and Mary's. It was the right thing to do. This cabin needed a family. It only held memories for Kade.

Mary was rocking Gideon when Kade walked in. She looked up at him and smiled. It was a happy smile. Kade seldom saw Mary smile, so this alone told him how things went last night. Kade smiled back.

"Mister Kade, I hate to have you leave this home," Mary said softly. "It's yers. We should be the ones to leave."

"Mary, this is just stuff," Kade answered, looking around the room. "I'll take some things with me. If I want anything later, I'll let you know. James and I can settle up on this after we see how it works out for us both." Kade looked back at Mary and laughed, "Honey, I can't keep hiring housekeepers and have them get married out from under me. I'll be better off in a room at Sarah's."

But his bravado left him when he stood in his bedroom. Here were his most treasured memories, moments alone with Sabra. What should he take? The pictures, of course, and his clothes, but what of the rest? Over the years, they had had things sent out from St. Louis. There was a dresser now, an off-the-floor bed, and a trunk that Sabra had used to store quilts and special items she saved.

Kade went to the trunk and lifted the lid. There was an extra quilt for winter, handmade by Sabra. Under it were some winter clothes, and under them was each of their children's first small outfit. And on the very bottom, wrinkled and pressed down from years and the weight of the clothes on top, was the dress Sabra had worn the night they said their vows. She had never cut it up for scraps, and she had never worn it again.

"I'll fold up the quilt on the bed for you to take," Mary spoke softly from the door. "Yer wife made it. It should go to you, an' James has one to bring here."

Kade nodded.

"An' this trunk holds yer life," Mary continued, watching Kade. "James said he'd bring up a wagon and haul it down for you."

Kade nodded again.

"Mister Kade, yer sure you want to do this?"

Kade nodded, but this time he turned to Mary. "It will take some getting used to, but it will be easier this way. She's not here. Staying here won't bring her back," Kade walked to the doorway and laid his hand on Mary's shoulder. "Put my things together for me and have James haul them down to Sarah's." Kade squeezed her shoulder gently before he turned and left. Like when Sabra died, and he couldn't put her away from him, Kade couldn't pack his own things up to leave. He knew that Mary would know what he needed to be packed. It was easier just to walk away.

The next few days were happy ones for James. He and Mary fell quickly into a routine, becoming comfortable with each other and the children. Emmett and Alice were clearly pleased to have James with them. Gideon was crawling now, and within days he was crawling to greet James when he got home. To James, acquiring this ready-made family was an easy move. He already liked the young'uns, and they were used to him.

On the fourth evening after he moved in, Noah told Emmett to go up to the loft alone when it was time for bed. "I'm older than you," he told his little brother. "So, I can stay up later."

Emmett grumbled, but James agreed with Noah. James had a feeling that Noah had something on his mind. He had been quiet and withdrawn these first few days. And Noah was right. He was working a man's job, helping Matthew with the farming and the sheep. He could stay up.

Mary gathered Alice and Gideon and took them off to bed, leaving James and Noah alone in the main room. James was working on a bridle that needed repair, so he sat at the table. Noah also sat there, working on some lessons Sarah had given him. Despite his job with Matthew, he spent an hour or two most days with Sarah learning to read and write.

"Ain't never told you 'bout how I feel," Noah said offhandedly, not looking up from his lessons.

"Hmmm, you got a right to keep your thoughts to yourself," James replied.

Noah's pencil stopped moving on his paper, tracing words. "I reckon it's good fer you an' Mary to be together."

"Makes me glad to hear you say it," James said seriously.

"Don't reckon I need me a pa anymore, but if I did, you'd be a good one," Noah still didn't look at James.

"I don't need to be your pa," James agreed. "If the need ever arises, I'm here. But just so you know, me and Mary are sort of a package deal now."

Noah nodded, not replying to that. When Mary came back into the room from putting Gideon down, Noah moved to get up. He gathered his paper and pencil, and put them on Kade's desk and went outside. James looked up at Mary and nodded. She had heard Noah's words.

When Noah came back in, he hesitated before he climbed the ladder.

"Night, James," he called. Then just as he started up to the loft, he added, "Night, Mary."

CHAPTER **9**

Reluctant Travelers – August 1881

J ake watched for his riders to come in from working on their last horses. It was mid-August, and in Jake's judgment, it was time to start thinking about heading home. Twin Peaks employed extra summer help now, so it wasn't urgent for Jake and his crew to return for the haying, but Jake knew that the Utes were getting moved west sometime before winter, and he wanted to get news of when that move would occur. Jake, Hawk, and Kasa wanted to see family before the army moved them to Utah. In the past, Jake and the others usually stopped at the agency and saw family when they traveled back and forth to the mountain cabin. But after the Meeker Massacre, the Utes didn't stay in the vicinity of White River as they did before. The band that Hawk and Kasa's mother was with was not in the area when Jake and the rest went through in early summer. He knew Hawk and Kasa were nervous about not seeing their mother this year and would want to find her before the Utes went west.

Jake watched Anna as he closed the gate of the corral. She was outside with a big pot of stew bubbling on the fire. He could smell it as he approached.

"Where are the kids?" he asked as he approached.

"Little Kade sleeps," Anna replied, "and I told the girls to watch him and be quiet. I don't want them out by the fire."

"I'll go get them," Jake told her. "I'll take them up to Kasa and Lathe's and see if Kasa wants help coming down. I'm waiting for Hawk and Lathe to get back. I think maybe we should decide on when we want to head home. I'd hate to delay and miss Snowbird before she and the Utes head out. I'm thinking another couple of weeks, and we should be leaving."

"Will the Utes really go then?" Anna asked.

"From the news I picked up at Steamboat a week ago, it sounds like they don't have much choice. The word was, there are troops being sent to escort the Utes west."

Jake went to the cabin door. Kestrel and Lark saw him gesture to them to come quietly and they scampered out, happy to get out of the cabin. At three years old, Lark held her arms up to her daddy, wanting a ride but Kestrel, more independent at five, walked by Jake's side.

"We'll be back," Jake smiled at Anna.

Kestral scampered ahead, winding through trees and jumping fallen logs while Jake, with Lark on his shoulders, walked along the path. They were heading through a stand of trees that separated the lower meadow from a smaller upper meadow. It was in the upper meadow that Lathe had built a small cabin several years ago. It was in this small cabin that Lathe and his wife, Kasa, stayed during the summer months. It was also in this meadow that Hawk and Bonnie had built a small cabin to live in during the summer.

Lathe and Kasa had two children. Three-year-old Slade Layton was an active little guy and already a great playmate to Kestrel and Lark. The baby, Jesse Matthew, was born in February. They were good children and Kasa was a capable, calm mother despite being only twenty. She and Lathe had married when she was sixteen. Jake's half-brother, Brown Otter, had been alive then and Lathe had given Otter two good horses for Kasa. With Brown Otter now gone, killed in the battle at Milk Creek, Jake was the closest to a father that Kasa had.

Jake found both Kasa and Bonnie working outside in the shade of trees. Kasa was helping Bonnie learn to make moccasins. Bonnie, who was married to Kasa's brother, was trying to learn many of the skills that Hawk expected his wife to know. They had been married a little over a year, and were both still adapting. They came from two different cultures, and for their marriage to work, they had to compromise and learn each other's ways. So far, it was working, but there were many challenges.

"You want me to take Slade back with me?" Jake asked Kasa. "He can play with the girls until you get there."

"Yes," Kasa agreed. "Slade has too much energy this afternoon. Take him and let Lathe deal with him. I will be down soon."

Jake nodded, and calling to the children, he started back. It was the custom of the three families to share meals in the evening. They enjoyed making a fire and sitting around together. Sometimes they ate down at Jake's cabin and other nights at Lathe's or Hawk's.

Just as Jake emerged from the trees, he saw Anna hurrying towards him, little Kade in her arms.

"Jake, someone comes!" she called anxiously, pointing down the meadow.

Jake stepped up his pace, picking up Slade and carrying him along with Lark. Visitors didn't necessarily mean danger these days, but they didn't often get visitors, and it didn't hurt to be careful. Jake went to the cabin and dropped the children there, warning them to stay inside until they were called. Taking his rifle, he went out to watch the approaching riders.

Two riders were making their way across the valley. It didn't take Jake long to set his gun aside. It was Sam and Luke, up from the ranch. Like the former mountain man he was, Sam rode with his rifle across his lap instead of in a scabbard. When he worked cattle or rode a horse that he was training, he used a rifle scabbard, but when he was simply putting on miles, the rifle sat in his lap, cradled in his big competent hands as if they needed the comfort of the gun as he rode. While the approach of Sam and Luke was a relief, there was still a concern. Jake wasn't expecting anyone from the ranch to come to the mountains. That could mean there was trouble or news from below that couldn't wait. Jake went to meet them.

"You boys lost?" Jake asked, reaching up to shake hands with the two men.

"Hell," Sam drawled, "I ain't never been lost a day in my life. Jest reckoned it time to come see this heaven on earth that you come to every summer." Sam surveyed the meadow, the sturdy cabin, and the welcoming fire in front and grinned down at Jake. "It is a mighty purty spot for sure. I can see why you love it up here."

Jake felt relief. If it were bad news, a death, or illness of some sort with loved ones below, Sam would have come with a serious demeanor and come right to the point. Whatever brought the men up to the mountain cabin would wait until later, when they were all together.

The sun fell behind the peaks, but light remained in the evening dusk as those nestled around the campfire finished their meal. The fire crackled and the three women quit fussing over serving the men and relaxed among them, listening to the conversations.

"Here's the big news since you left in May," Sam started, lighting his pipe. "James went and got married."

"You don't say!" Jake grinned. "Hell, he's hardly grown yet. Has to be Mary. Wasn't he sparking her this spring?"

"Yup, it's Mary," Sam agreed, filling the mountain people in on the summer events, ending with the return from Laramie and the secret wedding. "We'll have to figure out a time to shivaree them this fall. But they've got the little ones, so maybe we just have a big party. Can't let this go without something."

"For jest a kid, James jumped in with both feet," Lathe commented. "He's got a ready-made family with four kids already."

"James will handle it," Hawk said seriously. Swift Hawk didn't often enter into conversations, but when he did, his comments were well thought out. "He's always liked kids. And he is steady, not afraid of work. It is good for him."

"So where are they living if they got hitched so quickly?" Lathe asked. "I suppose Kade is looking for a new housekeeper?"

Sam glanced at Jake before filling them in on the new living arrangements. He wasn't sure how Jake would feel about his family home being turned over to another family.

"So, it's working out for them all, then?" Jake asked when Sam finished.

"'Pears to be," Sam answered. "No one's been complaining."

"How'd Thomas take it?" Jake asked.

Sam hesitated, thinking through his answer. "Thomas wasn't too happy with it when Kade first told him. We were all at the corral an' Thomas jumped Kade 'bout having strangers in his ma's house. You know Thomas. Takes him awhile to get used to change. But Kade jest leveled an eye on Thomas an' took him down a peg. Told him it weren't no strangers in the house, but friends. It was sort of sad, in a way. Kade jest looked at Tom and told him his ma wasn't in that house anymore. No sense in looking for her there. Then Kade jest turned an' walked away. Nothing more was said, an' Thomas got over it like he usually does."

Jake nodded. It was his father's place to decide that. Jake was okay with the decision. Like Kade, he knew his mother would approve. That was enough for him.

They sat in companionable quiet for a while before Jake asked, "So, you didn't come all this way just to tell us about James getting married. What is the real reason you came up here? It ain't sightseeing."

Sam took a puff on his pipe before continuing. "Kade went for mail at Dixon an' heard the army was called in to move out the Utes. Word was some of the northern Utes have already gone off to the Uintah Agency in Utah, an' some of those have already come back. Others have gone to join the Uncompahgre Utes in the south. Heard that Yellow Dog's band was one of the bands that went south," Sam paused in the story, thinking. "The government is getting tired of waiting. Sent a Colonel

MacKenzie an' about three or four hundred infantry an' cavalry out to get the Utes going. Kade thought you'd want to know. If you plan to head that way, Luke an' I kin take the horses home."

Jake nodded solemnly, digesting the news. He knew Snowbird, Hawk and Kasa's mother, and his own sister-in-law, was with Yellow Dog's band. Jake had already heard from travelers he'd seen along the river that Yellow Dog's band went south. Jake knew he'd have to go with Hawk and Kasa to say a final goodbye to their mother. Jake had cousins and friends in the tribe, as well. He had to go; he'd just hoped something would come up and the move wouldn't happen. He studied the fire, thinking.

"We'll get packed up tomorrow. Leave the next day," Jake decided. He looked over at Anna before speaking again. "I'm thinking we send the wagon with Anna, Bonnie and young'uns home with you, Sam." Jake saw both Anna and Bonnie sit up straighter in surprise. He knew they would not be happy with that decision, but he felt it was necessary. "We don't know the terrain down south," he explained, glancing between Bonnie and Anna. "We don't know how much time we have, so we need to make tracks to get south before the army moves the tribe. The wagon will slow us down. Hawk and I will help Kasa and Lathe with their little ones so we can move faster. I don't want to get down there to find the Utes are two weeks ahead of us, and we have to chase them all the way to Utah. It's best you and Bonnie go home with Sam and Luke and the horses." Jake could see that Anna wasn't liking this, but she wouldn't say anything now. She'd wait until they were alone in the cabin later.

The fire was about out when the men put away their pipes and headed to their blankets. Anna, Bonnie, and Kasa had long since left with the children. Jake stretched, using his moccasined foot to kick dirt on the hot coals. It wouldn't do to let a wind come up and fan the coals. He'd lived through enough smoke during the dry summer two years ago with its numerous fires in the mountains, to keep him vigilant about putting out his campfires. Nodding at Lathe and Hawk, Jake headed inside while the two young men followed their wives to the upper meadow.

The cabin door stood open, but the night was getting chilly. Jake pulled it shut behind him. Anna was sitting in the rocking chair, baby Kade in her arms. Not quite two, little Kade, or Kade Brown as they called him to distinguish him from Jake's father, was asleep. There was hope that Anna would not get pregnant while nursing, so she still nursed the toddler, planning to nurse him for as long as possible. It was hard traveling back and forth to the mountains with infants. Both she and Jake wanted more children, just not right away. Kestrel, almost five, and Lark, three and a half, had become good travelers. Kestrel rode her Indian pony most of each day, while Lark played in the wagon. Neither Jake nor Anna had enjoyed staying home from the mountain the year before when Kade Brown was an infant. They wanted to space their children so they could continue their summer trips.

Jake went to Anna and leaned over, taking the sleeping toddler from her, and carrying him to his bed of blankets. The girls were already sound asleep in their corner, but little Kade slept on blankets near Jake and Anna's bed, so that if the baby woke during the night, he was close to his mother and didn't wake the girls with his cries. Luckily, he usually slept through the night now, only occasionally needing a snack to tide him over.

When Jake turned to his bed, Anna was already taking her dress off and standing in her shift. Jake went to her and drew her close to him. He felt her curves through the thin fabric.

"Are you mad at me?" he asked.

Anna nestled close, and Jake felt her shake her head. After a moment, she spoke. "I'm not mad. But I don't like you going off without us."

Jake grinned to himself, leaning over to nibble on her ear. "You aren't going to go off like a crazy woman and try to burn my clothes this time, are you?" he asked, referring to a trip Jake made after Kestrel was born. Anna had gotten so angry that Jake left her behind that Kade found her throwing all Jake's things out in the yard one day planning to burn them. When Jake returned, it took him some time to get Anna over her mad.

"No," Anna smiled reflectively, "I won't do that, but you better behave while you are gone."

Jake grew serious. He knew Anna was a jealous woman with a vivid imagination. That was what got them into trouble the last time. "Anna," he began, "you should trust me by now. I have never looked at another woman since you came into my life. I gave you my promise. I don't want to hear any more foolishness."

"I know," Anna began slowly, "but it's not like you courted me. You bought me. You were stuck with me.

You might see someone that . . ." she didn't know how to go on, her words drifting off.

Jake laughed at that. "I bought you and then fell in love with you. Hell, woman, where is a half-breed like me ever going to get such a fine white woman for a wife? I should be more worried you'd find a lover when I am gone." He untied the string of Anna's shift, stretching the neck open so that he could push it off her shoulders. He leaned down, nuzzling her neck.

"Take this off," Anna whispered, pulling at Jake's shirt.

They found their way to the blankets they called their bed in this mountain cabin. It was a far cry from the off-the-floor bed in their bedroom at home, but they had never wanted to add more to this cabin, leaving it much the way it was the first summer that Jake had brought her to it.

"I'll never find another man," Anna whispered as they lay. "You are my man, my forever man."

"Well, good," Jake said. "I'm glad we got that settled 'cause I'm not giving you up. But I am sending you home with the children. I don't have a good feeling about this Ute removal." His fingers played with her breasts. "The Utes don't want to go, and the army is getting sent out to move them. I'm hoping nothing happens, but if it does, I want you clear away. I wish Kasa would stay back too, but it's her mother and her people who are leaving. I understand that, and if you, Bonnie, and the children are safe, I can better help Lathe and Kasa."

Jake sat beside Anna, running his hands over her body as she lay watching him. Anna had changed so much in the seven years since she had become his wife. She had been such a starved-out wraith, scared out of her mind when Jake bought her and took her off with him. Then, when Anna began to feel safe with Jake, she panicked that he would sell her. Now Anna was twenty-four, a grown woman with children. When Anna had all the food she wanted after he bought her, she filled out. Now after three children, she was wider around the hips, bigger in the bosom and soft all over. Jake liked the changes in her, the slight plumpness. He still remembered how Anna's bones stuck out the first time he made love to her. Anna was like a skeleton then with a tight skin pulled over the bones. Now she was all woman, warm and soft and inviting.

"You just come home to me," Anna murmured, her hands moving to him. "Whatever happens, you come home."

The Uncompahgre River Valley lay before them teeming with a sea of animals, people, wagons, and teepees. Jake had never seen so many Utes gathered at the same time and place. He doubted that Hawk or Kasa had either by the way they grew silent at the sight. Thousands of cattle, sheep, goats, and horses were grazing in the valley, and the teepees, lodges, tents, and campfires spread over several miles. Silently, they approached, weaving between grazing animals until they got close to the encampment. Apart from the teepees of the Utes were the orderly rows of tents of the soldiers. The soldiers weren't in battle-ready positions, nor were they threatening, but they were camped on the outside edge of the Utes villages. As Jake's group approached, the soldiers watched them go by, but they were not stopped and questioned.

Jake and Hawk rode ahead, searching the teepees for a sign of Yellow Dog's band. For the most part, they saw southern Utes, men and women Jake didn't know. They passed some of Colorow's followers, a band of northern Utes that were involved in the Meeker incident. From talking with some warriors of Colorow's band, Jake was directed another half mile deeper into the camp, where they found Yellow Dog. It didn't take long to find the teepee of Snowbird's brother and Snowbird herself.

Snowbird had been worried that Kasa and Hawk wouldn't arrive before they left. She was relieved to see them ride up. After some discussion, Snowbird and Kasa and the children disappeared into her teepee. Lathe, Jake, and Hawk stood visiting with Yellow Dog and other warriors they knew. Jake was glad to see Yellow Dog. Older than Jake's brother Brown Otter who died at the Battle of Milk Creek the year before, Yellow Dog had been a friend and contemporary of Jake's blood father, Blue Knife. Jake had heard much of what he knew about his father through his brother, Brown Otter, and through Yellow Dog. With Brown Otter now gone, it was a relief to see the old man who Jake had looked up to most of his life.

Just as Jake turned to his horse to begin to unsaddle, five soldiers rode up to them. They rode past Jake and went up to Lathe.

"Sir, you can't be here," one of the soldiers, a captain, said.

Lathe looked around him, puzzled. "I can't?"

"We are moving these Indians to the reservation in Utah," the captain said politely, "and it is part of our commission that they are to be kept apart from all white men when they reach the reservation."

Lathe looked around again. "This doesn't look like the reservation," he said mildly.

"Sir, we don't want trouble, but we have secured the boundaries here and are moving out in the morning. We don't have time to go looking for you again. You need to leave now," the captain said firmly.

Lathe was beginning to get angry. "Look, I have a wife here who just wants to visit with her mother. We are all together," here Lathe indicated Jake and Hawk, "and we will leave in the morning if we have to."

The soldier glanced at Jake and Hawk before answering. "Sir, you have to leave now, and they," he gestured at Jake and Hawk, "are not leaving at all. We have orders to take all Utes to the Uintah Reservation. These men are not leaving."

Until then, Jake thought Lathe was doing a good job of speaking for them and not losing his temper. But with these last words, he knew it was time to step in. Lathe was known for a hot temper at times. Having Lathe hauled off in chains to an army post wouldn't do.

"Captain," Jake began, stepping away from his horse and next to Lathe, "we are not from these bands. We are from a ranch north and east of the northernmost border of the Ute lands. We are just here to say goodbye to relatives. We don't want trouble."

The young officer was startled when Jake spoke such good English with no accent. He looked from Lathe to Jake before speaking. "Look, I have my orders. You," he pointed at Lathe, "have to leave. And you," he pointed at Jake, "have to stay. Those are my orders. If I have to get Colonel Mackenzie, my commanding officer, I will.

But he's going to say the same thing. We have our orders, and we cannot be seen not doing our duty."

"And if we don't comply?" Lathe asked angrily before Jake could stop him.

"We have our orders. We'll take you to the White River military headquarters and hold you there until we are told to release you."

Jake saw Lathe bristle at that. Jake stepped in front of Lathe and turning, he put his hand to Lathe's chest. "Lathe," he hissed, moving the young man backwards where he could speak quietly to him. "You won't do us any good getting hauled off."

"Jake," Lathe started impatiently, "I am not leaving Kasa!"

"Yes," Jake spoke low, but his voice was firm. "You are going to leave Kasa, and you are going to do that right now. Take one of the pack horses and part of our supplies. Ride away out of sight."

"Jake . . ." Lathe started angrily, but Jake pushed him back another step, and none too gently either.

"Listen to me, Lathe," Jake was deadly serious now. "I need you out there, following behind and waiting. Give us two, maybe three days and we will just drift away. When we do, we will need supplies. Look around, Lathe," Jake spoke reasonably, "There are, what, maybe a thousand Utes here? They can't keep track of us. Right now, you stick out like a white man in a sea of red. I reckon with you gone and none of us making any trouble, the soldiers will forget about us in a couple days, or if they don't forget, they won't care. We'll just drift out after dark. You stay back and watch for us."

"Jake, I don't want to leave Kasa and my kids," Lathe said with some desperation.

"I understand that," Jake said soothingly, "but Hawk and I are here. We won't let anything happen, and it will only be a few days. You make trouble here, and it could be months before we get you out of some military jail. And if you make me fight for you here, then we may have more trouble than that. Use your head, Lathe."

Lathe looked from Jake to the soldiers who were watching them, thinking through Jake's words. He looked towards the teepee his wife had disappeared into and met Hawk's watchful eyes. Finally, he looked back at Jake.

"Can I at least say goodbye to Kasa and the kids?"

"No, go now," Jake said firmly. "They don't know who your wife and children are. They only know my face and Hawk's. Let's keep it that way. Hawk and I can disappear pretty easy if we have to, but let's not put Kasa in that position. I'll talk to her. It will only be a few days. Trail us, but keep far enough behind that you aren't seen. When we drift, we will follow the trail back. With this many people and animals, it won't be hard."

Lathe looked at Hawk and then back at Jake. Slowly, he nodded, but just before he turned to his horse, he grumbled, "I'll go, but I damn sure don't want to."

"Hell, Lathe," Jake allowed a small smile, "I don't think much of this either, but I don't want to go to war over it. You look for us in two or three days. Stay out of trouble until then."

CHAPTER 10

Prejudice Raises Its Ugly Head - September 1881

Kasa took it well when Hawk told her the soldiers turned Lathe away. She understood the consequence of his trying to stay and agreed with Jake that they would be able to drift away unnoticed in a few days. She was happy to be with her mother for a few days, and she was glad they weren't all being turned out.

Jake and Hawk took care of their horses and set up a temporary camp near Snowbird and her brother's teepee. Men from Yellow Dog's camp stopped to visit. Hawk and Jake were busy catching up with friends and relatives.

But the atmosphere was bleak. The Utes were a nomadic tribe, as were most Native Americans. The Utes had traveled when and where they wanted for five hundred years. These were their ancestral lands, and they traveled back and forth between the northern and southern Ute tribes every summer. This move to Utah was different. This was not their idea, and they were not moving to the lands they loved. The Utes were angry, despondent, and frustrated in equal portions.

Almost fifteen hundred Uncompahgre Utes were gathered, and along with a few bands of the northern

Utes that joined them; it was a massive camp of Indians. With only three or four hundred military troops assigned to escort the Utes to Utah, things could get ugly. But basically, the Utes knew there was an unending supply of soldiers that the whites could call on. If the Battle of Milk Creek had taught the Utes anything, it was that success in one battle did not make the end of the war. They knew they were too few in number to fight the white army.

Jake felt the same frustration. He hated to see his friends and relatives being moved. He knew that technically, he, Hawk, and Kasa were expected to relocate with the tribe. But he also knew they wouldn't. Even if they were taken in chains to the Utah country, they would come back. They were part of Twin Peaks Ranch, and there they would return. Once they were home at the ranch, no one would bother them. But for now, they were part of the tribe, and the three of them watched with sadness as the people packed up and made ready to leave their homelands.

The first day of travel had been a trying day. The soldiers had made it clear that the Utes were expected to leave that morning, and there would be no more dawdling, no more excuses. So shortly after sunrise, the people began to move. Some rode their sturdy Indian ponies, some walked, some used travois to pull their belongings, and some had wagons. There was little organization. As the people got ready, they moved off, allowing those who were still packing to catch up. Some rode off in anger, scattering blankets, livestock, and possessions as they went. Some women and children were wailing and crying their despair at leaving. But soon, the scene was simply hundreds of wagons, travois, horses, ponies, dogs, cattle, sheep, and people, making their way westward. It truly was a sight to see so many Utes headed west, but it wasn't a good sight. Jake felt the pain of his people as he never had before.

It was late in the day when the hoard of moving people and animals simply quit moving. Scattering out over a mile, the people picked places to camp and got out cooking pots. A creek was nearby to get water, and the family units settled down for their meals. Jake and Hawk ate with Snowbird's family. She was living with her brother, but also camped with them was Hawk and Kasa's older sister and her husband. Together they all shared a meal, pooling the supplies they carried. As darkness came upon them, the fires in the bottom flickered for several miles up and down the creek. Yellow Dog had come to sit with them, and the men pulled their pipes out to smoke. There was little conversation. There was nothing they had to say, but instead sat together simply for the companionship.

As they were sitting, a group of young Ute men wandered close. Jake did not know these men. They were either Uncompahgre Utes or from a northern Ute band that he didn't know. Jake did not recognize any of them, although there were a couple of braves who seemed vaguely familiar. Maybe Jake had seen them when he went south after the kidnapped Meeker women. These men were maybe eight or ten years younger than Jake, mid-twenties instead of Jake's thirty-two years. They wound their way around campfires, haughty, arrogant, and, most of all, angry. Jake watched them as they kicked dirt on campfires or bantered with some of the young women. Jake knew these young men were trying to save face. This forced move was hard on all of the tribe, but the young men often blamed the older braves for their plight. The younger men wanted to fight, to resist, and the older ones said no. The older ones signed the treaties.

As the young men approached, one spun off from the rest and came to stand in front of Jake. As he got close, Jake knew he had seen this young man before, but he couldn't place him. The man's stance was belligerent, his face taunting.

"Why don't you leave, half-breed? You more white than Ute," the young man snarled in Ute.

Jake looked mildly up at the man. "You know me," he said, also speaking in the Ute tongue. "I don't know you. What are you called?"

"You came searching for the white captives last year," the man spat at him. "Take away what we won. My uncle had one white woman. You come with soldiers."

"You are Buffalo Rib," Jake said, suddenly remembering the aftermath of the Meeker incident. "I saw you in Douglas' camp. You didn't want to give up the women." He remembered this young man who was angry then too. Jake had asked another brave who the hothead was. That is why this man looked familiar. He was a White River Ute, after all, but one that wasn't from Yellow Dog's band.

"I am Buffalo Rib," the young man agreed. "And you are a white man to us. You will go back to your white people anyway. Go now. No one wants you here."

"I will leave when I want," Jake held his temper in check.

"Ha!" Buffalo Rib spat. "You will go sneaking off to your white woman, just like your father did, and leave the people behind."

This angered Jake, but he held his emotions inside. "My father had two wives."

"Your gutless father married a white whore and left the tribe . . ." Buffalo Rib began.

Jake came unglued at that. He sprang easily to his feet, taking the young man by surprise. Grabbing the man by his shirt, Jake shoved him back, slamming him against Snowbird's wagon, knocking the wind from him. "Never refer to my mother or father like that," he spoke low to the man. "Get out of my sight." Then turning the man away, Jake shoved him, watching him stagger.

Jake was just turning around as Buffalo Rib caught his balance, then pulled a knife from his side. Buffalo Rib lunged at Jake, slashing dangerously with the knife. Jake felt the knife cut through his shirt on his right side. He felt the pain of the blade and the hot blood running down his side. Jake dove for the knife, and catching the younger man's hand in both of his, he wrestled the man back. Again, Jake slammed the younger man against the wagon. Jake was stronger than Buffalo Rib and quicker, but Buffalo Rib had the knife and was lethal. Jake needed to break Buffalo Rib's grip on the knife. Jake did not want to hurt the man seriously, but he was angry. Jake forced the man back, fighting to keep the knife away. Slowly, Jake was able to force the hand with the knife down against the wheel of the wagon, striking it hard repeatedly. Buffalo Rib struck at Jake with his free hand, but Jake kept his body too close to the other man for the blows to do any real harm. Again and again, Jake slammed the hothead's knife hand down on the wheel until suddenly, Buffalo Rib's hand unfurled, and the knife dropped to the ground. Jake stepped back, back-handed the young brave, and kicked the knife away.

"Leave me," Jake growled, panting heavily, "before you get hurt." Then he turned and walked away.

Jake saw the ring of faces around them. The scuffle had drawn attention from campfires nearby, and there were many onlookers. No one spoke. Jake walked back to his seat by the fire, reaching down to pick up his pipe. That was when Kasa screamed.

"Uncle!"

The report of a gun didn't register on Jake until after he felt the searing pain in his upper left arm. Instinctively he reached for his knife and whirled. Buffalo Rib stood with a revolver, aiming it at him, smiling through bloody teeth.

"Die, half-breed," he snarled, and he took aim again.

Jake didn't stop to think. Staring at the muzzle of the gun, his left arm already going numb, he threw his knife. The gun went off just before the knife made its impact. The shot was wild, but the knife went true. Jake could hear the bullet sizzle through the air, but it didn't touch him. Instead, he watched the bugging eyes of his young opponent. Buffalo Rib staggered one step back, clawing at the knife. The hilt was sticking out of the man's chest, the blade buried deep. Buffalo Rib crumpled and fell.

Jake just stood, panting. His right side was on fire now, wet and slippery with blood. His left arm burned. But Jake kept looking at the man laying before him. The last thing he wanted was to kill the man.

"Come with me," the low, calm voice of Yellow Dog startled Jake. Without any more thought, Jake turned and followed the old man. Walking away, he heard wails of grief well up behind him.

.♠.

Yellow Dog led Jake to a not-too-distant small tent and motioned Jake to wait. Bending over, Yellow Dog went inside. Jake could hear the soft murmur of conversation coming from inside, but he was unable to make out the words, and he was too heartsore to care. He had had to deal with the white man's prejudice against him all his life, but never had he felt any intolerance from a Ute toward himself or his parents. This had come out of nowhere, and he was surprised at how much it hurt. How many others harbored thoughts such as these toward him? And the killing of a Ute man was beyond his imagination. Never would he have thought that would happen.

Yellow Dog emerged from the tent and walked to Jake.

"You go in," he said quietly. "Medicine Woman here take care of you. Then you get Swift Hawk and Kasa, and you leave."

"No!" Jake said forcefully, taking even himself by surprise at the vehemence of his tone. "I will not run. I did not want this. It was not my doing."

Yellow Dog regarded him thoughtfully, and finally he nodded. "I will ride with you tomorrow," he said. "We will talk of old times." Then the old man tipped his head toward the tent before turning and walking away silently on his moccasins.

Jake went to the tent, bending over to enter. It hurt his side to bend over, and a small grunt came out unheeded. With his left hand, he had balled up his torn shirt and held it tightly against the knife wound on his right side. Already the shirt was red with blood. The bullet that grazed his arm was not as serious, he thought, as it was only oozing now. The sleeve of that arm was blood-soaked too, but there wasn't a strong flow of blood.

A woman was inside the tent, going through a box on the ground. Jake saw bandages and bottles as she rummaged. She glanced up at Jake and motioned to him to sit on a robe near the one kerosene lamp that sat on a small keg. Jake gratefully sank to the ground, sitting cross-legged, watching the woman.

The woman was older than he but looked vaguely familiar. She was of average height but not as thick through the waist and hips as many of the older Native women became as they raised their brood of children. He saw only one set of blankets in the tent, so he assumed she lived alone or with just a husband, although she might be young enough to have children who were not yet grown. It didn't matter. He just wanted his wounds bandaged and to return to his fire for whatever reception waited there for him

"The side, it looks the worse. Let me look," the woman spoke in Ute.

"The side is worse. It is still bleeding." Jake said quietly in Ute.

The woman pulled the balled-up shirt away, assessing the wound, then pressed it back again and told Jake to hold it steady. She did the same with the arm. Taking a knife, she cut away the fabric of Jake's shirt, exposing the arm wound. It was a graze as Jake expected, and while still bleeding, it wasn't steady. The woman reached for some cloth she had in a pile, and folding it over and over, pressed it against his arm.

"Hold this tight," she ordered. "It will stop the bleeding and keep your arm out of the way of your side."

Mechanically, Jake reached up with his right hand and held the cloth in place, applying pressure. Again, the woman removed the bloody shirt from Jake's right side. Taking a wet cloth, she began washing his side, pressing the folds of the knife-slashed skin together like puzzle pieces, trying to see how they fit.

"I don't have any medicine for the pain," she said softly. "I need to sew it together."

"Do it," Jake responded.

The woman went back to her box and set out supplies. Jake watched her dully, his thoughts remembering the fight. *What could he have done differently? How could he have acted to get a different outcome? Why didn't Buffalo Rib just walk away after Jake took the knife away from him?* The thoughts swirled in Jake's head. Questions with no answers.

The pain of the needle brought him back to the present. He jerked once, then made himself ready. This was a bearable pain. He was ready for the next stitch.

"Where did you learn to do this?" Jake asked the woman. He wasn't really curious, but talking kept his mind from the fight.

She was fingering his side, pulling the flaps of skin together, assessing where to put the next stitch. "My husband was sick. He went to the agency doctor. He was there many days, and I stayed there with him. I watched the doctor as he worked with my husband and with others. When my husband died, I asked the doctor to teach me, let me live there. Now they call me Medicine Woman, and I make my own way."

Jake nodded, understanding what she was saying. As a widow, she would be dependent on a son or brother, uncle, or father. As a medicine woman, she would be taken care of by all. She had value.

"Your children are grown?"

"I have no children," Medicine Woman replied seriously. She gave no explanation and Jake didn't ask. It was enough to know that she was alone, and she saw a way to bring herself status and security. Jake could also see Medicine Woman was good at this. But it still hurt as she pushed the needle through his skin.

With the stitches in, Jake saw the wound was only oozing blood now. He watched as the woman took out bandages and rolled them tightly around his torso, holding the cloth tight against the stitches. It both hurt and felt good as the bandages pressed against his wound. When she felt the cut was covered adequately, she tore the ends of the dressing and tied it off snuggly. Jake grunted a little as she tugged on the knot to tighten it. He saw a slight smile touch the corners of her mouth.

Then the woman went to his arm. The bleeding had stopped when she removed his hand and the cloth beneath. She went for more hot water from the fire outside and washed this wound too. "This does not need stitches. It will heal," she said, poking at the thin line where the bullet had grazed him. "A bandage for a few days will be enough."

Jake nodded, letting her wipe off the dried blood and pull out the threads from his shirt that were stuck to the blood. She tore more of the shirt sleeve then looked at Jake. "The rest of this shirt needs to come off. It is worthless. Should I cut it off, or do you want to try to take it off?"

Jake contemplated the question and answered, "Cut it off. I don't think it's worth fixing." And it wasn't. The whole right side had been balled up to stop the bleeding, and then torn off to get it out of the way. What was left was two sleeves and the left half of the shirt. To lift his arms to remove these remnants didn't sound like a movement Jake wanted to do just then.

Expertly the woman cut off the shirt, throwing it in a corner. "I will wash and use for more bandages," she remarked. Nothing was wasted when there was such a need.

When his arm was bandaged, Jake watched the woman return to her box, looking inside. "Am I done?" he asked. He couldn't shake the despair he felt for the events of this evening. He just wanted to be alone.

The woman glanced over at him and then came to kneel before him. She took a wet rag and used it to wash his bloody hands, crusted and dried already. It was almost a caress as she wiped down his fingers, palm, and lower arm. When she was finished with his hands, she fingered the bandage around his body, running gentle fingers along the edges of his belly. "Too tight?" she asked.

"No."

She fingered the bandages on his arm, again gently feeling around the edges of the bandage. "Too tight?"

"No."

Medicine Woman rocked back on her heels, assessing Jake, and then she did a surprising thing. She reached up to his bare chest and placed her hands there, gently caressing the contours of his muscles. "You don't remember me," her words were soft, barely a whisper.

Jake was startled and looked closely at her. Her voice seemed familiar now that he thought about it. But he didn't know her. He didn't know who she was before she became Medicine Woman. He shook his head.

"You came to me a boy. You did not leave the same way," she whispered, her fingers moving along his chest, up to his neck, caressing.

"Sunlight," Jake murmured, surprise and recognition in his voice. "You were my first. I remember."

"I never saw you after that time," Sunlight said. "We never visited Yellow Dog's band again when you were there. But I heard about you. I knew you grew up to be a warrior. Brown Otter was proud of you."

"*Waugh*," Jake grunted. "He would not be so proud now after tonight's fight. It is not right to spill the blood of our people."

"Buffalo Rib was looking for trouble," the woman said icily. "He has been trouble for years. People keep away from him. Only his closest relatives will mourn him now."

"Still . . ." Jake began.

"No, it is done," she cut him off. "Maybe this was the one thing our people needed to go on and let the anger die. Maybe anger at the whites won't die, but it will between ourselves. We are an unhappy people now. But we should not blame each other."

Jake thought about her words. He was also aware of her hands. They were caressing him. He felt the gentle fingers as they moved along his chest, his good arm, his neck, and into his hair. He knew her intention just as he felt his body tingle at her touch. She was not the beautiful Sunlight of his memory but an older, wiser woman. Still, her fingers were skilled. Her mouth touched his chest and burrowed into his neck. He felt her contact; he smelled her scent. Jake wanted what she was offering. He wanted the guilt he felt to be washed away. She was offering to do that in the way a woman knows. And he wanted that release. He wanted the anger and guilt and frustration to be washed away. He wanted to lay with her, to lose himself in her, and feel cleansed. He wanted to forget, even if for a while.

Jake reached for her hands and held them. Sunlight leaned back and looked at Jake. Jake put her hands against his chest again, holding them tight, but his gaze direct.

"I remember how I felt that first time, and the two nights we spent together after that," he started softly. "I will never forget that time. And I feel desire for you now," he took a deep breath. "But I cannot. I have a woman. I have promised to be only hers." Jake set Sunlight's hands in her lap and released them. He fingered the wisps of hair flying free from her braids and tucked them behind her ears. "I have a lot of white blood flowing in me," he continued. "I have made a promise. Not all white men lie. I cannot stay with you. But I remember. And it was good."

Slowly Jake rose to go. Sunlight sat still, watching him. She spoke just as he was reaching for the tent flap to go outside. "I remember too. I remember those nights. You are a good man. Brown Otter would be proud."

Jake studied her for an instant and then nodded. Bending low, he ducked out of the tent and into the night.

They hadn't been riding long the following morning before Yellow Dog caught up to Jake and rode beside him. Neither the old man nor Jake spoke at once. They were content to just ride together. The morning was cool, and Jake was glad he had on a buckskin shirt that Anna had made for him.

Jake had walked back to his camp the night before shirtless, bandages white against his brown skin in the shadows of the campfires. He felt, rather than saw, the eyes that turned his way, watching him as he walked. He heard the voices quiet as he came near. At his camp, the eyes of his niece and nephew searched his face before Kasa finally spoke.

"Uncle, are you all right?"

"I'll heal," Jake responded solemnly. Then he went to his packs, found the buckskin shirt, and gently pulled it over his head. He tried not to wince as he moved his left arm. Then he sat back before the fire and picked up his pipe. No one else remained at their campfire, and no more words were spoken that evening.

Now the people had been on the move for almost two hours. There were questions Jake wanted to ask Yellow Dog, but he was working up in his mind how to do it. After all, he had all day. Buffalo Rib's words from last night still hurt, both about himself and his parents.

"You were there last night," Jake finally started, turning to look at Yellow Dog. "You heard the words Buffalo Rib said."

Yellow Dog nodded, but didn't speak.

"Was there anger against my father for taking my mother as a wife?" Jake asked. "Did the people feel he left the tribe?"

Yellow Dog hesitated, "No one felt your father left the tribe. He was there when we needed him. But we knew he was different. He had always been different, and he was accepted that way."

"How was he different?" Jake needed to know. He had never gotten the idea that his father was anything but part of the tribe. This was new territory for Jake.

"Blue Knife was my best friend," Yellow Dog began. "Your grandfather brought the family to our village at least once a year, and they stayed for weeks or even months. I looked forward every year to their coming. When Blue Knife and I were old enough to hunt together, we spent many days off alone. Knife came on his own when he was old enough and stayed with the tribe. When he married, he seldom went back to your grandfather's cabin. But he had lived many years as a boy in the mountain cabin with his white father and his Ute mother. That made him different from us. Your father often wanted to be alone, even when he was in our village. Because of that, he went off hunting often, and he went with every war party. It caused some problems with his first wife, Brown Otter's mother. Blue Knife was gone a lot. He would go off alone or, at times, with me."

"But how did people feel when he took my mother and lived at Jacob's cabin?" Jake had to know.

"I don't think many people understood why he didn't bring her to the village," Yellow Dog replied thoughtfully. "At first, I think the anger your mother felt from the braves was her biggest fear, and Blue Knife knew that. He wanted to protect her. It would not have been good for her if your father hadn't taken her for himself. Even as Blue Knife's wife, it would have taken a long time for her to be an accepted part of our village. But

Knife told me once when he visited the village, how it was with them. He told me of her songs, and the stories that she read from her books, and her work with her horses. Knife didn't want her to change. He didn't want her to change into what she would have to be if she came to the village. He never told anyone else that except me and Brown Otter.

"I visited them, and I watched your mother. I came on them once when they were racing their horses, and your mother was becoming great with child . . . with you. Before your mother knew I was there, I saw her laughing and riding that great black horse, jumping the creek and fallen logs. She was like a spirit. If she came to live in the village, she could not be like that. She would not fit in with us. I would not have wanted her to change if she were mine, but I would not have wanted to live away from the village either. It was the cabin your father grew up in. To him, it was just as much home as our village. He was my best friend, and I understood that."

"So, my father wasn't resented for his white blood or his white wife," Jake continued. After a pause, he asked, "Am I?"

Yellow Dog thought about that. "You are Blue Knife's son, Brown Otter's brother. You have always been accepted as one of us. But you too, are different. Unlike Blue Knife, you never chose to stay with us. Even in the summers, when you came to Jacob's cabin, you only visited us. No one expected you to stay, but some hoped it would happen. It was enough that you hunted with us. It was enough that you went with our war parties. It was enough that you were a good warrior and counted coup. Brown Otter always hoped you would marry and stay. But toward the end, Otter was glad you didn't."

Yellow Dog stopped talking for a while, riding on silently. Finally, he looked again at Jake. "You and your family helped us many times with cattle to eat when the government supplies didn't come on time, and the buffalo were gone. There was never resentment toward you or your family. You were just Rides the Wind with a white family as well as red."

"And now I have killed a Ute brave," Jake said. "Will I still be accepted?"

Yellow Dog snorted at that. "Buffalo Rib was a troublemaker. I am glad he wasn't from my village. He brought this upon himself."

They rode for a long time without speaking. The people, wagons, travois, and livestock were spread along the rolling plains, dust rising from wheels and hooves. The mountains behind them still seemed close, but they were receding. Finally, when wagons began stopping for a mid-day meal, Yellow Dog turned again to Jake.

"It is a good thing you fought Buffalo Rib," Yellow Dog said solemnly. "I too disliked the man's words against your father and mother. I would have fought him for that," Yellow Dog was thoughtful. "But I don't think this old man would have been a good match for Buffalo Rib. The outcome would not have been good, but not the same way," Yellow Dog grinned then, and Jake saw the approval in Yellow Dog. "But if I could have killed him, I would have enjoyed it."

Later that night when the fires burned low, Hawk, Kasa, and Jake quietly saddled their horses. They led the animals through the sleeping camp and around the soldiers' camp, carrying the two small sleeping children. When they were out of sight of the flickering firelight, they mounted their horses, and under a crescent moon, they began their long trip home. They all knew this might be their last time seeing these friends and relatives. This had been a journey of endings. It was with sadness that they rode away into the night.

CHAPTER 11

Not Too Old – November 1881

K ade walked briskly in the evening cold. It was dark by the time he got his horse unsaddled and settled in the corral behind Sarah's. He had been riding with James most of the afternoon, and he was getting chilled now that the sun was long gone from the sky. He smelled the woodsmoke from Sarah's and knew that she would have supper ready.

"You're late tonight," Sarah said as he came inside, shaking off snow from his boots.

"James was riding a new three-year-old colt, and it gave him trouble. We ended up quite a ways from home before he got it under control. Then we figured it need- ed a couple more miles just to get the message across," Kade grinned. "That son of yours is getting to be a good horseman. I was supposed to be with him to help if he needed it, but that crazy horse spooked into the woods, and there was no catching or stopping him. For a while there, I thought I might have to come back and tell you James hung himself in a tree. Then suddenly, there he was, ahead of me, and had the colt under control."

"I wish you wouldn't take those colts for their first rides outside in this cold weather," Sarah commented dryly. "Wouldn't it be better to wait until spring?"

"There's some advantages to winter riding. Usually, we can keep a young horse controlled by riding them into drifts if they get out of control," Kade said as he sat down at the table. "Get them into a drift, and one of two things happen. Either the horse plays out in the deep snow, and you gain control, or it's a soft landing if you don't. Problem today was that the colt started out so good we drifted too close to the trees. Then the darn animal started pitching. We won't make that mistake again."

Sarah set food on the table and they both began to eat. They made small talk, relaxed between themselves. When Will moved out over a month ago, Kade worried that he and Sarah would be uncomfortable together. But that hadn't happened. Kade had lived in James' old room now for over three months. It was working, this arrangement with him and Sarah. He missed the activity of the Snyder kids being in the same cabin, but he was content in Sarah's home. He wasn't alone, after all. And on many nights, they had visitors; Matthew coming to play cards or talk business, James bringing down the children, Thomas or Jake or Sam, wanting a game of checkers. But as the nights got longer and the evenings colder, the visits were fewer. Winter was like that.

So, he and Sarah had a routine of their own now. After supper, while Sarah cleaned up, Kade bundled up and made many trips to the woodpile, bringing in enough wood for the evening and the next day. Most nights, he also piled extra wood on the porch just in case he was delayed the following night. If there was one thing Kade detested, it was running out of firewood at the wrong time, like in the middle of the night.

When he and Sarah finished their chores, they mostly sat before the fire. Kade had an endless supply of old newspapers, sent out from St. Louis by Joe, that was picked up every couple of weeks from the Dixon post office. Reading them with only a flickering candle or their kerosene lamp for light took time. Kade had leather to repair some evenings, and for that, he sat at the table. Some nights, if his eyes were strained from reading, he played solitaire. Sarah usually sewed or knitted, rocking gently in a chair made by old Tom many years earlier.

Usually, Sarah left for bed first after bundling up to go outside. Then Kade would bank the fire and check the stove before heading quickly outside. If Kade worked it right, there would be a live coal or two in the woodstove or the fireplace in the morning that he or Sarah could coax into a flame. But if not, they had matches or flint. Life was so much easier now than when he and Sabra had first been married. They now had better access to supplies and mail. They simply had to ride a half day away to replenish any basic staples they needed.

This night was like the others. Kade had put away the newspaper and was playing cards at the table when Sarah went outside. When she came in, she went to her chair and gathered up her knitting, placing it in a basket she kept on the floor for that purpose. She went to the stove, took off the kettle, and poured hot water into a basin to take to her room for washing. But then, Sarah did a surprising thing.

"I'm not sure I have ever told you this," Sarah said softly, setting the basin on the mantle and turning to Kade, "but I am so glad you are here. I can't imagine how lonely it would be with Will gone, and I were all alone."

Kade looked up, surprised. "I reckon that works for both of us," he responded.

"It's still lonely, though," Sarah went on. "I mean, it's
. . . well, I . . ." she turned away from Kade before getting the courage to get her words out. "I sometimes just
can't face going into that room alone, seeing that big
bed and being alone."

Kade could feel her pain. He understood her loneliness. He couldn't see her face, but he saw her shoulders
shake ever so slightly and saw her hand go to her face.
He knew she was fighting to control tears. He got to his
feet and went to her, turning her toward him. He pulled
her into his embrace.

"You aren't alone, Sarah. I'm here," he said over her
head.

She clutched at him, burying her face into his shoulder. "God, I miss Jim so much. It's been over five years
since he's been gone. You'd think I would be used to it
by now."

"I don't reckon we will ever get used to it," Kade said
softly.

"I just don't want to go in there alone," Sarah repeated, and Kade felt her grip him harder as she said the
words.

"I'm not Jim, Sarah."

"And I'm not Sabra," Sarah replied. Then taking a
breath, she said, "But we are here, and they aren't. We
aren't too old to want . . . I mean," she stopped abruptly,
unable to go on.

Kade understood her need without her words. He
held her for a moment, thinking of a reply. He cared
about this woman. He wanted to get it right. "I need
to go outside. If you still feel this way, leave your door
open. If it's closed, I'll know, and it will be all right.
Whatever you decide will be all right." He felt her nod

against his chest. Then she turned from him, took up the basin, and went to her room.

Sarah's door was open, a candle flickering inside when Kade returned. He didn't let himself think about this. He just kept hearing Sarah's words, "We aren't too old to . . ." He felt those words; they had meaning to him too. Kade went to the stove, poured water into another basin, and took it to his room. Stripping off his shirt, boots, and socks, he washed. It was an evening ritual that he had ever since marrying Sabra. Some things are hard to break, not that he wanted to.

He went to his door and looked out again. Candlelight still flickered from Sarah's room through the open door. Going through the cabin, he set his candle on the table and blew it out. He went to her door and stopped, his bare feet noiseless on the wood floor.

Sarah sat in front of a low dresser and mirror, methodically brushing her hair. She had golden hair, long and straight when she freed it from the bun at the nape of her neck. Sabra's hair had been long and brown with golden flecks in it. Sabra would sit at night brushing it until he came to bed, or until she had brushed it one hundred strokes. Sabra seldom made it to one hundred strokes. Now Kade watched Sarah brush her hair. Kade knew Sarah was aware he stood in the doorway, but she didn't waver from what she was doing. Kade walked to her and took the brush from her. He drew the brush gently through her hair, feeling the silky sensation of the golden strands. Their eyes met in the mirror, and he set the brush down on the dresser top. His fingers pulled her hair back, away from her face. Then she rose, turning to him.

"Are you . . . is this . . . ?" Sarah stammered.

Kade bent over and kissed her. She came to him hungrily. He felt her press against him, felt her breasts beneath the thinness of her shift. He merely held her at first. They weren't kids. There was none of the exhilaration of youth, where they couldn't wait to get home. How many times had he and Sabra found a spot in the woods and lay there together because they couldn't stand to wait? There was none of that here. There was only a deep desire. Kade felt the same passion in Sarah, and he felt it in himself. Slowly he pulled her shift over her head.

The light was beginning to come in the window when Kade woke up. He was surprised. He was always up before dawn. He had slept hard, harder than he had in the last fourteen months. He glanced at Sarah. Her golden hair fanned out against the pillow. She had her back to him, spooning into him. Kade got up and padded naked to the fireplace in the next room, feeling the cold air on his bare skin. He searched for a live coal and, finding one, he fed it with paper and then kindling until a flame burst. He added logs then went to the stove and did the same. It wouldn't take long for the heat to seep into the room. He went back to Sarah's bedroom.

Sarah was awake and watched him as he walked in. He felt he should be embarrassed about being naked, but he wasn't. He climbed back into bed and curled up close to Sarah. She rolled to her back and smiled at him.

"Sleep good?" she asked.

"Hmmm . . . You?" Kade saw her nod.

It was too cold to throw the covers off, but Kade found his hand moving underneath, finding her and exploring. She was a bigger woman than Sabra. Sabra was so often outside with the horses. Sabra's body was trim and strong and soft. Sarah's was soft too, but she showed her age more than Sabra had. Sarah had thickened through the waist more, was wider at the hips from bearing five children, bigger breasted. She was not fat, but rounder than Sabra. And yet, as he lay there, he just thought about something. Something that had bothered him so much of his early married life. He smiled in the remembering.

"What are you smiling about? What are you thinking?" Sarah asked.

"I just realized something," he replied. "When Sabra and I first married, I was bothered by the fact that she had been Blue Knife's woman, had a child with him. I'm not proud of that, but it was in my mind, and in the early years, I couldn't get it out. There were times when I would, I don't know, challenge her, maybe? I would ask her if she loved him, or I would ask her what it was like living with him. She would tell me that she only loved me but that she had cared for him. That she had learned to care for him. Sometimes I pressed too hard, and she would get angry with me. But for years, I would come back to that every now and then. Finally, I guess I knew she loved me, and I got over it. But it was a thorn in my side for a long time. I couldn't understand what she meant when she said she 'cared about him.'"

"So why are you thinking about that now?"

Kade smiled down at her. "I am thinking about it because now I understand it," he said. "Sarah, you and Jim have been our good friends for what, thirty years? Now

Jim is gone but you are still my friend. I care for you. I will always love Sabra, but I care for you. I hope that doesn't hurt you."

Kade closed his eyes, recalling that terrible night when he lost Sabra. Then he opened his eyes and studied Sarah. "I understand another thing too," he continued. "When Sabra was dying, she said something to me. She told me to 'let Sarah comfort you.' I thought she meant let you cook me a meal or let you talk to me or, I don't know, maybe just be around to help. But then she said it would help you too; comfort you too," Kade stopped talking and pushed some strands of hair off Sarah's cheek. "She didn't mean that, though. She meant this. Sabra meant for us to find each other. How did she know that?"

Sarah smiled back at Kade. "That Sabra," she said fondly, "she told me the same thing, maybe a day or two before she died. I thought the same as you. Darn your socks or make you a shirt or send a pie to you, any of those things. I wasn't thinking sleep with you. But she was. She cared for us. Well, she loved you, but she cared for me. She wanted this to happen, didn't she?"

Kade smiled at that. "Her last thoughts were about how she could help us. I wasn't sure I could survive her dying. But she wanted us both to survive," Kade paused, fingers slowly caressing Sarah under the quilt. "Last night was good for us, I think. It was good for me, anyway. I hope it was for you."

Sarah pulled the quilt over her head, and he felt her nuzzle against the hair of his chest. "I'll tell you in a little bit," her words came out muffled. He felt her hands moving across his stomach and down, and he knew what her answer would be. The cabin would be warm before they came out from under the quilts this morning.

Kade was late getting to the hay lot that morning. The men had half of the first hay wagon loaded when he walked up. This was the first thing that had to be done every day once the snow fell. Every morning, the men gathered behind Matthew's to load the hay wagons. When one was loaded, three men would drive it out to the cattle in the valley and fork it out to the herd. The rest of the men would load the second wagon and go down the river bottom to the steers. There were too many cattle now to keep them all in the valley. Thomas and his crew separated the steers, all the yearlings, twos and three-year-olds, drove them down the river, and held them there during the winter months. In the spring, they sold the threes, which had now turned four, and the rest were driven farther along the river, well past where the ranch hands hayed, and there, the steers stayed all summer. In the fall, the ranch sold another package of steers. It all depended on the price and how well the animals had fared. The cows and calves were separated, the calves were locked in a large corral near the haystacks. When the second wagon went out, the men left behind would start forking over hay to the calves. The cattle needed to be watched carefully, gauging their condition. Sometimes a third wagon was loaded and taken out. In excessive cold, the animals needed more feed to help keep them warm. Kade was adamant that the cattle needed to come through the winter in good shape.

Kade differed from the big ranchers who ran cattle on the plains. There, the tough, primarily Texas longhorn cattle fended for themselves on the free grass. Free-range cattle, they were called, and while the ranchers lost some cattle every winter to the elements, it was cost-effective to let them survive on the free grass. But Twin Peaks' cattle could be sold in the spring and the fall because they were in good flesh. Kade predicted there would come one of those brutal winters that the plains could have. Some winter, the free-range cattle wouldn't survive so easily. Kade had ridden those plains and saw those winters during his trapping days. He wanted no part of that. He told his son-in-law, Jackson, that putting up hay for the cattle may be expensive and labor intensive, but it was worth it. So far, Jackson was still running his cattle on free range. But Jackson had a hay crew put up hay for his horses, and he did bring a small package of cows and calves home each fall. Jackson made that one small concession to his father-in-law.

"You're late this morning," Thomas called out. "We were beginning to worry."

Kade saw the rest of the crew grin. He was the oldest one there. They joshed him a lot about that. Matthew was almost as old as Kade, but he was the farmer. He didn't come to help with the cattle. Instead, Matthew had his own chores to do; taking care of pigs and milk cows. Noah was Matthew's right-hand boy and good help. Will, Sarah's eldest son, was also absent. He had his new cabin across the river nestled against the foothills. He kept the sheep in a fenced meadow behind his home. He had his own haystacks for the sheep, and he would be busy forking over hay to them. And finally, Jeremiah would be down at his lumber mill, grinding out boards from logs. The community was going to build a schoolhouse in the spring. There were going to be a lot of children soon who were school age. The community would have a schoolhouse for the children that would double as a big enough building where everyone from the ranch could congregate when necessary. Jeremiah would have boards ready when it was time to build in the spring after the snow melted.

"Boys, I slept good last night," Kade grinned back. "Damn, James about gave me a heart attack yesterday with that sorrel bastard he was riding. I was plumb wore out."

There were chuckles at that. James had already reported to Jake about the horse. They finished the first load, and Hawk, Sam, and Lathe took it out.

"You want to go with me again this afternoon?" James called to Kade. "I think I should get old sorrely out again right away before he forgets what he learned yesterday."

Kade looked at the young man and grinned. "Only if you stay away from the tree line. I don't fancy trying to keep up through them damn trees again."

They finished the second wagon. Kade drove the team, and James and Thomas forked the hay out. He knew they afforded him the somewhat easier job of driving the team, and he took it. He could feel the creak in his bones these days, especially when it was bitterly cold. He nodded at Jake, Army, and Luke as he drove by, the younger men already moving to the stack by the calves to pitch hay over the fence. The sun was getting high in the sky by the time the feeding was finished.

❧

A week rolled by, and then another. Sarah's door remained open each night, and Kade found himself going there after coming inside at night. He didn't oversleep again, but he slept well each night. After two weeks, Sarah rolled over to him after he crawled in beside her.

"Maybe tomorrow morning before you leave, we should bring your trunk in here?" she asked tentatively. "Doesn't seem to make much sense for you to keep walking back and forth from James' room to here each night. Your clothes will be here in the morning when the cabin is cold."

And that is what they did. Sarah also took Sabra's picture off the wall and brought it into her room. "Hang this where we can both see it," she said. "I like to see her too. Maybe I can get Mary to draw a picture of Jim from the photograph I have from Beth and Thomas' wedding. I'd like that."

They were comfortable together, Kade knew. Their deceased spouses didn't threaten them. They often enjoyed lying in bed, remembering the special times each had shared before Sabra and Jim left them. There was no jealousy. They were just two people who understood each other's pain and helped to drive it away.

James came in quietly. It was nearly midnight, but he knew the house well, and he made his way in the dark to his old room. He tapped on the door. "Kade, wake up," he called softly. There was no answer. He tried the door, and it swung open as he expected. "Kade, wake up," he spoke again. There was still no answer. He reached down to shake Kade, knowing where the bed was despite the night's gloom. But there was no body in the bed. There were two beds in the room, he went to the second, but no one was there. His eyes had adjusted to the gloom enough to see that the room was cleared out. The trunk of Kade's that James had carried to Sarah's cabin several months ago was gone too. What the hell? This was a development he hadn't anticipated.

James went to his mother's room. "Ma, where's Kade gone? I need to find him," he called out softly. He didn't want to alarm her after all. He saw dim candlelight as the door was pulled open. Kade stood before him with only his trousers on.

"Kade?" James inquired, surprised. Then he glimpsed his mother behind Kade, candle in her hand. "What the hell?" he said surprised.

Sarah came forward quickly. "James," she spoke firmly, "what is it you wanted that you had to wake us up in the middle of the night?"

James looked between them, confused. He hadn't expected this. "Thomas and Jake sent me for you," he said, looking at Kade. "There were wolves in with the colts. They want you to come. We may have to shoot some of the colts. They want you to come," he was almost stammering, repeating himself.

"Go fetch my horse from the corral," Kade ordered, turning for more clothes. "I'll be right out."

James stood, looking between his mother and Kade.

"James, go," his mother ordered, and James fled.

Kade looked at Sarah as James banged out the door. "Maybe we shouldn't have put off talking to the kids?" he said mildly. Sarah just nodded.

James had Kade's horse gathered and outside the corral as Kade came carrying his saddle. Kade threw on the blanket and heaved the saddle up. James stood still, watching, wanting to speak, and not knowing what to say.

"What the hell were you doing in my Ma's bedroom, Kade?" James finally exploded.

Kade had to smile at that. "You are a married man, James. Don't think I have to explain what goes on between a man an' woman."

It was probably the wrong thing to say; the question just struck Kade funny. But Kade's response only fueled James' indignation.

"Are you fucking my mother?" he finally exclaimed, anger in his tone.

Kade stiffened, losing his smile; he turned slowly to face the young man. "I'd be very careful in how you choose your words when you are speaking of your mother an' me, James," Kade said, his voice low and deadly.

James stepped back. He could see the anger in Kade. It startled him. Kade leveled a look at James and then turned and finished tightening the girth. He bridled the horse and swung on, not looking back at the young man. Kade kicked the horse into a lope. He was a quarter of a mile from the house when the track grew icy, and he slowed his horse to a trot. He could hear James behind him, catching up. When James had pulled up beside him, Kade turned to him in the darkness.

"So, you have an objection to my being with your ma?" he asked.

The question surprised James. He was full of righteous anger at seeing Kade in his mother's bedroom, but put like this, it gave him pause. He had to think about that.

"Well, no, reckon I don't have an objection, but it jest took me by surprise, is all," he stammered.

"Well, I reckon it took us by surprise too," Kade agreed. He looked over at James. "I won't hurt your ma, you know. We are both alone these days. It jest sort of happened, an' we feel comfortable with each other."

"Well, it would have been nice to know," James said grudgingly. "I was some surprised, you know."

"That probably was our fault," Kade conceded. "We've talked about telling you kids, but we jest kept putting it off," Kade paused. They were nearing the pasture where the colts were kept. "Would you give us a couple days, keep this to yourself?" he asked. "Your ma an' I will tell the rest. They should hear it from us." In the darkness, James nodded his head.

The scene that met Kade and James was bloody with dead and dying colts. These were this year's crop, both colts and fillies, weaned in the fall from their dams. They were being held in a small pasture between Jake and Lathe's cabins. Both Jake and Lathe had heard the ruckus and had gone to the colt's aid, but it had been too late for some of the colts. They had been able to shoot two wolves, driving the rest away, but the damage was done. Jake and Thomas had already put two of the colts down, knowing the young animals had sustained deeper wounds than the poor things could recover from. The men had four more colts haltered and planned to move them to the barn by Thomas' for safety and care. There were two other colts that Jake wanted Kade to decide about. They were good colts and he hated to lose them, but was the cost of their recovery, if they even could recover, too hard on the young animals themselves?

Kade's gaze hardened when he saw the colts. "Damn," he muttered, "damn, damn, damn." He inspected the two colts in question, holding a lantern above the colts. "This one may make it," he said gravely, "but you will have to carry him in. This other one you better put out of its misery. It will be more humane to kill him than try to save him."

Kade turned away and went to the colts that Hawk held. These colts were waiting to be led to the safety of the barn. A shot rang out loud, and despite expecting it, Kade jumped a little. He bent and looked at the wounds of the trembling animals. Straightening, he turned to Jake.

"Take Sam an' Hawk an' track the pack," he said, knowing the three men were the best hunters on the ranch. "Good chance the pack will be back, either here or to the sheep or calves. We can't put out sentries at night all over the ranch. Break up the pack. Either get them all or enough that they look for new hunting grounds."

Jake nodded, then turned to Hawk. "We'll get these colts in. You go home and get some rest. I'll get Sam and meet you here at dawn," he said. "We'll head out at first light."

Hawk's black eyes glittered in the moonlight, and he nodded back. A winter hunt was much better than loading hay wagons.

It was almost dawn before Thomas, Kade, and James got the colts to the barn, doctored, and settled in a pen. Kade had sent Jake off to get some sleep as soon as they had the five colts in the barn.

"I'll catch a bite of breakfast an' meet you at the haystacks," Kade told Thomas. "We'll be three men short, so it could be a long day." Kade looked over at James as Thomas headed to his cabin. "Don't think I'll ride this afternoon either," he said quietly to James. "Your ma an' I will probably be out visitin', but I'd jest as soon talk to Thomas an' Jake together, an' Jake might not be back for a bit. Give us a couple days."

The night was short for Jake and Hawk, but they were up and bright-eyed at dawn. Jake rode over to Sam's and filled him in on the night's events. By the time Jake was finished with the story, Sam was outfitted and ready for the hunt. They were saddled up and headed for Hawk's just as the mountain peaks could be seen outlined against a dusky sky.

At first, they could follow the wolves' tracks easily with the horses, but as the footprints led them higher into the mountains, they eventually had to leave the horses. Strapping on snowshoes, they kept doggedly on. The three men spread out, following the tracks as they veered one way or another, but always up, up, up into the high country. They had the wind on their side, blowing into their faces. The wolves would not catch their scent.

They had a plan. When there was evidence that the wolves were not too far ahead of them, Hawk, who was excellent with moose calls, would call for the wolves. If the wolves could hear the calls, they would be back to investigate. The animals must be getting hungry by now since they had been scared off of their kills the night before. Jake was banking on the wolves looking for a moose calf or cow for a quick meal. From the tracks on the ground, they felt they were following maybe eight to ten wolves. Jake wanted to get them all if possible. He didn't want a pack of wolves returning to the ranch.

It was just past noon when Sam motioned the others to join him. Pointing to the ground, they saw the coiled, ropey scat that indicated a wolf had passed by. It was still steaming in the winter cold, dark, and slightly dampish looking.

"They haven't been long by here," Sam drawled. "This scat is still dark. It gets lighter as it dries."

Jake looked around the terrain. They were coming out on a long narrow mountain meadow.

"Reckon we can fan out here. There's plenty of trees and rocks to conceal us. If they can hear Hawk," Jake said, looking around, "they might come back. They should be hungry."

Hawk and Sam nodded, looking around for the best hiding places. Hawk would stay in the middle, but Jake and Sam would move in opposite directions and find a spot to hide. Here they would sit and wait.

"They probably will come down through the trees, but Hawk, if you go back some, they may jest leave the protection of the trees before they get this far," Sam mentioned. "We'd want to see them before they came across our tracks and smelled us. Wolves can be pretty damn smart."

Hawk nodded and moved back into the trees. Soon he was lost to sight. Sam and Jake both moved off to find hiding places. They had just gotten concealed when they heard the long, lonely sound of a cow moose. The sound dwindled off, and the mountains were silent but for the rustling of leaves above them. After a bit, another lonesome plaintive call came from behind them. They waited. The best hunters were patient; Hawk, Sam, and Jake were patient.

Jake wasn't sure how long they waited, but he began feeling the cold seep into his bones from the inactivity. They would have to move soon if they had no results. It was then that he caught a glimpse of a shadow, coming along the edge of the meadow, still within the trees. The wolves were coming back on the side of the meadow nearer to Sam.

Another lonesome sound came from below them, softer now as if the moose were farther away. As the sound drifted away on the wind, a lead wolf broke from the trees. Jake was ready, but held his fire. He wanted more than the lead wolf. They had time to wait. The wolf came out fast, then slowed, circling. Farther up the slope, two wolves emerged, trotting easily out on the snow-packed meadow. Jake could see more shadows in the trees. The lead wolf was nearly on Sam when Jake opened fire. There were seven wolves in the open by then, but near the edge of the trees.

Methodically, the men sighted on the animals. Jake was aware that a third rifle also spoke so he knew that Hawk might have been farther downwind calling to the wolves, but he wasn't so far that he wasn't aware when the wolves emerged. Hawk didn't want to miss the hunt. When the guns went silent, six of the wolves lay dead. Another trailed a thick stream of blood. Jake was pretty sure the animal would not live to hunt again.

"Hawk, you want to trail that one and put an end to it?" Jake asked. "Sam and I will skin these. If it looks like the wolf will travel a long way, then leave it. I don't want to lose a man hunting a wounded wolf after dark. But I don't think this wolf will get that far. I just don't like any animal to suffer if I can help it."

Hawk didn't speak, just moved off and disappeared into the woods. Jake looked around at the dead wolves. "They were just being wolves," he muttered to Sam, "but they damn sure didn't have to be doing their hunting on our stock." Then Jake pulled his knife and went to skinning.

Hawk returned shortly after Sam and Jake had finished skinning the wolves. He was dragging a seventh pelt.

"Did you see any sign that there were more?" Jake asked.

"There were many tracks," the young Ute replied, "but I think they were tracks from before they turned back toward us. I don't think there were more."

"Let's get back then," Sam said. "It's gonna be cold soon when the sun goes down. Be nice to make it to the horses before dark, at least." Jake and Hawk nodded. They had used up a good portion of daylight getting to the wolves. It would be late getting back, and mountain cold was not something to fool with in the winter.

Kade was haggard by nightfall. He had driven Sarah, bundled up in a buffalo robe in their little cutter, to talk to Will, Martha, and Bonnie. The girls were surprised by the change in Kade and Sarah's relationship, but were pleased. Surprisingly, Will, the unmarried son, was not surprised. He grinned and told Sarah he hoped his moving out might bring about this change. Apparently, he was the only one who thought of that.

Because the day was late by the time they left Bonnie's, they had asked the girls not to mention the news to anyone for a day. Jake would not be back until late that night, if at all, and Kade wanted to talk to both boys together. While he would talk to the boys, Sarah could speak with Beth. They could leave that until the next day.

The next afternoon, Kade brought Sarah to visit Beth and caught both of his boys at the corral. Between feeding and the short days, they didn't ride as long these winter days, but most afternoons found them doing something with the horses. On this day, Hawk had gone home early to get some much-needed rest, and James had mentioned during feeding that he needed to split some wood. It was a good day to talk to Jake and Thomas alone. Jake was dragging from two nights with little sleep, so Kade got right to the point.

"Boys," he started, leaning up against the corral fence, "I need to visit with you a minute."

Thomas was doctoring one of the injured colts, and Jake was holding the little animal for him. They both looked up expectantly.

"Well, I jest wanted you to know that I'm living with Sarah now," Kade remarked, trying to sound nonchalant.

Thomas gave Jake a sideways glance before replying. "Pa," he started tentatively, "we know that. You been there for nigh onto four months. You feeling alright?"

Kade grinned suddenly. "I don't mean jest living in her house, Tom. I mean, I am living with *her*," Kade emphasized the word her.

Both men just stared. Jake began to grin as realization hit him, but before he could say anything, Thomas exploded.

"You mean . . ." he hesitated, drawing breath, "like *with* her . . . like a *wife* . . . in her *bed*?" Thomas' voice rose as he struggled to find words.

Kade sobered up, his smile leaving him. "That is exactly what I mean," his voice took on a hard note.

"Well, shit, Pa, Ma's not hardly cold in her grave!" Thomas spat out.

"Your ma has been gone fifteen months, one week, an' three days. You want me to include the hours? I am aware of jest how long she's been gone," Kade's voice was cold.

"Well, hell, Sarah is my mother-in-law! How do you think Beth is gonna feel about this?"

"I'm hoping she'll be an adult an' be glad her mother isn't alone anymore," Kade turned on his heel, and without another word, he headed toward the cutter sitting in front of Thomas and Beth's cabin. He had to get away before he said something he'd regret to Thomas.

As Kade walked away, Jake leveled an eye on Thomas. "You know, brother, you can be an ass sometimes."

Thomas looked surprised. "Shit Jake, our father is fu . . ."

"Don't go there, Thomas," Jake interrupted him. "Don't even think about saying that. Get your head out of your ass and think before you speak."

Jake left the corral and followed his father, catching up with him waiting for Sarah beside the cutter. "Pa,"

Jake said softly, extending his hand, "I think congratulations are in order. I'm happy for you."

Kade looked solemnly at his eldest. "Once again, the son I have with no blood ties understands me more than my blood son," he took the proffered hand. "Thank you."

"Pa, Thomas doesn't always think," Jake assured his father. "Give him time. He doesn't like change. He'll come around."

Unlike Thomas, Beth had no reservations about the relationship change between Kade and Sarah. All of Sarah's children welcomed Kade as their mother's partner. A few of them were surprised, but they all were aware of how lonely Sarah was.

The next order of business for Kade was to visit Molly. It wouldn't do for someone from Twin Peaks to meet up with a rider from the Anchor J and spill the news. So, the following day, Kade bundled up, caught his best saddle horse and headed off toward Molly and Jackson's ranch at first light. It was a half day of travel to get to the Anchor J, but it took longer with snow on the ground. Still there was several hours of daylight left when Kade rode into the ranch headquarters.

Molly was elated to see Kade. While Kade played with his little grandson, Molly bustled around the kitchen preparing a meal. Jackson came in shortly after Kade arrived, and they sat and visited while Molly worked.

"When we were in Cheyenne," Jackson began, "I met with an investor my father sent over from England. He had a magazine with him that was very interesting and spurred this man to contact me. It was a *Harper's Magazine* from November 1879, and the article was about the cattle industry in Colorado. My father mentioned I was in the cattle business in Wyoming, and that is how this investor happened to come to meet with me. I think you should read the article." Jackson went to a bookshelf, rummaged around, came up with a magazine, and handed it to Kade.

"I'll read it later. Tell me about it," Kade said.

"It's about a cattle ranch in southern Colorado that, in theory, makes thousands of dollars in a three-year time span," Jackson started. "With the free range, the price of the cattle we can get from Texas, and the demand for beef in the east, the profits are huge. It is based on a ranch size of four thousand cattle. My new investor is backing me for two thousand more cows in the spring. That will bring my herd up to over five thousand head."

Kade nodded his head thoughtfully, but didn't comment.

"Kade, you need to jump on this too," Jackson said seriously. "Do you even have a thousand cows?"

"Well, I imagine we are getting close to eight hundred if you count everything," Kade agreed, "but it takes a lot of manpower to put up enough winter feed for that many head. I don't think we want to build up much more."

"Well, that is just the thing," Jackson replied, warming to his subject. "You are missing out on all the free range you could take advantage of on the plains. I know you have free range in the mountains in the summer, but instead of going into the high country, you could turn the bulk of your cattle out on the prairie year around and cut down on your labor costs."

"We've discussed this before," Kade said quietly. "You know my thoughts on that. Those plains can be dangerous when you least expect it. When you hit a bad winter, you could lose it all. And I don't like to think about those cattle out there simply starving or freezing to death. It will happen one of these winters. Mark my words."

"I think you are missing out on a big opportunity here. Maybe you want to see if Thomas or Jake want to build up," Jackson continued. "I can find investors if they want to expand. And look at the prices of cattle! They were over $5.00 a hundredweight last spring and are still going up. There is a lot of excitement out there. There are a lot of men who want to invest in cattle right now."

"My sons can make up their own minds," Kade said. "I will tell them what you are saying. But as for me, I don't owe a penny on what I have. Our ranch has money in the bank. I'm too old to try to start an empire, even if that is what I wanted."

After supper, Jackson went to the bunkhouse to discuss the next day's activities with his crew. Kade helped Molly clear the table. The baby was put to bed, and the house was quiet as they worked. Kade knew what he had been putting off couldn't wait any longer. But it was one thing to discuss this subject with his sons and quite another to discuss it with his daughter.

"Molly," he began, "I need to discuss something with you." Kade found he was nervous. Maybe the reaction he had gotten from Thomas bothered him more than he knew.

"I knew you had some reason for visiting other than just playing with little Jack," Molly smiled at her father.

"Let's sit for a minute," Kade said, leading the way to the parlor. When they were seated, he started again. "Daughter, you need to know that I am living with Sarah now."

Molly nodded, waiting expectantly for more. She smiled at him to go on.

Kade realized that, like when he told the boys, he hadn't gotten his meaning across well. "I'm living with Sarah like I," he hesitated, searching for words he could say to Molly. "Like I did with your ma," he finished lamely.

Molly smiled and nodded, then suddenly took in a quick deep breath. "You mean . . . oooh," she drew the "oh" out long.

"Yes," Kade agreed, "I mean that."

"Oh," Molly repeated, "And how did Jake and Thomas take that?"

"Jake was fine with it, but I think it is safe to say that Thomas and I are not speaking right now."

Molly stared for a minute and then began to laugh. "I could have told you that would be the reaction of both. Give Thomas time, Pa. He will come around. He can be such a prig at times." Then she rose and going to her father, she knelt and gave him a big hug. "I'm glad for you, Pa. And I am glad for Sarah. You both deserve to be happy."

"You don't mind?"

"Pa, I know how much you loved Ma," Molly said sincerely. "And I know you still love her. You will always love her. I bet Sarah feels the same way about Jim. But Pa, you aren't even sixty yet, and Sarah is many years younger. Neither one of you wants to live alone for years and years. You will be good for each other."

"Where did I get such a smart daughter?" Kade asked fondly.

"Well, I got it from you and Ma with some help from my big brother, Jake," Molly laughed. "Thomas, not so much!" She got serious again. "Pa, I am sure whatever Thomas said to you hurt, but he will change his mind. He just has a hard time."

"I cain't see where it should matter to him," Kade began.

"Oh, Pa, think about it. Thomas knows Ma's dead. We all do. But he doesn't want more change. This is one more thing that he must get used to. Thomas is just a bit slower than Jake and me to understand," Molly smiled at her father. "I'm betting he'll sing a different tune by the time you get home."

Four days later, Kade got home late in the afternoon. He was surprised at how good it felt to walk into Sarah's cabin and feel her arms around him. He had enjoyed being with Molly and playing with little Jack, but home is always the best place to be.

Kade walked over to the haystacks the next morning to join the feeding crew. He took out a loaded wagon with Lathe and James. After a noon meal, he rode up to the horse corral. There was enough daylight left to ride a horse or two before supper. He saw Jake sorting off some colts. Thomas, Lathe, and James were already saddling up.

"Jake," Kade called, "sort me off what you want me to ride." Kade made it a point to ignore Thomas. He didn't want to come back to an argument.

Jake nodded and looked over the horses left in the corral. Kade watched him work through the horses, deciding on one and roping it. When the rope settled over the horse's head, it stopped and turned to face Jake.

"Pa," Kade was startled. Thomas had come up from the side. "If you were willing, Beth thought you would like to come for dinner on Sunday," Thomas said.

Kade looked at Thomas, trying to decide if there was any animosity in his son. "I reckon if Sarah is agreeable, we could do that," he answered cautiously.

"Oh, I spoke to Sarah while you were gone," Thomas said. "She is willing if you are."

"Well, I reckon Sunday it is then," Kade responded.

Thomas nodded, then turning, he walked away.

Kade watched Thomas as he returned to his horse. There was no apology, no explanation. But as Jake and Molly both said, Kade needed to give Thomas time. It felt good to have this son back again.

CHAPTER 12

New Worries - 1882

K ade jumped down off the hay wagon and surveyed the meadows. It was March, and the snow
was patchy at this time of year, much of it melting in the open areas. More snow could still come, but
spring was trying to arrive in the mountains. Here and
there Kade saw some green shoots poking up, trying to
get a head start on summer.

The hay wagons weren't loaded so heavily now. The
feeding was finished much earlier these days. Yesterday, Sam, Luke, and Thomas had headed towards a
distant mining town with fifty head of steers. Twin
Peaks supplied the miners with cattle, necessitating
a trip every other month to the mining camp when
the weather permitted. In another month, they would
take several hundred head to Laramie to sell. The cows
would be driven to the high country after they calved,
and the rest of the steers would be driven miles west
along the river to graze for the summer. The ranch
would buzz with activity until summer was in full
swing, and then the haying would start.

Kade liked this time of year. There was a promise
in these early spring days of new life. They had gotten through the winter, and everyone was ready to
get outside and away from the four walls of their cabins. The horse crew had more time for riding now too.

Kade preferred riding horses to forking hay to cattle. He looked forward to summer when winter chores were a distant memory.

Kade noticed Emmett and Alice on old Brownie leaving Sarah's. He waved them over.

"You two are heading home early," he smiled at them. "No lessons today?" Sarah had always been the teacher of the community, teaching all the children reading, writing, and numbers. With the big crop of children coming to school age now, they had decided to build a schoolhouse this summer and hire a teacher if they could. But until then, Sarah was helping Emmett and Alice when they came for milk and eggs.

"Miss Sarah ain't done any lessons with us all week," Alice chimed.

"She been feelin' poorly," Emmett added.

Kade looked toward the cabin. This was the first he heard of Sarah not feeling well. He certainly hadn't noticed anything in the evenings. "All week, you say?" he inquired again.

"Yes, sir," Emmett said. "Miss Sarah sends us to Mr. Matthew for the milk and eggs."

Kade nodded gravely at the two children. "Well then," he said, "you better get on your way an' make your deliveries."

As the children rode away, Kade headed to the cabin. Sarah had seemed alright when he left this morning. He wondered if the children had the story wrong. But as Kade walked into the cabin, he immediately knew the children were correct. He found Sarah sitting in a chair, vomiting into a bucket.

"Sarah, good God, what is wrong?" Kade moved quickly to her side.

She waved him away. "Get me a drink, please," she croaked.

Kade went to the pitcher and poured her a cup. When she had wiped her face and drank from the cup, Sarah stood up and faced him.

"What is wrong?" Kade asked again. He could see that Sarah was near tears.

"Oh, Kade," her voice trembled, "I think I am pregnant."

Kade just stood rooted to the ground, staring at her, letting the words sink into his mind. He had trouble wrapping his mind around the consequences of her words. Sarah being pregnant was not something he had anticipated at their age.

Taking his reaction as an indication that he was upset by the news, Sarah wailed, "Oh, Kade, I'm so sorry! I don't know how this happened!"

Sarah's words shook Kade out of his trance.

"Well, darling," he drawled, her words struck him funny, "if you truly don't know, then we could go into the bedroom there," he nodded towards their room, "and I could give you a demonstration."

Sarah stiffened, then stamped a foot, "Oh, Kade, I know that!" she emphasized each word. "But I don't know how I could get pregnant. I'm fifty years old! I'm too old to get pregnant!" She stood, wringing the towel between her hands and the tears flowed down her cheeks. "Oh, God, I have grandchildren, for goodness sakes!"

Kade saw she was losing control and he went to her, pulling her into an embrace. "Hey there," he soothed, stroking her hair, "it's alright. Children are a gift. We'll figure this out."

Sarah sobbed then. Putting her face into his chest, he felt her shoulders convulse. He patted her awkwardly until, finally, she quieted.

"I don't know what to do," Sarah barely whispered. "I'm sick every morning now. It starts just after breakfast . . . after you leave the cabin."

"Well, the first thing is you are going back to bed an' lie down," Kade ordered. "Then there will be no feeding the crews for you anymore. The younger women can take over the noon meals. I can cook supper. I have fended for myself before, you know." Kade thought a minute and then went on, "No more school. Maybe Martha can help Emmett an' Alice for an hour each day when they ride by with their deliveries. When we get a schoolteacher next year, they will get more learnin' then. For now, you have to rest."

"I used to get sick every morning when I had all my babies, but it always went away," Sarah murmured. "But this is much worse than before. I suppose it is because I am old."

"Are you sure you are pregnant?" Kade asked.

"Well, no, not positive, but I think I am. It's hard to tell now. I mean, I am not regular anymore so it's hard to tell," Sarah spoke hesitantly, "but I never completely quit having . . ." This women's subject was not something she spoke of to a man, even one who shared her bed.

"Well, let's jest give this a bit of time," Kade soothed. "You rest, an' we will just see what happens next."

"Oh, God, Kade," Sarah wailed again, her face against his chest. "We will have to talk to the kids again, won't we?"

"Let's jest give this some time and then we will see," Kade repeated, but the same thought had gone through his mind as well.

Sarah wasn't wrong. She was pregnant. It wasn't but another week, and Kade could feel the slight bump of a baby rising from Sarah's belly. The morning sickness lessened some, but never really left. Sarah found herself losing her breakfast so many times she quit eating breakfast. Lunch was not much better, and instead of gaining weight with this baby, she was getting haggard and thin. Sarah spent much of the day in bed, rising and trying to sit in a chair to sew or knit when she got bored. But often the sickness would return, and she headed back to the bedroom.

As the weeks passed, Kade began to worry. They had passed off Sarah's illness to the kids as just being overly tired coming out of winter. Kade made it clear to them that it was time the younger women stepped up and took over many of Sarah's responsibilities. Sarah's daughters; Martha, Beth, and Bonnie, were more than willing to take over feeding the work crews at midday, and Martha took over tutoring Alice and Emmett when the children rode by each day. Because Kade was loathe to leave Sarah for several days, he did not ride that spring to visit Molly. He just sent a message with someone from the ranch who was riding that way that he would come and visit soon.

By April, Kade decided that maybe it was time to get an expert opinion of Sarah's condition. It was a hard letter he wrote to his brother Joe, explaining this news.

Kade asked Joe to seek out a doctor and get an opinion about pregnancies in older women such as Sarah.

Kade rode the letter over to Dixon the next day. He had written Joe that he would check the mail in two weeks. He knew his brother was always willing to help, but he wanted to make sure Joe understood that time was of the essence, or at least Kade thought it was. Kade was concerned about Sarah's deteriorating condition.

Two weeks later, Joe's reply was waiting for Kade when he returned to the post office. Joe had gone to the doctor who had birthed Katie's babies. The old man also had a younger doctor with him in his practice. Neither doctor had ever treated a pregnancy in a woman of fifty. They had both read of it happening, but it was very rare. Considering Sarah's condition and how this pregnancy was affecting her, they both suggested that Kade bring his wife to St. Louis, where she would have the medical attention she might need. Kade agreed. Sarah needed to keep her strength up, and it wasn't happening here on the ranch.

It was dusk when Kade got home with his letter. He found Sarah rocking gently in front of the fire, trying to knit.

"How are you doing today?" Kade asked as he entered. Sarah had been in bed this morning when he had left the cabin.

"Maybe better," she smiled at Kade wanly. "I haven't thrown anything up since early afternoon."

"Have you eaten anything?"

"I just had some bread and jam," Sarah replied. "I'm hoping they stay down."

"I wrote to Joe, got an answer today," Kade handed the letter to Sarah. "Wanted him to get an opinion from a doctor in St. Louis. This is his reply." Kade waited to let Sarah read the letter.

"Oh, Kade," Sarah said, looking up from the letter after reading it, "I hate to think of going to the city."

Kade pulled up a chair next to Sarah and sat down. "I do too, but I hate more to lose you, and there is that possibility. This baby is not setting too well with you."

Sarah's eyes filled with tears. "You really think it's that serious?"

"Hell, hon, I don't know what to think," Kade reached over and caressed her cheek. "Ain't like I planned this in my old age. But we got to be smart here. I think we should go to St. Louis an' see a doctor. Joe an' Katie want us to stay with them. We can catch the train at Laramie."

"I suppose that is the best," Sarah answered slowly. "But darn, now we have to talk to the kids all over again. We have put it off too long as it is." She smiled up at Kade tentatively. "I didn't think this through very well last fall, did I, when I said I was lonely?"

Kade grinned at her. "Reckon, I wasn't thinking much then either," he said softly. "But I don't regret it."

The kids, even Thomas, took the news of Sarah's pregnancy well. They were surprised, yes, but also supportive. The same could be said for the rest of the community. No one had heard of a woman Sarah's age having a child, but Mattie remembered that when she was a child, a neighbor woman had sixteen children, and the woman was well into her upper forties when she had her last one. Sarah was only a couple of years older than that. Obviously, it could happen. What concerned them most was Sarah's health. She was not feeling well most days and was tired every day. They all agreed with Kade that Sarah should go to the city and see a doctor.

Kade and Sarah left within the week. It was early May now, and the weather was mild. Kade outfitted the light wagon with a bed for Sarah, and extra seats. There was just room for a trunk full of clothes and supplies they would need for the trip to Laramie. James and Emmett drove them to Laramie to bring the wagon back. Thomas had offered, but James was Sarah's son, and he wanted to be the one to travel with them. Will, James' older brother, was off looking at more sheep to buy, so he wasn't even home. There was no telling when Will would be back. So, James would take Emmett along for company on the drive home.

The first day was only a half day of travel as they stopped at Molly and Jackson's. As they pulled in, a surprised Molly came to meet them. She instantly recognized that Sarah was not well. Sarah was pale with tired lines on her face, and as Sarah let Kade help her from the wagon, Molly saw her lean heavily on her father. Molly raised questioning eyes to her father but didn't ask.

"Molly, girl," Kade began gently, "Sarah is goin' to have a baby. It's not goin' real well for her, so we are headin' to St. Louis to see a doctor."

"Oh," Molly couldn't think of anything else to say. But she could see the weariness of her stepmother, so she went to her side and took her arm. "Then we had better get you into the house and sit down. Or would you rather lie down?" Gratefully, Sarah went with Molly into the house.

The evening at Molly's was pleasant. Sarah was able to eat a little and then went to the spare room early. Kade sat up with Molly and Jackson, smoking before the fire.

"We didn't much plan fer this," he commented to his daughter. "It's been a bit of a shock. I never thought I'd have a child younger than my grandchildren. An' I don't want to lose Sarah because of this either."

"Pa, you just take care of Sarah," Molly responded. "That is all that matters. The rest isn't important at all." Molly thought a minute, then asked, "How did Thomas take it?"

Kade grinned at Molly. "Thomas is good. I think he regrets his outburst when we first told him we were living together. He never really apologized, but he's been considerate ever since. That's acceptable."

"Oh, Pa, Thomas is a good man, a great brother," Molly replied, smiling, "but he does hate change. I'm glad he came around."

"So, with you gone, will Jake still go to the high mountains?" Molly asked, changing the subject.

"I reckon," Kade answered. "Thomas and Matthew can handle everything that needs to be done at home. They have Will, James, Army, an' Luke there to help. Jake, Lathe, and Hawk will take their families an' head up when the snows up in the high country start to melt. I reckon they will head that way later this month sometime."

"Do you think any of them will ever just stay up there at Jacob's cabin all year?" Molly wanted to know.

Kade thought about that before answering. "I could never say for sure, but I doubt it. That meadow up at Jacob's cabin is too small for a big operation, an' it is plugged up with snow all winter," Kade took a puff on his pipe before going on. "But it is a great place to take our young horses. The trip alone toughens them up an' riding on those mountainsides in that high altitude is good for them. I think for Jake an' Hawk especially, the trip there an' back satisfies them. I think those two will always want to ramble some. Lathe takes after Jake too. He must be a throwback to old Jacob." Kade smiled, remembering the old mountain man he knew so long ago.

"Well, what about Bonnie? You think she will always want to travel there in the summer?" Molly asked. "I think Anna and Kasa are suited for the summers there. Being raised with the Utes and Pawnee has pretty much trained them for a nomadic life, but this is not what I expected Bonnie would like?"

"I've had my concerns about that too, an' so has Sarah, but I reckon only time will tell," Kade said thoughtfully. "I'll give Bonnie credit, though. She tries to learn from Kasa an' Anna many of the ways of the Indians. She tries to be the wife Hawk wants. Hawk tries too. But it is hard for both Hawk and Bonnie. They come from such different ways. So, we'll just have to wait an' see."

It was late when Kade rose for bed. He and Jackson sat late into the night and talked of the cattle business until they bored Molly. Promising to have an early breakfast ready before Kade left in the morning, Molly went off to bed herself. She had enjoyed this evening with her father. Although worried about Sarah, Kade had been relaxed and happier than Molly had seen him in a long time. Molly desperately hoped that Kade would still have Sarah with him when he eventually returned from the city.

The rest of the trip was uneventful. Kade and James took turns driving, and for most of each day, Sarah dozed on the mattress in the wagon bed. They camped at a creek in the late afternoon, knowing they could reach Laramie by afternoon of the next day. Sarah felt good enough to sit up with her son and Kade by the fire and eat a little supper before going off to her blankets. That was a good sign.

When they reached Laramie the next afternoon, Kade got Sarah settled in the hotel and headed for the train station. They would have to lay over a day to wait for the next train. That suited Kade. He had plans. Over breakfast the following morning, he brought up what was on his mind.

"Reckon, since we have a day here to waste, might be time I make an honest woman of you," he commented nonchalantly, glancing between James and Sarah. "What do you say to goin' to find that preacher who married Thomas an' Beth an' we make this permanent?"

"I thought this was pretty permanent," Sarah smiled, "but I like the sound of going before a preacher."

With James and Emmett standing with them, Kade married Sarah that afternoon. "Now, when I say this is my wife," Kade teased Sarah, "I won't be lying."

The four of them had a light meal at the hotel restaurant before Sarah mentioned that she needed to go to the room and lie down.

"Let me take Ma up," James said to Kade.

When James got Sarah to the room, he hesitated before leaving her. "Ma, I got something I want you to know before you leave," he said earnestly. "It's a secret still until we know for sure, but I want you to know now before you leave."

Sarah could see the suppressed excitement in her son. She waited, having a feeling she knew the news already.

"We think," James started, then corrected, "Mary thinks she is going to have a baby." James couldn't hide his smile.

"Oh, James, I hope so!" Sarah exclaimed. "Write us and let us know. How does Mary feel?"

"Like you, she is a little sick each morning but not bad. She's pretty sure she is . . ." James' voice trailed off. "She's a little scared. She's afraid the baby might be, well, like Gideon. You know her first husband got pretty ugly after Gideon was born," James finished.

"And what do you think?"

"Oh, Ma," James said happily, "I keep telling her it makes no difference to me. I think she believes me, but then the doubt comes again, and she gets scared. I'm just about busting and want to tell everyone, but she says wait. I had to tell you though. I wanted you to know before you left."

Sarah smiled fondly at her youngest. She reached up and pushed back a wayward lock of hair that had fallen over James eyes. She had done that since he was a little boy. Now he was a man with a ready-made family and his firstborn soon to come.

"How was I so lucky to have such a wonderful son?" she asked him fondly. "You are a good man and already a good father. Of course, you will love this child, no matter what color. And I will love it too. You tell Mary that. I will come back and love your child. No matter what."

⬩❦⬩

Emmett escorted Sarah onto the train while James and Kade carried the trunk between them. It was the first time any of them had been on a train. Emmett was all eyes, noticing the tufted seats with velvet covers.

"Oh, my," Sarah murmured to Kade when they found their berths, "I didn't think the accommodations would be this nice."

"This is first class, Mrs. Welles," Kade smiled. "Only the best. It's one of those Pullman cars. These seats fold together to make a bed you can sleep on, and there is a shelf above which folds down for me to sleep on. We can pull the curtain for privacy."

"Goodness, this must cost a lot," Sarah said doubtfully.

"Sarah," Kade said patiently, "you have done the ranch bookwork since you and Jim moved to the ranch. You know we have the money."

"I guess," Sarah said cautiously. "But I hate to think of all that is getting spent on me right now."

"We are both riding on this train," Kade answered firmly, "an' I intend to be comfortable. I don't want to hear about how much things cost. We have the money, an' I have more in St. Louis in investments. I don't care how much I spend as long as we both go home together."

The conductor announced it was almost time to roll, so James and Emmett said their goodbyes and headed down the aisle to the door. Sarah watched them disappear and then looked at Kade as she settled herself on the overstuffed seats.

"I wish we were getting off with them," she said quietly. "I've been too long in the mountains. I'm not sure what to think about a town anymore, especially one as big as St. Louis. I'm not sure I know how to act."

Kade chuckled at that. "You will do fine. Once we get to Joe's, Katie will take over. You have my word on that," he patted her hand.

James watched the train roll toward the east and wished his mother was not on it. More precisely, he wished she didn't have to be on it because James was also worried about Sarah. She wasn't well. He could see that this pregnancy was difficult and maybe life-threatening. He hoped the doctors in St. Louis would be able to help.

"Come, Emmett, I have one stop to make before we hit the mercantile for the list of things I need to take back with us," James said. "I'd like to head out by midday if all goes well."

"You going to that fancy house where I have to wait on the street?" Emmett asked.

James grinned. Damn, kids don't forget a thing. "I just have a friend there I need to see for just a minute," he said.

"I showed Noah the house last summer when we came for the fireworks," Emmett commented. "Noah said that whores live there."

James glanced down at Emmett, a frown on his face. "That's a pretty ugly name to call someone," he said.

"It sounds ugly," Emmett agreed. "What does whore mean?"

"Didn't Noah tell you?"

"I asked him, and he just said it was bad," Emmett replied. "He wouldn't say more. So, what does it mean?"

James looked around him. There were few people out on the boardwalks at this early hour. He stopped walking and turned to Emmett.

"It is a bad name that people call some women. It isn't a nice name."

"Why?"

"Emmett, how old are you again?"

"I'm nine. You know that."

James did know that, but he was trying to buy time. He had to think of a good way to explain to Emmett what the word meant.

"You are too young to know a bad word like that."

"Well, I think if Noah is old enough to say it, I should be able to know what it means," Emmett replied patiently.

"Noah shouldn't have said anything to you," James answered, "but I'll talk to him later about that. For now, you only need to know it is a bad name for a woman." James started walking again.

"So, did the woman do a bad thing?" Emmett trotted to keep up.

James breathed deeply, trying to stay calm. He was going to have a serious talk with Noah when they got home.

"Look, Emmett, sometimes a woman gets in a bind. She might not have money or a way to support herself. So, some women move into a big house like that, and men go there, and they talk, and sometimes they stay together for a night like a married man and woman might do. But they aren't married. People don't think that is right, so the woman gets a bad name."

"So, do you think it isn't right?" Emmett asked innocently.

"I think we just have to let people be people," James said, trying to stay patient. "I don't like to judge."

"So, are you going to go in and talk, or will you do the married thing?"

"Emmett," James started impatiently, "I am just going to go in and tell a friend who works there that your ma and I got married last summer. That is all."

They turned the corner and moved off Main Street, and the big house came into sight. James stopped short. Instead of the gaudy "Miss Tillie's Palace" sign above the door, there was a new sign that said, "Guns, Pistols, Ammunition, and Hardware," and next to the steps outside to the upstairs rooms, there was a sign that said, "Rooms to let, inquire inside."

"Wait here," James said as he reached the door.

Inside what was once Miss Tillie's parlor, James saw counters in front of tall shelves, filled with guns. The corner bar was gone, along with the plush chairs and settees. James went up to the man behind the counter and waited while he helped another customer.

"What happened to Miss Tillie?" he asked when the storekeeper looked questioningly at him.

"Sorry, cowboy, they been gone a couple months now," the man smiled. "Some of the girls have cribs on the other side of the tracks, I am told. Try there."

"I'm not looking for a girl," James said shortly, "just wondering where Tillie and her Black bartender went off to."

"Can't say," the gun trader said. "I only been here for a month. I been told that the new church in town has a fire and brimstone preacher who was talking about running Tillie out of town. This establishment is right off Main Street, and that didn't sit well with the righteous, having it so close to the good folk of the town. What I heard, Tillie sold the house, and as far as anyone knew, they loaded up what they wanted and, during the night, they were gone. I think if they were around here, someone would notice. Not many fat women or Black men in town," the man grinned.

James grunted. He turned and left the store. He had just wanted to tell Tillie that her words had helped him, and that he and Mary were hitched. James was surprised at how sad he felt that he wouldn't see Tillie and Charlie again.

"Did you find your friend?" Emmett asked when James rejoined the boy.

"No, but I saw a lot of guns," James said moodily. "Let's get to the mercantile and make tracks toward home. I'm sick of town already."

CHAPTER 13

Summer Jobs – Summer 1882

K ade folded up the paper impatiently and set it on the side table. The clock on the wall was closing in on noon but it seemed more like an eternity to him. He got up and went out the door to the balcony. He was restless and getting worse each day.

Kade leaned on the railing and looked out onto his brother's backyard. The wood and brick stable, tall and stately, was there, along with a small pasture where his brother's two carriage horses grazed. It was a pretty view, and he was grateful the room that he and Sarah shared in Joe's house had this nice balcony. Sarah could come out each afternoon and get fresh air without climbing stairs. The doctors didn't want her climbing stairs. They allowed her to come down for supper with the family, but that was all. It was either bed or a chair with her feet up on a stool that the doctors ordered for Sarah. If Kade was getting stir crazy, he wondered how Sarah stood it, but she never complained.

How long had they been in St. Louis? Too long, if how he felt was any indication. It was early May when they arrived by train. With Katie and Joe waiting for them, Sarah and Kade were hustled home in the carriage, and Sarah was taken up to bed. The doctors, both the old doctor and his new young partner, came the next morning. They examined and visited with Sarah for a long time in the bedroom while Kade paced nervously in the hallway. The doctors had studied their medical books and sent telegraphs to colleagues, asking about the care needed for an older woman in Sarah's condition. After seeing Sarah, they had a plan that included only certain foods and almost complete bedrest.

Now, three weeks later, Sarah was improving. Her face had lost its tired lines. She wasn't vomiting anymore. She was eating and gaining a little weight. Kade was still the only one who could see the change in her body, mostly at night when he curled against her, cradling her against him. Then he could feel the baby pushing out from Sarah's stomach. Soon, her skirts wouldn't hide the bump anymore. However, the more Sarah improved, the more restless Kade got.

He had fallen into a routine of sorts. Unless Sarah needed him, Kade had breakfast with Joe and Katie and walked with Joe to Joe's office. Kade bought a newspaper from a stand and returned home to read the daily. He had scoured Joe's library for books and took them upstairs to read while sitting with Sarah. Occasionally, there were letters from home that he and Sarah read over and over, discussing the news. On the days Sarah felt well, he was comfortable leaving her to Katie. The women enjoyed each other and often spent the afternoons sewing or knitting together in Sarah's room. Kade would escape the house then. He exercised Joe's team, cleaned the stable, or found odd jobs around the place to keep him busy - anything to burn off his restless energy.

His mind kept wandering to the mountains, knowing by the time of day what he would have been doing if he were there. Jake had sent a letter posted from Steamboat Springs. Jake, Lathe, Hawk, and the women and children had made the trip just fine. Before going to Jacob's cabin, they were spending two nights camped near the hot spring pools near Steamboat. There was a large corral at the edge of the Steamboat village where they put the extra horses for a day. Kestrel, Lark, and Lathe's little boy, Slade, were old enough to enjoy splashing in the warm water. Jake thought it would be nice to rest before pushing on to the cabin, and he wrote that the children loved the water. Kade had to grin to himself at the written words his son sent. He had no doubt that it wasn't only the children enjoying the water. Kade knew the place. He and Sabra had gone there, once when they were first married and again the last summer before Sabra got sick. There was something about making love to a woman in that warm silky water that was more than special. Kade's mind went back to those times with Sabra. He felt an almost physical hurt for the loss of their time together. Only the memories lingered.

Kade knew the warm waters were enjoyed during the day by the children, but he also knew three young couples were taking turns using the warm waters by night. Jake wouldn't write about that. Maybe Jake had no idea that Kade had been there himself.

So here Kade was, standing on a balcony, lost in memories. This would be a long summer, for the doctors strictly forbade Sarah from returning home. Despite his restlessness, Kade knew that staying in St. Louis was for the best. Sarah was better, but it was a long time until this baby was due. She was not out of the woods yet.

Kade took a breath and turned back inside. He wasn't finished with the paper yet. He gathered it up and sat down again in his chair, glancing up at Sarah. Seeing her watching him, he smiled.

"You still feeling pretty good this morning?" he asked. "Think you can eat soon?"

"Kade," Sarah said gently, ignoring his question. "Weren't you given some jobs to do while you were here?"

Kade was startled. "Well, that is only if all went well."

"All is going well," Sarah replied firmly. "At least for now. I think you need to start on your list. What was it Jake wanted you to do?"

Kade stared at her for a moment. "He wanted me to see if I could find Anna's people."

"And what did James want?"

"He wants me to go an' visit with Mary's brother if he were still in the same town."

"And," Sarah emphasized, "what did you want to do?"

"Well, I was goin' to look for a new stud horse, but I don't really need to do that," Kade finished lamely.

Sarah studied her husband for a moment before answering. "I need you to go and look for a horse. You will drive me to drink if you keep pacing around here like some caged animal," she said. "I'm fine. The doctors are watching me. Katie and her girl take good care of me. And you are driving me crazy. Just go," she hesitated, then added, "but keep checking in on me." Sarah smiled fondly at Kade.

*

At first, Kade had trouble making himself leave for more than a few hours. The first few days, he made the rounds of farms near St. Louis that were known to raise good horses. But he was not gone long any day. As that first week went by, Kade felt more comfortable leaving for a whole day or sometimes overnight if he traveled any distance.

He had in his mind the type of horse he wanted. He wanted a stallion that, mated with their mares, would bring some size to their herd. He saw in his memory the horse Sabra owned when Kade first met her. Coal black and big, Ebony had been raised by Sabra. His breeding was three-fourths thoroughbred and one-fourth workhorse. Ebony was big-boned from the workhorse bloodlines, but refined by the thorough-bred. Kade had, at the time, admired the horse from afar. But when Sabra was kidnapped and taken back to St. Louis, Kade had followed her, two weeks behind and riding her great black horse. It was then that he learned the extent of the horse's endurance. When Sioux war-riors came upon them on the prairie, Kade had asked the horse for everything, and the animal gave it. Miles later, when they long since lost sight of their pursuers, Kade slipped off the horse. Lathered with sweat and its sides heaving, the horse was all but spent. Kade jogged beside it, letting the animal rest while they kept mov-ing, putting distance between themselves and the Indi-ans. When miles later, Kade mounted Ebony, the horse had broken right back into his ground-eating running walk as if it hadn't just run for its life. Kade wanted another horse like Ebony. He wasn't sure if one was out there, but he would look.

Kade spent three weeks searching in vain. He saw nice horses, some he liked, but none he loved. Then Joe came home one evening with the news that a client of his had been in Illinois and had seen horses, such as Joe described to him, at a farm near Springfield. Kade thought he would go there on the stage and take a look. He might be gone a couple of days, or longer if he bought a horse and had to ride it home. He would telegraph Joe if he found he would be gone more than a week.

It took three days to get to Springfield, weaving between towns and stops. At the livery, Kade inquired about the farm he had heard of and hired a horse for the next day. Then finding a telegraph office, he let Joe know where he was staying. Joe would let him know if he needed to rush home.

No telegraph came urging Kade home. The next telegraph Kade sent two days later told Joe of his route home. He was riding his new horse, a four-year-old stallion. Depending on the horse's stamina, it could take Kade a week to get back. Not knowing the horse or his level of training, it was hard to estimate how long the trip would take, but Kade hoped to put on thirty miles each day.

Kade bought a used saddle from the livery. The horse had been ridden, but he was far from a finished saddle horse in Kade's estimation. He had been used as a stud for a month, and the animal was full of himself. But when Kade got him away from the farm and had the stud's attention, the horse had a ground-eating walk that reminded Kade of Sabra's Ebony.

This stallion was big with sturdy bones. He was what Kade would call "watchy," meaning the horse was always alert, often to the point of shying at new sights and sounds. At the moment, this stud treated every new sight and sound like a monster, afraid it would strike. Kade didn't worry about that. The horse had never been off of the farm. The stud would see plenty of sights and sounds before Kade got the horse to the mountains. Kade always liked a horse that paid attention. That went back to Kade's mountain man days. Sometimes a "watchy" horse meant the difference between life and death. A horse could often sense danger before a man did, before it was too late to escape.

By noon of the fourth day, Kade rode into Joe's yard. Both of Joe's carriage horses were geldings, so Kade turned his new stud in with them. There was the usual snorting and bickering common for strange horses when first mixed, but the stud was tired from the trip, and he gave way to the old geldings who thought they ruled the place. Kade didn't spend much time watching. He wanted to see how Sarah was feeling. It had been over a week since he had been home.

Sarah was glad to see him. She was doing well. Kade could see the color in her cheeks, and she had gained more weight. The wan look was gone, and she was rested.

"You were successful?" Sarah asked. She was in a chair with her legs propped on a stool.

"Very," Kade replied smiling, leaning down to kiss her. "This may not be as good a horse as Sabra's old Ebony, but I think it is a close second. He got better each day I rode him. A good horse takes time. Reckon I got a lot of time right now." Kade sat down across from Sarah. "Miss me?" he asked.

"Yes, but it was very peaceful with you gone and not pacing around here," Sarah teased him. "So, what is next on your list?"

"Trying to get rid of me already?"

"Yes," Sarah laughed. "But you don't have to be gone so long. So, tell me, where are you off to?"

"I'll go an' find Mary's brother if I can," Kade replied obediently. "Mary told me she came from somewhere near St. Charles, Missouri. Her first husband's brother had a mercantile in that town. I'll start there."

Kade laid over for two days before heading out again. He wanted his horse to get some rest, and he wanted a better saddle. The saddle he bought at the livery was cheap and didn't fit either him or the horse well. Joe told Kade there was a leather and saddle shop in town, so Kade visited there first. The saddle maker had several saddles ready to go, but Kade found just what he wanted in a used saddle.

Called a "Mother Hubbard" saddle, because it had a full wide skirt, Kade had seen this type of saddle used on the prairies near Laramie and by some of Jackson's hands. It was made in Cheyenne by two Collins brothers. This saddle was not old, having been purchased in Cheyenne and only ridden to St. Louis. The luckless cowpuncher who owned this saddle lost it in a card game, and the saddle eventually ended up in this saddle shop. It had been used just enough to get the "new" off it. Kade liked how this saddle felt to him and how it fit his horse. Since one of the Collins brothers had committed suicide the year before, Kade knew this saddle was a find, as there would be no more exactly like it.

The trip to St. Charles was easily made in a day. Kade made the main street of the little town along the Missouri River by midafternoon. Inquiring from the first local he passed, he was directed to the far end of Main Street where he came to Snyder Mercantile. He tied the bay at the hitching post, climbed the steps to the boardwalk, and entered the store.

"I need to speak to Mr. Snyder if he's around," Kade told the woman behind the counter.

The woman smiled and pointed to the back, where Kade saw a man unpacking a box of cans, setting them on shelves. The man was close in age to Kade himself. He had a pleasant face and an apron tied around his waist. As Kade approached, the man straightened and waited.

"Mr. Snyder?" Kade asked.

"That be me, Sanders Snyder. What can I help you with?" the smile was genuine.

"I have news of your brother if he were Albert Snyder," Kade was solemn.

The smile faded. "It isn't good news, is it?"

"No sir," Kade agreed. "He's dead."

"Margaret, I'm going in the back with this gentleman. Call me if you need me," Snyder called. Then to Kade, he said, "I think we need a drink."

The back turned out to be a kitchen with steps leading upstairs to bedrooms and a sitting room. Snyder went to a cupboard and took out two glasses and a bottle, pouring them each a shot.

"Albert is my younger half-brother," Snyder said, sitting across the table from Kade. "Tell me what happened."

Kade told him about the brawl in Laramie and that one of the cowhands from Twin Peaks was sent to break the news to the widow.

"I had hopes that going west might shape Albert up," Snyder commented. "I guess that didn't happen. What happened to my niece and nephews?"

Kade noticed that the man did not ask about Mary. "They are with their stepmother. She has remarried and lives at our ranch now. She had a child with your brother, though, before he died. A boy."

"Oh, shit. I never thought Albert would think of Mary as a wife. I just hoped she'd keep the children fed and clothed, and he would at least provide for them," Snyder shook his head. "I guess you are here to tell me she wants to send Albert's children back here to me?"

"From what I have pieced together from Mary and the children," Kade chose to ignore the man's question, "your brother may have tried to run the farm in the first months at the soddy, but then Mary had his child. The baby shows Black blood. Apparently, that sent your brother on a rampage. By the time he was killed, he had drunk and gambled most of his livestock off. Mary was wearing a dress made of flour sacks and the kids were in rags."

Snyder groaned at that. "Those poor kids . . . and woman," he murmured. "I should have kept them here, but to be frank, I just wanted my brother gone." Snyder looked up at Kade, "He was ten years my junior. When my father died, he told me to take care of my brother. Albert was just a kid then. Always in trouble. I got him jobs. I had him work for me. When he married the first time, I thought maybe he'd straighten up, and he had some good stretches. But he always followed the good times with bad. I'm sixty years old and still living above my store because I spent so damn much money bailing Albert out of trouble." Snyder drained his glass and poured another shot. "When his first wife died, Albert was a mess. I heard of the claim on the Wyoming plains and bought it and sent the family there. I set him up with livestock and told him he was on his own. I loved those kids and thought if I made Albert take the woman with him as a wife, he'd keep her. He was appalled at the thought. Everyone around here knew she had Negro blood, even though she didn't show it. Albert didn't want to show his face. I hoped if they got out west, where no one knew, that Albert would . . . Albert could pretend she was white," Snyder finished desolately. "I didn't think he'd ever treat her as a wife, but I hoped he'd provide for them."

"Sounded like it was pretty rough for them, especially Mary," Kade commented. "If our cowhand hadn't helped them, I reckon they would have starved out in the winter. And to answer your question, no, we don't want to send the kids back. Mary and her new husband have made a home for them. The kids are happy. I don't think they would want to come back anyway."

"Do they need money then?" Snyder asked. "I could spare some. It takes a lot to raise kids. I can't see your cowhand making that much."

Kade smiled at that. "The cowhand turns out to be the son of my late partner. We have a big enough ranch. There's no problem with providing for them. Mary just thought you'd want to know what happened."

Kade reached inside his jacket pocket and pulled out some folded papers. "Mary is a pretty accomplished artist. Did you know that? She drew some pictures an' sent them with me. Thought you might like to see your nephews an' niece." Kade opened the paper and smoothed it out. Mary had drawn a picture of James and her with all the children, sitting in front of the fire in the cabin. Gideon lay in Mary's lap, Alice in James' lap, and the two boys were seated on each side of them. They were all laughing and looking down at a checker-board. Kade was always amazed at how Mary could see a scene, pluck it out of her memory later, and put it to paper. It was a good picture of the family.

"Mary did this?"

"She's drawn quite a lot of pictures. She's good," Kade began. "But more important, she's happy. The children are happy. Mary an' James are expecting their first child this fall."

"What will this young man think if the baby comes out looking like the one in the picture?"

"We don't see color on our ranch," Kade said, "James knows the possibility, an' I can assure you; he won't mind. He's a good man."

Mr. Snyder knew where Mary's brother was living and gave Kade directions. The location was about two miles from town. It was July, and the days were long, so there were still several hours of daylight left. Kade thought that if he found Ezekiel Allen at home, he might be able to get miles down the road toward home by the time darkness overtook him. Then, Kade could leave the stud in a livery overnight and get a hotel room.

Kade saw the small shanty set back from the road as he approached. It was, as the Snyder man described it, small and stark. But as Kade approached, he saw that while the shanty was a poor house, it was at least kept up. The shingles were all there, the porch steps didn't sag, and the door was on. Because of the heat, the doors and windows were open. A neat garden was beside the dirt walkway, and a slight Black woman was hoeing the rows. Kade turned his horse in and approached. He saw the woman glance up and straighten her shoulders. She glanced around nervously.

"Ma'am," Kade asked politely, "would this be Ezekiel Allen's place?"

"Yes'm," the woman didn't smile.

"Would Ezekiel be here?"

"No, suh."

"Will he be back directly?" Kade looked toward the lowering sun. There were still a couple of hours of daylight left.

"What you want him for?"

Kade realized that the woman was scared. He had been away too long from civilization. He'd forgotten what it was like for a Black man or woman. Riding up here on his big fancy horse could mean anything to a Black person, and usually nothing good.

"Ma'am, I have news of Ezekiel's sister, Mary. I jest want to talk to him," Kade said gently.

"You know Mary?" the woman looked surprised.

"I know Mary," Kade emphasized. "She's doing good. I'd like to tell her brother that."

"He be home after dark," the woman replied, more comfortable to talk now. "He's working over at the Thompson place."

Kade had no idea where the Thompson place was and didn't want to traipse all over the country looking.

He could go back to town and wait and come back after dark. But it was hot and Kade knew the horse needed water. They had not crossed any streams on the way out and it was almost two miles back.

"Would you have a water trough my horse could get a drink at?" Kade asked.

"Yes'm," the woman nodded. "Out back. You're welcome to it."

Kade nodded his thanks, and dismounting, he walked the horse around the side of the house, taking care to miss the garden. He found the water, pumped some fresh into the tank, and watched the bay drink greedily. After the horse was finished, Kade pumped some more, splashed it on his face and neck, then drank deeply himself. The heat and humidity were high this day. He longed for the mountains.

As Kade walked back around to the front of the shanty, he heard voices drifting toward him. As he rounded the side of the house, he saw the woman had left the garden and was backing up toward her porch, her hoe still in her hand. A young man was coming up the dirt path, his horse following him. Even at this distance, Kade could see the woman's face. She was frightened.

"Now, Juba, I've missed you," the young man was saying as he advanced. He was grinning at the woman. As he got closer, he cut across the garden, blocking the woman's retreat toward the house. "Didn't you miss me?"

"I ain't known you was back, Mistah Randolph," Juba answered, her voice shaky. "I's don't work for your momma no more. I's a married woman now." She stepped backward, deeper into the garden as he continued to approach.

294

"Well, I got back last week, and I was sorely disappointed not to see you. I told my momma you should be working for us again. I told her I'd come right over and tell you to come back."

"Your sisters don't need no nursemaid anymore."

"My momma told me that, but I said you should work in the dairy. You were good there," he grinned at her, getting closer. "You remember the dairy, don't you, Juba?"

"Mistah Randolph, I's a married woman. You stay away from me now," Juba's voice rose as panic set in.

"Ma'am, I thank you for the water," Kade said casually as he emerged from behind the shanty. He saw the man freeze.

"Who are you?" the young man glared at Kade.

"I'm jest a traveler who needed to water my horse. This lady let me use the water tank."

"You can get on the road again then," the man was belligerent.

Kade surveyed the sky. "Reckon I might jest set a spell under that shade tree over yonder," Kade commented conversationally. "Ma'am, would you mind my resting for a while?" Kade tied his horse to the fence and casually walked across the garden toward Juba, careful not to step on the plants.

"I said to leave, Mister!" the young man thrust his chest out menacingly.

Kade kept coming until he was next to Juba. "Go to the house," he ordered low under his breath, giving her a gentle shove. Then turning back to the young man, his voice took on some menace, "I don't think it's your place to order anyone off. I don't much care for your tone."

"Who do you think you are?" the young man exploded.

"Let's jest say I'm a friend of the family," Kade said levelly. "An' I don't think you want to fight with me."

"You're just an old man."

Kade stepped forward into the man's personal space. "Try me," he said, but his voice was challenging. "You're nothing but a shitty little bully."

The man leaned down quickly, reaching into his boot. His hand came out clutching a small Stevens boot pistol. Before he could clear the boot with the weapon and straighten up, he felt the prick of Kade's big skinning knife against his throat. The young man froze.

"Think you might want to leave that little toy gun in your boot, boy," Kade said smoothly, "if you value breathing."

Slowly, Randolph pushed the gun back into his boot. Kade moved the knife back away from the man's neck slowly until just the tip touched under the man's chin. Kade used the knife to guide the man to a standing position. With the blade kissing the man's chin, Kade spoke softly.

"Reckon we are finished here," he said. "Now you jest back up an' get that horse out of this garden. Get on him an' go on down the road."

Randolph did just that. But when he mounted his horse, he looked down at Kade. "What's to stop me from just pulling this gun right now, old man?" he was belligerent again.

"Well, you could try," Kade nodded, his voice ice. "But the thing is, not many men can grab iron, shoot, an' hit anything, much less a moving man. An' I'd be moving. Now this toothpick I have," Kade fingered the blade, "it never misses. You want to have a go at it?"

Randolph didn't think about Kade's challenge for long. He wheeled his horse and hit a lope. "I'll be back," he threw over his shoulder.

Kade watched him go. Randolph had privileged white boy written all over him. He needed someone to take him down to size. Kade hoped it wouldn't have to be him.

"Mistah, I thankee," Juba was out on the porch, "but that man is crazy. He be back. You better go."

Kade studied the woman. She was young, maybe in her early twenties. A pretty mulatto woman, he could see that she was still scared.

"Who is he? How do you know him?" Kade asked softly.

"I was a nanny, worked for his momma at the Randolph farm. He's younger'n me, but it was his baby sisters I took care of. Harrison was at boarding school when I worked there, but he come home for holidays. Then he went off to university. Been gone three years. I haven't worked at the plantation for two years."

"I'd like to rest my horse," Kade said casually, "let him have some grass. Do you mind if I jest wait here for Ezekiel? He's your husband, right? Reckon I might be quite comfortable under that shade tree taking a nap." Kade indicated a huge old tree that shaded the side yard.

Juba nodded, and Kade hobbled his stud, letting him graze on the grass beyond the garden. Taking his rifle from the scabbard, Kade settled under the tree. If young Randolph returned, he'd have more than a knife handy the next time.

∗❦∗

Just before dark, Kade caught up the stud and tied him to the fence. He didn't want to be hunting a horse in the dark. Juba had long since gone to the house, but when she saw him moving, she came out and sat on the porch. There was no railing; she just sat with her legs dangling, waiting for Ezekiel.

"I ain't got no cider, but I got cool water from the pump if you like," she called to Kade.

"I'd be obliged," Kade answered. Taking the offer as an invite, he made his way to the porch and took a seat. He propped his rifle up by his side.

Juba brought him a tin cup of cool water, and he drank deeply. He surely missed the cool mountains. But as the darkness settled in, the breeze had a little bit of coolness to it. Evening was always a relief.

Ezekiel Allen was a tall man, thin but muscled. Kade saw him approaching in the dim light of the moon. By his walk and the slump of his shoulders, Kade knew Ezekiel was weary. He had probably put in a long day of physical labor. But when Ezekiel turned off the road and saw Kade sitting in the dim light of the shanty, he stopped dead and stood up straight.

"This man has news of Mary," Juba called out to him. "He's a friend."

Juba brought out tin bowls with some stew and gave one each to Ezekiel and Kade. Kade suspected the meat in it was squirrel. It had been a long time since he had squirrel, and he found it good. He wouldn't let Juba give him seconds. He figured Ezekiel only got half of his meal that night and maybe Juba less than that since they had shared with him. Kade wouldn't take more of their food.

Again, Kade told Mary's story. Again, he took out Mary's drawing and showed it to the couple. As Ezekiel and Juba studied the picture, Kade suddenly saw it through their eyes. Beside Kade sat Ezekiel, barefoot and in torn and tattered clothes, and Juba in a shapeless sack of a dress, patched and worn. In the drawing was James, cowboy hat pushed back on his head, neckerchief at his throat. James sat with one of his legs crooked over the other, cowboy boots and spurs on his feet. Mary had shaded her drawing with some of the colored pencils she had gotten at Christmas. Her light green dress had lace at the collar and was shaped to her body. The stark difference between the Allens and the Bates was noticeable.

"She looks good," Ezekiel looked up wonderingly. "She looks like a white girl. She gots a White family, 'ceptin' for the baby."

"She's jest Mary," Kade replied. "She's a good woman. They're happy."

Slowly, Ezekiel nodded. "I'm glad fer her. She had no chance here." Ezekiel looked at Juba solemnly. "She'll have a good life."

A silence settled between them while Ezekiel continued to study the picture. It was then that Juba spoke low to her husband.

"Harrison Randolph come by this afternoon," her voice was low.

Ezekiel looked up quickly. "What did he want?"

"Says they want me to come work in the dairy," Juba tried to sound casual. "Mistah Kade sent him 'way, but he was mighty mad when he went. He says he be back."

"He abused you, didn't he?" Kade spoke casually to Juba but direct. No sense in beating around the bush.

She ducked her head. "Yes'm."

"He'll do it again, won't he?"

"Yes'm."

"What can be done about that?" this time Kade directed the question at Ezekiel.

"I kin kill him," Ezekiel said without emotion. "They'll hang me then. Or Juba can kill him, an' they'll hang her. Or Juba can jest go there an' work at the dairy. That's where he wants her anyway," Ezekiel said bitterly, "an' jest let him have his way with her whenever he wants."

"So which way you goin' to play this?" Kade asked.

Ezekiel stared out into the night. When he turned to look at Kade, Ezekiel's eyes were hard. "I gotta kill him. I ain't giving Juba to the likes of him." Kade heard Juba draw a quick breath.

"What if there was another way?" Kade asked.

"Ain't no other way," Ezekiel said. "Ain't got no money to run. Ain't got nowhere to go. Means starvin'."

Kade turned to Juba. "You were a nanny. You good with babies then?"

"Yes'm. I like babies."

"We ain't been blessed yet," Ezekiel broke in, "but we are hopeful."

"That won't happen if you go an' get yourself hanged," Kade commented casually. He stood up, walked into the dark, and then turned back to the couple on the porch, coming to a decision. "I lost my first wife. My children are all grown with children of their own. I remarried an' my wife an' I are well beyond the age when you expect to have more children. Leastwise, we thought we were. My wife is in St. Louis now under a doctor's care. We expect a baby in August, an' it's been hard on Sarah. I'm thinking that at our age, having a nanny to help with the baby would be something nice for Sarah. Maybe for me too. Want a job? It would mean you'd have to go to Wyoming territory." Kade looked over at Ezekiel and added, "I can find you a job too."

Ezekiel and Juba just stared, then looked at each other. A smile lit Juba's face and she nodded. Ezekiel looked back at Kade. "Yessir, we'd surely want that."

"I pay my cowhands twenty-five dollars a month plus board. I could give each of you that, but for the first winter, you'd have to live in the spare room in our cabin. We couldn't get another house up before winter," Kade stopped, thinking. "Reckon, it would make sense to have you in our cabin, at least through the first year anyway."

"Mistah Kade," Ezekiel was confused, "that is white man pay. You mean to give us white man wages?"

"Well, will you work as hard as a white man?" Kade asked.

"Yessir."

"Then you get the same wages," Kade returned to the porch and sat again. "You got anything holding you here?" When Ezekiel shook his head, Kade went on. "It's getting late. I can put my horse out back with that old mule you got there for the night an' bed down here on the porch. How 'bout you gather what things you need, an' we head to St. Louis in the morning. I can find things for you to do in St. Louis, an' if I get you away from here, I won't lose my new hired hand to a hang-man's noose."

◆

Kade's return with Ezekiel and Juba in tow was met with some surprise, but after discussing the situation with Sarah, she agreed that help with the baby, at least the first year would be a benefit.

"Here you go spending more money on me," she complained. "If I get too expensive, you will probably divorce me."

"I've thought that same thing," Kade teased her, "but I don't think I can find another widow to put up with me." Then he grew serious. "I remember when our kids were little," he continued, "there were many a night when Sabra an' I had to take turns with a colicky baby. To be truthful, that is not part of fatherhood I look forward to experiencing again. Maybe this will help some."

There was a groom's room above Joe's stable that hadn't been used in a decade since Joe did all of his own chores for his two horses. Juba and Ezekiel cleaned it up and took their meager things there to wait for the baby's arrival. Joe found day work for Ezekiel in the area, and Juba began working in the house, getting to know Sarah, and helping Katie with anything she could. Kade sent the couple off the first day to a mercantile where Kade had credit. He wanted the couple to get two sets of clothes appropriate for their new lot in life. He instructed Ezekiel to get boots, jeans, shirts, and a hat, and left it up to Katie and Sarah to talk to Juba.

Sarah was comfortable right away with Juba, and as Juba became more familiar with the house and the changes in her and Ezekiel's circumstances, she began to relax around Sarah. Every night, Juba went back to the little room above the stable with food from the "big house" for their supper. The little room had no cooking facilities, and the amount and type of food that Katie sent with Juba each day astounded them. If this was any indication of what their life might be like in the Wyoming territory, they were ready to go.

After a week at Joe's, Kade decided that he better attack his last job soon. Already it was well into the third week of July. The baby was due about mid-August. He didn't want to be gone at that time. For this last job, Jake had asked Kade to see if he could find any relatives of Anna's. It had been eight years since Jake had ridden into a Cheyenne village and bought Anna, a white girl, then seventeen. She was a slave to the Cheyenne but had been raised by the Pawnee since she was eight. Jake had bought Anna intending to find Anna's family and send her home. But Anna's immediate family had been killed on the Oregon Trail and in the beginning, Anna couldn't even remember her whole name.

As the years passed and Anna became more comfortable with the English language, more and more things from her childhood were coming back to her. She remembered that her name had been Anna Curtis and that she came from a town somewhere near St. Louis. She could not remember the town name, but there was "New" in the name. That narrowed the search down some. Anna didn't remember being in St. Louis, only that her grandfather would go there to sell livestock. So Kade felt Anna's hometown was on the west side of St. Louis. Otherwise, there would be a good chance the family would have gone through St. Louis on the trek west.

Anna also remembered a cousin who she played with, a girl her age. The names Mary, Miriam, Marian, and Martha seemed somewhat familiar. She remembered a grandfather and grandmother, but to a little girl of eight when she left Missouri, they were simply Papa and Gra'mama.

There were six towns on the eastern side of Missouri with a name that began with "New." New Haven and New Madrid were quite far south, and Kade hoped they were not the right ones. He would leave them for last as they were so far that it would take him several days to hunt in those vicinities. He also felt they were so far south that those towns might be too far from St. Louis for most farmers to travel to sell livestock.

Kade decided to start with the two towns nearest to St. Louis, New Haven and New Florence. If he had no results there, he could go to New London, far to the north, or New Franklin, another day and a half to the west. Kade knew he was looking for a needle in a haystack, but he hoped for Jake and Anna's sake he could find some answers for them.

Kade started early, for it was a long day's ride to New Haven. The stud was rested, and they made good time. Kade rode into New Haven just before dark and found a livery for the horse and a hotel for himself. As soon as businesses opened in the morning, he started making the rounds, inquiring about a family named Curtis. At the mercantile, the storekeeper said he had no regular customers named Curtis. Kade was told the same at the post office; no families were nearby with the name Curtis who received letters in New Haven. But at the elevator, Kade hit paydirt. The grain buyer remembered once having a farmer by that name from north of New Haven come in and ask about the grain prices. But the farmer never came back with grain. The buyer was not surprised because it sounded like the farm was north of the Missouri River. There were only a few bridges in the area across the river, making travel with a load of grain difficult.

Kade left the next day and headed north. New Florence was about forty-five miles by the time he found a river crossing. He made the town by nightfall and got his horse put up for the night and a room for himself. First thing the following morning, he went to the mercantile, where the storekeeper knew of a Curtis farm about ten miles north. Getting directions, Kade saddled up the bay and headed out. He was tired of traveling in the Missouri heat and anxious to return to Joe's. He hoped this farm was his destination.

The farm came into sight, looking just as the storekeeper described it. Three homes were scattered haphazardly off the road around barns and other outbuildings. Kade could see fine fields with corn and small grains growing. He could see men in the distance with a team. It appeared they were pulling up stumps to prepare more land for crops. Because he passed by the houses first, he turned into the drive and went up to the first house. An older woman was hanging out wash, and the stud looked at the gently waving clothes suspiciously but didn't shy. The woman noticed Kade and walked across the yard to meet him.

"You lookin' for someone, Mister?" the woman asked.

"Ma'am, I am that," Kade replied. "Would this be the Curtis farm?"

"It is."

"Would you have had a Curtis family that went overland on the Oregon Trail seventeen or so years ago?" Kade watched the woman's expression change.

"My son and his family did," she said slowly, "but they all died. We was told they was all massacred by Indians."

"Ma'am, was there a girl 'bout eight then, named Anna?"

The woman's eyes widened, and she nodded.

"Ma'am, Anna didn't die," Kade said gently. "I know Anna."

For an instant, the woman just stared. Then she turned and took some steps toward the house. "Miriam, Miriam!" she called loudly.

A woman about Anna's age came to the door.

"Run to the fields. Get your father and grandfather. This gentleman says he knows our Anna!"

When the family assembled on the porch, there were quite a few of them. Miriam's husband came in with the men. There was also the older woman's husband. These were the grandparents of the family, the ones Anna remembered as Papa and Gra'mama. The son of these two would be the uncle to Anna and the father of Anna's cousin, Miriam. They all sat quietly as Kade told the story, downplaying the harshness of Anna's life with the Cheyenne.

"When my son brought her away from the Cheyenne, she was scared to death an' didn't remember English. It came back fairly fast, but her memories of her earlier years came slower. She an' my son fell in love an' got married. They have children now. Anna is happy. She fits in well on our ranch." As Kade finished, he opened the satchel that he carried and took out the family picture taken at Thomas and Beth's wedding. Just as he was going to point out Anna, Miriam interrupted him.

"Oh, don't tell us. Let me see if I can pick out Anna," she said, studying the picture. It didn't take long. Smiling, she pointed to Anna, holding little Kestrel in her arms. "This has to be Anna!"

The rest of the family studied the picture. It was old Mr. Curtis who noticed Jake in the picture. "This is an Injun!" he exclaimed. "What're he doing in with your family?"

"That is my son," Kade said patiently, not surprised at the old man's reaction. "That is Anna's husband."

An audible gasp came from the older people. Old Mr. Curtis leaned back, surveying Kade. "You're a squaw man?" His eyes were hard, and his tone was not cordial.

Kade gave the old man a level look, holding his temper in check. "Jake is my adopted son. My wife was married before me. Blue Knife was the son of a partner of mine. When Blue Knife was killed, I married Sabra an' adopted Jake. He was three months old at the time."

No one knew what to say about that. Kade pointed to Sabra in the picture. "This is Jake's mother, my late wife."

"He's still a goddamned Injun, what killed my boy an' his family!" Mr. Curtis exploded. "An' now he's ruined our Anna."

Kade took a breath before answering. This reaction was not unexpected but after thirty years of it, Kade was tired of strangers' reactions to Jake. Leaning forward, his hands on his knees, he looked directly at the old man. In a voice of steel, Kade spoke low but firm, "That man is my son. He's part Ute Indian an' had no part of your families killin'. If you want to know any-thing more about Anna, you will keep a civil tongue. I am proud to say Jake is one of the finest men I have ever known. I'm proud to call him son. I'll hear no one slander him."

The tension was palpable as the family sat rigid. Kade and the old man stared at each other. It was the older Mrs. Curtis who finally spoke.

"I reckon if Anna is happy, we have nothing to say about it," she murmured. "Did she suffer when she lived with the Indians?"

Kade glanced at Mrs. Curtis. "Anna was treated well by the Pawnee. She was with them almost nine years."

"And when she was with the Cheyenne?" Miriam asked.

Kade looked at the young woman before answer-ing. "Ma'am, you don't want to know about that. What is important is that Anna survived there, an' when my son took her away, she learned she was safe. She had enough food. No one hurt her. They love each other. That is enough."

Remembering, Kade took out a drawing that Mary had done for Jake and Anna. Anna had sent it with Kade in hopes he would find her people. He unfolded the paper and showed it to the family. Mary had drawn Jake and his family outside, sitting on the ground. Jake was leaning against a tree, with Kestrel on his shoul-ders and Lark in his lap. Anna was sitting next to him, half facing Jake and the girls. Little Kade Brown was standing, holding onto his father's shoulder, and Jake had reached out to Anna, his hand gently on the side of her neck, his fingers in her hair. What struck Kade in this picture was the expressions on the faces. They were all laughing. The joy of being together was evident. Mary had caught the love between them. As he handed the picture to old Mrs. Curtis, she gasped, and tears came to her eyes.

"Oh, my," was all she could say. Then after studying the picture some more, she looked up at Kade. "She is happy, isn't she?"

"I have letters from them to you too," Kade said, pulling two letters from his satchel. "You have to remember that Anna didn't remember any learnin', any readin' an' writin' before being captured. She is relearning some now, but it is slow. She's a married woman with three children an' doesn't have time to study much, but she is trying." Kade held the letter out to them.

It was Miriam who took the letter. "Let me read it," she whispered. She fingered the paper and then began to read.

Dear famly, I am good. I have two girls and one boy. I have a good man. I am happy. I have good cabn. I was sad to leev you. I have crik here like one we played in. I miss Papa lap and gramma apple pie. I member you. But hom is here.

Anna

The family was silent, digesting the words. Kade saw tears come to Mr. Curtis's eyes at Anna's mention of him. Kade knew the old man remembered too. Kade handed Miriam the second letter.

"This is from Jake," Kade said quietly. "He thought you might have some reservations about him so he thought he would write too."

Miriam read Jake's letter out loud.

Dear Curtis family. When I first saw Anna, my only thought was to get her away from the Cheyenne. She was starving and had been mistreated. I thought we could find her family and send her home. But at the time, she couldn't even remember her name or how to speak English. By the time she remembered who she was, we had married. I love Anna, and I love our children. We are expecting our fourth child this winter. I am part of a big ranch in the mountains of Wyoming territory. Anna will always be provided for and will always have a good home. I hope this will alleviate your fears about me as her husband.

Sincerely, Jake Bates Welles

"What does alleviate mean?" Miriam looked up at Kade.

Kade grinned. That was a big word. Kade wondered if Jake had to look it up in the dictionary of Sabra's. "Reckon it means something like eases your mind," Kade answered.

"He sure writes pretty," Miriam said.

"Jake's mother was firm on her children talkin' an' writin' well. Another woman in our community taught the children, but Sabra insisted they study. We may be from the mountains, but my children know how to read an' write," Kade commented. Kade looked at old Mr. Curtis. "I understand your dislike of Indians. You lost family to them. But those Indians were not my son's people. He's a good man. Anna could do no better, even if her husband was white. You have my word on that."

❦

It was afternoon the next day when Kade came in sight of Joe's home, sitting on the rise at the end of a long drive. He was glad to be back. He knew the stud would be ready to have some rest. But this last trip had been a good one. Jake and Anna would be glad to know about her relatives in Missouri. And after the somewhat rough start, Kade had enjoyed spending the day with the Curtis family. They wanted to know all about the ranch and Anna's life. Mrs. Curtis and Miriam insisted Kade wait while they wrote letters to send back to Anna. The afternoon had gone quickly. It was late before Kade returned to New Florence and got a room.

As Kade rode in sight of Joe's home, he saw a figure get up, waving his arms. It was Ezekiel. He had been sitting in the shade, leaning against a big tree. Now he stood, waving frantically at Kade. Kade was instantly alert.

"Mistah Kade, Mistah Kade," Ezekiel called excitedly. "It's Miss Sarah! The baby comin'!"

Kade put spurs to the bay, and the horse leaped forward. It was only the end of July. It was too early. A feeling of dread rose in Kade.

CHAPTER 14

The Wicked and the Righteous – July/August 1882

The three men sat on their horses, surveying the cabin before them. They were a rough lot, clothed in a mixture of buckskin and homespun. They sat patiently, watching a fire burning in front of the cabin heating a large kettle.

"This cabin weren't here before. It's new," the oldest of the men remarked. "This ain't Kade's cabin. Kade were the trader."

"Somebody must be in the cabin, Ed," the man next to him said. "That fire is being tended."

"What you think we are waiting for?" Ed replied disgustedly. "You think I want to go barrelin' in 'til knowin' what are there?"

Ed McDonald was a big burly man in his mid-forties. He had roamed the mountains for twenty-odd years, mostly doing odd jobs, hunting, or stealing when there was an opportunity. He had visited old Tom Grissom, a former mountain man, in this valley maybe ten or twelve years earlier. He remembered then that Kade Welles had traded goods and hides and that Kade traded with the Indians. He probably had money hidden away too.

"We heard the cattle bawling when we turned north," Ed said, thinking out loud. "I'm thinkin' that the menfolk are down at the headquarters by the river valley workin' cows. That is a couple miles from here. But makes sense to be careful. I'm thinkin' we kin jest mosey down this trail, check out this cabin an' any other'n we come on until we get to where I recollect Kade's was an' then high tail it over the ridge an' head out with whatever we can find. Should be food if nothing else, but I bet we will find some greenbacks, maybe some silver."

It was then Kasa came out of the cabin with a load of clothes. She dumped what she had into the kettle. Taking up a wooden paddle, she stirred the clothes in the hot water, steam rising from the water. Intent on the washing, she didn't see the three men, partially hidden by trees high on the ridge overlooking the cabin.

"Wal, now," Ed murmured, "will ya look at that? That is one fine squaw." His eyes met the other two, and they smiled.

The men waited, watching Kasa. She stirred the kettle for a bit more, then put the paddle down and went to the cabin. Of one mind, the three men urged their horses forward. They had their animals tethered in the trees behind of the cabin when Kasa came outside again with bedding. Split up, the men approached Kasa from both sides of the cabin.

Kasa was startled to see two men coming toward her from the trees. Dropping the linens, she turned to race to the cabin for a weapon. Instead, she ran right into the waiting arms of Ed McDonald. She screamed, trying to pull away. But Ed was a big man, and his grip was strong. With arms around Kasa's waist, he dragged her inside the cabin. She screamed again and again, struggling against the man.

"Charlie, look on them shelves for anything we kin use," he ordered. "Billy, you come help me with this bitch."

Out of the corner, little four-year-old Slade came, screaming at the men. "Leave my mama alone!"

Ed backhanded the little boy, and the child was thrown backward. Kasa screamed in Ute to the child, ordering him to stay back with his baby brother. She tried to break free, but she was no match for the two men. They held her tight between them, and the big man pulled a knife from his side.

"Ain't you jest the prettiest little bitch," he crooned, slowly slicing the knife through her dress, popping buttons and tearing fabric. Kasa struggled wildly trying to pull back, and his knife slipped, nicking her breast. A red line of blood bubbled up. She screamed again, and this time, Ed backhanded her. His hand gripped her torn bodice and pulled hard, ripping the dress and her shift away from her.

"Throw her down, Billy," he growled, "I'll show her what she's good for."

Between them, they threw Kasa down, and she screamed again, fear and anger combined. Ed knelt and pulled the fragments of the dress away from her, his hands rough on her chest.

"I git her next," Billy said. "You leave enough fer me."

Ed stood and unbuttoned his trousers. Kasa, seeing her chance kicked at him. But he stood to the side, and she only gave him a grazing blow to the leg.

"Goddammit," Ed raged, "Charlie, come hold her legs. I'm ready."

Charlie left off what he was doing, and kneeling, grabbed Kasa's legs, effectively pinning her down between the two men. When Ed lowered himself onto her, she screamed again, a high animal scream of pain, hate, and fear.

Anna was drawing water from the brook when she heard Kasa screaming. She froze, listening hard. Again, she heard Kasa. This wasn't Kasa playing with little Slade. Anna's instinct told her that something was very wrong. Running to the cabin, she grabbed the revolver that Jake had given her years earlier.

"Kestrel, run to Mary's! Something's wrong at Kasa's! Run fast! Get the men," Anna was almost out the door when she turned back to issue another order. "Lark, watch little Kade!"

While Lathe and Jake's cabins were out of sight from each other, with a hill between them, it wasn't very far. Anna ran, knowing Kasa needed help. As she rounded the hill and the cabin came into sight, she saw the horses tied to the trees beyond the cabin. Anna knew there were strangers here. The cabin door stood open, but Anna couldn't see inside. She ran across the yard to the door, revolver ready.

Anna instantly took in the sight before her as she entered. Kasa lay, her clothing torn off, body exposed. Anna saw that there were three men, but the closest one had his back to her. This man held Kasa's legs and was a clear target for Anna. In front of him, a big man was lowered onto Kasa, grunting and pumping with pleasure. The third man was holding Kasa's arms. Anna didn't think. She just raised the gun and fired, hitting the first man, the one on Kasa's legs. The shot went true into the man's back, less than six feet in front of her.

Holding Kasa's arms, Billy had been intent on watching the show, already anticipating his own turn. But, the change in the light as Anna came through the door alerted him. Billy was on his feet rushing her before Anna had time to cock the pistol for a second shot.

Kasa felt the weight come off both her legs and arms at almost the same time that she registered the sound of Anna's gun. Startled by the roar of the pistol, Ed jerked up, giving Kasa her chance. She struck at him. Pulling away, she turned over to her stomach, trying to claw her way out from under the man. But she wasn't strong enough. Ed, glancing behind him, took in the scene. Charlie was lying with a blood-soaked hole in his back. Even at a glance, Ed knew Charlie was dead. From the corner of his eye, Ed saw Billie with another woman backed up to the wall, wrestling with her for her gun. Ed turned back to Kasa, and reaching forward, he grabbed her hair, pulling her back to him.

"Fuckin' bitches killed Charlie," he fumed, "but I'm gonna finish this first."

Jake about had enough of the gelding he was riding. A big five-year-old, the horse had been left home this summer because of an injury. The roan had a whole summer to run free. Jake had told James to let the animal heal, and when Jake came back, he'd work with the gelding again. Nothing like a summer off to create a barn sour horse, and this one was big, strong, and cantankerous.

The slow pace of the cattle had frustrated the colt, who wanted to get home. Now they were almost home, and Jake decided the horse needed a few more miles and lessons taught to him before quitting for the day. The crew pushing this herd of steers was large enough to handle the sorting. They wouldn't need Jake. He rode up to Thomas.

"Hey, I am going to take this colt around the loop before quitting. He needs more miles. You have enough help, don't you?" Jake asked, fighting the roan who wanted to keep moving toward home.

"Yeah, we don't need you," Thomas agreed. "I've been watching him, and I figured you'd want to ride on. See you later."

Jake turned the colt away from home and put the spurs to him. Even after the several miles they had ridden already, the colt wanted to bog his head and buck to get his way. But Jake expertly took hold of the reins and got the horse lined out, zig zagging some as the colt kept trying to head home. *Damn colt, anyway,* Jake thought. He'd been home less than a week and was already fighting with a horse.

Jake rode east a mile and then found the trail that they called the loop. This was a well-traveled trail they used when working with young horses. It ran north, away from the river and skirted the side of the ridges that sat behind the cabins of Thomas, James, Jake, and Lathe. When the young horses were ridden on this trail, they knew that home was right over the rim. The colts would want to go up and over the steep hills to get home. But the loop trail went farther north, through ravines and over rocky elevations, until it wound a half mile north of Lathe's cabin and came down to the home meadow. For a young horse, being so close to home and not allowed to go in that direction was a learning experience. For a barn sour horse like the roan that Jake was riding, it was a lesson. The loop was several miles long, and with all the ups and downs, by the time a horse came out at the end and started toward home, the animal usually had a whole different outlook on life.

Jake knew he must be beyond James' cabin by the way the colt kept trying to turn to the left and climb the hill. Jake put spurs to the colt and pushed him forward. Not long after that, Jake saw a pile of horse manure on the trail ahead of him. He stopped his horse and stared. It wasn't that horse manure on the loop was unexpected. But this was fresh, still slick and damp despite the morning sun. There were no other riders out today. Everyone was either in the hayfield or helping Thomas. Jake's eyes searched the ground. There were many hoofprints, but that was expected. This was a well-used trail. Jake and Lathe had both been on it yesterday, for that matter. But the fresh horse manure meant at least one horse had been over this trail in the last couple of hours. And the ranch's saddle horses were either in the meadow grazing or being used. The mare bands were pushed up into high country for the summer. There shouldn't be any horses on this trail today.

Jake urged the colt forward, noticing how the horse stepped off the trail, missing the manure. Jake looked forward. He saw no movement for as far as he could see. What business would anyone have in coming up here? The only place this trail led was far to the north and down around to the meadow, then turning to the south, passing the cabins.

Jake came to a decision. As much as he hated to give in to the colt, they were going over the top of the ridge toward home. It would be a tough climb and a steep ride down on the other side, but nothing that wasn't doable. If Jake turned now, he would come out just past Thomas and James' cabins. From there, he could turn north and see if he could intercept anyone riding the loop as they came from the far end of the meadow.

The colt thought he was heading home, so he was more than willing to scramble up the incline and over the top without protest. Going down was steep in places, but the colt was sure-footed, having been raised in these mountains. Just before Jake made his final descent, he noticed movement along the path coming toward James' cabin. It was Kestrel, and she was running as if her life depended on it. Jake put the spurs to his horse and took the last incline dangerously fast.

Kestrel saw him coming off the ridge, and her little arms waved frantically. Jake spurred his horse and rode up to her. Reaching down, he grasped her arm and pulled her up into the saddle with him.

"Kestrel, what's happened?"

"Mama said run. Kasa screaming," the little girl was panting, trying to catch her breath. "Said run to Mary's for help, to get the men."

Jake nodded. "Then you do that. Run fast, and I'll go ahead and see." He set Kestrel down, and lashing his horse, he was off. The horse had no more fight in him. He was in a dead run in two strides.

When Jake came in sight of Lathe's cabin, he took in two things almost instantaneously. First, he saw the strange horses tethered by the tree line. Second, he caught a glimpse of Anna in the doorway. He heard the gunshot, saw a figure barrel into Anna, and then she disappeared inside the cabin. He didn't pull his horse to a stop, only slowed it as he drew close and dismounted on the run.

By the time he reached the cabin door, Jake's revolver was in his hand. It was chaos inside. Kasa and Anna were both screaming. Slade was wailing from his corner, and two men were shouting obscenities, beating on the women. Ed was on the ground, pulling Kasa back toward him, his bare buttocks telling his intent. Anna was backed up against the far wall. A man in front of her was showering her with blows. Jake took it all in and knew the revolver was too risky. If he aimed at Kasa's attacker, he took the chance of the bullet going wild. Slade and the baby were in the line of fire. If he shot Anna's attacker, the bullet could go right through the man and into Anna. He switched hands on the gun and pulled his knife. Jake never missed with the knife. In one fluid motion, Jake let the blade fly at the bare-ass man. He heard it thump into the man's back and heard the man's grunt, but Jake was already turning toward Anna and her attacker. Switching the gun back into his right hand, he took one step closer.

"Leave her," Jake spoke, his voice almost a growl.

Billy froze, one hand grasping Anna's hair, the other balled into a fist. Slowly the fist relaxed, and his arm began to lower, inching toward the gun in his waistband.

"You ain't goin' to shoot me in the back, are you, friend?" Billy asked, his back still to Jake.

"You're not my friend," Jake replied. He caught Anna's eyes over Billy's shoulder. Jake nodded his head off to the side. Anna needed to get out of the line of fire.

Anna barely moved but gave an ever so slight twitch of her head that she understood.

"We's jest funnin' some," Billy said, wanting to buy some time.

"Don't look like my wife is having fun," Jake's voice was a snarl. "Turn around, mister, slow."

Billy suddenly reached for his gun and meaning to pull Anna in front of him as a shield, he turned. Pulling her by her hair, Billy tried to draw Anna to him, but Anna had a different idea. When Billy reared back to pull her off the wall, she collapsed. He had a good grip on her hair, and his hold on her hair had to hurt, but her dead weight pulled Billy off balance. He realized he had lost Anna as he would need two hands to raise her. Instead, Billy dropped his grip on her, whirling, gun in hand, looking for a target. He didn't find one. Jake fired as soon as Anna dropped. The first shot only caught Billy in the hip, throwing him off balance. Billy's answering shot was wild. Jake's second shot missed entirely, but the third was square in the chest. Billy staggered once and then went down, tripping backward over Anna.

Jake pulled Anna up and held her. Then they both went to Kasa. Kasa had crawled to Slade and Jesse and had the children pulled into her lap. Anna let go of Jake and knelt by them. Jake watched for just an instant and then went to the bed. Pulling a quilt from it, Jake went to Kasa and covered her. Kasa was sobbing uncontrollably, rocking the boys while Anna held them all. Jake glanced around the cabin. Three dead men, one bareassed. Blood and bone matter on the floors, wall, and even on Anna and Kasa. Jake's blood boiled. These men had come into his niece's home and defiled her. For the first time in his life, Jake wanted revenge. He wanted to wipe away these sights and the knowledge of what came before.

"Are you all right," Jake knelt by Anna, trying to be calm. "The baby?" Anna was six months pregnant. She had taken a beating.

"I think so," Anna replied. "It's my face that hurts."

And indeed, it was her face that took the worst of the man's blows. Her nose bled, and her lips were cut and bleeding. Already the bruising was showing up on her face. Jake put one hand on Kasa's shoulder and another to Anna's waist. They were sitting like this when Lathe and Hawk burst in.

There was no need for words. Lathe went to Kasa and, kneeling by her, reached out to comfort her. She pulled back.

"Don't touch me," she cried, "I am ruined. I didn't fight hard enough!" She raised the quilt to her face, sobbing into it.

"That is not true!" Anna spoke fiercely. "There were three of them. You were fighting, but they were too many."

Jake rose and, taking Anna's hand, he pulled her up. Lathe needed to be with his wife and children. Jake looked at Hawk and saw Hawk's rage. It mirrored his own. Hawk looked at the dead and pulled his knife.

"Hawk!" Jake spoke harshly. "Not here."

Hawk looked at his uncle. "They forced my sister," Hawk's voice held malice. "It is my right."

"Yes, it is our right," Jake agreed. "But not here. You and I will take them away. We will not do that here." Jake nodded toward the door. He could hear more men coming. "It is our way, but not their way."

Sam and Thomas were the next ones to reach the cabin, then James and Matthew. They stopped dead inside the cabin taking in the destruction, reading the signs. The men stood, unable to fathom the violence that had happened in their midst. Jake could see that he would have to be the one to take charge.

"Get these men strapped on horses," Jake commanded, his words clipped. "Hawk and I will take them up to a ravine above here. There is an overhang there we can chip out, and it will collapse and cover them. I want them gone."

"We will help you bury them," Matthew said. "It will be too much for the two of you."

"No!" Jake spoke more sharply than he intended. Taking a breath, he continued, speaking more calmly. "Matthew, I need you to help Lathe take Kasa and Anna to my cabin. They can't stay here tonight." Jake turned to James, "Go to Bonnie and tell her Hawk will be late. Let her know."

Jake surveyed the room. "Thomas, can you get Beth or maybe Martha to come up and help Kasa and Anna? I don't know how long I'll be."

"I'll go with you to get these bodies covered," Sam drawled casually, looking hard at Jake. Sam, the former mountain man, understood precisely why Hawk and Jake had to take the bodies. Sam knew and understood what would come. Jake gave Sam a steady look and nodded.

When the bodies were strapped on horses, Jake turned to Anna. "You going to be all right?" he asked.

"Yes, you go," Anna looked at him and he could see the anger in her. "You make them go to next life without . . ." she didn't finish but her eyes brimmed with tears.

Jake nodded to her, giving her arm a slight squeeze. "It will be taken care of," he told her. She was Indian now, with Indian ways, despite her white skin.

These hills and valleys were Jake's playground growing up. He knew every creek, every ravine, and every clearing. He led the way now, leading one of the dead men's horses with its burden. Jake, Hawk, and Sam rode for almost an hour before approaching an overhang in the ravine they were following. As kids, Jake and his brother and cousins would ride up here and play under the almost cave-like outcropping. Over the years, there had been erosion, and Jake counted on that erosion to work for them. They could lay the bodies as deep as possible and then hack away with pickaxes and shovels until the top collapsed.

Jake didn't want these men in their cemetery. They didn't belong there. It was true that the Cheyenne who attacked their ranch six years ago were buried in a mass grave at the bottom of the burial ground, but that was different. The Cheyenne were making war on Twin Peaks, just like they had made war on Custer. They came to kill, and maybe do worse, but it had been a fight between men. This was different. These were white men who came to steal, hurt, and rape. They were no better than rabid dogs. Jake still boiled, remembering the scene he walked in on.

Between Hawk, Sam, and Jake, they unloaded the bodies and dragged them under the overhang. Sam surveyed the area and then turned to Jake.

"Reckon, I'll go up above and see where we might want to start picking at the rocks," Sam said casually. "If you see any movement under this ledge, call out. I don't want it to collapse on you."

Jake nodded. He understood Sam. Sam was getting out of the way, leaving Hawk and Jake to their task. Jake imagined that Sam had seen his share of scalping and mutilating, but this wasn't Sam's play. This was Jake's and Hawk's.

Hawk had already started carving up the bare-ass man. Jake let him. Instead, he went to the man who had beaten Anna. Jake had only scalped once, when he rode with a Ute war party when he was nineteen. He had killed for the first time then. He hadn't liked the scalping, but he knew it was expected of him. He couldn't shame Brown Otter by getting squeamish. It was easier when the adrenaline still flowed fierce through his veins. This was different. The adrenaline had long since worn off. It was replaced though, with a burning anger, with righteous rage. He went to work with knife and hatchet. When he was finished, there was little to recognize of the man's features.

It was dark when Hawk reached his cabin. He saw the fire in the fireplace through the open door. He knew Bonnie was waiting for his return. James would have told her what happened, but she would be waiting to hear from him. Kasa and Anna were Bonnie's friends. She would be worried.

Hawk unsaddled his horse and turned it loose in the corral. Then, taking his bounty, Hawk went to the cabin.

Bonnie turned and saw him, smiling with relief at her husband's return. Then she stopped dead, seeing what Hawk was carrying. Hawk was covered with blood, and he carried the scalps of three men. With horror, Bonnie recognized the private parts of the men.

"Hawk, no!" Bonnie's face was stricken. "Get those out of here!"

Hawk regarded her solemnly. "These are mine."

"No!" she could barely speak, "Not in my house!"

"It is my house too. These men hurt my sister," Hawk was firm, his voice cold.

Bonnie backed away from him. "That can't stay here," her voice took on a high, almost hysterical pitch.

"It is my right," Hawk said, no emotion showed in his face. "You are my woman. You should understand that." He turned and finding a peg on the wall, hung the bloody string on the wall.

"I will not live here with them!" Bonnie screamed at Hawk.

He regarded her solemnly, but made no move toward the bloody trophies. Bonnie stared, then turned. Grabbing up a shawl, she brushed past Hawk and out the door. At first, she didn't think about where she was running, but eventually, she knew. Her mother was in St. Louis. Bonnie was running instead to her older sister. Martha would understand. Martha and Sam would take her in.

Even for the beginning of August in the mountains, the days had been warm. Jake sat, leaning against the cabin wall watching the sunrise, feeling the cool breezes on his face. He held his tiny newborn son in his arms, wrapped in a light blanket. He didn't need to keep this baby warm. It was not alive, after all.

About midnight, Anna had awakened, writhing in pain. Jake had gone for Martha. Anna was in labor, and it wasn't normal. The trauma of the day and the beating she had taken had brought this baby over two months early. A perfectly formed little boy who never took a breath. A boy, black fuzz on his head already. A son.

Jake sat with Anna afterward, with the baby between them. They talked, Anna cried, and they decided this perfect tiny child would only be "Baby Welles" on the cross. Finally, Anna cried herself to sleep, and Jake picked up this baby and carried him outside. Leaning against the cabin wall, he had a lot to think about.

Sam and Martha left before dawn. They mentioned that Bonnie was with their children. They would come back in the morning. Sam would notify Matthew. Jake wanted to bury the baby before the sun got too high in the sky. Anna would not go to the burial ground. She was emotionally and physically spent. The blows had battered Anna, and she was bruised and sore. The premature birth had been violent. Anna would stay in bed and let Jake put this baby in the ground.

A horse and rider were coming slowly down the meadow. Jake could see it was Hawk. Jake wondered if Bonnie went home after Sam and Martha returned. Jake doubted it. It was so close to morning then that surely Bonnie would stay at Martha's until it was light out. Hawk may not know about the baby, but he would be coming to check on Kasa.

Hawk rode his horse up to the cabin but did not dismount. "How is Kasa?" he asked Jake in Ute.

"She finally slept sometime in the night. Lathe came out for a bit and then went back to sit with her," Jake replied. "Mary and James have Slade, Jesse, and my kids. The children needed to be away for a bit. Alice and Emmett will keep them busy."

Hawk eyed the bundle in Jake's lap. "And Anna?" he asked.

"She had our son last night. Stillborn," Jake closed his eyes and leaned his head back against the wall. "Anna is sleeping now."

"Let me see," Hawk spoke softly.

Jake turned back the blanket. The tiny boy baby, pale white as new fallen snow, lay in his lap. Gently, Jake fingered the fuzz on the little head. "He would have been a warrior. He is perfect."

Hawk studied the child. "He sleeps with our ancestors now."

Silence fell between the two men, and Jake covered the baby again. Finally, Hawk spoke. "I am going to the reservation. I will see my mother."

"That is a far piece away," Jake replied. This was unexpected.

"I have time," Hawk said, his face a mask.

"Bonnie going?"

"Bonnie ran off last night. I waited for her to return. She did not."

Jake wanted to ask Hawk what he did to cause Bonnie to run. Hawk was his nephew, but it wasn't his business. Jake knew the anger for what had happened was still in Hawk when they parted the evening before. There still was a fury in the man. And Hawk went home that way. Something had set Bonnie off to run, and Hawk didn't look like he was trying to work it out. Instead, he was leaving.

"You have mares in the mountains with ours," Jake commented. "You have a wife here. You coming back?"

"I will go to the reservation and visit my people," Hawk replied noncommittally. Then he turned his horse and rode away.

Jake watched Hawk fade away and then stood up. He couldn't help Hawk now. It was time for Anna to say goodbye to the baby. It was time to go to the burying ground.

As Jake walked past Thomas' cabin, the door opened, and Thomas, Beth, and their four-year-old Jennie came out and fell into step with him. Beth was expecting, her dress not hiding her pregnancy any longer. They would have their second child by Christmas.

At the burial ground, Sam had already dug a small hole. Jeremiah and Will stood waiting, a small, simple wooden casket between them. When Sam spread the news at dawn, Jeremiah had gone to his stockpile of lumber and had chosen the boards he needed. The casket was small, but Sam had lined it with a soft rabbit skin, and Will and Jeremiah carried it between them.

Jake nodded to the people who had already gathered. Matthew and Mattie were there, along with Rachel and Army. James and Mary had brought all the children down, both theirs and Jake's and Lathe's. Bonnie, Martha, and the children were there. The only ones missing were Lathe, Kasa, and Anna, the families from Jackson's Anchor J ranch, and of course, Kade and Sarah. It touched Jake to see them all here to support him. He hadn't asked for a funeral, but his family and friends would not let this child go into the ground alone.

Matthew spoke a few words over the casket. Then the little box was lowered into the ground, and Will and Jeremiah filled the hole. When the ground was heaped and smoothed, Matthew asked Jake if there was anything else he could do. When Jake shook his head, the families began to disperse. Jake stood by the little mound, his face grave.

After the rest of the people had descended the hill, Jake sat down. He wasn't ready to leave yet. So lost in thought was Jake that he didn't hear Matthew return until he stood above Jake.

"You are hurting," Matthew said softly, "but I think it is more than just the loss of this child." Matthew slowly lowered himself down to sit beside Jake. "Do you want to talk about it?"

Jake closed his eyes and thought about how to answer. "Those men were evil, and I do not regret killing them. Is that a sin?"

Matthew thought about that. "There are many places in the Bible where God slays the enemies of Israel. There will always be men who need killing. Evil men. Even I have killed, you know that. But a verse in Micah says, 'And I will execute vengeance in anger and fury on the nations, such as they have not heard.' You did no more than that. You executed vengeance on evil men."

"But after," Jake hesitated, thinking. "Would God take this child from us for what I did after? Did I cause this baby to be born dead?"

"I am not sure what you mean," Matthew started slowly.

"Hawk and I, we took the bodies up to bury under a rockslide. We were both filled with anger," Jake looked at Matthew and then away. "We mutilated the bodies. They were a pulp when we were done. And I gloried in it. Would God punish me for that by taking away my son?"

Matthew sat silent for a while before he spoke. "'The righteous shall rejoice when he sees the vengeance; he shall wash his feet in the blood of the wicked.' I remember that from somewhere in the Psalms. You did no more than that. You only sought the vengeance that the wicked deserved. God wouldn't take your child because of that. Those men took your child, not you."

Jake nodded but said nothing, head bent, eyes to the grave.

"Jacob," Matthew said softly, using Jake's given name, "it also says in the Psalms, 'Let the wicked be ashamed, let them be silent in the grave.' Put those men away from you now. Go home. Anna needs you." Matthew struggled to his feet and looked down upon the younger man. He reached down and laid his hand gently on Jake's shoulder. "Let the wicked be silent, Jake, both in the grave and in your mind. Let them go to hell. Don't go with them."

New Beginnings - Late Summer 1882

Kade didn't even take the horse to the stable. He left the animal tied to the hitching post, knowing Ezekiel would put the stud away. Kade took the stairs three at a time and found Katie watching for him in the hall. The wait seemed like an eternity to Kade before the young doctor came out to speak to him.

"Your wife is doing reasonably well right now, Mr. Welles," the young man said. "This could be a long night, so I'd suggest you get some rest."

"This is too early," Kade said worriedly. "We didn't think the baby would come for at least another couple of weeks."

"You have to remember that your wife wasn't getting her menses regularly," the doctor replied. "The baby's due date was just an estimate. Because your wife was so ill for so long with this pregnancy, she has not gained a lot of weight. It has been hard to gauge. The baby might be very small."

"But she's doing all right?" Kade asked.

"The labor is not hard yet. I'm hoping that this will not be too hard on Sarah," the doctor said, "but only time will tell. For now, all is well."

Joe pressured Kade into going to the study with him and they sat there, sipping a beer. Kade didn't like being so far from Sarah, but standing in the hall wasn't doing any good. The doctor did not want Kade in the room.

The afternoon light dimmed. Juba or Katie came regularly to assure Kade that Sarah was still doing well. Ezekiel came in and told Kade the horse had been taken to the stable. Kade finally sent Joe to bed and returned to the upstairs hall. Pulling a chair out from another bedroom, he sat, waited, and worried. He could occasionally hear Sarah or one of the doctors talking, but he couldn't make out the words. Finally, well after midnight, he heard the voices inside the bedroom raised, encouraging Sarah. He heard her cry out once, and then suddenly, all went quiet. Kade hovered by the door, holding his breath. He wanted to hear something, anything of Sarah or the baby or both. Suddenly, he heard a slap and the tiny cry of an infant. Then he heard Sarah. She was laughing, or maybe crying. Whichever it was, Kade knew it was the sound of joy. At sixty-years-old, Kade was a father again. In his mind, he sent up a simple prayer of thanks.

The doctor allowed Kade in briefly to see Sarah after she and the baby were cleaned up. The tiny little mite was lying on the bed, nestled against her mother. Sarah, weariness etched on her face, smiled at Kade.

"A daughter," Sarah whispered. "I seem to have a lot of daughters." Sarah could hardly keep her eyes open.

"A pretty little thing," Kade said, reaching for Sarah's hand. "Best I get a daughter at my age. Don't think I can keep up with a growing boy anymore." Kade squeezed Sarah's hand. "You sleep now. I'll come in the morning."

Sarah barely nodded, and Kade knew she was already drifting off. The baby too, was sound asleep. Slowly, Kade nodded to the doctor, and they both backed out of the room.

The morning was bright, sunshine streaming in from the windows when Kade was allowed back in with Sarah and the baby. Sarah was rested, and the baby had nursed. The doctors had been by and thought both mother and child were doing remarkably well. When the room finally cleared, Sarah looked up at Kade.

"Do you want to hold her?" she asked softly.

Kade nodded. He leaned over Sarah and picked up the tiny baby, carefully cradling it in his big hands.

"My God, Sarah," Kade exclaimed. "She don't weigh but a feather!"

Sarah smiled, and Kade, looking at Sarah, smiled back. "She is a feather, isn't she?" Sarah said. "Marie was my mother's name. I wanted to call her that. But I know you, Kade Welles, you won't ever call her anything but Feather. So, let's name her that. Feather Marie Welles."

Together Kade and Sarah wrote a letter to Twin Peaks, to all their children and friends, telling them that Feather had arrived, and both mother and child were healthy. It was early August, and neither Kade nor Sarah had any idea that on this morning, Jake was burying his newborn son.

September couldn't come fast enough for Kade. Sarah gained weight and strength every day, but because Feather was so small and the pregnancy had been so hard on Sarah, they felt they had to wait until the baby was at least six weeks old before traveling. The couple both yearned for the mountains and their family there. When Jake's letter arrived, telling of the outlaws who came to the valley and how they had hurt Kasa and Anna, it was hard for Sarah and Kade to be so far away.

Bonnie's letter came next, telling that she and Hawk were having difficulties and that Hawk had ridden off to visit the reservation. Bonnie did not elaborate. She wrote that she was home in her cabin waiting for his return. She was fine. Will was building up a good number of sheep, having bought more during the summer. His new business was complete with a sheepherder who had the flock in the higher mountains for the summer. Will and his new herder had several dogs, and one had given birth to seven puppies. Will thought his sister, Bonnie, might like the comfort of having a pup with her now when she was alone, so Will had brought her a puppy for companionship.

Mattie and Matthew wrote that the hay was up. They had hired extra men from Laramie to help with the haying this summer. The ranch needed even more hay now that Will had such a large flock. In early July, a handful of Utes had wandered in. They were dissatisfied with the reservation in Utah and had left for the summer to hunt. They had stopped by to visit Jake and Hawk, but at the time, Jake, Hawk, and Lathe were at Jacob's cabin. James had known one of the braves, and he had talked the men into staying and helping hay. Matthew wrote that the Utes were good help for a couple of weeks, and then they had taken goods for their pay and ridden off. The Indians had left as quickly as they came.

Jeremiah had all the lumber needed for the schoolhouse stockpiled and when the hay was all hauled in, the extra men hired for haying stayed on. Jeremiah and the men had the floor done and were raising the walls. Matthew hoped the building would be finished before Kade and Sarah returned. Jeremiah's wife, a schoolteacher before she married Jeremiah, was searching for a teacher who would come out for the winter to teach.

James wrote that he was busy with the young colts left behind that summer by Jake. Mary and the children were all doing fine. The baby was expected in December. Alice and Emmett were excited about another baby in the cabin. Gideon was beginning to talk and getting into everything. Noah was off most of the week helping either Matthew or Will but usually came home one night every week to be with the family. They were all waiting for Sarah and Kade's return.

With each letter, Sarah and Kade only yearned for home more. So finally, Kade wrote his last letter home telling the family they were booked on the train to arrive in Laramie early on the morning of September seventh. Kade requested that someone meet them in Laramie with a buggy and a wagon. Kade sent a list of supplies he wanted filled and asked that everything be purchased and packed up, ready to go when the train pulled in. Neither Sarah nor Kade wanted to stay even one day in town. After eating a meal at the hotel dining room, they wanted to head out and leave town behind. The mountains were calling them home.

James and Noah were at the train station when the train arrived. It didn't take long for Kade and Sarah to climb down the steps, little Feather in Sarah's arms. Juba was with them, much to the porter's dismay. The porter had tried ordering Juba to another car instead of first class, but Kade would have none of it. Juba was to stay and help his wife. Ezekiel, though, rode with the bay stud. Kade intended to ride in the livestock car with the horse himself, but Ezekiel insisted. Ezekiel felt more comfortable with the animals.

With Noah escorting the two women and baby to the hotel restaurant, James, Ezekiel, and Kade went to unload the horse from the train. James was impressed with the big bay and offered to take the horse to the livery. He would get the horse some breakfast and then harness the two teams. The wagon was already loaded, and James would pick up the family at the hotel when he had everything ready.

"I's go with this young man," Ezekiel said. "I's help him with the teams."

"You haven't eaten," Kade replied. "You better come with me an' eat some."

"No, suh," Ezekiel said firmly. "Only be trouble should I go in a hotel. You can git the baby's nursemaid in, but not this Black man. Jest be trouble. I be fine."

Kade regarded Ezekiel and then nodded his head. "You may be right, Ezekiel. I'd fight for you, but today I jest want to go home. I'll bring you something to eat." Kade nodded to James. "Take him with you an' bring the buggy up to the hotel when you are ready. I'll ride the bay."

James and Ezekiel walked toward the livery.

"Mistah Kade say you married to my sister?" Ezekiel asked.

James smiled. "I am. Mary is excited you and Juba are coming."

"You sure?"

"Of course," James replied, puzzled. "It will be nice for her to have family with us."

"She ain't gonna be able to pretend she's white with us'n around," Ezekiel said solemnly.

James stopped and looked at the older man. "Ezekiel, Mary's not ashamed of the blood that runs through her. I'm not, either. I know there's some people who want to make you and her ashamed of that, but it won't happen at our ranch. We don't care. Time you trusted some of us white men." They walked on in silence before James said, "You know I have distant cousins who are Indian, don't you?"

"Yes'm, Mistah Kade told us'n 'bout his son."

"Well, there is also Jake's niece and nephew at the ranch," at least James hoped that Hawk would return to the ranch. "What do you think about Indians?"

"Reckon they's jest people, right?"

"Exactly," James agreed. "And that is just what you and Juba are, just people." As they came to the livery, James handed the bay's lead rope to Ezekiel. "Take him in and get him some water and feed. I'll catch up the teams."

"Yes'm, Mistah James."

James pulled up short and looked at Ezekiel. "No, I'm not Mister anything. I'm your brother-in-law. I'm just James. Might stick in your craw a bit, but that's who I am."

Turning, James went into a corral and sorted out his four horses. As he haltered them and headed to the gate, the livery groom came out to help him.

"By gad," the man said to James, "I ain't never seen a Negro in my whole life, an' I jest seen my second one in two days!"

"Second one?" James asked, distractedly.

"Yup, jest yesterday there was a Black man come in to get supplies," the man said. "He drove a wagon in an' left the horses here for some feed. Left an hour later. Headed to the mercantile, then out of town."

"Someone new around here then?" James asked.

"I ain't been in town but fer a couple weeks, but Bert said the man used to work at the whorehouse what got run out of town last winter."

James turned to the stable hand. "Say where he was going?"

"Hell, I don't know my way around town yet, but Bert used to cowboy around here. He might know," the hostler replied. "He owns this place."

"How long will you be?" Mary asked, watching James roll a blanket and an extra set of clothes into a pack to tie behind the saddle.

"Not sure," James replied, "but from what the livery owner said, it sounded like Marcus might be at a place in the mountains a little over two days west of Laramie. There was a homesteader out that way who used to come in, but he packed up when his wife and in-laws died from consumption. Bert thought maybe Marcus had bought that homestead. I got general directions, but it might be tough to find."

"How far do you reckon it is from here?"

James thought a minute on that. "Hard to tell, but from the details that Bert gave me, it might be as close as a day away from here, maybe two. I'll give myself four days, and if I don't find him, I'll head home. But I could be farther out and take me some time to get back, so give me a week before you start worrying," James ruffled Mary's hair.

"I ain't goin' to go worryin' myself over you," Mary ducked her head to hide sudden tears.

"Well, I'm going to worry about you then," James teased. "Don't you go having this baby without me."

"I got two more months to wait for this baby," Mary said. "I ain't plannin' on havin' it early. You jest better git back."

"I will. Thomas said he and Beth will look in on you. Reckon Kade and Ezekiel will too. Just take it easy," James warned. "I have enough wood to get us through the whole month, so no chopping, you hear?" James ran his hand through her hair gently, then turned and left. He was almost down to the horse corral when he heard Mary call to him.

"You tell her I say thank you. Tell her I's much obliged."

James stopped and looked up the hill at Mary. "I reckon to do just that," he said, "from both of us."

As James rode past Matthew's cabin, Noah came out from the corrals, riding his horse. At fourteen, Noah was considered a man and did a man's day of work. He had two horses in his string now. He generally helped Matthew and Will, which didn't require much horseback work. If he went on fall gather, Jake would cut out a couple of extra horses for Noah then, but on a daily basis, he could get by with just two saddle horses.

"Where you heading this morning?" James asked when Noah got near.

"I'm taking care of Will's pigs first," Noah replied. "He's off to the sheep in the mountains again. Then I'm supposed to take the milk cows out and help at the schoolhouse after. Matthew doesn't need me today."

"Learning carpentry now, are you?"

"I like it," Noah replied. "But I like working with Matthew the best."

James nodded at that statement. Matthew and Kade were the patriarchs of this ranch, and everyone liked and respected them. James knew that Matthew, with his deep faith in God, was a good influence on this young boy. Someday, Noah might ride colts with Kade or work cattle under Thomas, but for now, James was glad Matthew took the boy under his wing.

"What did Will tell you to do while he was gone?" James inquired.

"You should know, he's your brother," Noah grinned at James. "Will jest pointed at the hogs and the barn and said, 'Do what needs doing.'"

James laughed at that. It was no secret that Will was not much of a talker. Eight years older than James, Will had never been James' playmate. But Will had lived in his parents' home until after Kade moved in two years ago. That summer, Will built his cabin and barns on the other side of the river, nestled against the foothills. James remembered playing checkers with Will when they both still lived with Sarah. Night after night, James hardly heard Will say a word. He might grunt, point, or groan, but to get a word out of Will, James felt like he had to rope it and pull it out of Will's mouth. Will had always been a quiet child, but now he was a godawful silent man.

At Will's, James waved goodbye to Noah and followed a trail made by Will and the sheep, climbing to the higher slopes. He'd follow this trail until it turned off the wrong direction. James wasn't sure where Will's flock was grazing. Maybe, if he were lucky, James would come upon the flock and catch a meal with Will and his sheep herder.

When the sheep trail turned west, James left it and headed east, knowing he'd get no meal with his brother that day. By instinct, and his general knowledge of this mountain country, he felt he had to go more toward the east. He traveled much of the day without seeing a sign of a man. Late in the afternoon, he topped a ridge and sat, staring out at the expanse of mountain slopes, tree covered, a mixture of pine tree green and aspen gold. As he searched the horizon, James saw a thin wisp of smoke a couple of miles in the distance. It might not be where Marcus disappeared to, but if it was another homesteader, maybe the settler knew where there were other cabins. At the least, this might be a place to catch a meal and stay for the night. James kicked his horse, and they began to descend the slope. He wanted to make that smoke before dark.

James saw the buildings as he broke through the trees and came out on a pretty mountain meadow. There was a low log barn with a corral against it. Two horses were in the corral, and they threw up their heads as they sighted James. There were two cabins, one larger with a covered porch. The smaller cabin sat close to the bigger cabin with a dog trot connecting them. James could see wood stacked in the dog trot where it would stay dry.

A garden was in front of the cabins, and a woman was digging in it with a spade. The woman had her back to James. From that distance, James could see that this woman was stout, but not overly fat. Miss Tillie would make two of this woman. James felt instant disappointment. He must be in the wrong place. He only hoped these people had news of other homesteaders in the area.

The horses in the corral nickered to James' horse, which alerted the woman. She turned and faced James as he got close. James pulled up his horse sharply, surprise and shock making him exclaim, "My God! Miss Tillie, it is you! Are you well?"

Miss Tillie laughed back at James. "Don't I look well?"

James lost his voice then, not knowing how to respond. He dismounted, giving himself time to think. This was indeed Miss Tillie, but instead of the immense woman he remembered, she had lost a great deal of weight. She was not thin by any means, but she was not obese. A trace of the beauty James remembered from the photograph he'd seen at the brothel was there, just in a woman twenty years older.

Tillie was dressed in a calico dress, demurely buttoned to her throat. The raucous woman he'd known in Laramie was hidden beneath a proper frock. James wasn't sure what he expected to find, but this was not it.

"I mean," James stammered, "you look good, but have you been sick? You've . . ."

Tillie laughed again, and it was that boisterous laugh he remembered. "I'm fine. I just seem to do well out here in the mountain air. Lots less to carry around now. What brings you to these parts, cowboy?"

James found this safer ground. "Looking for you," James replied. "Wanted to tell you I got married. Wanted to thank you for that. Mary too; she sends her thanks."

"Well, that is good news. You better put that horse in with ours. We have a stall in the barn, but there is already a horse in it. Come to the big house. Marcus will want to see you. He'll have supper ready soon." Tillie shifted her burden of freshly dug-up potatoes in her apron. "You better plan on staying the night too. Got catching up to do." She turned to the cabin, and then thinking about something more, she turned back to James. "I go by Susan now. Tillie and Black Charlie don't live here. Just Susan and Marcus."

James stepped slowly through the door of the cabin and stopped in surprise. The large main room was both kitchen and parlor. In it were several of the gaudy settees and chairs that he remembered from the brothel in Laramie. Bright golds and reds were arranged around the room. The table was one of the beautiful round tables from the main parlor of Miss Tillie's, where often a card game could be found in the evening. A gold and green carpet was on the floor, a piano in one corner, and a bookcase against the wall.

"Holy! Are you in business here?" James asked in surprise, wondering how customers could find this place.

Marcus stood by the stove, stirring a pot. "Mistah James, it is good to see you. Susan will be out in a minute. She's washin' up. And no, we ain't in business here. But

Susan wasn't going to leave her fine things to that mob that wanted us out. So's we just brought 'em with us."

James surveyed the room again. "Well, it sure is comfortable in here . . . and bright."

Susan came out of an adjoining room then in a clean dress. This one was also a conservative dress which was somewhat out of place in the gaudy furnishings. She motioned to James to take a seat, and he sat in a tufted settee, remembering the luxury of it from Laramie.

"So, you came looking for me, did you?" Susan began.

"Yes, ma'am, I did," James replied. "Wanted you to know about Mary and me and that we are going to have our first child before Christmas. Wouldn't have happened without your help."

Susan smiled at that. "That is good to hear. She seems a right nice young gal. You are happy, aren't you?"

"I am," James smiled warmly. "The kids are all doing fine, and we all get along. I always dreamed of having a big family. Never thought it would happen all at once, though."

"You did jump in with both feet, didn't you?" Susan commented. She leaned back in her chair, surveying James. "You have filled out. By God, I believe you look your age finally. You aren't looking like a little kid anymore. Having a woman in your bed every night must suit you."

James colored at that, the blush spreading up his neck to his face. But he grinned back at Susan, "It suits me. I like the commotion of a family," James hesitated, then changed the subject, "So how did you two come to be way out here?"

Susan grew serious then. "There was a new preacher in town, and he was preaching about all the sin in Laramie. He thought a whore house a block off Main Street was the worst," she laughed bitterly. "One night, we had a brawl, and one of our customers pulled a knife. Before it was over, there were several cut up. No one was killed, or we might not have gotten away, but that put us in the limelight, so to speak. The town council got in the act, and I could see we would be driven out. I knew a businessman who wanted my building, so I just up and sold him the place. I knew the owner of this homestead, and he wanted to sell it, so I bought it sight unseen. Marcus and I hired a couple of wagons, loaded them up with furniture, and headed out of town one night. I never looked back."

"So, who lives next door?" James asked. "I saw curtains on the window there."

"Rosie came with us," Susan replied. "The rest of the girls went to a new place out beyond the train tracks or just left town, but Rosie wanted to stay with us, so we brought her here."

"So, Rosie is your only girl then? Are there any customers out here?"

"Rosie isn't working," Susan said quietly. "She was caught in that knife fight. She's got two ugly slashes across her face. They luckily didn't disfigure her badly, but the scars will always be there. She probably wouldn't be able to go anywhere but to a crib, and that's a poor end for a working girl. She's been with me too long to let that happen," Susan smiled gently. "She was a farm girl before taking up the trade. She wanted to come here with us and said she'd help with chores for her room and board. It is working out," Susan chuckled, "and Rosie's a kept woman now."

"Kept woman?" James wasn't familiar with the term.

"Rosie has a man."

"No shit?" James was surprised. "I'm sorry, forgot myself," he apologized.

Throwing her head back, Susan laughed at that. "Still the gentleman, aren't you, James?"

James just grinned back. "So, she's married?"

"Now, cowboy, you know that doesn't happen with the likes of us, but she has a steady man who comes and visits," Susan explained. "Rosie has her own cabin. He gives her money for her needs. Comes when he can. Only says if Rosie takes another man, he's gone."

"So, how long do you think this will last?" James wondered.

"Who knows? From the gentleman's end, I can't say, but from Rosie's, it is the best she can hope for, and she's content. She won't let anyone else in her bed. This is too good a deal for her. She's thankful for what she has." Susan thought about that for a moment and then added, "And I think she really cares for this man. He seems a good man, a quiet man. You'll get to meet him shortly. He's here now, and they come over here to eat. Rosie's cabin doesn't have any cookstove, just a heating stove. She takes all her meals with us."

"Can you make a living on this place?" James asked, changing the subject.

"Don't need to make a living here," Susan answered. "Marcus and I have money saved. My house made us a lot of money. I like working in the garden, though, and so does Rosie."

"You must do the heavy plowing then," James looked at Marcus.

"I's a house nigger," Marcus replied in a wheedling Southern drawl, but his wide grin belied his words.

"You quit that nigger talk," Susan admonished Marcus. She turned to James, "Marcus has kept me safe for over twenty years. He wanted to keep me out of the trade, but a Black man cannot make a decent living for himself, much less for a woman too. He grew up in the fields and has the mark of the lash on his back to prove it. I swore he'd never go back there, and I plan to keep it that way. Luckily, Rosie's man came along at just the right time this spring to plow up a garden for us. But don't you fault Marcus none; he will do whatever we need. We both will." Susan glanced fondly at Marcus.

"Set up to the table, you two," Marcus said, carrying a steaming pot. "Food's ready. I'll call Rosie." Marcus set the pot on the table and went out the door. James heard a pounding on the cabin next door, and Marcus came in grinning. "Let's see how long it takes them."

The three of them had their plates full when Rosie entered. She stopped abruptly when she saw James.

"Oh, hello," Rosie said, surprised. James recognized her at once. Two angry welts cut across one side of her face, the healed scars of a knife. Behind her came a tall man. With the light from the setting sun coming through the door, it wasn't until the man moved into the cabin a few steps that James could see him.

"Well, hello, brother," James drawled. "I take it the sheep are doing just fine."

Will Bates froze, a crimson blush spreading up his neck to his face. Susan looked between the two men and began to laugh.

"I'll be go to hell . . ." she said. "I should have known."

◆

James thought the meal might get awkward then, but it didn't. Will did what he did best. He sat, ate, and didn't say a word, barely looking up at the rest. Susan, Marcus, and James carried most of the conversation, with Rosie chiming in at times. The food was good, and there was plenty of it. When they finally finished and pushed back from the table, Will spoke his first words.

"What brings you, James?" he asked, glancing suspiciously between James and Rosie.

"Susan and Marcus are old friends of mine," James answered easily. "I came to find them and make sure they were doing all right. And you?" James asked innocently.

"Shut up, James," Will responded, getting up. He went out to the porch.

"Why don't you men go have a smoke," Susan said, "and let Rosie and me clean this up."

James got up from the table and joined Will on the porch. Marcus didn't follow. Will pulled a pipe from his pocket and studied it. Taking a pouch out, he filled the bowl, but not having a light, he just held it in his hand.

"So, how'd you find this place?" James asked Will.

"Heard rumors in town. You?"

"Livery owner saw Marcus in town. I heard when I went for Ma and Kade."

"I thought you and Mary were doing good," Will stated.

"We are," James answered, then realizing what Will was implying, he went on. "Susan did me a good turn when I was courting Mary. Mary had reservations about marrying again. Susan talked to her last year when we went to Laramie in July. Changed Mary's mind. I just wanted to tell Susan we were married."

"That's all?"

"I know what you're implying, Will, and it isn't so. I didn't even know Rosie was with them here. Don't care neither," James said shortly.

"You been to the house in Laramie then?" Will wanted to know.

"I been around some," James answered, knowing Will was talking about Miss Tillie's Palace.

"You been with Rosie?"

"Does it matter?"

"Could."

"Well, it shouldn't," James said impatiently. "I don't plan on being with her here, that's for sure. I don't plan on being in any woman's bed but Mary's."

Will just grunted at that. Silence settled between them. James could hear the women inside, and shortly they came out.

"Think I'll turn in then," Rosie commented, heading for the little cabin. Without a word to the rest of them, Will got up and followed her. James watched him go. That was so like Will. Just walk away without a word.

Susan settled into the chair next to James, and Marcus came out and joined them.

"So, that is your brother," Susan did not say it as a question.

"That is my brother. He's about as different from me as a man can be."

"I'm not so sure of that," Susan teased. "That blush must be a Bates trait. And I think you boys have the same kind of appetite."

"Well, the food was good," James replied.

351

"Wasn't the food I was referring to," Susan laughed. She was rewarded by the color that crept up James' neck and face.

❧

James, Marcus, and Susan stayed up late into the night. James could see that the couple was starving for news and visitors. After living for years with the public, the mountains could be a lonely place. If Will was the only visitor they got, they didn't get much news from him.

James enjoyed the conversation as well. Both Marcus and Susan came from a different world than he had experienced. They both came from the South, but over the years, they had lived in cow towns, mining towns, and cities. Some of the places Susan talked about were hard for James to imagine, having never been to any town larger than Laramie.

James spent the night in Marcus's room. A small cubicle with a small cot and dresser, it was in the corner of the house farthest from the stove. The nights were not yet cold, and James found it comfortable.

"I hate to turn Marcus out of his room," James told Susan.

"You aren't," Susan replied wryly. "It isn't like he uses this room. This room connects to the main bedroom by a hidden door behind that wardrobe. But you don't know that."

"Right," James responded, understanding. "You are careful, aren't you?"

"We are," Susan answered. "This might not be the South, but we don't want any trouble. Other than Rosie, you are the only one to know, and only because you guessed long ago."

"It will stay that way," James said seriously. "Maybe someday things will change, but until then, your secret is safe with me. I am just glad you have this much."

"You are a good man," Susan patted James' cheek fondly. "Stay that way."

James could smell coffee when he woke in the morning. Marcus was by the stove, a big batch of scrambled eggs cooking in one pan, bacon frying in another.

"Smells good," James stated. "Do you do all the cooking?"

Marcus looked up from his pans and smiled, "You don't want to eat Susan's food. She can bake a good cookie and sometimes bread, but don't let her near a frying pan. She gets distracted and burns everything."

"I do not," Susan chimed in from the doorway. "You just like to cook."

"That's true," Marcus smiled at her. "Holler at Rosie," Marcus said, and shortly they heard the pounding on the cabin next door.

Rosie and Will came in almost at once. Apparently, they were ready for breakfast. The food was flavorful and filling, and James ate heartily, knowing it could be late when he got home.

"I'm heading out after eating," James commented to Will.

Will nodded. Between bites, he mumbled, "I'll ride with you."

With breakfast over, James went for his horse while Will went to Rosie's cabin for his bedroll. James had his saddle thrown on his horse when he saw Will come out of the cabin, saddlebags over his shoulder. Will stopped and stretched, surveying the yard. Just as he took a step forward, Rosie came out behind him and reaching around Will's waist, she pulled him back to her. Will froze for a moment, then suddenly turned on the woman. James saw a flash of white leg as Will pulled her skirts up to get his hand under them. Then he picked her up and walked Rosie back into the cabin, kicking the door shut with his foot.

James snugged his cinch, but not too tight. He had a feeling that Will wasn't quite ready to head out. James led the horse to Susan's porch, tying the animal to the hitching post. Marcus was sitting on a chair on the porch and grinned at James.

"That happens a lot," Marcus said. "You in a hurry?"

James and Will had been riding for almost three hours before Will finally broke the silence. James was determined not to speak first.

"You going to mention this to Ma?" Will asked.

James looked at his brother in surprise. "You think I'd say anything?"

Will just shrugged.

"Let's see," James said casually, "how would that conversation go? Maybe like, hey Ma, I was visiting this madam of that brothel in Laramie that got run out last winter, because, you know, we got to be friends when I used to visit there and when I got to their place . . ."

"Okay, sorry," Will interrupted him. "I wasn't thinking."

"Brother, you don't do a lot of thinking sometimes, by what comes out of your mouth," James laughed.

"Shut up, James," Will responded.

"So why don't you just marry Rosie and bring her home? Wouldn't that be better than having to ride here . . . what, every month?" James wanted to know.

"Good god, I can't marry her," Will almost exploded.

"Well, I know she was a working girl," James said, trying to be tactful, "but who would know out at Twin Peaks?"

"If you know, must be others," Will answered. "But it isn't that."

James waited, but Will didn't go on. Finally, James asked, "So what is it?"

"I don't want anyone in my house."

"You don't want anyone in your house?" James repeated, incredulous.

"Can't stand all the noise," Will didn't look at James.

"Noise?"

"You know, all the jabbering a woman makes. Well, men too." Will said. "I can't even stand it when Noah has to stay over sometimes. I tried once, you know."

James looked at Will, studying his older brother, wondering what he meant by that statement. He searched his memory. "You were writing some woman in Missouri, weren't you?" James ventured. "Whatever happened to her? Didn't you go to meet her at Laramie? A couple years ago? After Thomas' wedding? Did she stand you up?"

"Didn't work out."

"I remember you said that when you came home without the woman. But how didn't it work out?" James pressed Will.

"She married that cattle buyer, Jenkins," Will said evenly.

"So, she gets off the train to meet you, and she marries the cattle buyer instead? Kind of quick, wasn't it?" James was confused. "How'd she even know him."

"I took her to lunch."

"Son of a bitch," James exploded. "Will you just tell me what happened? Do I have to pull every word out of you?"

Will looked at James and then ahead but finally relented. "I met her at the train, we ate lunch at the hotel, and I got her a room. I met her for supper, but I couldn't stand the constant talking. I mean, she wanted to know about the ranch and the family. Just questions and more questions. We got a table, and I looked up, and there was Jenkins. I heard he'd been wanting a wife. I got up, told him to come sit with this woman so she wouldn't be alone. I told the woman it wasn't going to work with us, and I walked out. I heard they got married two weeks later."

"You just walked away, leaving her with a stranger?"

"I was a stranger. What difference does it make?"

James just shook his head. "So, you just walked out on her and rode home?"

"I visited Rosie first."

"You are a strange man, Will."

"Shut up, James."

CHAPTER 16

Prayer of Thanksgiving – Fall 1882

T he horses were sorted and ready to be let out of the corral. It was time to head to the high country for the fall gather. Every man in the community except Matthew, Will, and Kade were saddled and ready. A remuda of saddle horses was sorted, enough for the week to ten days the gather would take. Each hand had sorted out the best animals from his string.

"Going to be different this year," Thomas commented to Jake as they mounted. "Was hard when we didn't have Ma, but now with Pa staying back, it just don't seem natural."

"Changing times, little brother," Jake answered. "Pa wants to stay with Sarah and the baby. Reckon it's time we step up and let him step back." They reined their horses away from the corral. "But you're right; it doesn't seem right. Leaves a hole."

Jake looked at the crew, all trusted men. Mostly family to Jake, like his half-brother Thomas, distant cousins Jeremiah, Lathe, and James, and friends married into the family like Sam and Army, and the one lone hired man, Luke, who had been with them for five years. The only young man missing was Hawk. For Jake, that left another hole in the crew.

"I'm going to stop over at Bonnie's," Jake said to Thomas. "Check that all is fine there before heading out."

"I think Will and Kade were going to watch out for her," Thomas replied distractedly. The remuda was being let out of the corral.

"Hawk's my nephew," Jake said quietly. "I need to check on her myself. I feel sort of responsible in this."

Thomas nodded, understanding. "Catch up then. We won't wait."

Jake left the rest of the cowboys trailing the horses, heading them to the trail into the mountains. Instead, he rode across the meadow and headed north. Bonnie and Hawk's cabin was the farthest one on that side of the valley.

As Jake rode, he thought about his last conversation with Hawk, as Jake sat with his dead baby son in his arms. At the time, Jake thought Hawk would calm down when he got off by himself. But when Bonnie turned up at his cabin late in the afternoon that same day, Jake knew Hawk had not turned back.

"Jake," Bonnie had said that day, "I need your help. Can you come home with me?"

Jake had left Anna sleeping and walked with Bonnie to her home. She was confused and scared and wanted his reassurance that Hawk would come home. When Jake asked Bonnie what had happened the night before, she tearfully told him.

"Jake," Bonnie said, "Hawk was so cold. He just stared at me like he hated me. Then he turned and put that . . . those . . . oh, God, it was awful. I just ran. I thought maybe he'd come after me, but he didn't."

"How can I help?"

"Can you take it out of the house?" Bonnie implored. "I can't go in there with those hanging there."

"I'll get rid of it for you," Jake said.

"No," Bonnie admonished, "you can't get rid of it. Just put it somewhere . . . maybe in the back of the cabin, where I don't go. Put it there. I won't throw away Hawk's . . ." She couldn't name the bloody string of scalps and man parts.

"I can do that," Jake had told her.

They had walked quietly together for a while until Bonnie could talk again.

"Jake, I don't understand any of this," Bonnie started. "I don't mean the killing of those men, or maybe even what Hawk did, but to bring that home and think that I would let that . . ." She had to stop again, unable even to use descriptive words. She took some deep breaths and continued, "I mean, you are Ute, and you wouldn't do that, not to the men or to Anna."

"Bonnie," Jake said gently, "I did do that. I was part of it. I never thought I would be, but we were both so angry. I kept seeing what those men were doing when I got to the doorway. Kasa and Anna were being hurt. They were being hurt in the worst way. I never felt hate like I did that day."

"But you didn't take any of those things home," Bonnie was surprised. "I mean, you wouldn't do that to Anna?"

"Honey," Jake said gently, "Anna wanted me to do that." He saw Bonnie look up at him with wide, surprised eyes. Jake went on. "Bonnie, remember when I warned you and Hawk that you come from different backgrounds? I never imagined this would be part of it, but it is. Hawk did nothing more than what would have been expected of him if he lived with the tribe. Not just expected, but praised. Remember, Anna was raised by the Pawnee. She expected revenge to be taken against those men. If I had taken scalps . . . trophies, home, she would have welcomed them. It was me that couldn't do that. That was the line I couldn't step over. I might be able to take revenge, but I couldn't take those things into my home. I was not raised in the tribe. What Hawk couldn't understand was your reaction. In his anger, he couldn't see who you are. He just saw you rejecting him."

They walked on in silence then. When they reached the cabin, Jake had Bonnie wait outside. He went in and took the bloody string of items off the wall and carried them behind the house, finding a notch to hang the string. He called to Bonnie then, letting her know it was safe to go inside.

"Will he come back?" Bonnie asked softly as Jake turned to leave.

Jake pondered that question before answering. "I hope so," Jake replied. It was the best he could do.

So here Jake was now, almost two months later, riding back to Bonnie's to check on her. He had done this several times a week since that awful day. Bonnie was his nephew's wife and was herself a distant cousin to Jake. And Hawk had not returned.

The cabin door was shut against the October chill, but the little pup Will had given to Bonnie heralded Jake's arrival. No one would sneak up on the cabin with the little dog around. Bonnie pulled on a shawl and came out into the yard. Jake watched her come slowly to stand by him. Bonnie had not said anything, but he knew she was carrying Hawk's child. She was beginning to show. Sadness radiated from her.

"You are off to gather?" Bonnie asked.

"I am," Jake answered. "Will you be fine?"

"Will and Kade will watch out for me," Bonnie said. "James was here yesterday and chopped enough wood for weeks. I am such a bother to all of you."

"You are not a bother. I just wish I could help more," Jake hesitated, then asked, "When is the baby due?"

Bonnie looked off across the meadow before she answered. "Maybe March? Or early April."

"Bonnie, I could write a letter to the agency. If Hawk is there, he will get it."

"No," Bonnie was firm on that. "I don't want him to come back because of the baby. He has to come back because he wants to; because he wants me."

Jake nodded. He understood what she was saying. The marriage couldn't be held together if only the knowledge of a baby brought Hawk back. Hawk had to return on his own. His choice had to be a life with Bonnie. And Jake, truthfully, didn't know what choice Hawk would make.

It took half a day for the men to get to the big upland meadow where the shack was built to hold supplies when the gather was happening. Jake caught up with the rest of the crew long before then. The men always looked forward to fall gather. They camped outdoors, ate around the campfire, and rode the surrounding hills for days. Jake remembered when fall gather was truly a family affair as the whole Welles and Bates families went, but now, with Sabra gone and most of the young women home with little children, it became an event only for the men. It was different now, the language and the food much rougher. But the camaraderie was still the same, although, without the presence of women, a bit more off-color.

As the remuda was driven into the holding corral, Jake noticed there were already several hundred cows and calves grazing in the expansive meadow. A wisp of smoke from a campfire in front of the shack rose lazily into the sky. And there, in front of the shack, stood Hawk, skinning a deer that he had hanging from a tree. Jake rode up to him.

"Looks like you been here a few days," Jake observed.

"Thought I'd make up for being gone."

Jake nodded, but felt irritation rise in him, "You could have checked on Bonnie."

"Bonnie left me."

"Bonnie is in your cabin, waiting for you," Jake said impatiently. "She's been there since the day you left."

"Why didn't her sisters or brothers take her in?"

"She didn't want anyone to take her in," Jake spoke angrily. "She just wanted those goddamn scalps out of the house."

"She took them out?"

"I took them out."

"You got rid of them?"

"Bonnie wouldn't let me get rid of them," Jake tried to be calm. "She said only you could do that. I hung them behind the cabin."

Hawk went back to his skinning. Jake watched him, then turned and stripped the saddle off his horse, turning it loose to graze. Finally, Jake turned back to Hawk.

"Hawk, what is it that you want?"

Hawk's knife stilled as he thought about an answer. "I went to see my mother, my sister, and my uncle. They are not happy in the Utah country. The Utes from there are not happy that our villages have joined them. The promises from the government are not being honored. I rode out with some of my friends. We went to our old lands and hunted in the mountains. Many whites have moved in. The whites complained. Soldiers came and told us to leave. I didn't want to go back to the reservation. I came here."

"Hawk, what is it that you want?" Jake repeated the question.

Hawk glanced at Jake and then back to the deer. "I want our old life back, our old lands."

"You want a Ute woman in your teepee?" Jake asked. "You want to live in the village?"

Hawk did not answer at once. He worked on the carcass. "I see no woman sharing my robes," he finally murmured.

"Well, here is what I see," Jake retorted, trying to control the anger in his voice. "The old ways are gone. You can want them, but you won't find them. The Ute lands are gone. The white government took it. I can't change that. No one is powerful enough to change that, to get our Ute lands back. But you have land, Hawk. It is not the land of our fathers - lands that stretched farther than a man can ride in a moon. But it is here. You are a part of this land, first because you are Ute and next because you are my family and married to this family. You have land here, and in a few years, you will have a government patent on the land you and Bonnie filed on. That is your land, and part of Twin Peaks Ranch is yours. You have a choice. It is for you to decide where you belong."

"Bonnie left me. I have no woman."

"Bonnie ran from you when you expected her to be something she is not," Jake countered. "She went back home to wait for you. She is in the cabin because she thought you would go there when you returned. It is for you to choose."

"Bonnie went back to our lodge?" Hawk had to think about that. "I will speak to her then when we are done with the gather," Hawk did not look at Jake, intent on the deer.

"You have a lot of daylight left today," Jake told the young man. "You have saved us time already with these cows you have gathered. I'll send James back with you. Take these cows home. James can come back tomorrow. We can get along without you for a day. Go home, see Bonnie, and make your choice. Then come back and tell me your decision."

It was after dark when James and Hawk got the cattle to the home meadow. As they hit the valley floor, Hawk turned off. The cattle would spread out and bed down. This valley was home to them. They would stick around. It was time for Hawk to go home and make his choice.

Hawk rode to the corral below his cabin and unsaddled his horse, turning it out in his pasture to graze and rest. Hawk was surprised as he climbed the hill to the cabin to see a small dark shape come barreling out of the shadows, growling and barking. A dim light was coming from the cabin and when the door opened, Bonnie stood, pistol in one hand, candle in the other.

"Bonnie," Hawk called softly.

Bonnie turned toward the sound of his voice. "Shep, no," she called to the dog. "Don't kick him," Bonnie said to Hawk.

"You have a dog."

"I have been alone," Bonnie said quietly, "I feel better with the dog."

The two stood, Hawk in the dark, Bonnie only a dim silhouette in the doorway.

"Are you coming in?" Bonnie finally asked.

Hawk didn't answer, but he came forward, and Bonnie backed up into the cabin. She turned away from him and set the candle and the gun on the table. The fire crackled in the fireplace, and the cabin was warm.

"You are fine?" Hawk asked.

Bonnie stood, with her back to him. "I am fine."

"I missed you," Hawk said softly.

Bonnie turned then, and Hawk saw her. His eyes widened as he took in her shape, the evidence of the child to come.

"When?"

"Maybe March or April," Bonnie replied.

"When did you know this?"

"I guessed. When you left, I thought I was, but I wasn't sure," Bonnie answered. "I am sure now."

They stood regarding each other. Then ever so softly, Bonnie spoke once more. "I just want your arms around me again."

Hawk came to her then, pulling her to him. She clutched him, tears wet on her cheeks. Fiercely, she said, "Don't ever do that to me again."

"Do what?" Hawk whispered, "Leave you, or bring home blood trophies?"

"Don't do either."

"I won't then," Hawk told her, holding her tight.

With the cattle home from the mountain, and before the winter snows became too deep, there was much to do. Will and his Mexican sheepherder moved Will's sheep home and sorted off the big lambs. These were driven to Laramie and sold. Will's sheepherder took his pay, and boarding a train, he started his long journey home to his wife and children in Mexico. The herder had instructions from Will to be back in Laramie on the first of May if he wanted his job back.

The choicest of the Twin Peaks' fat cattle were butchered and hung in smokehouses and cellars, safe from bears. It took days for the men to get enough meat for every family. When the men were finished with the cattle, they went to Will's farmstead and started to butcher the hogs. Again, enough animals were harvested, so each family had pork hanging in their storerooms. When the crews were done with the meat needed for the community, they butchered enough hogs to fill two heavy wagons. In the November cold, the carcasses quickly froze. Will and Luke drove these pork-laden wagons to a mining town, where they sold them. Unlike cattle that could be driven to a market, it was easier to transport carcasses after processing the hogs. For pork, the cold of winter was when the meat could be transported without spoiling. The miners paid dearly for the frozen meat.

Between butchering the cattle and hogs, the men sorted the cattle into separate groups, cows, calves, steers, and bulls. Each herd was moved to its winter pasture. The cows stayed in the meadow with the saddle horses. The bulls went to the east along the river and the yearling and two-year-old steers went along the river to the west. The calves were weaned and enclosed behind Matthew's cabin in a large corral. It took the rest of October and most of November to complete these chores.

As time allowed, Jake, Lathe, James, and Hawk would get in rides on colts. Sam and Jake took a dozen finished horses to Laramie in early November. Jake had an order there for the horses. Winter was beginning to set in by the time Jake returned. It was the third week of November and soon the snow would be so deep that the cattle would need to be supplemented by hay. The storerooms and cellars were full. Woodpiles were stacked against cabin walls. The settlement was ready for the long winter.

On one unusually mild day, Jake and his crew had taken horses out, taking advantage of the nice afternoon. The days were getting so much shorter now. Snow had come, but it was not deep yet.

Hawk turned out the colt he had ridden and turned to saddle his personal horse. It was a mile to his home, and he didn't intend to walk there. Jake too, turned his colt out and turned to his nephew. The other men had already left for their dinners.

"How's Bonnie feeling?" Jake asked.

"She's good," Hawk replied. He tightened his cinch, then turned to his uncle. "We have much to be thankful for. You worry about us, but Bonnie and I, we will make it. This summer was bad. But we are good now."

Jake nodded. He did worry about Hawk and Bonnie, but the young couple seemed to be working things out.

"It is not me that you should worry about." Hawk mounted his horse. "My sister is not right. Lathe is not right."

"I know," Jake said sadly. "I don't know how to help them. Lathe stays away until late. He comes home after we are in bed. I notice it more now that the darkness comes so early."

"What does my sister say?"

"That's the worst of it," Jake looked off into the distance. "She doesn't say anything. She eats and goes into her room with the boys. Anna says Kasa does well with the children and the chores when they are alone during the day, but then she withdraws to the bedroom with the boys after supper," Jake sighed. "I don't even know where Lathe goes off to these nights. He just puts his horses away and then disappears. Maybe I should track him."

Hawk had reined his horse away from the corral fence, but he stopped and looked back at Jake. "Lathe is at his cabin. He is tearing it down. He builds a big fire and works in the light of it. I can see the firelight from my window. I do not have the words for him. You should go."

Jake thought about what Hawk said as he trudged up the hill to his home. Lathe, Kasa, and the two boys still lived with him and Anna. They stayed in one bedroom, and Jake and his family used the other. They had done this the first winter when Lathe and Kasa were married, but then Kestrel was the only child. Now, Jake had three children, and Lathe had two boys. They got on well together, but the cabin was crowded. Thankfully, Anna and Kasa were good friends. Two women in one home could be a problem, but it hadn't been for them.

Jake had seen a change in Lathe and Kasa since the summer. It was an expected change at first after the attack. Kasa was withdrawn much of the time. She had never returned to her cabin, not even to gather her things. Lathe and Bonnie had brought down what was needed. Lathe mentioned going back to their home, but when Kasa panicked at that, Lathe had given up the idea. Jake told Lathe to spend the winter with them, and then in the spring, see how Kasa felt about moving home.

Now, into late November, Lathe stayed out later and later each night. Kasa never mentioned Lathe's absence. Instead, she made him a plate of food, left it covered with a cloth on the table, and went to her room as soon as supper dishes were cleaned. Jake could hear her in with the boys on most nights, telling them legends of Coyote or singing to them in Ute. Eventually, it would get quiet, and Jake would see the candlelight go out from under her door, and he knew Kasa and her children were in bed. After Jake and Anna were in bed, he would hear Lathe come in.

Supper was almost ready when Jake walked into the cabin. He played with Kestrel, Lark, and little Kade. Jake would lie on the floor and let the kids crawl over him, and he would buck them off. Four-year-old Slade also got into the fun of it, while Kasa sat rocking with Jesse in her arms. Jesse, not yet two-years-old, was fearful after the violent attack that summer and seldom roughhoused with Jake and the others. Wounds of the mind were hard to heal.

When Kasa picked up her two boys and went to the bedroom that night, Jake went to Anna.

"Does she say anything?" Jake whispered. "Do you know what is going on with Kasa and Lathe?"

369

Anna just shook her head. "She won't say anything. Just says Lathe is working and will be home late."

"I'm going out to talk to Lathe then. This has gone on too long. Hawk told me where to find Lathe," Jake shrugged into his coat. "Don't wait up for us."

When Jake rounded the hill separating the two homes, he saw the bonfire that Lathe had burning on the far side of the house. The cabin's front wall was gone, and the used logs were piled neatly in the front yard. He couldn't see Lathe yet, but he heard the *tat-tat-tat* of a hammer. When Jake rounded the corner of the cabin, he saw Lathe. Lathe was breaking out the chinking between the logs, hammering it into pieces.

"Lathe," Jake spoke calmly, "if you want to tear it down, we can all help. You don't need to work on it alone."

"No matter," Lathe said, not looking up at Jake, "I don't have anything to do now anyway. Might as well start."

"I suppose you could take time for supper," Jake observed. "See your boys."

Lathe didn't answer. He just kept chipping at the chinking.

Jake watched him for a few minutes before speaking. "Lathe!" Jake said finally, raising his voice over the sound of the hammer. "What drives you, man?"

Lathe didn't turn toward Jake, but his hammer stilled. "I can't go home until I am so fuckin' tired that I can sleep." The words came out soft.

"Come to the fire," Jake commanded. "Talk to me."

Reluctantly, Lathe turned toward Jake, and the two men went to the fire.

"What's eating you?" Jake asked.

Lathe shook his head and wouldn't look at Jake. Lathe still had the hammer in his hand and began to hammer it against the frozen ground. Finally, he looked up at Jake and began to talk.

"Kasa sleeps with the boys. I moved them to their pallets on the floor a couple different times, but she just goes rigid, turns away from me," Lathe hesitated. "It's been four months. She gets worse." Lathe threw the hammer down and raised haunted eyes to Jake. "I sleep on the floor in the boys' bed."

Jake sat silent. He had no words to help.

"If I stay out here and get tired, really worn out, I can sleep when I lie down. So, I stay out," Lathe stood up and paced. "I just want my wife back," he finally said. "I just want Kasa to be happy again."

"Does she speak to you?"

"Not really," Lathe sat down again. "If I reach for her, try to hold her, she goes stiff, and if she says anything at all, it is that she sees them. That is what she says when she wakes from the nightmares. She sees them. She might let me hold her then until she gets calm, then she turns away from me. I can't reach her."

Jake thought about that. "She sees them. Those men?"

"She will push me away saying that."

"Lathe, you have to make Kasa see you," Jake said slowly. "I don't have any damned idea how you do that, but you have to try. She has to see you. You can't let her keep remembering them."

Lathe nodded, looking into the fire.

"And that isn't going to happen if you are out here," Jake said sternly. "You have to face this. It might take a long time, but those boys need you too, and staying away isn't going to change anything."

Again, Lathe nodded, but he sat as if he were defeated. "Come, let's put this fire out and go home," Jake said, "before it gets too late."

The cabin's main room was empty when Jake and Lathe entered, but candlelight peeked out from underneath each bedroom door. With a nod to Lathe, Jake went to his bedroom. He couldn't help his cousin anymore.

Lathe lifted the cloth over the plate on the table and looked at the cold food. It didn't look appetizing. He took the slice of bread and chewed it thoughtfully, gazing at the flickering light coming from under his bedroom door. Finally, taking a breath, he went to the door, opened it, and went in.

Kasa sat rocking with both of her boys in her lap. They were both asleep. Startled, Kasa glanced quickly at Lathe, and then her eyes dropped. She lowered her head, leaning it against Slade's hair and closed her eyes.

Lathe watched her. This was how it went with them now. It was as if she blamed him for the hurt that she withstood. As Lathe stood, a thought went through his mind. It was no more than a hope, but it gave him a direction, a pathway. He stripped off his boots, shirt, and trousers. Standing in his gray union suit, he studied his wife. Then finally, he went to her, scooped up little Jesse, and laid the sleeping toddler on the pallet on the floor. Running his hand gently over the little boy's head, he got up and went for Slade.

Lathe had to slip his arms between the child and his wife to pick up the four-year-old. As his arm touched Kasa, she flinched. "I do it," she said, starting to rise.

"No," Lathe said firmly, "I will take him." He felt Kasa go still as his arms slid under the sleeping child and raised him off her lap. Kasa never looked up.

After covering Slade and Jesse with a quilt, Lathe stood up. He backed away to the bed, their bed, and sat down against it. He watched Kasa. She didn't move or look up.

"You need to come to bed, Kasa," Lathe said gently.

"I will soon," she replied, making no move to get up.

"You need to come now," this time it wasn't a request. Lathe tried to speak calmly, but his words were firm.

Kasa glanced up at him swiftly, then stood. She turned away from him and began to take her clothes off. Very quietly, Lathe slipped out of his long underwear and climbed into the bed. He didn't want to frighten her, but Jake was right. Staying away wasn't going to change anything.

"Leave it," Lathe said when Kasa reached for her nightgown. In the flickering candlelight, he saw Kasa freeze, hand halfway to the nightclothes hanging on the pegs on the wall.

"Leave it and come to bed," he spoke softly, hoping it would calm her.

Kasa did not turn but backed up to the bed and sat on the edge. She leaned toward the candle, but before she could blow it out, Lathe spoke again.

"Leave it. Let it burn."

Kasa just sat. In the light from the one small flame, Lathe could see Kasa's bare back, and a slight tremor. Was she cold or frightened? Lathe thought maybe both. For four months he had gotten to this point and then pulled back. He didn't want to hurt her or frighten her. But he was tired of walking away.

"Lie down, honey," he whispered softly, holding the quilt open. "Let me cover you."

Kasa lay down, turning on her side away from him. Lathe gently laid the quilt over her, tucking it snuggly around her. He waited, giving her time. After a few minutes passed, he put his hand on her shoulder, pulling her gently onto her back.

"Turn over so I can talk to you," he said.

Kasa did as he asked but kept her face turned away.

"Kasa," he spoke so softly, she could hardly hear him, "what do you see?"

It took a moment for her to answer. Taking a shuddering breath, she said, "I see them. They laugh at me, rip my clothes, look at me, hurt me. I see them."

Lathe sat up so he could see her face, being careful not to pull the quilt off her. Her eyes brimmed with unshed tears.

"Kasa, look at me."

She did not turn her head. Gently, Lathe took her face in his hands and turned her toward him. "Kasa, look at me," he repeated. "What do you see?"

Her eyes flashed to him, and then they flew off to the side. "I see them," she whimpered.

"No," Lathe said, his voice firm. "Look at me. Look at me, Kasa. What do you see?"

This time she looked at him, and her eyes fixed on his. She swallowed, "You."

"You see me? Have I ever hurt you?"

"They hurt me."

"I know, honey. They were bad men, evil men. But they aren't me," Lathe saw her eyes waver. "Look at me, Kasa." These words were not so gentle. "Look only at me."

Kasa watched him then, her eyes wide. Very gently, Lathe caressed her face, running his fingers through her hair, around her eyes, tracing her cheeks. Then he started to talk again.

"Do you know when I started to love you?" When Kasa gave no reply, he went on. "Remember the first time, the first year you came to the mountains with your mother and father? I saw you out picking berries, and I stopped to talk to you. Do you remember?"

Kasa watched him, and ever so slightly, she nodded.

"We talked and ate berries, and it was getting late. I gave you a ride home on my horse," Lathe traced her mouth. "I let you off before we got home so no one would know we were together. Remember that?" Lathe was rewarded with another slight nod.

"I didn't know love then, didn't recognize it, but I think I started right then, loving you," he smiled fondly at Kasa. "I remember wanting to do more than ride with you."

"I know," Kasa whispered.

"How? How do you know?'

"You grew big behind me. You pressed into me," her eyes were serious, but she didn't appear scared. She was listening, remembering.

"You little imp," Lathe chuckled softly, "you never told me that. I didn't think you'd know." His hands caressed her throat, then her shoulders, reaching under the quilt.

"Do you remember that day, when my cabin was almost done, and you walked through the meadow?"

"You showed me the inside."

"I did," Lathe agreed. "And we kissed." He leaned over and kissed her gently. She did not pull away. "We wanted each other. Do you remember?"

Kasa nodded. "You wouldn't take me," she murmured. "You said you couldn't without my father's permission."

"Hmm, but you took me, didn't you?" Lathe slipped his hands to her breasts, gently moving over her softness.

"I wanted to."

"I gave your father our two best horses, and he sent you to me," Lathe breathed. "Do you remember?" Lathe leaned over Kasa, his lips brushing her nipples. She did not flinch. She was listening to him.

Lathe continued talking softly, and his hands moved over her. If her gaze wavered at all, he would pull her back to him with the memories. "Do you remember, Kasa?" he would ask. He reminded her of their wedding day when they spent the whole day in his half-finished cabin. Did she remember Jake coming and pounding on the walls? Did she remember going to supper that night and how her mother gave her a new dress made of soft doeskin. Did she remember how uncomfortable he got when they were almost home to Twin Peaks that summer, and he knew he would have to face his family with a new wife. A new wife he had not married the Christian way.

"You were afraid your father would not let us be together," Kasa said.

"Pa married us at once," Lathe said. "And then we lived that winter here with Jake and Anna. Do you remember?"

Lathe could feel her under his touch. She was still but not rigid. She was concentrating on his words more than his hands. He felt as if he were going to explode, moving so slowly. This is not how they would have made love before. She would have come to him.

She would have loved him, wanted him. Lathe wanted that back. But instead, he moved slowly. He only hoped he wouldn't run out of things to remember or that she wouldn't panic.

His fingers reached between her legs, to her most private place. He gently felt her, probing. He felt Kasa jerk slightly.

"Look at me, Kasa," he repeated once more. "I am here. Like I was on our wedding day. Like I was in the hot waters near Steamboat. It's me." Her eyes searched his. He kissed her gently, his hands caressing. And then he felt it. The slightest movement of her hips, the deeper breath, a little moan. Her body was responding. Lathe did not hurry. He wanted to, but he knew he could ruin this so easily. He just sat beside her, loving her gently with his hands and his mouth and his words.

It seemed an eternity before Lathe heard Kasa speak. "Lathe, come to me," Kasa suddenly whispered. "Take me."

Lathe almost couldn't breathe at her words. But a thought stopped him. Those men had held her down, climbed on her, and hurt her that way. He was afraid she would panic. He laid back on the bed beside her on his back.

"You come to me, honey," he spoke softly, pulling her to him instead.

She rolled toward him, and he helped her, lifting her hips over him. He felt her touch him, guiding him into her. Then slowly, ever so slowly, she sank down on him.

Lathe had only once in his life been beaten severely by his father. He had been fourteen and had been cocky. He talked back to his father, using the Lord's name in vain, repeating it for emphasis. That was something that Matthew never allowed from his children. Blasphemy had no place in the Jorgensen household. Matthew hadn't taken the strap to Lathe then like he had when Lathe had been a disobedient child. Matthew had struck Lathe with his fist, and Lathe, being full of himself, had repeated his curse. It had not gone well. Lathe had never seen fury in his father before. The kind, gentle father was gone. Never again would Lathe look at his father and think him reticent or retiring. The wrath of God was in his father that day, and it was frightful.

Now, as he felt Kasa rhythmically moving above him, he looked up at her and smiled.

"Sweet Jesus," he whispered, his heart full. Deep in his being, he knew he wasn't using the Lord's name in vain. He was saying a prayer of thanksgiving.

CHAPTER 17

Twin Peaks – Spring 1883

Jake pulled his horse up to let him rest. He had just climbed a grueling hillside, testing the horse for endurance and sure-footedness. This young horse had withstood the test. It stood, head low, breathing hard but not spent. If Jake had another slope to climb, he knew the horse could still give him more. But Jake didn't need more on this day. He was just on a training ride, not a life-or-death race. There was only one steep downhill trek left, and they would be home anyway, for they sat on the tallest ridge overlooking the main buildings of the ranch. Below them was home.

There was no one place where the whole ranch could be seen. That was perhaps because so many of the men who built their homes had been wanderers, mountain men, or of Indian blood. Men who valued being alone. They picked the places to build their cabins where they at least felt alone, even if they were part of this sprawling ranch.

From where Jake sat now, he could look down and see the twin log homes of Matthew and Kade far below him. It wasn't Kade's original home; that was up the meadow where James lived now. These two homes were built in the first years of the ranch by the two farmers, Matthew and Jim. Now, with Jim dead almost seven years, it is Kade and Sarah's home. Jake couldn't see his father's original cabin, where James and his brood lived, or his brother Thomas' cabin next to it, but he could see two twin spires of fireplace smoke well up the valley. Even farther up the valley, he could see two more twin spires rising on this cool May afternoon. That would be his home, and next to it was a new cabin Lathe and Kasa built. The fear of being alone never entirely left Kasa, so Lathe built a new home next to Jake and Anna's house.

Jake twisted in the saddle, looking almost over his shoulder to the valley's west side. He couldn't see Sam and Martha's cabin, or Hawk and Bonnie's farther out still, but he could see their smoke. It was Saturday afternoon, and Jake knew he was probably the only one still out riding. Sam and Hawk would be home by now, chopping firewood, hauling water into cabins, or playing with their children. Bonnie had a baby boy at the very end of March. You would think Hawk had done all the work of birthing himself, as proud as he was of this baby. He had already picked out the child's first horse, keeping it in his pasture behind his cabin. Hawk would know that horse and have it superbly trained by the time the child was three.

A movement below caught Jake's eye and he turned back to the river valley. His father, Sarah, and little Feather were on their way to the river, walking slowly. That Feather was a tiny mite. Kade was carrying Feather on his shoulders and had one arm around Sarah. Sarah carried a fishing pole. Jake grinned. If his mother were the one with Kade, they would probably be carrying a blanket, too, and it would be everyone's cue to stay the hell away. But maybe Kade was too old for that nonsense. Still, his father's arm around Sarah pulled her close, and even at this distance, he could see them smile at each other. Jake was happy for them. They both grieved so for their lost spouses. It was good they found happiness again.

Another movement caught Jake's eye, and he saw his daughters, Kestrel and Lark, on their ponies, loping to catch up with their grandfather. Kade might be a father to a baby daughter, but he was still the beloved grandpa. Kade had time for all his grandchildren. Kestrel would come to Grandpa and get him to ride out with her. She wasn't allowed to ride out of eyesight of the ranch if she were alone, but with her Grandpa, they could climb the slopes and explore the ravines. Kestrel was definitely the spirit of her grandmother, Sabra. Kestrel wasn't happy if she wasn't on a horse.

Jake studied the river valley below him. The schoolhouse was finished in November and sat in the valley across from the twin cabins. A schoolteacher had been found, a friend of Jeremiah's wife's family. The young man had come from far away Chicago to teach at the ranch. Mr. Charles Tanner was only seventeen and not at all suited for the West. Small and retiring, he was the youngest son of a storekeeper and had no chance of becoming a part of the family business with three older brothers vying for it. Charles hadn't even ridden a horse before coming to the ranch. But he was interested in the ranch and wanted to learn.

The school had four students the first year. Sam's TJ was seven, along with Jake's seven-year-old Kestrel. Mary and James' Emmett, at eleven, and Alice, eight, rounded out the first class of students. But there were more on the way. Sabra Lark, Sam's John Henry, and Lathe's Slade Layton, all five-year-olds, would follow in the fall. And several younger ones would join their older brothers and sisters in the coming years. With the amount of young married folk, Jake knew that more babies would arrive.

James and Mary's Noah, at fifteen, refused to go to school. He was a ranch hand now and had only a sprinkling of learning. Mr. Tanner wanted to learn to ride a horse and participate in some ranch activities. He wanted to learn how to shoot and hunt. So, James made a deal with the young schoolteacher. Noah spent half a day with the teacher every Saturday, studying reading, writing, and numbers. Then in the afternoon, Noah would take the young greenhorn out to learn about ranching, farming, and hunting. There were less than three years between the two boys, and Noah flourished with the responsibility of teaching the teacher.

There was a new structure being built beside the schoolhouse. The walls and roof were up, and the windows and door would soon be installed. Two of the three men hired on as summer help last year had come back in April, promised another summer job. Kade had put them to work erecting a new building. Kade was going to start a trading post. Saying he started out in this country trapping beaver and trading with the Indians, Kade guessed he would end in a similar way with his own trading post. The cold was seeping into Kade's bones, riding the young horses during the winter. Kade vowed his riding days were about over, other than riding with his grandchildren and eventually with Feather.

The ranch had always paid retail price for the needed supplies, and then freight was added on to that if a hired wagon did the hauling. Kade had goods for his store ordered at wholesale price to be delivered to Laramie. At the end of the month, Twin Peaks' wagons would haul the supplies out. The ranch itself would benefit from having a trading post here, but settlers were also moving in. Even Jackson and Molly would find Kade's goods closer to reach than going to Laramie. Kade would have enough business. The schoolteacher planned to stay the summer and help Kade start the store. Charles Tanner was a storekeeper's son, after all. He'd be good help.

The horse had quit breathing heavily and stamped impatiently, restless to move on. Jake shook himself from his thoughts. It was Saturday. There was always much to do on a late Saturday afternoon. He'd collect his two daughters from their grandpa and head them home. Jake needed extra water hauled in for the Saturday night baths. His mother had started a tradition before Jake was old enough to know about traditions. Sabra had been firm on Saturday night baths, and the family seldom missed them. As a boy, Jake resented bath night. It was a lot of work for the oldest son, hauling in bucket after bucket of clean water from the brook, and hauling bucket after bucket of dirty water out after he and his brother and sister washed. Then, they were sent to bed early so his mother and father had the privacy of the main room with the tub in front of the fire. As a youngster, he remembered hearing his father chuckling and his mother giggling, wondering how they found a bath so funny. It took him the first Saturday night after he and Anna got their own home to remember those nights and appreciate bath night. Damn, it was almost as enjoyable as the hot springs near Steamboat. Maybe the tub was a bit cramped, but in a house filled with children, the privacy of bath night was not to be wasted. Lathe and Kasa and their boys were in their new cabin now. Yes, Jake should gather the girls and head home.

He glanced once more at the landscape below him. Twin Peaks was more than a ranch. It was a community filled with his family and friends. For all the good and bad that had happened here and in these mountains, he knew of no better place to live. These were his people. This was his home.

"Come on, bay horse," Jake murmured, "time we make tracks. Special people down there waiting for us." He urged the horse forward, finding the path down the steep incline. It was time to go home.

ACKNOWLEDGEMENTS

I want to thank the people who have helped me get this book to fruition. My sister-in-law, Dayna, who is my first editor and helps me send my manuscript on to the publisher looking like I know my grammar! We know who the grammar genie is!

Then there are my first readers. Of course, Dayna was one of them. But I want to especially thank Renee and Adele for their insights and comments as they read this story. Your encouragement has spurred me on to continue my stories, and I thank you for that.

Thank you to W. Brand Publishing and JuLee Brand for your continued support of my novels. I hope my stories never let you down.

ABOUT THE AUTHOR

Johny Weber is a retired assistant professor at Northern State University in Aberdeen, SD. Since childhood, her life has revolved around horses. Marrying a rodeo cowboy, she moved with him to the plains of South Dakota where they both competed in rodeos and then turned to a ranching lifestyle. Her career in education began by teaching first grade in 1975 and by retirement, she was teaching graduate courses to teachers in a state-funded program. Johny and her late husband raised a son and daughter on the prairies of the Cheyenne River Indian Reservation. She now enjoys time spent with her children and grandchildren and traveling with her horse and dog to ride the mountains of the west in the summer and the deserts of the southwest in the winter.

Also available in the
Mountain Series

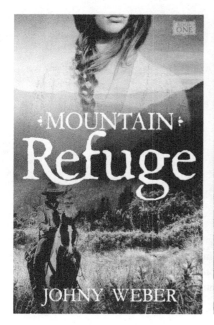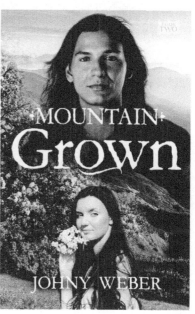

Book One,   Book Two,
Mountain Refuge   *Mountain Grown*

Made in the USA
Monee, IL
05 January 2025

73764658R00236